Micky's ...

(growing up in '60s ...

By

Mike Ricl...

CW00407624

Introduction

If you venture deep into this book, I should warn you, you may start to feel old.

I began writing these weekly pieces seven-years ago, in 2017.

I have collated them and they describe aspects of my life about growing up in London in the sixties (without the flowers in my hair) and seventies (without excessive use of mousse).

The first six-months were a bit rambling, if I'm really honest, but then my editing got slightly tighter – so persevere, please. I think it's worth it

My main hope was to make people laugh, but also remind them of the halcyon (and this is the last time I use a big word) days when we were all much younger.

I sincerely hope it makes you laugh and also metaphorically (I lied about the big words) takes you by the hand and leads you down Memory Lane towards Noddy's "Dark, dark wood".

Laughter is good for the endorphins. So, let's protect those endangered species.

So, sit back, with a cup of cocoa, enjoy and feel increasingly ancient ☐and try and keep awake.

But most importantly, as we say in south London – be lucky.

Having been born where Albert Speer died, and Sir Alexander Fleming discovered that if you left bread out long enough it'd save going to the pharmacy within St Mary's Paddington to get penicillin, my parents decided that a room in a road just off Baker Street wasn't the place to bring up their little Mickey Mouse. So we emigrated south of the river (it was before 8pm so cab drivers were happy to take us) to a 1936-built block of flats located on Balham High Road, SW17. My maternal grandmother lived there, next door to my aunt (her sister), who was sponsored by Embassy before they got into snooker, and their step/real dad respectively.

Because I was moved there when I was only nine months old, my early memories are negligible but, as I lived there until I was 15 (we had to move as my mother had run out of maintenance people and shopkeepers along Balham High Road to shag) I collected many memories. I will choose this vehicle to share with you.

Having started with a leading Nazi, this first chapter will end with one of my most vivid memories.

Within Du Cane Court, the flats of which I mention, there was small dairy-cum-grocer's shop that most of the tenants would visit this each day. In the 600 plus flats you could count the number of children living there on the fingers of two hands, one of which having had an accident with the bacon slicer in the dairy. One of the other children's mum was German. I remember her one day saying to my nan and me that her cousins had all been in the SS and that you could not have met nicer people.

I can only assume, within the Third Reich, they never had "take your cousin to work day"?

My nan lived next door to my Auntie Vera. Her husband, my Uncle Ted, was a semi-professional band leader. This took him up to town every Friday and Saturday evening. To occupy herself during my uncle's absence, she would go 100 yards across Balham High Road to a gaming club frequented by the Krays called the 211 Club.

Situated at 211 Balham High Road, the 211 Club used to be the Balham Conservative Club. Pre-Ron and Reg it boasted several bars, snooker tables and a massive garden. As the 211 Club the snooker tables were replaced with gaming machines and blackjack tables.

One evening my Auntie Vera was entertained by Jack "The Hat" McVitie. Sadly, she never left her flat with her autograph book, so she may have lied, although she isn't currently a central support of the then recently-built Westway.

When not in the 211 Club she would smoke Embassy cigarettes. My job was to count them. She was saving up for a set of new towels - "you can never have enough towels, Michael", she would say (in between coughing). Sadly, she died of emphysema. Looking back, she should have been saving for a new lung, the towels could have waited. She could have used my Uncle Ted's vest; he did.

In addition to being a professional smoker, my Auntie Vera was an accomplished pianist. It was decided she would teach me. After two lessons and being severely wrapped over the knuckles with a steel ruler I decided that Kendo (with me not being armed with a stick) would have been less painful.

However, it was my Auntie Vera who, when I was six in November 1963, came out of her flat to greet me and my nan en route back to my parents' flat, with the news that Kennedy had been shot. I assumed, given her violent nature and the company she kept when my Uncle Ted was away, that perhaps she'd been the person who'd shot the American president. In Du Cane Court they had lovely gardens, but not a grassy knoll to be seen, so my Auntie Vera was innocent.

One of the flats in which we lived in Du Cane Court had its windows backing out onto a courtyard. Any sound would echo around. By the law of averages, one of the inhabitants within the 627 flats (we counted them all one wet Bank Holiday Monday) would be a mad person. Mr Philips was that man in our block.

I remember one hot, summer evening, when the windows were open but a quiet air of peace hung over SW17, when an utterance, through the silence and reverberating around the courtyard came from said Mr Philips: "Turn that fucking radio down!" He shouted like the opening of Billy Cotton's Showband programme and then suddenly back to a silence like a grave.

We think that Mr Philips may have previously been a Radio Caroline DJ and was never reconciled to the fact he was no longer afloat. He certainly wasn't mentally.

Gateway to the South (coast) revisited – 4

On a rare break away from the flats dominating Balham High Road, I was sent away on several summer holidays with my paternal grandparents. Many of my teenage years were spent in Greatstone which is on the Kent coast and near to the Dungeness power stations. Wearing a safety suit when the tide went out precluded playing on the beach and certainly gave me a dodgy bowling action as I tried to twirl my leg-breaks (this is not a euphemism).

In 1973 I was on holiday in Greatstone. This was my O-level year where I set a record for spending the least time in the school hall during the exams. I feared the worst. The realisation came from a call home when I duly reported in and spoke to my mother - one of the two parents who had, throughout my secondary school career, been constantly told that "Michael could try harder".

She told me: "We opened the envelope and you got one O-level; your father's bleedin' furious".

But all was not lost, as, over the series of many summers, I learned the names of all the engines on the Romney, Hythe and Dymchurch railway and learned, having read the Dr Syn novels, believed that life as a smuggler may be the employment route I was destined for with my one O-level. Or, as my O-level had been in English Literature, I thought of being a Scottish King, a miserable prince in Scandinavia or a man who removed thorns from lions.

I never made it as a smuggler, the barrels were too heavy and found that absinthe made me come out in a rash. Also, I don't suit a bandana - it messes me hair up.

Norway: null points

Starting next week Norway, a country famous for regularly achieving "null points" at Eurovision, ranting racist (but with very good knowledge of UK history) football commentators and introducing the world to the word "Quisling", is to start switching off its country's FM radio signal.

I am sure there will be many Norwegians from Oslo to Narvik who may not possess a digital radio. There may be many inhabitants of Hammerfest who only own transistor radios. Their only form of entertainment from next week could well end up being "pin the tail on the herring".

This move to digital-only radio will also happen in the UK and I'm reminded of the joy different forms of radio has given me over the years as well as increasing my myopia.

The block of flats in Balham where I used to live had, when it was first built in 1936, radios installed into every flat. They would play the Light Service (this had programmes with a lot of people saying, "can I do you now, sir?", the Home Service which was mainly news read by virtually anyone except William Joyce, and the Third Programme which cheered everyone up during the war years playing mostly Mahler.

By the 60s most of the radios hardly worked. In my Nan's flat it still worked but you had to go inside a cupboard in which it was housed. I spent many hours inside this cupboard listening to programmes such as "I'm sorry I'll read that again" and deciding which Mahler symphony I liked the least. As well as the radio, also inside my Nan's cupboard lay the central heating system. It was very hot inside the cupboard. I remember after 30 minutes of "The Clitheroe Kid" I'd lost half a stone. After the radio stopped working, my Nan would hire out the cupboard to apprentice jockeys hopeful of a ride at Epsom.

I also had a transistor radio and would listen under my covers to the Top 30 on Radio Luxembourg. Under torchlight I would write down the charts as they were played. This is something I've never admitted to my optician - or psychiatrist.

I remember listening to a lot of sport on medium wave, police activity on short wave (always handy when living so close to HMP Wandsworth) and long wave with my ear very close to the in-car speaker to Test Match cricket when not in the country, but you could see it from France.

I will bemoan the move to purely digital, but first it will be manifold Norwegians who will no longer be able to tune in to "De Bueskytter - the everyday story of fjord folk"

Cough up, it might be a gold watch

The Queen has made her first appearance since going down with some lurgy, which is possibly this bronchial virus which has been going around. Having missed two major church services, I assume she'll excommunicate herself?

It seems that many people have been affected by this illness which hangs about for three weeks and makes you sound like Jane Austen and Frederic Chopin before being carted off to a sanatorium in Eastbourne. I've already started saving up for a blanket and bath chair. I knew those Green-Shield stamp books would come in handy.

In the mid-60s, peoples' minds were temporarily taken off the ever-decreasing lengths of skirts as a possible smallpox scare hit our island. Everyone was encouraged to get inoculated against this killer disease; I remember queuing up outside my doctors on Balham High Road to get mine. Similar to going to foreign climes and the need to have a little bit of typhoid or West Nile fever injected into you (you have to feel for the people of the West Nile having such a vicious disease named after their home town – it'd never happen in West Hampstead) the vaccine for smallpox is the bovine disease, cow pox. When this first began in 1796 satirical magazines showed cartoons of patients growing little cows from their limbs.

My mum got cow pox. It meant two things: if she got smallpox she'd be stuffed and secondly, she couldn't be inoculated against it. While she was ill she was forced to wear a bell, get milked twice away and only answered to the name of Daisy. It was rather typical of my mum – she and ailments went together like Pete 'n' Dud, Ron and Reg, Julian and Sandy. She rarely took me to school as she'd often have "one of her heads" – as a youngster I wonder quite how many heads she possessed? Could she remove them like Frankenstein's monster? Was the *The Exorcist* based on my mum and her head-swapping ability?

Sadly, my mother could also pick up diseases by hearing about them on the TV. There could be a documentary about Dengue fever on the telly one night, by early morning my mother thought she had the early symptoms. Always embarrassing being dropped at the school gates when one of your parents is ringing a bell screaming 'unclean'.

Swimming with the fishes – but only with the aid of a float

My parents were vituperative. I heard a lot of bad language growing up. In addition, my Nan would point out rude words in the Bible (a fairly short exercise given its general message) and her sister and next-door neighbour, my Auntie Vera, was often to be heard, through the paper-thin walls, informing my Uncle Ted that perhaps he should have "never have left the f*****g RAF".

So no real surprise that, armed with an ostensible lack of vocabulary, a rude word was destined to come out of my mouth before puberty.

My mother would befriend families who had certain skill sets I did not possess and try and impress them on me. One such family, who attended the same primary school in Balham as me, were the latest focus of attention for my mother; this family were half-human and certainly half-fish as they were all, to a haddock, prolific swimmers. Oddly, they all had rubbish memories too, but they did like a three-inch high deep-sea diver.

Living on the fourth block of a block of flats meant there was no real necessity to learn to swim. To this day I'm grateful the family of swimmers didn't try high-board diving. This might have been tricky, we never possessed a paddling pool, but my mum did own some big saucepans.

And so it was that I was sent to learn to swim at Balham Baths – in the mid-60s this was a swimming pool four-parts chlorine, six-parts urine.

The first two weeks were easy. The lessons were held in the shallow end, which measured 3'6" – I was a tall eight-year-old, so I felt like Johnny Weissmuller – and all I had to do was keep hold of the bar and kick hard.

By week three the bar wasn't exactly raised, rather to be taken away. We were to let go of the bar. Suddenly the three-and-a-half feet depth became the Mariana Trench.

"Take your hands off the bar now, Michael," was the request of the swimming instructor. (The name Michael still fills me with dread: Michael means you've not tidied your room; Michael means you're late for your tea and Michael in this instance threatened me with my whole life flashing before me as I'm taken down to unfathomable depths by an angry coelacanth).

As the request of "take your hands off the bar now, Michael" turned into an order reminiscent of Harry Andrews in The Hill I looked at my imaginary wristband (not the one they give you in exchange for your clothes) and thought "What Would Mother Do?" I decided the course of action was similar to hers when she'd often ruined my egg and chips and told the swimming instructor that I would not "take my hands of this f*****g bar"

You could have heard a pin drop except this was Balham Baths with a million screaming, splashing children and those not in the pool, intent in giving the hot chocolate machine a good kicking.

The swimming instructor walked off. Lesson over, I assumed. Never assume, my mother would warn me in later life, assumption is the mother of all cock-ups.

After I'd got dressed and removed the actual rubber band (and a layer of skin as it was wet and on too tight) I went to find my newly-Piscean parents. As soon as I was reunited with them, my father marched me off to where the swimming instructors gathered and forced me to apologise for my bad language. It was 15 years later that I used the F-word again, terrified I'd use it in earshot of an acquaintance of Mr and Mrs Sweary.

My fear of swimming never subsided, so imagine how awful it was, once at my new grammar school in Tooting, to be informed that swimming lessons happened every three to four weeks.

Oddly, the school swimming baths were at Latchmere Baths in Battersea (which entailed getting about a dozen buses for each trip). Latchmere Baths at that time was situated next to the Lambeth Coroner's Court. Bit ominous, I thought.

After the third trip I learned a new word: verruca.

Clueless of what one of these was, I soon discovered that, by having one, you were excluded from swimming. I would get one of these – real or otherwise. If Amazon had been around in 1969 I'd have ordered a box full. "People who liked verrucas also liked genital herpes and anything by Jackie Collins."

With the fourth swimming lesson imminent I approached the PE master saying, "Please sir, I have a verruca" – I clasped my hand tightly to my ear as I was still anatomically ignorant of its location. "In which case," answered the PE master "you'd better go and play cricket".

As I played cricket for the 1st XI (and it was the turn of the 1st XI to go swimming) I was sent to play with other pupils who believed cricket (in this case) were the entomological kind, googlies were the things we'd had checked at the First Year cough 'n' drop test and a leg break could land you in A&E (provided you'd got a signed exeat from the PE master).

Despite playing, hampered with an imaginary verruca, I returned the best bowling figures ever during that year's games days and scored 569 not out.

I still can't swim, but I can toss up a wrong 'un.

Don't drink the water

The post-Christmas season historically offer us a plethora of travel ads. It's cold and wet in the UK, so travel advertisers are encouraging you to seek warmer climes.

Having been on the receiving end of much moaning from my mother, my father succumbed and booked us on our first foreign trip. We were heading for Majorca.

It was the summer of 1968. If Frankie Valli had had number dyslexia he'd have sung a song about it.

My mother had previously been to Bognor, Brighton and Bournemouth. Because she'd had little education through not going to school during the Blitz, she'd only really mastered the letter "B", so her vacation destinations were alphabetically limited.

We set off from Luton Airport to Palma. It was only when we stepped onto the tarmac that we realised my mother had a fear of flying.

Earlier we'd been delayed several hours; we'd all been given vouchers to the value of 2/6 (12 and a half pence in today's post-decimalisation days). Mother took mine and got herself more alcohol. We had to walk from the departure lounge (less lounge, more outside toilet) across the tarmac onto a plane which wouldn't have looked out of place during the Berlin Airlift.

While my father was carrying copious bags of duty free, my task was to get my mother onto the plane. In 1968, when I was 11, I was very slight and so weak I couldn't even pick up a discus during school athletics, let alone throw it the required distance to avoid getting detention. So, getting a five-foot seven, 35 year-old adult on the plane was an incredible feat. Not blessed with the persuasive powers of the brothers Saatchi I simply dragged her like a caveman brining a sabre-tooth tiger back for tea.

Several weeks before the trip we were encouraged, lest you caught Spanish Tummy, to take tablets with the snappy name of Entero-Viaform. The packet did what it said on the tin as there was a cartoon man gripping his stomach featured on the packet.

Even with the preventable medicine, my mother still got ill. This had followed on very quickly with her contracting cow pox, having one too many of her "heads" and now she had Balearic Belly. My father vowed never to take her abroad again. He didn't. It was back to Bognor next summer, there was less chance of getting Bognor Belly there.

Thunder snow

For nearly 60 years I've listened intently to the weather forecast and have built up a vocabulary second only to my mother's prolific and prodigious swearing repertoire. Today I have learned a new one: Thunder snow. Ok, two words. This is what arrived in London today. Should I get Virgil Tracy to get his snow-shovelling mole out of a Thunderbird 2 pod and save us all? I'd suggest a Thundercat saving us too, but all their names were unimaginative, especially Sabre-Tooth Tiger-o. Although I did like Elaine Paige in the stage show.

It will be talked of as an Arctic Blast. "Bet you look good on the dance floor" being my favourite hit of theirs.

Aside from pigeons, my other fear is thunder. I rarely pull rank at work, but my one instance is that, if it is thundering, someone stays in the office. If there is no one there I have an inanimate green frog who protects me.

My holiday hell would be chasing thunder storms across the US. If I inadvertently went on such a holiday I'd probably choose to lie (with aforementioned green frog) in the glove compartment. They tend to be quite large in American cars.

Half a sixpence

On Monday 14 February 1971, when I was nearly 14, the UK currency system changed from the Roman Denarius system over to decimal (named after the Roman god of decorations - which is why Christmas is in December). On the same day, Belgian farmers illegally entered the EEC building in Brussels with three cows. Some of those cows went on to form UKIP.

It was on this day that I would have preferred to have been attacked by a mad, Flemish-speaking cow, as my mother had ordered me to teach her this new-fangled method of money.

I have mentioned before in this vehicle that my mother's education was limited given her own mother keeping her away from school for the duration of the war. A consequence of which, although my mother could read, she was unable to write and certainly couldn't add up (she thought that calculus was a former Roman emperor, multiplication was a song by Little Eva and division was a town in Wiltshire).

I had to teach this woman that, as from today, 240 was now 100. I had more chance of successfully teaching my pet goldfish long division without using the aid of a sunken ship and a diver.

It was one of the most painful evenings of my life. Given that I would go on to fail Maths O-level three times (I think it was three), it was like the blind leading the blind. If we'd have involved my maternal great-grandmother it would have been the blind leading the blind, as she was blind.

Sadly, she'd "gone to meet the angels" when I was six. I always assumed the Angels were a family she knew who owned an old peoples home for blind people and my great-grandmother had gone to stay there.

I was never going to get my mother to get her head round the fact that half a crown was going to be 12 and a half new pence.

"Halfpence," she questioned, "will they be cutting the coins in two?" So, her adding up ability was poor, but she could do simple division.

The only good thing, in mum's eyes, was that £500 was still a monkey.

However, this potential problem was averted as my mother, not yet 40 and certainly not looking it, was tall, stunningly good looking with blonde hair and blue eyes. She might not have been able to add up, but she managed to get a lot of things from various shopkeepers the length of Balham High Road for free. Well, when I say free...

She couldn't spell, but, from the carpet seller on Balham High Road, she would never go short of a new shag-pile carpet. Quite apposite, really!

It's not as we know it, gym

It would appear that many people living in the borough of Epsom & Ewell (twinned with Gruinard) have made it their New Year's resolution to go to a gym; *my* gym.

More than a working week on since New Year, my normal Saturday morning trip to the gym - where I attempt to lift three times my own body weight and chat about just how far Ian Hutchinson could throw a ball (many members are Chelsea fans, which makes talking about the 2012 Champion's League final awkward) - have been marred.

Early on a Saturday morning, because the gym staff is not quite aware of what programming might be vaguely inspirational, one of the four TVs usually has an old film on. I caught the end credits and saw that Robert Donat was in this week's. Perhaps it was The 39 Steps? It might explain why people were clinging onto the wall bars as if going over the Forth Bridge or being chased by a young John Laurie. There is always a kids' cartoon channel on too. This has beneficial as it means I am now up to speed with every series of SpongeBob SquarePants (I still can't see how he breathes).

Something vaguely sporting would be good - even if it's an old episode of Question of Sport with Henry Cooper in.

My point is this: There seems to be an inordinate amount of new people at the gym. So much so, even if I'd wanted to, I would have been unable to watch the derring do exploits of Richard Hannay, as all the machines facing the TVs were taken. Where were these people last year? Probably having medicals or got the DVD Paula Radcliffe: Live at the Apollo for Christmas?

The same happened on the train, during this week of strikes on Southern Rail. Several Southern commuters were clearly on my train, especially one woman, who peered out the window and talked into her phone saying, "Motspur Park?" – what did she expect on SW Trains? Grand Central? Munich Hauptbahnhof? The Island of Sodor?

The problem with this (hopefully temporary) problem is that it breaks up the 5.41am to Waterloo bridge club. You really don't need someone as your dummy if they don't know that Motspur Park is not one of Saturn's moons. Also, they don't want to play bridge, they want to play "beat your neighbour" – too many swingers parties if you ask me.

One man and his 140-year-old dog

Sport, living in Du Cane Court, was always restricting. With never more than 10 children living in the flats, team sports were forever challenging – even if we included our imaginary friends (of which, being an only child, I had an entire family) we'd never make up a full XI.

Even with both Tooting Bec and Wandsworth commons nearby we still chose to play most of our sport around the garages which were round the back of the flats. In those days, there were very few cars, a consequence was that our "playing field" was quite safe. The only traffic tended to be pedestrian in the form of the head porter, Mr Hurst, and his dog, Blackie (this was the 60s).

There were several "NO BALL GAMES ALLOWED" signs up and around the garages. Mr Hurst's job was to manage this. Sadly, Mr Hurst, an ex-prison warder, had been bitten by a prisoner in HMP Wandsworth and consequently walked slowly and with a limp. As did Blackie, who was the wrong side of 20 – and not in doggy years. Despite being the human equivalent of 140, the dog was quicker than the man and would waddle into view first. There were two ways into the garages and, as the dog entered at one end, we would gather up our sporting equipment and leg it the other way. We were never caught and mercifully so as child-biting was still allowed in the mid-60s.

When we did get to play, and were Labrador-free, we would invent games for two or three people. The only problem was the low level of the garages. If someone decided they were going to Wes Hall and get a ball to rear up, there was no option other than tipping it onto the rooves of the garages. Subsequently, we became very adept at climbing walls onto the garages to retrieve our balls. Word had it that Sherpa Tensing lived in the flats and mastered his climbing skills on the rooves of the garages in Du Cane Court. We once found a set of clamps and, putting two and two together, made Everest.

We had to decide on a set of rules when the cars were about, and it was possibly one summer to be given out caught one-handed off a Ford Cortina.

Martha Longhurst's Vineyard

People of a certain age (mine or older) will always remember where they were when they heard President Kennedy had been shot.

I was in the corridor on the third floor of Du Cane Court, where I lived in the flats on Balham High Road. I was six and a half and I had just left my nan's flat as she escorted me up one floor to my parents' flat.

I spent more time with my nan than I did with either parent. In the mornings I would go there for bacon and eggs (I blame her for my subsequent high cholesterol) and I'd read her *Daily Mirror*. I think my nan was a communist and her Russian controller was Andy Capp. I also spent evenings there, and watch *Double Your Money* and *Take Your Pick* with her. Or I'd play while she watched *Coronation Street*.

On this particular Friday in November 1963 we had left my nan's flat and suddenly, ubiquitous Embassy in mouth, came my Auntie Vera out from her flat: "Kennedy's been shot" reported Auntie Vera. This meant nothing to me being relatively oblivious to US politics and assumed it was another character from *Coronation Street* being killed off; although it did strike me as being quite soon after the tragedy of Martha Longhurst's "death" under the collapsed viaduct.

Five years later I was playing at a friend's house in Oakmead Road, near Balham Station, when his mother entered the room where we were trying hard not to take one another's eyes out with his new *Johnny Seven* (multi-action) gun. "Kennedy's been shot" she said. I thought, *"Either this woman is very behind with the news or another character has fallen off his mortal thespian coil from* Corrie".

Similar to my mother wishing to pursue the half-human/half-porpoise family and introduce me to swimming, my friend's mother and teller of grave (albeit slightly outdated) news had just started sending her son to elocution lessons. That academic year he was due to start at Emanuel and his mother had decided that a futile gesture was needed. He was to attend classes to make him more articulate through learning poetry.

These lessons took place in a semi-detached house in Tooting.

Because the problem with having elocutions in Tooting is that there is a danger that you may come out speaking worse after the course than when you originally started.

People living in Tooting in the late 60s believed consonants were Asia and Africa, a vowel was a very small rodent and a semi-colon was what posh people in Fulham had irrigated.

I met him years later when we were in our early 20s. The lessons hadn't worked as he sounded more like Eliza Doolittle, only with a deeper voice, but he did know every Philip Larkin poem off by heart. Really handy working in a hospital.

When I see an elephant fly

It is Majestic Wine now, but years ago, in its place on Balham High Road, sat the Balham Odeon.

If you went there now you'd be more likely to get Burgundy rather than Butterkist and Chianti rather than Kia-Ora.

I was never a regular there for Saturday morning pictures. I went twice and both times they were showing "Emil and the Detectives" so I assumed, having learned the plot and most of the dialogue, it was pointless attending much after that as this was clearly the only film they showed. My mum was quite relieved as my clothes would end up being soaked courtesy of someone above me accidentally dropping their Jubblies on me.

In 1970, my dad took me to watch George C. Scott as the eponymous hero in the Oscar award-winning film Patton: Lust For Glory. The film had a profound effect on me as, if ever, as a teenager I even got close to speaking to a girl, I'd be so pleased that I'd run off down Balham High Road, bowling imaginary leg-breaks and whistling the main theme.

In 1963 my mum took me to the Odeon to watch The Scarecrow of Romney Marsh. The film, based on the books published in 1915 by Russell Thorndike (Sybil's brother), tell of a vicar by day and smuggler in 18th century Kent coast by night. In the 1963 film version Patrick McGoohan (Dangerman and The Prisoner) stars as the innocent vicar who, as evening comes and there is rum to be collected, dons a scarecrow mask. If it had been used in the Wizard of Oz they'd have had to have made it X-rated. It was scary and, to a particularly sensitive six-year-old, too much and before I could break the film projector with my screaming, my mum took me out of the cinema.

The next time I went I didn't last the 100% of the film. Dumbo, which my mother thought less violent, was the next thing I saw Well, I saw up until Dumbo's mum is trapped in the fire. Again, before I could flood the Odeon with my tears, I was hastily removed.

I work in a business where I have to negotiate. People who know me and know of the Dumbo story realise that, if the negotiation isn't going their way, all they have to do is say, "Run, Bambi, run."

I assume Jubblies aren't sixpence anymore.

Bob-a-Job weak

Even though the British government passed the Abolition Act in 1833, 140 years on, slave labour was still very much in evidence in the form of small boys in shorts going from house to house offering their services (experienced or otherwise) for the price of a shilling (5p).

This was Bob-a-Job week, encouraging Cubs and Scouts to take part. These were the days before Beavers – a name clearly resulting in the research group determining the name being made up entirely of adolescent males.

It would seem, after exhaustive research among my gym buddies, that I may have got off lightly with the tasks they had to do for a lowly shilling. I didn't have to walk dogs (or lose them), nor peel the entire crop of Ireland's potatoes in the early 60s. My task, given I lived in a block of more than 600 flats in Balham, where animal ownership was not encouraged and there had been a potato blight while I was studying for my Signaller's Badge, was relatively light. I polished letterboxes; I didn't lose a single golden retriever, nor did I prepare a single chip.

After these Herculean tasks were accomplished, the donor would hand over the shilling and sign the card you carried. The money earned went towards the needs of the Scout pack. I always dreamed of getting a bigger woggle, but surgery wasn't as advanced as it is now.

The letterboxes in Du Cane Court, where I lived, were quite small (although luckily bigger than a postcard) and therefore didn't have much brass round them to clean. My nan and her sister lived in the flats too and were sufficiently menacing to ensure I had a large database upon which to work. Other tenants would rather part with a shilling than have my nan eff and blind at them in the communal dairy or have my Auntie Vera threaten them with a lighted Embassy.

I still have allergic reaction to Duraglit and am currently suing the Scout Association.
I guess Bob-a-Job was a pre-cursor to Just Giving.

It was ironic that I'd have to charge a shilling for doing things round the flats whereas my mum did most activities for nothing. There was a woman who knew her woggles.

A lighthouse moment

I wasn't terribly lucky with adventure-filled trips away with school or paramilitary organisation (my Cub group did go camping, but only in the field behind the church of St Mary's on Balham High Road – about 100 yards away from where we'd weekly shout "dyb, dyb, dyb". The field was still considered dangerous and we were inoculated against Dengue fever four weeks before. There were always rumours Anthrax had been placed there during the war.

I remember, when they were at school, paying for my kids to go to America, Israel and Berlin. I spent a week on school journey in 1968, in Cliftonville.

Cliftonville is a sub-district of Margate, on the Kent coast. In 1968 it was twinned with Roswell. I remember two trips away for the minus-two-star hotel where we were staying - one was to the North Foreland Lighthouse. I decided there and then that a career as a lighthouse keeper was unlikely. Ironically, after failing my O-levels for the second successive time and my dad taking me to an industrial psychologist, I was told that perhaps a career in lighthouse-keeping might be on the cards as I knew what a lightbulb was. And knew that a very big one was needed to make the lighthouse function. He did ask me how many people does it take to change a lighthouse lightbulb, when I answered "fish" it was then that he suggested a career in advertising.

Looking back, I'd have enjoyed working alongside the sirens who lure sailors onto the rocks on the east Kent coast. Although at just over 11 years of age the only siren I knew was the noise coming from one as I tried to sleep most evenings in my ground floor Du Cane Court flat, as the police arrived to attend to happenings in the dance club on Balham High Road opposite.

The second trip was to a farm. About 100 yards away from the farm told me I'd not be making a point of tuning in each morning to listen to the programming on Radio 4. The smell was like some form of olfactory torture. There, also, even at 11, seemed something quite wrong with what was happening with cows' udders on the farm. The smell still lingers - like Virol and calamine lotion.

Secondary school trips at Bec Grammar were slightly more exotic. We went abroad twice. This was pre-tunnel and we travelled by boat to Boulogne one year and (despite our behaviour on French soil) Dunkirk the following year.Everyone wanted to buy flick-knives (those days they were more in evidence than croissants) and cigarette lighters, whose flames were based on those emitting from the oil rigs in the North Sea.

We were all packed off by our various mothers with enough supplies assuming we'd either we'd never return from this foreign field or they'd hope we'd introduce the French to the joys of family-sized packets of custard creams. The French were never given this opportunity of sampling custard creams as all were eaten (as if hovered over by a judge with a stop-watch from the Guinness Book of Records); they were all consumed before the journey back. Therefore, on the second journey, we were packed off with Joy Rides and Kwells.

Vive la France – where is the nearest chemist?

From Balham to Bayern

Football allegiances, I believe, can be categorised into three sources: supporting your local team (very laudable), glory seeking (glory seeking), and parental indoctrination (who pays for your food?).

Balham United, of which the caretaker at my school (St Mary's on Balham High Road) kept goal, was my local team growing up. They never featured on the ladder you could get at the start of the season in *Shoot* so I followed my dad's team. Dad went to Stamford Bridge for every home game and was a massive Chelsea fan (or Speedway as they had that when he was going, let's stick to Chelsea or this article will become irrelevant very quickly).

Throughout the 1966/67 season my dad would take me to the Bridge. This was a time when football violence was becoming endemic and I was conscious of the intimidating atmosphere. Dad and I would walk from our flat in Du Cane Court to Tooting Bec Station and get the 49 bus towards the home of Chelsea FC.

My dad was so keen to make me a Chelsea fan he took me to ex-Chelsea player Frank Blunstone's shop on Lavender Hill and got me a Chelsea kit with a number 9 (Peter Osgood) on the back. There was no sponsorship, no team name. The Chelsea logo on the front and the number 9 on the back.

On Saturday 20 May 1967, Chelsea lost 1-2 to Spurs in the FA Cup Final (which this year, as I write this, will possibly be contended between non-league sides, Sutton and Lincoln – modern day Balham United equivalents). I had decided, from my armchair, that this team was rubbish and the quest for a new team began. I was, I hasten to add, more interested in cricket, but peer group pressure insists you follow a football team; my thought now was which one?

I was (I believe I still am) an only child. A consequence of this was that I was sent to bed, most days, exceptionally early. In the summer the sun would be shining, but my mum's little Mickey Mouse, was forced to have his beauty sleep.

Fortuitously, because of my dad's passion for football, screamingly early bedtime was delayed on the school night of 31 May 1967, 11 days after I'd spurned the Blues like a rabid dog.

There wasn't the proliferation of football on the TV in 1967 – if you've got a big enough satellite today you could watch football 24-hours (especially if you like hard-fought cup games in Timor Leste). This game was the first, live televised game after the English FA cup final.

The game was between Rangers (whom I assumed were from Canada) and Bayern Munich (could have been from anywhere). The event was the European Cup Winner's Cup Final. Dad explained it had been the previous season's equivalent of the FA Cup winners in various European countries in a knock-out competition. The cup doesn't exist anymore and has gone the way of other pan-European tournaments like the Inter-Toto cup (Toto split from Inter and went on to record Africa). Chelsea weren't going to compete in that next season, obviously, which highlighted my need to change footballing support.

The game started at 7.30 (perilously near bedtime). I didn't care that I was unaware of the competition, both teams meant nothing to me. I was in my jim-jams, but allowed to watch TV. It was on this evening that I had a Damascene moment and realised there was a God - and he was possibly German. The game was 0-0 after 90-minutes. Dad realised the importance of the game (I couldn't give a monkey's - I was staying up late). Extra time started (as far as I was concerned it was probably nearly time to get up it was so late) and after 109-minutes Bayern Munich scored. The score remained at 1-0. Bayern had won the mouthful tournament the European Cup Winner's Cup. A team of winners.

So, glory seeking it would be and the team I would support would be the team not from Canada, Bayern Munich.

During the following few seasons I wondered why Bayern Munich were never on *Match of the Day* or *The Big Match*. Wolverhampton Wanderers seemed to be on it a lot but they'd not won anything in Europe. Derek Dougan wasn't even singing the song for the Northern Ireland Eurovision Song Contest entry.

There was no such thing as the internet those days (which may have affected my eyesight even more if there had have been) so no way of keeping up with my new team's news. The absence from football programmes in the UK was a conundrum for me.

It wasn't until we started learning O-level Geography at Bec Grammar and focussing on north west Europe that I realised exactly why Bayern Munich had never featured having David Coleman commentating on a cold Tuesday evening at Stoke. The glory seeking also kicked in during the 1970 World Cup finals in Mexico where six of the 11 West Germany players played for Bayern.

50 years on, Balham United possibly don't even exist, Tooting & Mitcham have never threatened to win the Champions League, so continuation of following Bayern Munich has carried on. This is the 16th season I've had a season ticket and can say "where is the nearest chemist?" in German as well as my name, age and inside leg measurement. I was there on Wednesday against the Arsenal and these days Thomas Müller has replaced his namesake Gerd as my hero. *Auf geht's Bayern* (I think my clutch has gone). If Bobby Tambling had scored a hattrick on 20 May 1967, my Saturday morning travels would be slightly easier. He didn't, so 1,100-mile round journey every other weekend is now routine.

Odd-shaped balls

I was fine playing football on the cinder pitches of Tooting Bec Common for my school, St Mary's, Balham. I'd play at left back, not really getting involved as – even though they were an old pair – I wore glasses.

I'd worn glasses since I was five; my dad established I needed them having spent an afternoon of not picking his chinaman round the back of the garages of the Du Cane Court flats where we lived. I think my dad invented the *doosra* and was Balham's answer to Muttiah Muralitharan. I was taken to David Mercer, the optician in Tooting High Street to get fitted with NHS glasses, which had just been paraded at the Paris Fashion Show (not).

When I first went to Bec Grammar School in the Autumn of 1968 I was abruptly introduced to rugby. I'd never seen, let alone try and get one out of a loose ruck, such an odd-shaped ball.

Because of the inherent danger of having a fellow classmate handing me off (this is a rugby phrase and not a euphemism, there were rarely happy endings in my short rugby career) my glasses could easily break, thus rendering my myopia even worse. This was the boy who couldn't read the large letter at the top of the opticians' chart with his right eye covered.

Our teacher for rugby (and oddly General Science) was former Bec Head Boy, Bob Hiller. Mr Hiller was, as a former pupil and England's full back (I thought George Cohen was England's full back such was my knowledge of rugby), untouchable.

We had two rugby tops: navy blue and white.

Without my glasses, I would see three balls coming towards me; it never occurred to me to go for the middle one. Having spent 80 minutes (which seemed like 80 days, there is a ring to a book entitled *80 days round Tooting Broadway*) my shirt was still spotlessly white. I didn't get involved at all. I'd stand, freezing to death, on Fishponds playing fields, like Molesworth's Fotherington-Thomas; thinking Arcadian thoughts and nothing about rugby. Mr Hiller, in his infinite wisdom, decided I needed to get dirty and forced me to rub mud over my shirt (he was clearly sponsored secretly, in those days of rugby being an amateur sport, by Daz).

I stupidly told my mum.

My mum, in turn, and even more stupidly, wrote to Mr Hiller. No one has the right to make her little Mickey Mouse dirty for no ostensible reason. I was a marked man.

Luckily, I redeemed myself in the summer as I was, for a 10 year old quite a good cricketer and had inherited my dad's finger-spinning ball skills. I was deemed so good I was sent to play for Wandsworth and to report to Al Gover's cricket school. However, this was time off school and I never went. I bunked off. I could have been the next Shane Warne; I was never going to be the next JPR Williams.

My padlock's bigger than yours

It is ironic, given my most feared lesson at Tooting's Bec Grammar School was PE, that I now religiously and willingly attend a gym on a Saturday (Bayern home games permitting) and Sunday (when not serving as an acolyte at the Epsom & Ewell Buddhist Temple for Latter Day Saints).

At Bec we had a PE teacher (for teacher read sadist), Mr Scrowston, who you couldn't have made up. He didn't tend to mix with the other teachers and had his own "office" which housed an awful lot of rugby balls, hurdles and shot puts. There is a line in the film Hospital where the star, George C. Scott, suggests one of the nurses was trained at Dachau. I often used to think that Mr Scrowston learned how to teach cross-country running there as he dished those out as punishments.

I could never fully understand why I was so rubbish at PE. I had good hand/eye coordination, but could never climb a rope, jump a buck or successfully execute an angled-head-stand (with or without the aid of my partner).

I recall one moment when Mr Scrowston entered one of the classrooms, prior to us sitting a particularly important geography exam, to tell us the results of the PE tests we'd had the previous week. I and two other class members (out of thirty) had failed to achieve a single point and were therefore punished with a cross-country run at our earliest inconvenience.

In the 4th Year, double history preceded PE. I would sit in abject fear of what was about to happen in the bowels of the school gymnasium where the surrounding wall-bars I swear had been made from the bones of former pupils who'd also obtained 0% in their PE test. This innate fear explains why I remember precious little about why Home Rule was considered a good idea by the then PM William Gladstone. Oddly, I did remember that Gladstone's hobby, aside from tree-felling, was rescuing fallen women. As a very immature and naïve 15 year old, I believed that "fallen women" were clearly women with inner ear problems and that Gladstone was always hovering on the corners of streets near Westminster ready to break the fall of these ill-balanced women.

It wasn't until I'd read back copies of *Parade* in Ron and Don's barbers in Chestnut Grove, Balham that I realised why I'd never make it as a doctor, and certainly never a gynaecologist. Nowadays there is no one telling me I'm windy, a particular synonym for cowardice in Mr Scrowston's eyes. During an inter-house cricket match I was facing some particularly hostile bowling and before one ball I had walked towards square leg. "Richards, you're windy" announced Mr Scrowston, "cross country run!" – I was automatically given out and sent to run around Wandsworth Common – twice!

The only torment I get at the gym is from 50% of the members who are Chelsea fans and taunt me with memories of the 2012 Champion's League final. I blame myself as I turn up every weekend with my shirt with number 25 and the name "MÜLLER" on the back.

This week at my gym they introduced a new security system: one involving padlocks. You had to provide your own and it seems that not only does peacocking prevail in the showers (I blame the water being cold, so I don't take part in that) but now it seems the bigger the padlock the more important you are in the changing rooms. There are some padlocks which wouldn't look out of place at Fort Knox.

But not only have you got to remember bringing a padlock, you must have a sports-related number for the combination. I have a very good friend at the gym who has decided, as his combination, to have the 1988/89 Chelsea formation (see, there is no escape). Genius - until Graham Roberts becomes a member of our gym.

I have a small padlock (enter your own gag here) which needs no combination number. Consequently, I now have padlock envy. I spent an hour jogging, rowing and doing things on the cross-dresser this morning wondering, if I had a padlock with a combination lock, what that number would be? I decided on 1868, the year Gladstone first became prime minister. Because, whenever I think of Gladstone, I think of doing PE and that is motivation enough. Although, I look back on my Bec PE lessons and even if I'd have tried trying to vault over a horse, I may have saved time by not needing a vasectomy.

Tooth hurty

As a kid, I could have easily become either a dentist or a crack addict. The dentist was the preferred option as a child as I'd visit two – one on the corner of Ritherdon and Balham High roads, the other on Crescent Grove facing Clapham Common. Both were huge houses and, because I was nearly 30 before I physically lived in a house, I wanted to own a massive detached Victorian house when I grew up (toothless or otherwise).

Because my diet was very sugar-heavy – you could buy four shrimps and a Jubilee Bag for less than a sixpence and you could raise your cholesterol level in most Balham sweet shops for less than half a crown (the exact monetary value of a portion of big, big carpet-cleaning 1001) – my trips to the dentist as a young teenager were more regular than the mandatory six-month visits. I would (officially) go in April and September. April was chosen as invariably I'd be on school holidays. One year my mother sent me on my birthday: Happy Birthday – here's your present of an amalgam of mercury, copper, tin and zinc – hardly Gold, Frankincense and Myrrh!

Nowadays a drug called Lidocaine (originally invented by a swimming dentist who was a regular at the Tooting Bec lido) is used for pain prevention, when I went, and you didn't have gas, the drug was cocaine. It was injected, you didn't have to bring your own rolled-up 10-shilling note, although, if you did possess a 10-shilling note, imagine how many Jubilee Bags you could buy? Death by sherbet dab!

The dentist lived on-site with surgeries and waiting room on the ground floor, no doubt above this there were countless rooms filled with recently-extracted rotting teeth. The dentist must have been wealthy living in such palatial splendour, but this, to me raised one question: why were the magazines in the waiting room always out of date? Before one appointment (in the mid-60s) I read, with relief, that Crippen had been apprehended and mother was one year so pleased Mafeking had been relieved. She knew a Mr Mafeking and wondered if this was something she'd been involved in!

There was always a disappointing selection of magazines, not like the barber's whose waiting area was stocked with copies of *Parade* and *Health & Efficiency*. It was only when I went to get my haircut that I took such an ardent interest in naturism. The only chance of sneaking a look at a pair of boobs in the dentist's waiting room was if they had the 1958 edition of *National Geographic* which featured ladies from a remote village up the Amazon wearing nothing but a fish-harpoon.

Although I think about it I wouldn't have wanted to be a dentist – all that halitosis. Plus, you'd never have a decent conversation – unless your patients had the gift of being able to talk with the entire *Screw-Fix* catalogue in their gobs. Although I would like to use the word gingivitis at work more. Gingivitis derives from the fact that St Vitus was ginger. Open wide.

"A handbag?"

While there was plenty of mischief to be had growing up in Balham and Tooting, I was fully occupied during most evenings as I sang in two choirs (they met Tuesdays and Fridays and because of some event on Mount Sinai some years before, twice on Sundays – although you did get wine) and I attended an amateur dramatics group Mondays and Thursdays. I knew all the words to *Hello Dolly* by the age of 16, but ironically went on to have three children.

Every year the Am Dram society to which I belonged would perform a pantomime or musical once a year as these would create the biggest interest to the not-too-discerning musical public of SW12/7.

My first thespian part was as the man servant in *Me and My Girl*. I had one line, "This way, Mr Snibson" as I ushered the star of the show into the front room for him to introduce the upper classes to The Lambeth Walk. It took me several weeks to master the line and to decide the correct inflection on each word: "**THIS** way, Mr Snibson", "This **WAY**, Mr Snibson". I even contemplated method acting and becoming a man servant for a year, but the play was set 60 years prior as manservants were fast becoming a thing of the past.

From this, I slowly progressed and, because I could sing, was given the part of Buttons. Luckily it was *Cinderella*. A mate of mine was also in the group, but not a good an actor; he got given the part of Pontius Pilate. It took him until the end of the final show to realise this wasn't the biggest part he could have got.

One of the songs I had to sing was The Ugly Duckling, famously performed (and written) by Danny Kaye and latterly Mike Reid. It was in the style of Mike Reid – bringing Danish folklore into Cockney reality – was what the producer expected of me. Because I could read music, I sang the song using all the notation suggested on the sheet. After I'd sung the song the producer complimented me and said I'd sung it wonderfully. Sadly, he added, I'd made it sound like a church motet. Think Chas 'n' Dave singing the Mozart Requiem only in reverse.

One of the disadvantages of Am Dram was having to wear make-up (I was never allowed to use my own) which showed up under strong lights. The smell still lingers (like *Virol* or calamine lotion, which was liberally applied when you had chicken pox) as did the make-up itself if you were mid-teens and hadn't quite discovered washing (or girls). During show week and after every performance I'd go into school the next day. I think I was the only person at Bec Grammar ever to play an entire house rugby match wearing full stage make-up.

The zenith of my amateur thespian career came when I was given the part of John/Ernest Worthing in Oscar Wilde's *The Importance of Being Earnest"* Luckily there were no songs to sing inappropriately, but there were many lines to be learned. However, and not for the first (or last) time in my life, work got in the way and a consequence of me having to be on some advertising course and missing several dress rehearsals, the play never went ahead. Oh well, that's showbiz, I guess. Plus, I never got to say the words, "This way, Lady Bracknell"!

Lice, damned lice and steel combs

There were, at various stages throughout your school career, times when medical matters loomed on the disinfectant-smelling horizon. Although it seemed to go up a gear at secondary school.

At St Mary's Primary School in Balham I can only remember seeing a nurse a few times – each time armed with a steel comb (these were the days when buzzing combs had yet to be invented) and a glass of disinfectant. After the visit of the nit nurse your hair stank of Dettol and was probably highly flammable until bath night.

Secondary school was like an episode of M.A.S.H. compared with primary school.

In the first year at Bec we had the cough and drop test. I failed. I was given a card which said "Ascended right testicle". I took this home to my mother who knew one of the three words. I explained to her what this meant. She was livid. Not at the fact I'd had an undescended testicle but that I'd not been diagnosed with malnutrition. I was disturbingly skinny as a kid and was given Virol – a malt extract probably designed by dentists as it was 101% sugar. Because, as my mother put it,*" I looked like something out of Treblinka"*, she was disappointed I'd been told I had something she only knew 33% of.

In the second year, we had BCG tests – this was to check if any of us were going to get TB (or consumption if you were examined by an older teacher or the King's Evil if your school doctor had been reincarnated from medieval Europe). It was also to prevent any of us becoming 20th century Elizabeth Barrett Brownings – which was unlikely as no one was very good at poetry in my year at school.

The procedure was called the Heaf Test (named after the then PM, Ted Heaf) involved having, what appeared like a multi-staple gun on your arm. It was quite painless. You waited a week. If the mark of six spots had gone, you got the BCG injection (and sent to play rugby immediately after); if the mark was still there, you got another note to take home to your parents suggesting a chest x-ray. Mother was furious, a year on and still no diagnosis of malnutrition. Plus, Virol wasn't cheap

We never got tested for Rubella at our all-boys school. I assume, once Brexit is officially triggered, Rubella will go back to being called German Measles?

How do you solve a problem like Gerd Müller?

1973 was a momentous year: we joined the EU and (more importantly) I took my O-levels. Due to EU legislation, these are now called GCSEs.

The day I got my results has been recorded before:
https://mikerichards.blog/2017/01/05/gateway-to-the-south-coast-revisited-4/

To celebrate this grand union, the three new entrants, Great Britain, Ireland and Denmark played football against the six existing member states: Belgium, France, Italy, Luxembourg, the Netherlands and Germany (well, the bit of Germany not run by the Stasi). The game was held at Wembley, with the West Germans insisting no Russian ran the line. For the Six (as they were known) there were many players you'd have had in your team up the common – Beckenbauer, Netzer, Gerd Müller and the Dutch player, Neeskens. The Three had Arsenal, England and Ford Open Prison right back, Peter Storey.

It was fantastic seeing these great players from differing nations playing for two super teams. Of course, we have this today: it is called the Champion's League. In 1973 this was a massive novelty as we celebrated joining the Common Market.

The year before we'd been celebrating the onset of the three-day week and my school had merged with the school across the rugby field and imaginatively called Bec-Hillcroft before they discovered Ernest Bevin once shopped at Tooting Broadway Market.

I was taken out two-thirds through my 4th year at Bec and sent to Emanuel. I passed the entrance interview with the headmaster, not because of my academic prowess (I defy anyone who went to Bec to have had as much red biro strewn over their homework) but because the head was drunk and I could successfully juggle three empty bottles of Gordon's Gin.

While this move in theory was sensible, in practice it was a disaster. What my dad and I had underestimated was the different syllabuses between the two schools.

Having learned every nook, cranny and ox-bow lake along the Rhine Rift Valley, I soon discovered my newly-acquainted fourth-form classmates had been learning about northern America. I knew about Essen, they knew about Eskimos.

I knew every (bloody) word of *Pygmalion* while my fellow English Lit pupils pranced about the Quad (that's what they called the playground at Emanuel) pretending they were Lady Macbeth; some of them were quite realistic as they were going through puberty and you never quite knew which octave they'd speak in. Some were handy with a dagger too.

Having done special music at Bec and could hum most of the overture to Weber's *Der Freischutz*, my fellow musicians at Emanuel knew every single line to Britten's *A Ceremony of Carols*. I was 121 years behind!

I never bothered with science at Emanuel as giving the answer of "is it a little pip?" to the question "what is a pipette" during my first chemistry lesson, I was destined never to tamper with a Bunsen Burner ever again.

During the exams themselves I remember spending as little time possible in the hall which doubled as the exam room at Emanuel; I left most exams after 30 minutes.

I do remember being asked for Music O-level to write a short biography of Federic Chopin. Having swapped schools, I was blissfully unaware of him and knew more about Peter Storey. I liked to think, if he hadn't got involved with fraud after finishing his football career, he may have written polonaises, etudes of even a three-year (rather than minute) waltz?

So, as we are about to countdown to leave the Common Market we joined in 1973, I've no regrets I never continued French O-level at Emanuel. In two years' time, if I travel to France, I shall simply speak slower and louder.

So long, farewell, auf Wiedersehen, adieu, as Baron von Trapp, who came on as a substitute for Berti Vogts in that 1973 Three vs Six game, would have said.

No laughing policeman

The couple living in the third floor flat below my fourth-floor flat in Du Cane Court often came to complain to my parents about the noise I made. They had no children, but they were massive golf enthusiasts (and with hearing like bats as far as I was concerned). One day, rather than listen to me re-enact the Cassius Clay/Henry Cooper 1966 fight, they invited me to go, with them, to the driving range at Addiscombe.

I loved it and was hooked.

During the summer holidays my friends and I would walk to Balham station and get the Tube to Morden (several of my fellow-travellers believed, once we exited the station, we'd fall off the end of the world. After several trips, there was more chance of being invited to drive a trolley-bus down Balham High Road) to play the championship course which was Morden Pitch 'n' Putt.

Whenever I visit other golf clubs and am asked to enter my club's name, I still write *"Morden Pitch and Putt GC"* – probably one of many reasons I've never been invited to be a member of the R&A.

Having bought a putter and a sleeve of Dunlop 65 balls from Balham Woolworth's, I practiced for hours in my bedroom.

In between pulling down the big, old houses on Balham Park Road and erecting the new houses, thus creating Hunter Close, there lay a building site. This was, for a very brief period, to be our Augusta.

As a teenager, and having mastered my putting rather than doing my geography homework and having bought a selection of second-hand clubs from the second-hand shop on Balham High Road near the Duke of Devonshire (I think it may have been called *Décor*), we were all set for the Balham Masters.

We played one Thursday evening and, even though I say so myself, hit the ball quite well. It wasn't until the following day, that the police informed me of exactly how well I'd hit it. Unbeknownst to me I'd smashed one of the windows of one of the Du Cane Court flats. Equally ignominiously, the window belonged to one of Du Cane Court's minor celebrities: Harry Leader.

Harry Leader was the front man of the highly originally-named band *Harry Leader and his Band*. He had appeared on the radio and briefly, as he'd discovered Matt Monro, in the popular weekly TV programme *This Is Your Life*. This fateful evening, I had a local bobby tell me: *"This is your golf ball!"*

Our cause wasn't helped as the police refused to believe the answer *"choir practice"* to the question, *"Where have you been this evening?"* and then, as all of us thought we were heading for a 10-stretch at Albany High Security Prison (we were only 16 and horribly naïve) they found a book one of my fellow-golfers had purloined: *Boys and Sex*. Because the book was confiscated, many of us within the group didn't discover masturbation until well into our twenties. (Luckily my eyesight was already dreadful and this possibly ensured its arresting).

I still play golf, but have this dread, whenever playing at a course where you're playing near a clubhouse, that, if I were to break another window, the Sweeney will arrive before you can say *"get your trousers on – you're nicked"*. FORE!!!!

To bin or not to bin

When I was a kid, recycling meant taking your bike on a journey you'd made before. Nowadays, courtesy of Al Gore (one of few celebrities never to have lived in Balham), we're asked to save the planet; one way, other than using less deodorant, is to have different receptacles for differing items of rubbish.

In Du Cane Court on Balham High Road, on every floor, there was a room, inside which was housed the "dust chute". You gathered up every item of rubbish – be it Spangles wrappers or old spaniels –opened the lid of the dust chute and chucked everything through one hole into a ground floor giant dustbin, from which the idea of the Daleks came. While the dustbins within Du Cane Court never wanted to master the universe, they did have more brain cells than most of the porters.

I left SW17 and the communal dust chutes of Du Cane Court to live in the oxymoronic London Borough of Sutton. Sutton is not in London. I have since emigrated further under the remit of Epsom and Ewell Council and my bin count from my youth has tripled. Just in case there is another war I have be-friended people who still live in the London Borough of Sutton. A new recycling system has recently been imposed and, as one Suttonian friend and fellow cross-trainer tells me, they have sixteen bins! They are all different colours.

There is a two-week amnesty where the residents of Sutton can make mistakes. However, there is a cloud of fear which now lurks over the town. If you've recently had a row with your neighbour, you can claim an extra two-weeks grace by applying to: *Stasi@sutton.gov.uk/wheresyoubinisbinputtinthebinsoutwheresyoubin*

For anyone moving into the area, here is the colour guide:

Green	Grass
Fawn	Dead grass
Grey	Ashes
Magenta	Plastic
White	Brown glass
Brown	White glass
Beige	Dull neighbours
Orange	Fruit peel
Royal Blue	Old Chelsea shirts
Dark Red	Old clothes if you're a butcher or surgeon
Olive	Old comics
Yellow	Old Post-It notes
Peach	Stones from fruit

Turquoise	Any item of rubbish which is hard to spell
Khaki	Old Japanese soldiers who still believe the war is still raging
Red	Old books (geddit?)

If you're colour-blind and live in Sutton – get yourself an estate agent!

Orange is not the only coach

As a teenager, and because we didn't own a car, I would spend many a Sunday afternoon in a coach, destined to a variety of stately homes in Surrey, Sussex and Kent.
We would travel with Orange Luxury Coaches from Eaton Garage, at the bottom of Marius and Balham High roads.

I was, by the time I was 13, the only person in my class who knew that the main resident of Penshurst Place (a popular venue) was Sir Philip Sidney; several of my classmates, when talking about "what did you do at the weekend?", thought he may have played for Red Star Belgrade. (He didn't, as he had a career-ending knee injury while writing *Astrophel and Stella*)

I assume the reasoning behind my dad's thinking was that these journeys would improve me? In my opinion, watching the John Player League on the TV would have improved my leg-breaks.

The destination was always known in advance; we never ventured on mystery coach tours. One mystery to me, given, in my humble opinion, most of my fellow-travellers must be over 200, if they were a day, was how no-one ever died *en route*.

The coach driver would always count everyone back onto the coach. It still puzzles me to this day how we'd still not be on a 99% full coach waiting for a double centurion not to have made it back due to collapsing amongst Anne Boleyn's begonias at Hever Castle!

Another abiding mystery also remains: wherever the destination, in any of the southern-eastern Home Counties, the journey home was always broken by stopping off at The Black Eagle pub. This pub was situated near the vaguely amusing (if you were a teenager and had borrowed his mate's *Boys and Sex* book) Badger's Mount; and near, which I always, in a child-like way thought even funnier, Pratt's Bottom. We could have travelled to Whitby Abbey, we'd have still visited The Black Eagle!

I believe, in the days before Sat Navs, that all Orange Luxury coach drivers were descendants of King Arthur and The Black Eagle lay, like a series of Neanderthal burial mounds in SW England, on a ley-line linking Balham High Road and Ightham Mote.

The Black Eagle no longer exists, but if there had been an eighth ancient wonder of the world, this would have been it. Should have been in the top seven as you never got chicken 'n' chips in a basket at the Hanging Gardens of Babylon!

A relay baton is not just for Christmas

I was never going to be Balham's answer to Jessica Ennis; although I did enjoy the annual sports day during my final year at St Mary's primary school in Balham. It was our chance to become the next David Hemery, Bob Beamon or Mary Peters if you were big-boned (I enjoyed her singing duo with Lee).

Reports of my ever-decreasing sporting career has already been written about here: https://mikerichards.blog/2017/02/26/odd-shaped-balls/

Our school sports day was not within Beijing's Bird's Nest or under the record-breaking sheets of Perspex construction which is the Olympic Stadium, Munich. No, we walked to what is now called Tooting Bec Athletics Track & Gym. In 1968, the year of our sports day, it was a dilapidated cinder running track where the caretaker was called Jim.

It was the only year and only activity when we were divided into houses, a foretaste of being in Delta House the next year for my first year at Bec. I look back and wonder why we weren't named after famous people who'd lived in Tooting: Hardy; Lloyd George; Gibbon; Harriott? (OK, I get why).

We undertook all the normal races: 100 yards (the only meters in SW17 in 1968 were the ones you'd put half a crown in for the heating); 200 yards; the relay race (with a sherbet fountain being used as a relay stick) and, because we were only 11, the three-legged race.
There were 15 boys and 15 girls in our final year, the three-legged combinations were quite egalitarian. I was partnered to a girl (soppy though that may seem to any 11 year old reading this).

I'd been taken several times to my dad's place of work (an advertising agency in Gloucester Place) a consequence of which was that, when I grew up, I wanted to be part of this Mad Men world. My three-legged race partner wanted to be a golden retriever!

Ostensibly this is a major advantage: faster over 100 yards, more desire for running and a wet nose (handy extra moisture if there's a photo-finish). Sadly, there were disadvantages too – she wasn't a bloody golden retriever being the most obvious (ironically, she was prone to puppy fat). Also, I was 11, theoretically, my partner, mentally, was 77 years old. Not a good age for sprinting.

The prizes were bars of chocolate for first and packets of Spangles for second and third. Sadly, my partner was not incentivised as she was after some Winalot or a tin of PAL (Paired with A Looney).

Ironically my three-legged race partner craved a career in advertising but failed to get in the Andrex ads as she had a fear of quilted paper. I believe she is doing stunt work in the backs of cars selling insurance.

If you have a sports day coming up, don't partner with someone who wants to be a golden retriever when they grow up – get someone who aspires of being a whippet or a greyhound and get one of their parents to throw a pretend rabbit at the finishing line.

Swearing in

We were late getting a colour TV. I was nearly 20 before I realised snooker didn't involve varying shades of grey balls.

In 1970, when I was 13, colour TVs were the domain of the rich – or if you had relatives working for Radio Rentals.

In the 60s and 70s when I was growing up, very few people owned their own set.

We rented a series of black and white sets from Mr John in Balham Station Road. Although I never ran our family finances, we never seem to pay for any of the sets' rental or maintenance. Saying that, my mother's way with most of the traders in Balham & Tooting ensured we never paid for that much. It would appear, with Mr John, that payment enough was simply listening to him talk. And he could talk. He knew 1,001 things to do with a burned valve. He would regale you with these uses during most visits.

On 11 April 1970, my dad and I were invited to watch the FA Cup Final pitting together the Lionel Messi-esque players of Ron Harris of Chelsea against Billy Bremer of Leeds in colour. We knew the owners of the colour TV, they ran the hardware shop, HH Thomas & Son on Balham High Road. The owner wasn't a massive sports fan, but knew of dad's Stamford Bridge allegiance, hence the invite.

Despite having a senior job in advertising and being well-read, dad was staggeringly vituperative. He made Roy "Chubby" Brown sound like Mother Teresa.

Chelsea went 0-1 and 1-2 down and as Jack Charlton's mis-timed header went in, and Mick Jones' quick reaction follow up to Allan Clarke's assist, my dad was clearly having some mental Davina McCall moment as someone somewhere was imploring him not to swear.
(Dad was bright enough to be accepted to have an audition for "Fifteen to One". Sadly, because of this massive swearing vocabulary, he failed the audition).

Eighteen days later we watched David Webb, in his Royal Grey shirt, bundle the ball over the line to win the replay for Chelsea, in the comfort of our own flat, together with dad's mandatory 40 Senior Service. It was better for dad's health that he could eff and blind at home, rather than teaching the children who lived above the hardware shop to learn words they never knew could be used as verb, adjective and adverb all one sentence and so many times over 120-minutes.

I can't remember when we finally got a colour TV, but this didn't matter as mum's favourite programme was *The Black and White Minstrel Show*, so it was academic how sophisticated our TV was.

Breakfast at Tooting Bec

I don't suit Lycra. I've not got the legs for it and a penchant for *Twix* and *Picnic* means I don't possess the correct-sized stomach for it either.

I still commute to work. Last week I boarded the Tube at Morden; by the time I got to Clapham South I was surrounded by people clad in Lycra. On board, not only was I the only person wearing a tie, I was the only person not sporting garish-coloured trainers.

I began work in 1974. I lived in Carshalton and would ride a series of mopeds and motorcycles to my great aunt's flat in Flowersmead on Balham High Road. I would ride down Huron Road and while stopped at the lights at the bottom of Ritherdon Road my great aunt would see me and wave from her kitchen window. I would park my bike and drop off my protective clothing. I was an only great nephew and my great aunt's self-appointed task was to fatten me up as you would a goose to produce *foie gras*. She would prepare a selection of breakfasts which would rival those on the menu at Simpsons-in-the-Strand.

I was invariably late arriving in Tooting and after being force-fed breakfast, by the time I got to Balham Station to get the Tube to Charing Cross where I worked, I was hoping against hope that the Northern Line had been replaced by the Japanese Bullet Train.

In 1974, as I travelled to work, I, along with virtually every other male commuter, had a suit on. My first suit was purple - I looked more like a Bishop than an advertising agency messenger. (I once confirmed several people innocently standing on Stockwell Station).
In 1974 smoking carriages were still in operation. A Tube train would arrive at Balham and you thought you'd got lucky as one was more empty than others. By the time you got to Clapham South, you'd found out why. I was never a smoker; the only cigarettes I bought had a card inside depicting one of the *Thunderbirds* characters They don't exist anymore and travelling up to town, it would appear people wearing suits don't either.

Gyms are clearly open early in the City, either that or these fellow passengers are all competing in the *Tour de France* and have got horribly lost. These days "dress down" abounds. Most men can't cope with "dress down" and to them, this is not wearing a tie. On the busy Northern Line, people dressed in Lycra and wearing trainers are never going to offered a seat – they are all far too fit and unneeding. In an effort to getting a seat on the Tube, I have started wearing a selection of badges: *"I have a hernia"* was one of the more successful. I've toyed with *"Baby on board"* except I was found out when a pregnant woman suggested I'd simply eaten too many *Picnics*.

A mo, A mas, A mat (sic)

Unless you liked to sing along to *Songs of Praise*, Sunday evenings in the late 60s and early 70s, were interminably dull.

It didn't help that homework had to be done: Latin words learned (*expugnare* – to take by storm, being one of the few I can remember – because you're always using the phrase "to take by storm"!!); ox-bow lakes to be drawn and trying to remember 101 uses for a pipette with a 102nd being you use it to hold chemicals in. For me, the evenings were even deadlier because Sunday afternoon had gone the way of all flesh.

Sunday afternoons were fun. My dad and I would walk from our flat in Du Cane Court, with our football (me in my Peter Osgood kit (Thomas Müller hadn't been born, so Peter Osgood it was)) via my mate's house in Oakmead Road to Tooting Bec Common. There were lots of kids involved and with them came their respective dads. One of the dads was a basketball referee and tended to take Sunday-afternoon-up-the-park- football quite seriously and was disturbingly honest in his decision-making. Many a time the game would come to an abrupt halt as this man would say, *"Oh, Simon, you've played me offside!"*. He clearly didn't know the local rule that there was no offside unless a dog, larger than a spaniel, had peed on someone's anorak, which doubled as a goal, and still stood between keeper and striker.

The trudge back with Simon's dad still disputing an offside goal was the start of people petitioning for video refereeing. It also meant Sunday evening was looming and deciding what to have with my spam sandwiches and glass of milk.

I have, in previous posts, alluded to my parents' insistence of me going to bed early https://mikerichards.blog/?s=bayern ; Sunday evenings were the worst. However, one Sunday evening, 5th October 1969, my dad announced that I could stay up late as there was a new show on the TV which I may like. It could have been the testcard, I'd have been happy staying up late.

I was 12 and at 10.55pm, the time - in my mind – when milkmen were probably getting up, the programme started; it wasn't the test card, it was called *Monty Python's Flying Circus*. It had a massive influence in my life. The show moved to midweek early in the series and me and most of the entire class of 30 in my form at Bec would re-enact the sketches throughout the day the next day.

I didn't know anything about the Spanish Inquisition nor Marcel Proust (and how to summarise his works in 15 seconds) what we did know it was funny. Our favourite re-enactment was the man at the start of the programme staggering, out of breath, as he moved towards the camera and would only get to say "It's…".

We would stagger up the stairs of the 155 taking us back to Balham High Road from school doing this. Bet the conductor (not to mention the other passengers) must have loved it! We would cough and wheeze and once at the top of the bus shout "It's". But when you had a Red Rover, you were a king.

Strings, very much attached

Brains never had NO string coming out of his torso.

This may, on the face of it, appear tautological; I was at the gym (I go for the provision of latte and selection of back copies of *Woman's Realm*) and on the TV, facing the cross-dresser (or whatever the machine is called), was a new, horrifically-updated *Thunderbirds*. And Brains had no strings!

I was brought up on a TV diet of Gerry and Sylvia Anderson puppets. As a second year at Bec Grammar, several of the fourth formers called me Joe 90 – if only I'd had magic glasses, like my ostensible *doppelgänger*, I could have stunned them as if they were Russian spies trying to kidnap a leading British optician.

As a younger kid, pre-*Supercar, Stingray* and *Thunderbirds* (I'm too young to remember *Torchy the Battery Boy*) I would (literally) watch *Watch with Mother* with mother. I have a theory that children's eyes cannot discern string until well into adolescence. Bill, Ben and Little Weed would have been inanimate objects if it wasn't for the wonder of string (a girl who lived in Du Cane Court with me wasn't allowed to watch it, lest it affected her diction – because *so* many people from Balham & Tooting have gone on to be members of the Royal Family!). Without string, no one from the Tracy family would have been able to rescue anyone locally, let alone internationally.

This was an age of innocence, although this didn't stop my Guinness-fuelled mother trying to suggest a *ménage-à-trois* between Spotty Dog, Mrs Scrubbit and Mr Woodentop! Barbara Woodhouse would have wanted that banned.

Being an advertising man, I was always surprised they never used Captain Black and Captain Scarlet in *Oli of Ulay* ads – showing before and after; the Mysterons clearly worked Captain Black very hard.

I think string should make a come-back on TV and would welcome *Britain's Got String; Ant 'n' Dec's Saturday Night String* and *String Come Dancing*.

And Muffin the Mule is finally legalised.

And smile!

It was after the 1964 Farnborough Air Show that I decided not to a pursue a career as a professional photographer. I was seven in 1964 and had been given a second-hand Box Brownie camera by my parents.

A Brownie camera was a cumbersome device which was operated nearer your groin than your eye. Unlike cameras of today, where the resulting images are immediate, in 1964 you were beholden to the local chemists (to the tune of about three weeks) on the outcome.
In 1964 a selfie wasn't a photograph, it was something your parents warned you would eventually make you go blind.

By 1964 the Box Brownie had been around for 64 years, so wasn't exactly in the forefront of camera technology. Lord Lichfield used his to prop up a wonky table.

At the time of the 1964 Farnborough Air Show I was invited by a fellow classmate at St Mary's Balham, who lived in Streathbourne Road in Tooting, to join him and his parents in his parents' Austin Cambridge to travel to the Hampshire village which hosted, every other year since 1948, the world-famous air show. Packed off with Kwells and thermos flask full of chicken soup, I was allowed to take my camera.

If George Eastman had known how I was about to crucify his industry, he'd have never have invented Kodak.

We travelled to Farnborough, I took my full reel of 24 pictures, I wound it on after every shot, I never exposed the film, I'd not covered the lens with my hand (or penis - not that I was doing this naked), I'd carefully removed the film, proudly presented the film to the man in Boot's on Balham High Road and prepared to wait the mandatory three weeks (waiting for my O-level results was not as excruciating - although the results equally horrific).

At the end of the three weeks I walked from my flats the other side of Balham Station to Boot's on the High Road to collect and revel in the fruits of my labours of recording one the world's greatest air shows.

I paid my money and looked at my 24 individual efforts. I saw 24 minuscule black specks on a grey background. My attempts to capture the beauty of the then new VC10 had failed miserably. I'd have had a better definition on a photograph if I'd having been standing in Farnborough photographing an ant walking along Streathbourne Road.

A year later, David Bailey released his iconic picture of the Krays; it was this harsh reality which decreed I was never going to make it as a professional photographer. I have never picked up a camera since and am only grateful I never watched Tony Curtis's portrayal of Houdini.

More Dr Carrot than Dr Goebbels

I would have probably never made a good soldier: myopic; cunning implement to make it appear I'm flat-footed; never had a fight; not a massive fan of foreign food (so overseas posting would have been out) and I'd probably have an allergic reaction to the uniform. (I don't suit brown).

Having swapped schools after the middle term of my fourth year from Bec to Emanuel, the only consistent was the regular activities of the CCF (Combined Cadet Force). A chance for teenagers to dress up in military uniform several sizes too big, be shouted out by masters more often (and louder than normal) and to brandish weapons considered obsolete before the outbreak of the Boer War.

A group of us travelled via or from Balham every day *en route* to Clapham Junction. When it was CCF day travelling was like *The Borrowers* meets *Dad's Army*.

CCF wasn't compulsory at Emanuel, there were two alternatives: there was Scottish country dancing with the headmaster (not appealing in an all-boys school, although this was the man who was drunk during my entrance interview when he allowed me to join the school – it certainly wasn't based on academic ability) or a thing called *Taskforce*.

Taskforce was organised by the Divinity master; it involved us pupils visiting old people near the school and doing good generally. Two of my classmates and I were sent to visit Mrs Tyler, who lived in a terrace house just off Lavender Hill, just past Clapham Junction Station.

Mrs Tyler was built like she was training to be England's Strongest Woman, she was also the loveliest woman living in SW11 and a great sport. She was visited, regularly, by her daughter, who would also do her shopping. Our visit was, ostensibly, superfluous.

When we first arrived, she would get us to make a cup of tea – something three teenage boys could just about do in 1973 - and get the Custard Creams out her daughter had kindly supplied earlier.

Once settled, we would turn the TV on and watch the horse racing (at Mrs Tyler's behest, I hasten to add) the entire afternoon. Nowadays, whenever I watch Channel 4 Racing I also get a waft of Custard Creams. And to think, we could have been running around the playing fields of Emanuel, face covered in dubbin and with a perpetual itching where you were never quite sure if it was the texture of the uniform or visitors from a previous occupant.

Mrs Tyler was so welcoming me and my mates visited her during our holidays. I even grew carrots for her in the ground outside my flat in Du Cane Court. I felt she'd probably done this when she was my age so I hoped home-grown carrots brought back the memories of hating Hitler.

Even though my friends were playing soldiers, sailors and airmen on the Elysian fields of Emanuel, I look back and think there was probably more chance of being shot walking up Lavender Hill to Mrs Tyler's house than if we'd been behind the chapel at Emanuel pretending the music master was Himmler.

If I had have done CCF, I think, if I'd made it to Field Marshall, I'd have had Arding & Hobbs as my HQ. At least the carpets would have been of high quality.

Flagging a dead horse

Before email, people would communicate with one another using semaphore flags. Luckily for me, in the late 60s (just before the invention of email) one of the badges available for attainment within the 3rd/14th Balham & Tooting Cub Group was a Signaller's Badge. There was an option of learning how to work an Aldis lamp, but we were poor and couldn't afford the giant light bulb.

Having created two flags out of an old pair of red and yellow pants (they were never going to become fashionable) and a couple of Mivvi lolly sticks I was sent by Akela (the she-wolf who ran the Cubs) to a house in Holdernesse Road, Tooting, to learn how to spell out H-E-L-P-M-Y-B-O-A-T-I-S-S-I-N-K-I-N-G.

The house was owned by the father of a fellow pupil at St Mary's, Balham, and the dad's ability to send messages using flags meant there was no ostensible need for a telephone (there were, however, several discarded yoghurt pots and bits of string strewn around the house – in case of emergencies, the father would say).

The badges available these days for Cubs are manifold: Entertainer (I've done 50 stand-up gigs, so feel over-qualified); Home Help (I bought a duster on the doorstep last week and have almost mastered how to use it) and Local Knowledge (I pointed out where the Gents was on Ewell East Station the other day). If I were a Cub today I'd have an armful; as a Cub in the 60s, I achieved two badges – Signaller and Collector (dad was a prolific smoker and acquired boxes of matches which I would collect and stick in a scrapbook). It was the smelliest submission ever, said Bagheera (Akela's deputy).

I never graduated to the Scouts as cooking was introduced towards the end of my Cub career and this looked potentially quite dangerous with sausages clearly having a mind of their own.

As you get older, you hark back to the "good old days" and I sit in my office praying for the Internet to go down, because I never need an excuse to get my semaphore flags out. This is not a euphemism.

Wot, no fags?

I never smoked when younger; consequently, I am over seven-feet tall. Well, I smoked for about a fortnight when was 14, and because my growth was dramatically stunted, I now stand at six-foot (when not slouching and sporting Cuban heels).

My mother smoked about forty JPS a day, my father 50% more in Senior Service, my maternal grandmother smoked Weights and her sister was seemingly sponsored by Embassy (for interesting facts about collecting Embassy coupons, please see https://wordpress.com/post/mikerichards.blog/54 - new readers start here!).

Temptation was all around. Cigarettes were sold at the porter's lodge within Du Cane Court where I lived; if you didn't want either smoking-like-a-trooper parent catching you, there was a newsagent in Glenburnie Road in Tooting which would sell them individually (you'd have to go in the newsagents a great deal if you were collecting the coupons for sheets – or a new lung).

In the early 70s no one realised the inherent dangers of smoking – cigarette sponsorship was everywhere: I'm surprised my Auntie Vera wasn't as good a snooker player as Alex Higgins although I did have another Aunt who had a similar physique to Jocky Wilson. Cigarette ads were always on the back covers of men's magazines. Whenever I went to the barbers these magazines were always evident although before I was put on the bench and my mother explained to the barber in broken Greek (from whence the barbers had come) I'd never noticed the ads – I was too busy reading the thought-provoking articles which graced the likes of *Penthouse* and *Men Only*.

Luckily for me I never really ventured past sweet cigarettes (arguably worse for your teeth than actual fags were for your lungs) – I would pretend I was smoking, but never had the street cred for this to look realistic as I'd be constructing the Thunderbirds puzzle with the cards I'd collected.

Smoking saw off most of my aforementioned relatives; although my mum always maintained there was nothing more satisfying than sucking on an old Churchwarden!

"Where's your mother gone?"

Each week I would receive five shillings as pocket money from my Nan and five shillings from my great aunt. I got nothing from either parent as they suggested any additional income would put me in a different tax bracket. At 13, in 1970, I thought a tax bracket was something which held up book shelves.

I would, soon after pocketing my 10 bob, be quickly relieved of it by the man behind the record counter in Hurley's, a small department store on Balham High Road.

There were several listening booths within the record department; you could listen, in relative private (and without anyone shouting out "turn that bleedin' noise down, Michael"), and no one would ever know you were a closet Clodagh Rodgers fan.

75% of my pocket money would go on buying a single record. (There's not much you can buy for seven and six these days, mainly because pre-decimalisation currency in no longer legal tender).

Despite the unendearing fiscal lessons taught by my mother, I would occasionally buy her records she'd ask for. She was a massive Motown fan and I remember buying the Detroit Spinners' "It's a shame" and Freda Payne's "Band of gold".

One week my mother went rogue.

She'd taken a liking the Scottish group, Middle Of The Road. In June 1971, when seven and six had become 37 and a half pence, I went to the record counter at Hurley's. I approached the assistant and innocently inquired after the number one hit of this aptly-named middle of the road pop combo. I had long hair at the time and believe the assistant anticipated me asking for something by Jimi Hendrix, Eric Clapton, Humble pie. His assumptive world (and mine) was about to come crashing down:

"Have you got *Chirpy, chirpy, cheep, cheep*?" I asked.

"No," replied the assistant, choking on the absinthe he'd had hidden in his Thermos flask, "I've been like this since the accident."

Middle Of The Road went on to have two others hits: *Soley, Soley* and *Tweedle Dee, Tweedle Dum*; following on from *Chirpy, chirpy, cheep, cheep*, I naturally assumed either the lyricists were very unimaginative or had dreadful stammers.

Embarrassed after the *Chirpy, chirpy, cheep, cheep* incident, I took my custom to Harlequin Records, also on Balham High Road. It was there, buying singles, that I learned to spell badly courtesy of Noddy Holder.

Well heeled

Aged 60, I'm glad I don't need my mum taking me shopping.

Aside from flirting with most shopkeepers along Balham High Road, mum would take me to buy clothes, get my haircut and purchase shoes.

Last week I was set to buy a pair of shoes and was reminded about the many pairs we'd buy in the Clark's near Tooting Bec Station.

I loved the exact way they measured the length and width of your feet – one of the measuring instruments tickled; I can fully understand how people develop foot fetishes. I never did, as my mum told me this was a guaranteed way of catching Athlete's Foot (or was it VD? Either way, it's why she never made it to be Surgeon General).

The thing which most fascinated me about this shop was the pneumatic system which ferried money around. There was a complex system of tubing which went around the shop. Mum would buy my shoes (invariably brown sandals – how I was never bullied at school never ceases to amaze me) and in doing so handed over the money. This was placed in a tube and sent, ostensibly at twice the speed of sound, around the shop to a cashier, hidden from sight (probably had corns and therefore not a good advertisement for the shop). Any change, and a receipt, returned, as fast, through this magic system.

Last week I went to buy a pair of shoes (without my mum, I hasten to add). I found a pair I liked and asked, "Have you these in an eight?"

"I shall go and look," replied the small, Scottish female assistant, who had the demeanour of having several unsatisfied customers out the back in a cauldron.

After a few minutes, she returned.

"We haven't got these in an eight, but we have them in a seven-and-a-half?"

I can only assume she was expecting replies such as: "Oh, that's fine, I was thinking of chopping half an inch of several toes" or "That's OK, I never fully put my heel into the show anyway" or "Fantastic, that could immediately solve my verruca problem!"

I left the shop barefoot. It could have been worse, she could have replied: "An eight? I assume you have a small penis?"

Can't see for the trees

Living on the fourth floor of a block of flats as a kid didn't exactly get you at one with nature. There were two breeds of birds which would circulate around the courtyard of my Balham block of flats: pigeons and sparrows. I established (with the help of my *Observer Book of Birds*) that pigeons were the larger of the two species. Anything else which might have inadvertently flown into my courtyard were regarded by me as smaller or larger pigeons. A kite, would be a pigeon with a large wing-span, a pterodactyl would be regarded simply as unlucky for the other tenants if it chose to land on their *Grobag*.

Even with Tooting, Clapham and Wandsworth commons all nearby, I still had no tuition, and therefore comprehension, of the difference between trees. I remain incapable of determining between an oak and a Rocky Mountain Subalpine Fir (although, I seem to recall, there weren't many of those springing up to great heights in Balham during the 60s and 70s thus emulating a Canadian skyline).

My most immediate access to nature was the communal pond in the front gardens of Du Cane Court where I lived; inside the pond swam very large goldfish. It was rumoured they weren't actually goldfish, but coelacanths. This would figure as, in my child opinion, many of the flats' residents were like the walking dead, so having prehistoric fish in the ponds was logical.

My awareness of flowers is not dissimilar on a knowledge scale. I know what a daffodil and hyacinth look like as we had to grow them at primary school (I only once got a coloured certificate for first prize when I delegated the growing to a green-fingered uncle, I still can't go past a garden centre without feeling guilty). Living in near Epsom racecourse these days means I know what heather looks like. I also know it has a smell like that of having peed yourself a week ago, (not that that is a habit of mine), although this could be the people selling it in clumps? (I assume the smell is the people selling it as you wouldn't buy some given the lingering odour, and, why would it be given the epithet "lucky"!?).

But it is birds where I most struggle and wish I had a greater knowledge. My *"I-Spy Garden Birds"* is still in pristine, almost virgin state. I do have a garden now and have a bird table with many seed-filled containers hanging off it. While I know what a robin looks like (years of growing up watching *Batman*) I am still blissfully unware of the difference between a goldfinch and a collared dove; although I did see some tits once, but that's only because the woman opposite can't afford decent net curtains!

Phew, wot a scorcher!

In 1976 there was a heatwave like the one we are witnessing today in southern England. I had begun the second year of my advertising career that year and it was at this point that I realised just how glamourous an industry it was: I received a free T-Shirt from one of the clients of McCann Erickson for whom I worked, the National Water Council, encouraging everyone in the UK to "save water". Mine had the then TUC leader, Len Murray, embossed on the front encouraging me to do just that. (I don't quite see how this helped save water and is one of the reasons the T-shirt shop in the Atacama Desert in Chile, the driest place on Earth, shut down after only two weeks).

1976 (or 4673 if you were in Shanghai) had James Callaghan as Prime Minister from April; West Indian cricketer, Michael Holding had match figures of 14-149 against England at the Oval; Southampton beat Manchester United one-nil in the shock result of the FA Cup Final, Franz "Bulle" Roth created the same winning score-line for Bayern Munich in their third successive European Cup Final; in June of that year the "Cod War" (see what they did there?) between Iceland (the country, not the shop where "mum's gone to") and Great Britain ended (this was of huge personal relief as I was on stand-by and had worn a sou'wester through much of April and May); and the heatwave persisted between 22nd June and 16th July, instigating this need to save water.

One of the thoughts of the "Save Water" campaign was to bath with a friend. This threw up so many social problems: if you like, every evening, at bath-time, to re-create sinking the Bismarck, and you want to play the Kenneth More role, you do not want someone the other end of the bath acting as the French coastline; if you're sharing with a member of the opposite sex, you have the dilemma of choosing between Mr Matey and Miss Matey bubble bath; if you like the radio on during bath-time, remember, not everyone likes Wagner and worst of all, if you're sharing a bath with someone with a bladder control problem, what Archimedes had as his *eureka* moment, you'll have as your urethra moment.

On the plus side, we all learned that drought wasn't spelled with a "W".

Mangled

My nan used to let me play with her mangle (this is not a euphemism).

In her south London flat kitchen she had a table, underneath which, magically lived a mangle which not only helped removed excess damp from clothes, it also ensured you had one bicep big than the other – think of my nan was a precursor to Rafael Nadal.

She owned a mangle because she did not possess a washer/drier. Neither did my parents. When I was a child in the early 60s washing machine brands were unknown: a *Whirlpool* was something they had at posh swimming baths; *Indesit* was something you got if you ate too quickly and *Bosch* was 15th century Flemish artist obsessed with fish, torture or people being tortured by fish.

A consequence lack of family ownership of a washing machine meant we used the launderette opposite our flats on Balham High Road.

This week I discovered a shop where I get my shoes re-heeled, doubles as a launderette. While queuing to collect my good-as-new shoes I was reminded of the launderette on Balham High Road where my mum would take me and convince me the drying machines were actual TVs. I spent hours watching an entire drying cycle wondering why I never saw anyone from *Emergency, Ward 10!*

The shop was identical and almost in some time-wrap, the only difference being that packets of *Tide* now costs more than two-bob now (or would do if *Tide* still existed) and the actual machines, old-fashioned though they looked, probably don't take a couple of half-a-crowns to get the washing started any more.

If you needed your washing moved from washer to drier and then subsequently folded, you could give the woman running the shop a few extra shillings. This was quite ironic as my mum would offer "additional services" to most shop-keepers along Balham High Road for nothing.

Hell's kitchen

I've not eaten semolina since 1962.

Even with a dollop of jam to hide the malevolence of this dish, if the Devil were to publish a recipe book, semolina would be on page one; if I were Prime Minister for a day, I'd put semolina up there with all the major Class A drugs as a banned substance.

In 1962, the year I started school, semolina was the staple dessert in my south-west London primary school. If ever there was a pudding which also acted as an emetic, it would have been the St Mary's Primary School's pudding from Hell! If I'd have been War Minister, I'd have infected the remote Scottish island of Gruinard with it, rather than anthrax, which was chosen to deter invading Nazis.

However, living next door to the school meant I rarely attended school dinners. When I did, semolina would invariably be on the menu; this followed on nicely from the salad we were given, whose constituent parts were made up more of caterpillar than that of lettuce.

School custard had nothing going for it, either, unless you needed the skin to reinforce your wicketkeeping gloves. Leathery would have been a masterpiece of understatement.

Not only was the food frightful, the women serving it were just as bad. In our school, we had Mrs Roberts. Mrs Roberts, we believed, had trained, as a dinner lady, at HMP Parkhurst. Poor woman also had a dreadful limp – probably been involved in a custard-related accident during slopping out?

The only nourishing treat we'd be given was an annual slice of chocolate sponge, although I've probably eaten more edible carpet.

There were, back then, ostensibly, no such things as food allergies nor did the school ever entertain thoughts about giving us anything vaguely nutritional, as I assume there is in abundance these days within schools? No one was vegetarian and if you'd have asked a kid at my school *what's a vegan?*, they'd have probably replied it was the character John Thaw played in *The Sweeney*?

And is there honey still for tea? I bloody hope so, but I'm not putting any of it on my semolina!

Hold the bells

I was never going to make it as a professional recorder player; I don't like the taste of *Dettol*. I often see young kids on the train to work with musical instruments twice their size strapped to their backs. This was never a choice at my 60s primary school.

For music lessons we had to play a recorder that's end was more chewed than the end of a pen ravaged by the most nervous person in the world. If you were lucky you'd get to play a triangle (this smelled less of *Dettol*) or, if you were teacher's pet, the Glockenspiel. The set of hand-bells, which could have acted as knuckle-dusters, weren't issued to the more violent kids in the class! Whenever the teacher said the word "maracas" you'd have 15 boys giggling to themselves (although 50% not knowing quite why).

In the final year at St Mary's, my primary school in Balham, there was the opportunity of learning the violin. This was made attractive as it meant missing part of a maths lessons. (I can only assume that Einstein never had access to a tambourine when a child). I can't do long division, but I can play *Baa-Baa Black Sheep*.

I carried on, much to the chagrin of my parents, playing the violin when I went to secondary school. I played third violin (mainly because there weren't eighth violins) in the Bec School Orchestra. My murdering of the third violin part of *Die Meistersinger von Nürnberg* would have had Richard Wagner turning in his Bavarian grave.

There was clearly no vision of any of us becoming decent musicians – none of the Beatles played the triangle; I hate to think what damage Keith Moon might have done with a Glockenspiel hammer! And there wouldn't have been as much wonder of Jimi Hendrix playing *Hey Joe* with his teeth on a castanet.

The music aspect (in spite of the overriding smell of disinfectant) of music and movement classes, however, was the better half; moving about the school hall pretending to be a tree wasn't as much fun as playing with your maracas. Although, even though I say so myself, I did make a very good larch (even if I was only wearing pants!). I do, however, blame my myopia on over-doing the maraca-playing!

You know how to whistle, Mick, don't you?

If there'd been an O-level for whistling, I'd have got an A*.

My nan used to say, "here comes *Whistler's Mother*". which was curious given that this was an 1871 painting, rather than some sort of noise.

Rather than whistling, looking back, I should have been reading. Reading, when it came to school exams, was a more constructive ability to have than whistling.

Having passed my 11-plus in 1968, I set off to grammar school. I choose to go to Bec, a grammar school in Tooting (an educational paradox if ever there was one). The summer in between schools I was sent a reading list. The list contained about 20 books – none required a whistling accompaniment.

I was never a great reader as a kid and the summer of '68, when Jimi Hendrix and rioting French students were making headlines, was no different. I read the first chapter of *Rodney Stone* (a Gothic mystery written by Sir Arthur Conan Doyle and about 1% of the reading list) and decided that perfecting my leg-break and learning to imitate the call of garden birds of south-west London or members of *The* Goons (which I can still do – so look out *Britain's Got Talent*) was a better use of my time.

Throughout my teens, rather than reading books, I would read comics which were bought for me – *Beano* and *Shoot* being the two which were regularly procured. If there'd been a question about Roger the Dodger or Lord Snooty, rather than Lady Macbeth, during my English Literature O-level, I may have got a better grade.

Rather than reading (and learning) *Juno and the Paycock*, I was fully occupied making sure the free ladder from *Shoot* magazine was up-to-date with the movements of the First Division football teams.

While I can't remember how many pounds of flesh Shylock wanted, I can remember that 70s Arsenal striker John Radford's favourite food was "steak and chips in the Olympic Café, Neasden".

Or was John Radford one of the twins in *The comedy of errors*?

Luxembourg Calling

Until I was 13, I thought music was probably best heard under a thick blanket.
Armed with transistor radio, torch, blanket to muffle the sound of the transistor radio and ears which would make a pipistrelle bat jealous to listen out for potentially vituperative parents, in the evenings I would listen to Radio Luxembourg. I also had a pencil and paper to list the midweek Top 20. Unlike the BBC, who had their Top 20 inside *Pick of the Pops*, Radio Luxembourg's offering was midweek. My bed had so much stationery in it, it resembled a branch of WH Smith.

Because we lacked money, and to earn a few bob more, my father had a twice-weekly evening pools round around the back streets between Tooting High Street and St Benedict's Hospital. My mum would drive him in our Austin A40 to his destination and follow him round (like kerb-crawling except my dad didn't have the opportunity to stick his head in the car to ask "inside or out"). I would sit in the back, listening to my radio. These were days before car radios (which kept car radio theft down to a minimum). I would sit, one hand on the radio almost glued to my ear and the other on a pencil to write down the chart as it was unveiled.

Eventually we'd head home with my dad having been to one too many houses with people hiding behind their respective sofas. The chart, at this point, would only be about mid-way, so my sheet, with the numbers 10 to 1 remained blank.

By the time my strict parents had sent me to bed (ostensibly to sleep) the top five were yet to be revealed. Once the light was turned off, my listening post was hastily erected; important items were produced from under my pillow (this must have confused the Tooth Fairy). My writing kit and torch came into their own as I rapidly wrote down (probably not grammatically correct) songs like, "Signed, Sealed, Delivered, I'm Yours".

My interest in music coincided with my rapid eyesight decline (I have since learned my myopia was, due to another hobby discovered as a teenager, not helped, either). I don't think this was aided by some of the 70s bands having ridiculously long names – why couldn't groups be called Lulu or Dana? Why choose Dave, Dee, Dozy, Beaky, Mick and Tich? If I'd have wanted to witness such names I'd have watched episodes of *Trumpton*.

Bus-spotting (like train-spotting but with less heroin)

Although destined, as a bit of a geek, to become a train-spotter, an unnatural affinity to trolley buses deigned this was never going to happen.

As a kid, my nan had a grassy-knoll-type flat whose window overlooked Balham High Road. I would spend hours staring out of this window making a list of the buses travelling up and down the street.

I didn't need an especially large sheet as there were only three routes: 88,155 and 181. I'd sit, eating my nan's Callard & Bowser's toffees (she had no teeth, so toffees were a complete waste on her) recording each bus as it passed. I would do this until I spotted my Auntie Vera's alighting from here 155 as she returned from her job at Freeman's near the Oval.

Sometimes a complete spanner would be thrown in the works by the appearance of a 711 Green Line Bus. This vehicle never stopped at any of the two stops I could see so, in my mind it never existed – a bit like the little-known philosophical theory, Schrödinger's Bus. It certainly was never entered onto the toffee-covered list.

In the mid-60s, when I was around eight, my Auntie Vera decided she would take me on a trolley bus. We travelled on a 155 to Wimbledon where we picked up the trolley bus to Belmont. It might as well have been to Belize, such was my geographical lack of knowledge anywhere outside SW17. Ironically, I now live near there (Belmont, not Belize, where I still don't quite know where it is, it is only near Belmont alphabetically).

Three years on and I had my next out-of-Balham experience. I was selected to play for the school cricket team. The first fixture was away at Sutton Manor (now Sutton Grammar). I stood, with my dad, on the platform at Balham, looking in a direction I'd never been before (dad had assured me they'd all been lavender fields the week before). I assumed that, before we even got to Sutton, we'd have fallen off the end of the world.

When I changed schools from Bec to Emanuel I discovered several of my new form-mates were into plane spotting. I asked my dad if this would possibly be something for me? He replied saying: as long as I knew what an ME109 looked like, I'd probably best stick to bus-spotting. Any more fares, please?

Sign of the Ford Zodiac

There should be playtime in the workplace. Fifteen mental minutes when you can run around before going back to your office, sweating like a pig before creating more content for your last primary school year county project; never has so much rubbish been written about Middlesex as there was by me in my south London primary school in the late 60s.

Within my school most boys wanted to play professional football or cricket (we weren't allowed in the girls' playground, which was no bad thing as this was where the threat of kiss chase lurked and, as a ten/eleven-year-old boy, all girls were considered soppy). (My mother had warned me that using other peoples' toilet seats would induce VD; for me, kiss chase was simply the start of a slippery slope towards a life of contracting sexually-transmitted diseases. My mother's Chinese lantern presentations on the subject make me wonder how I ever talked to girls, let alone realise that kiss chase may well have been better fun than three-and-in).

In the confines of the boys' playground, we'd emulate Peter Osgood or Colin Cowdrey – some of the boys who weren't very sporty played cover drives like Peter Osgood and chested balls down and volleyed them like Colin Cowdrey. This was our desire, except for one boy in our class. He wanted to be a Ford Zodiac.

While we would hope, while we were running around, that possibly there'd be scouts from Chelsea or Fulham or Tooting & Mitcham if you were slightly more realistic; this one lad was hoping to have someone spot him from the Dagenham Motor Works. We all wanted to be footballers, he wanted to be a faux-wood dash board, leatherette steering wheel or alternator. We were trying to make the ball swerve off the outside of our foot like Pele, our mutual classmate would run around, changing an imaginary gear like Marcel Marceau.
I never got to play for Chelsea, but then,50 years later, I've never had to replace my clutch. Although I think I've started to leak brake fluid.

Flatulence will get you everywhere

Did people fart less in the 70s?

Because of the changes at Waterloo Station throughout the summer I have had to experiment and vary (in case I'm followed) my journeys home.

This week I travelled from Victoria, via my home town of Balham, *en route* to suburbia. I was lucky as I was the only person in a carriage of four banks of four seats. That was until a late-boarding passenger got in my compartment and proceeded to sit next to me. Did I have some invisible sign above my head saying *"This man is lonely, sit next to him"*? But this was the second time that week where this had happened to me – empty carriage, then suddenly I have a new friend. Had I been horrible in a previous life and this was some form of commuting karma on the 18.50?

My all-too-close neighbour began to entertain himself with that evening's *Standard*. Chewed pencil in hand, he duly went about completing the Sudoku. I've never seen anyone complete one so quickly; but then, I've never seen anyone using the number 24 in one of the squares before.

Sudoku done, on to the crossword; and cryptic one at that. I thought this man would struggle with *"Hot beverage (3) "T" something "A""* let alone dig deep into his knowledge of Greek mythology to seek out possible answers. However, I was wrong as the man next to me wrote *HAEMOGLOBIN* as one of the answers. A considerable feat on two counts: one, it's not the easiest word to spell and two, it's not easy to get an eleven-letter word into seven-letter spaces! He had completed the crossword (before we'd even got to Wandsworth Common) by using the word *haemoglobin* as every answer. I assume he'd just learned the word?

However, it was just outside Balham when the flatulence began. Was this due to excitement of the speed in completing the *Standard* puzzle page? Too many bubbles in his second can of *Stella*? Or bad diet?

I began commuting in 1974, the same year McDonalds opened their first restaurant in the UK. Before then, when I'd frequently visited my paternal grandmother in her council flat in St John's Wood, the only food people would have on the train would be housed in Tupperware boxes (Tupperware was introduced into the UK in 1946 when the containers were used more for somewhere to put your ration book rather than actual food).

Before the influx of fast food, the only times you'd hear "take away" would be at primary school and if you're nan had been collected by people in white coats as she's thought she was Joan of Arc again (one of the many dangers of owning a three-bar fire).

Nowadays, food available (especially at train stations) is manifold. People will eat couscous (not remembering these were the people fighting in Kenya during the 60s); Sushi was the girl at school with a lisp and Vegan was one of the main characters in *The Sweeney*.

We are lucky in London that we have greater choice than we did in the 60s and 70s, when you had on one hand, top-end (unattainable) restaurants and hotels and at the other, cafes, where you came out smelling of what you'd just eaten and with nothing in between.

I'm going to write to British Rail asking them for a selection of new signs on their carriages: "NO FARTING", "NO LOW HAEMOGLOBIN" OR EVEN "NO ONE ELSE"

More tea, Vicar?

Geneva unconvention

Whenever I see the spurting fountain of Lake Geneva, I don't think of many a closing scene of the "Confession of" film series; I think of Alexandra Bastedo.

She was my first crush.

Sadly, for me, when she first appeared in front of me (albeit through a small black & white screen playing Sharron Macready in "The Champions") she was already 22, I was barely 11. I loathe to use the word *rousing* in a public forum, but there was something about her which made me instantly regretting having started at my all-boys grammar school in Tooting two weeks prior, coupled with being a member of an all-male choir. When was I ever going to meet someone like Sharron Macready? I learned, after a few weeks at Bec School, that this kind of person wasn't going to be teaching geography (let alone biology – I would have to make do with learning about the reproduction system of amoebas, rather than getting sex education in an after-school class from Alexandra Bastedo).

I would watch "The Champions" avidly, every Wednesday evening during 1968 and 1969 with my nan in her south London flat while we ate Bird's Eye's Cod Fillet and chips (as only nans can make chips). I often wondered what it would have been like having Alexandra Bastedo bringing my cod and chips? If she smoked copious amounts of Player's *Weights* and had no teeth – quite similar!

This new-found affinity with girls had clearly kicked in. I procured, and stuck across most of my bedroom wall, a gigantic poster of Nancy Sinatra wearing pink, thigh-length boots (in which I assumed she'd walked).

I look back and feel I could have got lucky with Alexandra Bastedo as she'd dated Omar Sharif. Sharif was famed for his Bridge-playing ability - I was rather good at *Beat Your Neighbour*. No brainer, Alexandra.

The Champions ran for thirty episodes and was used in several other countries. In France, it was called *Les Champions* – which was, coincidentally, the name of the bloke who ran *Nemesis*, the organisation for whom Sharron Macready was employed as a spy-cum-doctor.
Next week: Why I tried to learn Italian in case Claudia Cardinale ever moved to Balham!

An aardvark is not just for Christmas

I was a dog owner for half a day.

I was 10 and my mother thought she could win Cruft's; the procurement of a West Highland Terrier would show us the road to victory.

What my mother had not anticipated was the trickiness of owning a dog while living on the fourth floor of a block of flats. I think she'd anticipated the dog either being on an extremely long lead or possessing the ability to fly (perhaps she thought she was buying a Harrier rather than Terrier?)

My mother also found out, in these fateful few hours of dog-ownership, that un-house-trained dogs giving no warning of doing a pooh, nor have the talent to order a lift to the correct floor to get to down to the communal gardens.

To be fair to the dog, during these morning hours, my mother had been sporting her newly-acquired curlers which would have loosened the bowels of most living organism.

By lunchtime, with a very nervous and understandably incontinent dog, the dog was returned to its previous owners, the people who also owned *La Patisserie* on Balham High Road. They had got rid of the dog as it had (literally) eaten all the pies. The dog had now been returned to be a perpetual menace to a selection of Fondant Fancies.

To avert my being so distraught over the loss of the free-poohing dog, my mother promised me a pet (as long as it wasn't a dog, obviously). I fancied an aardvark, but mother said it would ruin her newly-laid shag-pile carpet with its burrowing. I had (and still have) a terrible fear of birds, so a budgie, parrot or pterodactyl (we'd just started studying dinosaurs at school and hadn't got as far as the extinction bit) were all out of the equation.

I chose a mouse, which I unimaginatively called *Jerry*. Its toilet habits were similar to the terrier, only on an acceptably smaller scale. Throughout the 60s, 70s and most of the 80s, I never owned another pet, having lived in various flats scattered around south-west London.

I now live in a house and an aardvark is back on the agenda as I have an ant infestation and it will save me money on the special powder. I think one would make a great pet, although a right bugger if it ever caught a cold!

Don't shoot the messenger

43-years today I started work. With two O-levels you tended not to be placed on the fast-track graduate scheme; you were, however, almost over-qualified to be a messenger.

My role for the first three-months of my advertising career was as a messenger. My role was, twice a day, to travel to Fleet Street, where most for the major UK national newspapers were and representatives of most regional newspapers: 63 Fleet Street housed the *Southampton Evening Echo*, 85 the *Portsmouth News* and *Sunderland Echo*, 107 was the *Isle of Wight County Press* (handy if you wanted to know what was going on with cats and the rooves of Ventnor supermarket car parks). I had to collect newspapers in which my company's clients had run advertisements.

During my three months I worked out I could save the money I'd be given for bus fares by walking from the agency in Howland Street to Fleet Street (this is how money laundering begins).

Because I travelled alone I would rest in the Wimpy on Bride Lane or Mick's Café on Fleet Street. I would dream that, with all the savings I was making on fiddling expenses, I'd open my own café, which, of course, would also be called *Mick's Cafe*. I also found that, if I'd drunk too many ice-cream floats in the Wimpy, there were very nice toilets, where *Kent Messenger* was on 76 Shoe Lane.

On one occasion, for our client Martini, I was given an A-Z and told to go to Brewer Street to collect a copy of *Men Only*, where the client had an ad on the back cover.

I'd never been to Soho before. Not knowing where the offices of Paul Raymond Publications were exactly, I walked quite slowly down Brewer Street. As I walked down the street thinking the lighting bill must be quite large, a man suddenly appeared from a doorway to distract me from my utility costs ruminations. "Would you like a girl for the afternoon?" he asked. I thought to myself, is this a bit like having the school hamster for a weekend – a temporary loan? And would he be supplying the girl equivalent of sawdust and sunflower seeds? I replied, "No thank you, I need to get this month's *Men Only*" – he looked at me and, seeing the thick lenses of my glasses, assumed this was probably not the first time I'd sought out a copy!

I found the building and, after asking the receptionist for a copy of that month's magazine, waited as several scantily-clad women walked past me. I assumed there'd been some failure in the building's air-conditioning.

(Sadly) I never returned to the building and the nearest I ever got to seeing scantily-clad women was an old woman in a bikini on a beach in Hythe, plastered over the *Kent Messenger*. I'd often wished to see similar pictures in my local *Balham & Tooting News*, but a topless Alf Dubbs was the nearest I ever got.

I look back, 43-years later and wondered that I should have thought less hamster more beaver!

Now wash your hands

Singing "Happy Birthday" is sufficient time to clean your hands. This should take about 20 seconds, unless your friend, to whom you're singing happy birthday has been called, by his or her Welsh parents, Llanfairpwllgwyngyllgogerychwyrndrobwllllantysiliogogogoch, in which case, this will take the best part of a fortnight.

I'd heard this "Happy Birthday" theory on the radio the other day. However, it didn't occur to me that it'd be the song written by a couple of Louisville sisters in 1893. So, after I'd "powdered my nose", I stood by the office wash basin and began to sing, in the style of Stevie Wonder, "You know it doesn't make much sense, There ought to be a law against, Anyone who takes offense, At a day in your celebration". Four minutes and 45 seconds later (the length of the 1981 hit) not only were my hands certainly clean, they were also bleeding profusely with all the rubbing.

I really shouldn't believe everything I hear on the radio. I've never been the same since I heard Lord Haw Haw play "Flowers in the rain" on Radio One's first day.

Beat Your Classmates Out Of Doors

While at my Tooting grammar school I honed my skills as a card shark. Well, played a lot of rummy.

During a wet playtime, this would be our classroom-bound pastime. No money was ever exchanged, although we could have played for tuck-shop-bought doughnuts, although this would have made the desks incredibly sticky; I'd struggled with secondary school education enough without having jam smeared over pictures of Gladstone and Disraeli in my history text book.

When I changed schools in June 1972 to go to Emanuel, rummy was not the card game of choice during wet playtimes. Because it was a posher school, some of my new classmates played bridge.

Before embarking on my fifteen-month sojourn at the Clapham minor public school, the only card games I'd ever played, aside from rummy, were Beat Your Neighbours and Newmarket. Although I'd only played Newmarket on Boxing Days with family friends. We'd play for halfpennies – how none of us ended up attending Gamblers Anonymous sessions I'll never know!

During these wet playtimes I'd look nervously on, but very quickly arrived at the belief that bridge was like rummy, only with more cards, the word "trump" was used a lot - a word I'd only heard my Nan speak, but this was a euphemism rather than something of an advantage - and there seemed to be a lot of inactivity for one quarter of the players.

I was eventually allowed to play. I say play as I seemed to spend an inordinate amount of time being the "dummy". If I'd have known this would have happened I'd have done some research before like buying the *1972 Titch and Quackers Annual*.

It was the posher kids in my class who played bridge. I assume their parents ran bridge evenings which, given we were all living in suburbia, probably led to swingers' nights; although you wouldn't have wanted to be the dummy there unless you actively wanted your eyesight to worsen.

I rapidly realised that bridge was not for me and decided to extricate myself from this elite group. With the cards dealt for another rubber (bridge seemed to full of comedy words) and me being, yet again, the dummy, I watched, and as soon as the second card was placed on the jam-free desk, I shouted "SNAP!!" The look I received could have been a real-life representation of an HM Bateman cartoon. I grabbed my suit jacket (of course they didn't have blazers!) and went outside to contract hypothermia. I never played cards since, the withdrawal as legal currency of halfpenny bits simply accelerated that.

I found it strange that no one in my class at Bec or Emanuel wanted to play Happy Families. I always fancied Penelope Plod, the policeman's daughter.

Rubber's off, love

A book is not just for bedtime

With the exception of Rupert the Bear annuals, growing up in the 60s didn't offer the choice of books available to kids today.

My book collection consisted of a second-hand 1958 Denis Compton annual, an *I-Spy Zeppelins* (probably third-hand) and three of the set of twenty-four Noddy books; I remember vividly Noddy Book No. 4, entitled: *"Here comes Noddy again"* – this was about Noddy being kidnapped, not his sexual prowess.

I have three grandchildren, two of whom are nearly one year old. Their combined libraries would rival those of the British, Bodleian and Balham!

One series which dominates the twins' bookshelves is *"That's not my Something"* (like puppy, kitten unicorn). The premise is the first five double-pages features puppies, kittens or unicorns not belonging to the reader. The sixth double page spread reveals the ostensibly lost puppy/kitten/unicorn with the phase, ***"That's my unicorn** – its head has a massive stick coming out of it!"* (or something like that)

We never had books this exciting growing up, and I pondered if we had, what they'd have been?

"That's not my ration book; all the stamps are missing!"

"That's not my home-made go-kart; none of the constituent parts are stolen!" or,

"That's not my TV; Bonanza's never in colour, therefore a valve has blown and the set's on fire!"

Night, night children everywhere, unless you happen to live in the dark, dark wood, as featured in Noddy Book No. 4.

Three pounds, seven & six for the guy?

These days, fireworks are in evidence seemingly every weekend from the middle of July until actual Bonfire Night. This was never the case when I was growing up in the 60s. Were Paines or Standard fireworks so expensive back then that buying them was so prohibitive?

In the *Economist* newspaper they show inflation by way of what a McDonald's Big Mac costs across the globe. Perhaps they could introduce the cost of a Brocks' Roman Candle?

I do recall writing my name with a sparkler for (seemingly for an hour) for sixpence. The massive battery with a flame on the end my Nan used to light the gas with was my sparkler replacement during the non-firework season. Sadly, not as spectacular as a sparkler, except the time my nan inadvertently left the gas on and I nearly set Balham alight causing a fire reminiscent to that of the Crystal Palace one in 1936.

In our flats, families would club together to contribute a few fireworks for us kids to enjoy round the back of the garages in my Balham block of flats. My overriding memory was not that of the firework display or a rogue Katherine Wheel coming off a garage wall and heading (as if programmed) towards the Head Porter, who nobody liked, but that of home-made toffee supplied by one of the mums. Looking back, we didn't have the selection or an ostensibly endless supply of fireworks that seem in abundance these days. It's not because we couldn't afford it, it's just that all our savings were used up paying dentist's bills!

Martial aids

I could have had a black belt in karate, but only attended six lessons.

In 1975, I started karate lessons in a Portacabin next to the A&E department at St George's Hospital in Tooting. At the time, I didn't know whether this was ironic or simply a precaution if someone were to hit you with a roundhouse kick they'd just mastered while you were still trying to work out how to tie the (nowhere near black) belt keeping up your trousers.

I had an aunt, who lived in Flowersmead on Balham High Road. As her only nephew she took a great interest in what I did. However, the character in Richard Sheridan's "The Rivals", Mrs Malaprop, could have been based on my aunt; she invariably got the place names just slightly wrong where I went to undertake my activities.

My aunt would shop, while visiting my nan, her sister, in the dairy housed within Du Cane Court, where I also lived. She would announce proudly to the other shoppers that her nephew went to Karachi every Tuesday. The other shoppers were probably thinking: "4,880 miles? Every Tuesday? Bit of a trek, just for one day? And those who knew what I did for a living would probably ponder: Didn't know there *were* advertising agencies in Western Pakistan."

Because of my love of cricket as a kid, I'd frequently visit The Oval and Lord's. I'd often be accosted by other tenants inside the flats genuinely asking if I was alright, or more to the point, cured? My aunt had told people I'd been to Lourdes.

I was never very good at playing cricket, perhaps I might have done better if I'd had Our Lady as a coach, rather than Alf Gover?

Being a grass

In the 70s, aside from wearing outrageously flared jeans and growing your hair longer than your mother, there was a massive desire to display Pampas grass in one's front garden.

In all innocence, wanna-be Percy Throwers would go to their local garden centre (or, more likely, florist, as this was the 70s) to buy up flora from the south American mountainside. Unbeknownst to these amateur horticulturalists, having Pampas grass in your front garden advertised houses where swingers' parties might take place.

In the 70s, I lived in a fourth-floor flat and as such had no Pampas grass our window box – no bad thing, as this might have attracted abseiling swingers – although, they'd have been given a suitable welcome by my mum, but warned about not taking off their safety helmets.

Not everyone had Pampas grass in their front gardens. Which begs the question, what might other floral displays have secretly indicated? What did a pot of begonias hide? The housewife inside had an even better display of begonias? Was a front garden full of poppies indicating the house was actually a clandestine crack den? Anyone designing some massive phallus out of a privet hedge clearly saw no need for Pampas grass.

Pampas grass would always remain outside due to the leaves being particularly sharp. Anyone not knowing that could bleed to death before throwing their car keys into an old ashtray advertising Kensitas. Always a dampener at any party, a guest bleeding to death (especially if you've just hoovered), unless the paramedics, who arrive, enjoy dressing up in a uniform and can throw a set of ambulance keys into an ashtray at short range.

I now live in a house but while I have no Pampas grass growing outside, I do have a barbed wire fence which sends the message: *thank you, but my drive doesn't need re-surfacing*.
Next week we'll be discussing people who grew Pampas grass in their *back* garden.

Legging it

I've not really got the physique for leggings. I have long legs but, because my tummy's sponsored by *Picnic*, and my body is less a temple, more a row of terraced houses in Bolton!

During my 42-years of commuting up to the City from various SW London stations, I've noticed an increasing amount of my fellow travellers wearing leggings. And it seems the earlier the train, the more multi-coloured the leg attire.

This is a relatively new fashion.

Years ago, on the early train, you'd expect to see either people in suits or men in overalls carrying either a spirit level or a tool box – both of which would be paint-splattered (do they come with paint already splattered or is the new owner presented with a small tin of *Dulux* and left to their own devices?

But back in the 70s, during my early years of commuting, there was not the proliferation of gyms there are now. If you wanted to keep fit or build your body, you'd buy a *Bullworker* or send off for the Charles Atlas Body-building course, advertised every week in the *Sunday Express*. I never sent off for one as I like the taste of sand being kicked at me at speed.

My question is this: are these legging-clad commuters actually going to a gym or preparing perhaps for the *Tour de France*? Last week a man got on at Clapham Junction wearing leggings together with a jacket and shirt on. Is this all the rage now too? I've not been to Paris Fashion Week for a while now, so I'm out of the *haute couture* loop. Or possibly the leggings are too tight it affects blood flowing to the brain and manifests itself in the ability to coordinate clothes either side of your waist?

I'd like to see bowler hats returning to commuters' outfits; if you're swapping this for a pair of leggings then, like pregnant (or very lazy) women sporting "Baby on board" badges, have a sticker which says: "My personal trainer knows lots of Latin".

Would you like to fly?

In the 60s, my parents often threw parties in our two-bedroom flat in Balham. Although I was not allowed to actually attend these parties (always fun being sent to bed at seven o'clock in the middle of Summer), 10 yards away from the actual party, I could hear everything: laughter, smoker's coughs, music from our tiny record player.

Both parents loved their music and had eclectic musical tastes, so there was a wide choice available to be played on the record player.

At one party in 1967, when I was 10, and at a very late stage of the evening's entertainment, I'd endured passive smoking as a selection of Sinatra, Big Bands tunes and mum's Motown records played. The, around 1.00am, I heard the playing of the newly-released song by the Fifth Dimension: "Up, Up and Away"

It then came on a second time and thought, *"this song is extraordinarily long AND quite repetitive"*. OK, so you've got a beautiful balloon – move on!

After the third time, I started to believe this was some form of parental torture, or, I'd travelled to my own fifth dimension, a dimension where they only have one record.
After the fourth play, I started to hear the front door opening and closing.

During the fifth, the door activity increased.

The song played for a sixth and final time. All the guests had left, encouraged by my father's low boredom threshold and heavy drinking as he'd simply played the song until everyone had left.

Neither parent appeared for a week and I became feral. However, I had learned every single word of, "Up, Up and Away", which, ironically, was what all the party guests had done.

He's leaving (leaving)

Harlequin Records on Balham High Road would be where I'd weekly part with most of my pocket money. I'd mostly buy Motown Records, except one week when I bought something completely different, which I wrote about here https://mikerichards.blog/2017/06/18/wheres-your-mother-gone/

It reminded me of one purchase I made in 1973 when Gladys Knight (ably supported by her Pips) sang about her man (who'd not quite made it as the superstar he'd assumed he would become) who was leaving Los Angeles and venturing back (having dreamed, pawned his hopes, sold his car, albeit old, and bought a one-way ticket), to Georgia.

My question is this: what if he'd got to Grand Central Station in LA at 11.59pm only for the train doors having shut 30 seconds before midnight, as is the done thing these days on British Rail?

Gladys could have written a follow up; and needn't have given up her world (his/her/our world)? She may have had to buy a platform ticket, but this would have saved a great expense with her train fare. Although the returning man would have to buy another car – would Gladys inform him that buying another *old* car would be a false economy?

Although, he's already down as he's got his ticket to Georgia and the LA Railways were notorious in the 70s for not giving refunds. He could have become the first Uber driver in LA? Whatever he did it couldn't have been complex as he was seeking a simpler place and time. Although this suggests Gladys believed LA and Georgia were divided by some time and space continuum.

At the end of the song Gladys says she's "gotta" board the midnight train. Knowing her luck, having very recently lost her man, there'd be a massive queue at the Ticket Office with some arse trying to pay their fare using luncheon vouchers or a student, with five bags, asking if it would be cheaper if they travelled via Rio de Janeiro?

Her world is his, his and hers alone. Unless there are leaves on the line just outside Surbiton.

Having the decorators in

Balham Woolworth's was the only place worthy of buying Christmas decorations from when I was growing up in the 60s.

The choice was a pack of lick-it-yourself paper chains and, well, that was it really, unless you count baubles for Christmas trees made out of material which would decompose before Twelfth Night.

Nowadays houses are decorated with lights brighter than ones used at Colditz and festooned with various Christmas-related mammals on rooftops – Reindeer, Snowmen, Father Christmases or, if you lived near pagan arsonists, Wicker Men. These decorations are in evidence shortly after Easter or, at worst, after the clocks have gone back – thus taking full advantage of the darker nights.

In the 60s, my task was to stick the paper chain paper together. It was probably the only colourful thing in our flat, unless you include the yellow ceiling courtesy of mum and dad's *JPS* and *Senior Service*s respectively. Thankfully I wasn't colour blind, so the lead up to Christmas (or Advent as Latin speakers call it) was like Joseph and his limited-coloured dream coat. Only primary colours were used with these aforementioned paper chains. But what you did get, and only for Christmas, was dehydration. Even though we were only in a small flat, to create a chain going from the four corners of the lounge, took a lot of licking. I'd have been more hydrated if I've polished off a packet of Jacob's Crackers.

We did have a nice tree though, although neither parent got the timing of the flashing lights right and when anyone visited they'd be handed a card saying: *"this lounge features strobe-lighting"*. The speed varied between the North Foreland Lighthouse to a club in Ayia Napa! Wonder if Chris Rea's set off yet?

Pret a baby Jesus manger

If Joseph had chicken pox during the birth of his son, Jesus, I could have played him with authority during my primary school nativity play.

Every year, during the 60s, at my south London primary school, I'd get selected for a major part and every year I'd contract a children's illness and be unable to smell any grease paint or hear any crowd roaring. The only smells I smelled were Vick, a selection of grapes and calamine lotion.

When I was due to play Melchior I had mumps; selected to play the innkeeper I'd caught German measles; and when invited to play Mary (it was a progressive school) I'd got a particularly virulent strain of scarlet fever – which any amount of gold, frankincense or myrrh wasn't going to shift.

With the teachers/casting agents increasingly fed up with my inability to play a leading role, I was given the part as the back end of a stable donkey (although I managed to make it less stable). I was going to enter into this properly and include the Stanislavski method of acting by spending months at a donkey sanctuary. I didn't because, knowing my luck, I'd have contracted foot and mouth and have been put down.

There is now room at the inn as they've had a particularly bad review on Trip Advisor!

A verruca is not just for Christmas

In the 70s, I sang in a church choir in Balham (anything to get a place in Heaven). At this time of year we would visit the now extinct St James's Hospital (I accept no blame for my singing being the catalyst for its closure).

I never had fond memories of the hospital; I was in constant fear of having to remove my clothing as we walked and sang (who said men can't multi-task?) between wards. This fear stemmed from having to go to St James's to have a verruca examined, only to be asked to take off all my clothes. It was mid-Winter and I've never looked my best naked when there's a chill in the air.

We would sing for an hour and then rewarded with mince pies in the hospital refectory; although, it was reward enough (as a teenager) sharing a table with loads of nurses to whom I'd have willingly demonstrated my verruca in true St James's investigatory style. However, a teenage lad with mince pie crumbs round their mouth and all over their Christmas jumper was unarguably unattractive.

After the hospital we'd convene to The Hope on Wandsworth Common (mince pies can be very dehydrating). A consequence of this visit ensured that during Midnight Mass at least one choir member, at the beginning of each verse of "Once in Royal David's City", popped out to the topically holly-infested outside toilets of St Mary's Primary school.

These were the days before pub closing times were extended, so the church was packed (with a third of the congregation wondering why the band wasn't terribly upbeat and why were too many songs about donkeys on the juke box?). Although they were soon topped up with a Communion wine sharpener – certainly the ones who didn't fall down the (particularly if you've had a few) steep chancel steps.

This year I've asked Santa for a nurse's outfit. Knowing my luck, it'll be delivered by someone who was once in *Emergency Ward 10* as they'll be 100!

Happy Christmas, mine's a verruca.

Keep taking the tablets

When I was nine my New Years' resolution for 1967 was to give up Class A drugs.

My mum would force-feed me Virol and Haliborange tablets to ward off flu, consumption and, because of the 1965 scare, small pox. Because of these theories, my mother never made it as a GP.

Having missed a Haliborange tablet one day, one day I took two; I feared I would never leave our communal bathroom, such was the ferocity of the Vitamin C overload.
It was apparent: if I couldn't handle Haliborange tablets, tolerating heroin, cocaine or Skittles (which has the effect of what I assume LSD is like) was always going to be a no-no.
Because fitness is today is what small pox was in the mid-60s, I will see new people at my gym within the next week. They will come until they give up going to the gym for Lent.

But beware anyone coming to my gym as there are protocols: at the weekend the cross-trainer is reserved for my mates who, for several decades, have been menacing in the Shed end at Stamford Bridge. The free weight area is not open to people who are heavily tattooed, think they can lift six times their own body weight or are incapable of training alone. This area is for people discussing the various footballing merits of Palace, Sutton United and AFC Wimbledon. The armchairs are not in this area for aesthetic reasons.
There will be people, for two months only, believing they are potential Olympic rowers; their action betrays them demonstrating they are not so much Steve Redgrave, more Vanessa. There will be others doing a spin class for the first time and would not have witnessed nausea quite like it since they went on the decrepit Soviet-run rides within Sokolniki Park, Moscow.

My New Years' resolution will be to drink less Absinthe; it may have worked for Picasso, but then I've always been rubbish at drawing women with three ears and a nose on the top of their heads.

Happy New Year – keep off that cross-trainer. And the Absinthe.

A right old pen and ink

In the late 60s, during my last year in primary school, I had Osmiroids; luckily it was a C of E school and the on-site nurse (caretaker) had a cream for such things.

Actually, I had a single Osmiroid and I didn't need a soothing ointment, I had ink. Almost a millennium ago, I remember the first days back at school; a new term, together with a new exercise book, but having to learn to write not only with ink, but write with an italic pen – produced by Osmiroid.

I would never submit my handwriting to a graphologist and risk the involvement of the Police (in my defence, I think I was a doctor in a previous life, although dressing up in a nurse's outfit is strictly behind me now. Honest.).

A new exercise book was always a thrill at school, although not as entertaining as getting a new text book, which you would have to cover with discarded wallpaper (or, if you really wanted to annoy your parents, wallpaper still on the wall). You always felt for the kid whose history book was covered in deep red flock wallpaper.

It was the only time I would write neatly; at least for one page!

At our school on Balham High Road, we had specific lessons teaching us to write with a fountain pen in italics. I don't think I've written in italics since 1968. Geography is a tricky enough word to spell, without having to slant every single letter writing it out too.

I still own a fountain pen, but am better off drawing cats with it than I am writing proper sentences – I can never read any notes I've written, even after five minutes.

Writing in italics should be left for people who like calligraphy. As for me, I've never really been that interested in bell-ringing.

Re-shuffling off this mortal coil

When I was a kid a cabinet reshuffle for me meant my mum clearing out some old 78s to make room for some new plates she'd bought and possibly doing some light dusting; this week has been slightly different, although vinyl is making a comeback.

I remember, when I was 18, getting a letter from my local Tory MP (Robert Carr) congratulating me on becoming 18. I have voted Conservative ever since, even though my middle name is Vladimir.

My first vote was in 1975 (I don't count helping Mary Hopkins and The Muscle Man to win *Opportunity Knocks*) but was disappointed, having successfully voted "Yes" for the Common Market entry referendum, not be sent any winnings from Ladbrokes (or personally delivered by Ray Winston).

Before this, my second-hand voting experience was with my Nan in the booths inside what was Balham Congregational Church hall. She would take up the kind offer of the local Tory activist to drive her to the polling station – where she would vote Labour. I would look back wondering why such massive (unsharpened) pencils were used and why they couldn't have afforded better string – and were the pencils *so* valuable that they had to be tied down?

Still waiting to be called to be Postmaster General and hope Teresa May doesn't know I've run out of stamps.

No pints of lager, but a packet of crisps

I only won one prize at school. In 1967 I was 10 and got the RE prize because the new vicar of our local church was from Australia and I knew who Don Bradman was. The prize would have been more deserved if I had known that St Michael (no relation) was the head of all the angels rather than a brand of clothing.

The prizes were given out at a ceremony in Brierly Hall, attached to Balham Congregational Church. My father, proud of this achievement and secretly hoping I might join a monastery, therefore reducing the family food bill, decided we would celebrate.

An 88 bus was hailed and we ventured towards the Windmill on Clapham Common.

This was the first time I got to sit outside a pub with a Coke and a packet of crisps while my father remained inside, no doubt regaling the regulars inside that his son was to be the next Billy Graham (Dad harboured thoughts I'd be the next George Graham).

I would go on to sit outside many other south-west London pubs as dad played cricket locally. I've had Cokes and whole potato fields' worth of crisps outside the Hope, Surrey Tavern and County Arms. And I wonder why I have high cholesterol?

Still, at least I know there are nine commandments. More lager, Vicar?

Taking the biscuit

You never see broken biscuits anymore.

There is nothing better than a box (preferably a large tin) of M&S chocolate biscuits. However, growing up in the 50s and 60s, such opulence was found only in the houses of film stars and sultans of Brunei.

On Balham High Road there was a grocer (Battershill's) where my mum and my nan would buy their groceries. As a treat, they'd occasionally purchase a packet of broken biscuits. These weren't packets of proper biscuits which some maniac had attacked with a mallet; these were an assortment of reject biscuits all thrown together into one bag. I can still smell them – bit like Virol and banana-flavoured penicillin – these things, like a top song (or an awful song like *Mother of Mine* by Neil Reid), stick in your sense memory.

The problem with these biscuits, by default, was that there was a more-than-average amount of crumbs in the bag. A consequence of eating said biscuits was that, while watching Alexandra Bastedo in *The Champions,* you'd get enough crumbs over your lap and that week's *Beano* to make a base for a cheesecake.

Is there honey still for tea? No, but I've got half a bourbon!

Doppelgänger warfare

Although a fan of the output of Gerry & Sylvia Anderson, I'll never forgive them for introducing the UK public to my Doppelgänger, *Joe 90, in September 1968.*

This was the month (and year) I started secondary school at Bec Grammar in Tooting; it was not the thing to have such a look-alike.

Being in the first-year was tough enough with the older boys insistent on demonstrating the inner workings of the school toilet system or nicking your tuck shop-bought iced bun, without looking horribly like the latest ITV puppet incarnation.

Both Joe 90 and I had blond hair and glasses (although I didn't work for the Secret Service), but the difference being Joe's glasses could make him speak Russian fluently, whereas mine couldn't even help me conjugate the simplest of Latin verbs!

I think it's usually a term of endearment, being given a nickname at school, and Joe 90 stuck for several terms; I would have preferred to have looked more like Captain Black, Troy Tempest or even The Hood.

I guess, given it was an all-boys school, it could have been worse. I could have had a passing resemblance to Lady Penelope.

"Home, Parker?"

"Sorry, m'lady, I have a PE lesson!"

Oi, oi, saveloy

To paraphrase Lady Bracknell: to have two chip shops nearby is handy, to have three is bad for your cholesterol.

Growing up in Balham we had three very different chip shops (although I wonder why they were called chip shops as chips were such a small percentage of what they sold).

One, in Tooting Bec Road, had built-in entertainment next door where if you inserted an old penny into a slot you'd see a model train going around in circles. I hate to think how many minutes I'd spend chewing on a saveloy (a food product basically made up of all the rubbish they don't put into sausages) watching this toy train go around.

A chip shop on Balham High Road was the newest of three within walking distance of my flats, Du Cane Court, and you went there if you wanted to improve your conversational Greek.

But easily the most interesting (for me) was in Chestnut Grove where the wall was covered with West Ham memorabilia.

It was the place where I first learned about exotic football clubs like TSV 1860 München. The Hammers had played and beaten them in the 1964/65 European Cup Winners Cup final and photos of this victory were strewn across the shop. I was about 13 when I learned that Martin Peters wasn't actually a type of fish.

I never read a paper as a kid, I never had to, I would always get my news from the back of a piece of rock salmon. It was imprinted back to front and went through my teenage years thinking I'd mastered a foreign language.

Or that Queen Victoria wasn't dead after all.

Whistler's mother

"Here he comes - Whistler's mother" would be my nan's retort as I'd skip through the dark corridors of Du Cane Court on Balham High Road where I lived until we emigrated to Carshalton in 1972.

I'd only whistle when happy and this would have coincided with me having talked to a girl – I would run down Balham High Road (I assumed no girls lived outside of SW17) whistling the main theme to Patton: Lust for Glory. I felt I was on top of the world, like the eponymous General George S. Patton addressing the troops at the start of the 1970 film.

To demonstrate multi-tasking is not just a girl thing, I could bowl imaginary leg breaks while running and whistling. Not unlike the kid in the 1982 Channel 4 film P'tang, Yang, Yipperbang – although he had John Arlott in his head, I had George C. Scott chipping away in mine, like Jiminy Cricket (which is quite apposite).

If I'd have pursued this talent, rather than the more ostensibly glamorous route of being in advertising, I could have been the next Percy Edwards or Roger Whittaker. I could have released a re-worded version one of Whittaker's famous ballads and written about leaving old Balham town. Or copied Percy Edwards with some of his bird impressions.

My nan always said I was a bit of tit; I could have proven her right and sounded like one too.

There's not an awful lot of coffee in Bal-Ham

When I was a teenager, growing up in the 70s, coffee was still regarded as relatively exotic; but it was just called "coffee". In the Wimpy on Balham High Road, one of the two hot beverages on offer was coffee. It cost 8p and tasted as such.

We rarely had it at home; we drank tea. I insisted on PG Tips being bought for the cards you got inside enabling me to learn about "British Butterflies", "Adventures and Explorers" and "Notorious Nazis". I would force-drink my mother until I owned an entire set.

One day, my nan introduced me to coffee: frothy, hot, milky coffee. Although it smelled fantastic, it was far too hot to drink immediately - you'd needed it to cool down. Because my nan had made the coffee by boiling milk in a saucepan (oddly enough she didn't own a *Gaggia* machine) the moment it started to cool, a layer of skin would develop. This could be removed with a spoon although, hanging off the spoon, it looked like something out of the *Quatermass Experiment*! It was enough to put you off coffee for life and why, I believe, lids are put on take-away coffee cups nowadays.

Today, courtesy of Messrs Costa, Starbuck and the Roman Emperor Nerro, there are copious amounts of choice of coffee, size of cup and type of milk. However, you'll have needed to have attended several terms of conversational Italian evening classes to be able to pronounce *cappuccino* and *latte* correctly and a good grade at A-Level to order *caramel macchiato*. It becomes easier - the more you have, the more your teeth have rotted away.

Still, in 1972, it was worth paying 8p for a cup of coffee, if only to dip your Wimpy Frankfurter into.

Arrivederci, Balham.

Stamps of authority

I tried to get money out of an ATM the other day by mistakenly using my donor card; I had far too many loyalty cards in my wallet. I either needed to shed a few or buy a bigger wallet, a small travel bag or basket-on-wheels like my mum had.

There are very few shops these days where you're not brandishing two cards – one to pay with and one to collect points. Three, if you're trying to break into the till.

Unlike in the 60s and 70s when you'd collect Green Shield Stamps or cigarette coupons, you knew exactly how much you had – eight and a half books or half a hundredweight of Embassy coupons.

Because of this lack of knowledge of the worth on your loyalty card, I'm always hearing (predominantly in coffee shops): "Have I got enough points on this card?", "No, you have 2p". An ignominious silence descends. In recovery mode, the question to the barista is: "Oh, where's that flag from?" "Tuvalu." More silence.

But it is (no pun intended) rewarding redeeming points, even when you've paid over several hundred pounds to earn a couple of free ginger nuts in Costa.

Don't get me wrong, these cards are useful; the alternative would be carrying around several bulging (freshly-licked) Green Shield Stamp books or several million Embassy coupons – you'd certainly need a bigger wallet – or a very strong elastic band.

I wonder, if I sold one of my kidneys, could I get the points put onto my Boots card?

Beaker people

During the 60s and 70s, petrol stations started offering gifts when purchasing fuel. This was a relief for those into collecting memorabilia, but living somewhere where a vintage petrol pump might dominate the lounge.

The advantage being that 1970 World Cup coins were smaller than the actual pumps.

There was an Esso garage on Balham High Road where my parents would fill up our Ford Poplar. I would as, a 13 year-old football fanatic, insist on visiting this garage; it was the only way we'd ever get Peter Bonetti into our flat.

As the years progressed (and you were prepared to queue for days during the 1973 oil crisis) you could collect glasses. I can only assume the principals at Standard Oil and British Petroleum believed that people in the UK, while owning cars, failed to possess a drinking receptible and were visiting tributaries of the Thames to drink water with their hands.

Soon many houses I visited had sets of glasses out of which you'd drink your squash; although always mildly tainted with the taste of four-star.

Some garages offered a dream, rather than faux cut-glass beakers, with the gratification of manifold sets of Green Shield Stamps; my parents would drive for miles looking for the biggest multiple.

Although, you'd easily swap several tigers in your tank for quintuple Green Shield Stamps.

Waiting for a queue

Have people stopped queuing for public transport? I've been promising myself, since 1974, the year I started commuting, to attend a travelling in London assertiveness course; it would seem this is becoming ever more urgent.

On the platform at Bank Station, connecting the Waterloo & City Line to Waterloo, there are markings behind which people would, with their rolled-up umbrellas, bowler hats and copies of the *Times*, wait patiently for the *Drain* as it is affectionately called, to arrive.

Not any more they don't, plus the umbrellas have been replaced by invisible-to-the-wearer back-packs (probably containing a small person), whose sudden movement can remove an eye before you can say Captain Hook. Oblivious, they carry on listening through their headphones to something like "The Clash sing Edith Piaf".

The markers on the platform are still very much there, but their existence is spurned.
I've noticed too that people no longer queue at bus stops.

Historically you'd form an orderly queue behind the bus stop. These days people congregate around the bus stop, mimicking vultures in the Nevada Desert, mentally preparing themselves to see the word "Due". This three-letter word pumps adrenalin through passengers' veins as they lie in wait.

The bus is spotted and it is as if someone angelic host has said "On your marks...", as there is an almost indiscernible shuffling towards where the bus door will open. The bus arrives and the ensuing pandemonium is on a par with a Boxing Day sale where tellies are suddenly available for under a shilling.

Planes are now boarded by the number on your ticket, this should be introduced for buses with priority given to people who never paid more than 10 bob for a *Red Rover*.

A complete gîte

Having avoided being sent to elocution lessons when I was 10 in 1967, my first taste of foreign languages, aside from my Nan speaking in rhyming Cockney slang to confuse her neighbours, was a year later at secondary school where they tried to teach us French.

Day trips to Dunkirk and Boulogne didn't help. Although did introduce us to cigarette lighters whose flames made oil rigs in the North Sea look tame - and flick knives.

But this was hardly immersion. The only immersion likely was us trying to dump our Divinity teacher overboard just pulling out of Dunkirk harbour.

During our French lessons we were instructed solely to conjugate verbs. Because that happens in everyday foreign languages – not. Whenever trying to buy a fresh baguette on holiday in a gîte in a town which formerly housed U-Boats, you will not be saying to the *Boulangerie*, "I bake, you bake, he, she or it bakes, you bake (several of you baker types), we bake, they bake" you are English and, therefore, you speak slower and slightly louder, as if the baker is slightly mutton: "Have. You. Got. Any. Bread?"

Latin was just as bad. And useless, unless you wanted to study etymology or become a personal trainer. Most Latin lessons involved us reading books about wars involving towns/cities/nations being taken by storm. We learned the Latin verb *'expugnare', meaning* to take by storm. I cannot remember, since my last Latin lesson in 1972, ever using the words "to take by storm" – although if I'd have supported Millwall that might have been different.

But, because English is the universal language, all we need to do is go to an evening class and learn how to say, in several languages: "Two beers, please", "Where is the nearest chemist?" and "I think my clutch has gone!"

Auf wiedersehen, pet.

Open and shut case (but not Wednesdays)

Growing up in the 60s, Wednesday was always half-day closing on Balham High Road. Having worked for over 40 years, I realise these shopkeepers needed a break.

As a kid I thought otherwise; perhaps they lent their shops out to wannabe Mr Benns – thousands of people swarming in from various parts of SW12 and SW17 to train as a lion tamer? Or they went into a temporary four-hour hibernation – like human tortoises? Or were secretly setting up radios made from cat gut or crystal meth (or whatever it was when wireless meant some massive wooden thing which sat on your mantelpiece) in which to contact Martians or Martins as Martin was a popular name in the 60s.

There is no such thing as half-day closing these days, if anything the complete opposite, with shops open every day. Odd, as one of the Commandments is: "remember the half-day closing day and keep it holy."

Aged 10 I was not the head shopper in our household. Looking back, I wasn't aware of any black-market cows residing in my Balham flats ready to produce milk at any time after 1.01 PM on a Wednesday. Or a handy seamstress, ready to knock up a top should you get a last-minute dinner date invite.

Did these shopkeepers do moonlighting or voluntary work? One had clearly done nothing as he'd said on Wednesday afternoons he did voluntary work for the RNLI. This was believable when you were 10, but having started geography lessons at secondary school and realising Balham was 60 miles from the nearest coast, he'd have had to have had particularly good hearing to have heard the rescue siren.

Just taming lions - back in 10 minutes.

Bugger Bognor

I only went to a holiday camp once; in 1967, along with half of Balham, we decamped (no pun intended) to Bognor Regis (so called because a monarch discovered swearing there).
I'd never been on a holiday where there was so much barbed wire; I told myself, as we drove our Ford Poplar through the camp gates, that Alsatians really were the friendliest of dogs.

I spent a week there. As a 10 year old boy, and because washing was anathema to me, I wore my newly-bought, from Frank Blunstone's Soccer Shop on Lavender Hill, Peter Osgood's No.9 Chelsea shirt the entire week. Dad refused to buy me a Gerd Müller top; to be fair, there wasn't much call for these in Clapham Junction. My friend from school came too, he wore a No. 10 Fulham shirt – denoting Allan Clarke (the footballer, not the lead singer from The Hollies).

There was an inordinate amount of sport to be played.

A consequence of the first book my dad bought me being the *MCC Coaching Book*, throughout the week I scored plenty of runs with my Colin Cowdrey bat (heavily aided by the fact that a tennis ball was used).

The week culminated with the lads vs dads football match.

If you're 10 you really don't want to be playing against a team of people several feet taller than you, slightly stockier and several having had many games in the Southern League under their ever-growing belts. "Chasm" wouldn't even get close to a word describing the difference in class (Or height. Or weight).

The first (and last time) I ever went for a 50/50 ball was against 35 year old Ron, who had been turning out for Hillingdon for years. Having previously innocently played on Wandsworth Common, where the toughest tacklers were squirrels, this was an eye-opener.

That summer of '67 I played the innings of my life, realised I'd never make the first team of Hillingdon FC and discovered snooker, darts and pool – this was subsequently reflected in my O-level results.

"Ronnie's up!"

Yoof Club

In 1969 I was destined to be the next Eric Bristow as I won the darts tournament at my local youth club.

Sadly, the promise of being the successor to the *Crafty Cockney* (I didn't attend elocution lessons, so was halfway there) was never to be; although my 14.3% O-level pass rate suggests that a misspent youth was evident.

My auntie Vera trained me, from an early age, to regularly hit double top – she'd tried to teach me piano on her Blüthner piano, but realised early on I'd be less Liberace, more Lazarenko. I was a dart prodigy; what Mozart was to symphonies, I was to 160 check-outs.

The youth club met in the hall of my old primary school in Balham. It did seem odd, as a 12 year old: A) going back there **not** singing *Hill of the North, Rejoice* (which we seemed to sing every week during assembly), B) no sight of a recorder or Glockenspiel, and C) it was dark outside.

We were fed copious amounts of orange squash in the days when people didn't realise the dangers of E-numbers – it's a curious sight, watching a group of pumped-up teenagers trying to play table-tennis as if killing a large rodent.

We'd also play snooker – well, I say snooker – the tables were the size if Fred and Joe Davis had been three-foot midgets, with less felt on the table than a very tiny piece of *Fuzzy Felt*. However, it was an escape from parents, homework and Glockenspiels.

The evening of the darts final arrived – which I'd breezed through to, beating several eleven-year-old girls in the process. I'd been practising trickier check-outs with my aunt the previous night only for the other finalist to have succumbed to Scarlet Fever (not brought on (as we all believed) from watching too may episodes of *Captain Scarlet*). So, by default, I won.

Although, to this day, I still think *oche* is something played at posh schools.

"High on a slightly-blurred hill…"

1966 is fondly remembered in England mainly for winning the World Cup. For me it was the year I was forced to watch The Sound of Music without my glasses.

I had been wearing glasses since I was five and now, at nine, while I didn't need them all the time, I did require them for watching TV and any film involving both Julie Andrews and Christopher Plummer.

In the summer of 1966 I visited for the first (and last) time, the Isle of Wight. I stayed at the Ocean View Hotel which was a lie on two fronts: there was no view of any ocean (you could barely see the Solent) and it was more boarding house/prison than hotel. Nearby Parkhurst was probably modelled on the routine there.

One evening's entertainment was a trip from the "hotel" in Shanklin to the Odeon at Ventnor. We drove the 3.7 miles there and had bought tickets for the blockbuster musical from the previous year. It was, after we collected our tickets, when I discovered I'd left my glasses back at the hotel. 3.7 miles was deemed too far to return to fetch them and my mother insisted I watch the film and suggested I squint (another reason she never made it as an ophthalmologist) through the entire 174-minutes. In Germany they had a shortened version for their own cinema-going public which lasted only 138-minutes – I can only assume the scenes involving the Nazis were left out.

Watching the film with very indistinct vision meant I didn't think the goatherd was all that lonely – I could see three of them; Maria didn't have a few favourite things, she appeared to have bloody hundreds and, in the scene where they sing: *"So long, farewell, auf wiedersehen, adieu"* I wondered, with ostensibly 50 or more children (several of whom were 16 going on 17) on the staircase, how on earth it didn't collapse?

Climb every mountain? Which one, I can see a couple?

If Bill & Ben met Pablo Escobar

Box sets are a relatively new phenomenon.

And Netflix doesn't mean curtain twitching.

Until 1967, when BBC2 began broadcasting, the choice on your TV was threefold: BBC, ITV or OFF. No video was connected; DVD sounded a bit like something you caught off a stranger's toilet and satellite was what Russians had launched into space a decade earlier to spy on other countries rather than broadcast Home and Away.

In the 60s the only box you had was one to keep jewellery in – or a hamster if you were a boy. And binge watching didn't exist unless that's what you called viewing Coronation Street twice a week.

In the 60s there were no devices for recording, so if you missed an episode of a favourite programme, you'd be reliant at school/work the next day to be told loosely and inaccurately what Meg Richardson had been up to – without sounding too much like Benny.

I wonder what it might have been like in the 60s if box sets had been available?

Could you have watched Emergency, Ward 10 for five hours at a stretch? (that's an awful lot of catheters).

And what if the Flowerpot Men's garden had been set in Medellin, Colombia and Weed really was weed?

And rather than watching both series of The Crown back-to-back, the only time you actually saw the Queen was on Christmas Day – although if she'd have discovered how to make crystal meth before Prince Charles was sent to Gordonstoun, you could have merged several series into one and saved valuable viewing time.

I started watching The Wire, but gave up when I discovered it wasn't about an electrician.

An imaginary bunny is not just for Easter

I first encountered the Tooth Fairy in 1961.

I never actually met her (or him) and assumed they lived in my Balham block of flats as you wouldn't have wanted to walk down the High Street in the middle of the night. But I was told that he/she/it carried sixpences to replace missing teeth. I worked out, in a JP Morgan-type of way, that I could stand (or lie, as I was invariably in bed when the Tooth Fairy visited) to eventually gain 10 bob, as I had 20 baby teeth.

This was my first experience of profit and loss as my gain of sixpence per tooth was quickly negated by my mother charging me a shilling to protect me the night the Tooth Fairy was coming from the Bogey Man. By the time I started the juniors in primary school I was heavily in debt to my mother.

Sixpence is worth £1.14 these days. If you haven't got a note for your child/grandchild then there is the danger of leaving sufficient coins under their Flopsy Bunny pillow to potentially cause copper, nickel and zinc poisoning. Might this be something the Bogey Man could protect you from?

I was destitute aged seven as Christmas was also heavily taxed: the sledges needed to be hired (there was great demand at Christmas, so the prices artificially inflated); reindeers aren't cheap to keep and I was told there was a congestion charge for sledges (even though this wasn't enforced in London until 2003); plus, half a sprout and mince pie crumbs cost several guineas in 1961.

Obviously, approaching 61, I realise neither the Tooth Fairy or Santa exists (I discovered this aged 14 – as if adolescence wasn't tough enough) but today, if there isn't a huge amount of chocolate for me, I shall be a very unhappy Easter Bunny.

It's in the jeans

I've never owned a pair of blue, denim jeans.

I'm probably in that 0.01% of the world's population where a pair has never been in my wardrobe, but I was never realistically given the option.

Rather than spend money on a pair of Levi's or Wrangler's, the only option to me was the Tesco Home 'n' Wear on Balham High Road.

As a teenager in the early 70s, I earned no money, so was reliant on my mother as my clothing benefactor. This benevolence sadly only stretched the 500-yards from our flats on Balham High Road to the non-food Tesco shop further down the road – not for me anything from Reno, Nevada or Greensboro, North Carolina! Tesco Home 'n' Wear, Balham was the only choice. A consequence of this non-option was that I never owned a pair of blue denims from a famous brand. The only thing shrinking in my bath as a teenager might have been blue, but certainly wasn't made from denim.

The same fate struck me with shirts. I so wanted a Ben Sherman shirt; the option I was given was one from Trutex (might as well have been Artex – arguably more fashionable and at least I could have covered my ceiling with it).

Trutex was to Ben Sherman what Hot Hits and Top of the Pops records were to the songs' original artists. Similar, but the collar, designed like the hat on The Flying Nun, gave it away that it was not the real thing!

I've never been that fashion conscious – probably scarred by the disastrous Haute Couture forced on me as an adolescent. To me, as a teenager, a kaftan was a dog known for its long, shiny hair; flares were things you activated if marooned at sea and (until Eurotrash was aired on Channel 4) I thought that Jean-Paul Gaultier was the best full back Paris Saint Germain ever had.

Gloves aren't off

I was told, after winning a new client, that my presentation had been "entertaining". The person telling me this hadn't actually been at the meeting, but they had heard and asked why?

"I used several glove puppets," I replied.

I hadn't, but it did remind me of my (rather too many for a boy) massive collection of soft toys I'd accumulated as a kid – including many glove puppets.

I have an early picture of me, aged four, throttling Sooty. As a kid, growing up in the 60s, many of the children's programmes I watched invariably had glove puppets as part of the merchandise. I was never that interested in string-puppets (although Muffin the Mule had been legalised by the time I was 10 in 1967) but my loyalty remained with things you could stick your hand into (I should have been a vet rather than choosing a career in advertising).
My favourite was Willie Wombat (still illegal in some States in the US) – Willie Wombat was to Tingha and Tucker as Knots Landing was to Dallas.

As an only child, and with a collection of glove puppets large enough to form several football teams, I would invariably re-enact big football games in my bedroom (although doing this didn't stop me having bad eyesight!).

One evening in mid-June 1970 Willie and Wendy Wombat became Gerd Müller and Uwe Seeler and snatched three late goals for a very antipodean-looking West German team against an England XI consisting of Sooty, Sweep and Sue as the front three. No contest.
I'm still technically a member of the Tingha & Tucker Club. The newsletters have dried up due to Tingha and Tucker moving the America to work on a koala stud farm. However, if ever I feel nervous I simply sing Auntie Jean's Wibbly Wobbly Way.

Next week: Why Twizzle defies every aspect of modern day health & safety.

Not a sniff

Hay fever was the reason I failed my O-levels. I should know, I'm a doctor, well, I once owned a plastic stethoscope from a 1960s doctors and nurse kit.

The hay fever season has returned to these shores (probably from Russia); I remember back to being 16 in 1973, sitting my O-levels and contracting, for the first time, Allergic Rhinitis - which is the correct medical term for hay fever and not the name of the cross-eyed rhino in Daktari.

My desk, inside the hot, imposing, alien school hall on Battersea Rise, looked more like a chemist's than a work station. If I'd had a bottle of ointment to treat marsh ague, some pampers and a box of prophylactics I could have rivalled Balham Boots.

I never had hay fever before and went to every exam armed with pen; Piriton; a Penetrol inhalant - which unblocked noses with power like that of a flame thrower - paper hankies, cloth hankies - all with a big "M" on (and a diagram of an oxbow lake, which I'd sewed on the night before my Geography O-level) and lucky, or not in this case, Gonk!

I also had a slide rule which proved more useful during my music O-level – underlining the name Chopin - than it did when I sat my maths O-level!

Despite having a desk which resembled that of a 15th century alchemist (I could turn base metal into Kleenex) I didn't do very well with my science exams. Not so much not knowing my arse from my elbow, I didn't even know my amoeba from my element's tables.

Gesundheit!

Personification of Evel

I think it was Evel Knievel who once said: "You wait ages for a London bus, then 14 come along at once". I was, despite owning a moped aged 16, never destined to follow the exploits of the master bus-vaulter.

In 1972, aged 15, my parents emigrated from Balham to Carshalton (it could have been Neptune, it seemed so far away). Transport back to family still in Balham would be a problem so my dad said he'd pay for me to get a motorbike.

Armed with a selection of Premium Bonds, illegal Singapore currency my dad had brought back after National Service and a handful of pretend coins from the Co-op, I travelled back to SW17 to purchase a Harley Davidson. Sadly, they never produced a range of mopeds, so an Austrian-built Puch Maxi S was procured.

The shop I visited on Garratt Lane, Tooting was called Elite Motors. Growing up in 60s/70s south London, "elite" wasn't a word we'd heard much, so we unwittingly called the shop "e-lights" (the shop is probably now selling vaping mechanisms).

Elites did well out of me; I bought three bikes there. However, I was more Mr Sheen than Barry Sheene and after a succession of minor accidents felt there was some supreme being telling me it was time to learn to drive.

On my travels back and forth from Balham to Carshalton, I remember vividly riding through Mitcham Common and the temperature dramatically dropping several degrees. I could have ridden blindfold and known exactly where I was – although this would have consequently entailed more arguments with the bridge over Mitcham Junction station.

I miss not having a bike, although my most embarrassing biking moment is still etched in my brain: having toppled over at Amen Corner, Tooting, I was asked by a frail, old woman if she could help get my bike upright again? It was at this point when I realised that old people act as very good fulcrums.

I won't ever be attempting vaulting over buses any time soon as my Red Rover is about to run out.

Deeper throat

I've not had barley sugar since 25 May 1967.

My nan had a cupboard like a confectioner's and contained an assortment of sweets primarily designed for sucking. If there'd been a warning fifty-one years ago on one specific packet I'd have not missed Cubs.

Dressed in Cub shirt, adorned with collector's and signaller's badges and newly-won felt sixer's appendage, shorts, socks (together with garters holding them up) and woggle in correct position (enter your own gag here), I was all prepared to shout "dyb, dyb, dyb", play handball, run like a Banshee round Balham Baths' adjoining hall and splatter over-cooked sausages to every part of the hall's kitchen, my nan proffered me one last sweet from her store.

I'd never had barley sugar before and felt it would make a change from her usual offering of Acid Drops or Callard & Bowsers Toffees. It would be the last time too as, after a nano-second, because it stuck in my throat. The natural melting time for a barley sugar boiled sweet is around the best part of a decade (the time it felt this thing was stuck in my throat). Cubs had to be attended at all costs, if only to see how far up sausages on too high a gas would ascend into the air.

I spent, ostensibly, hours and hours, being fed water as hot as possible to try and melt the stubborn barley sugar – was suffering third degree burns in my throat worth not being shouting at by Akela?

Eventually the sweet melted sufficiently for it to move through my throat. Cubs had been and gone and the sausage safe for another week before I returned as a maniacal Fanny Craddock.

I sat down, relieved; my nan to put the TV on – the 1967 European Cup Final between Celtic and Inter Milan was taking place. I had been a hero like the Celtic players that night. Less than a week later I saw, in the Radio Times, they had the European Cup Winner's Cup Final on TV. Glasgow Rangers against some team which I'd never seen on the Big Match. Perhaps I might bunk off Cubs again?

Russian fly in the ointment

I was seven when The Man from U.N.C.L.E. first aired on the BBC. I immediately wanted to be Napoleon Solo and sent off to become a member. A few days later, with membership card proudly in my hand, I believed I would be a master spy before I took my Eleven-Plus.

During the series I always had my concerns about Solo's sidekick, the enigmatic Illya Kuryakin; consequently, I wasn't really surprised when he popped up, dressed as a British RAF officer, in Colditz – but that's why Russian spies are so clever and clearly have a variety of seamstresses working tirelessly in their Gulags.

As a seven year old the name of U.N.C.L.E.'s nemesis, T.H.R.U.S.H., meant nothing to me. I'd yet to buy my first Observer Book of Song Birds and was unlikely to contract any sexually-transmitted disease (mainly because my mother told me never to sit on any strange toilets). Looking back, Napoleon and Illya were unlikely to quash their arch-enemy by rubbing a soothing ointment on them. Although eradication was the name of the game, I guess.

The show which rivalled The Man from U.N.C.L.E. on ITV was Danger Man – I also wanted to be John Drake and would stalk the corridors of my Balham block of flats seeking out enemies of the state (I suspected most of the cleaners and believed that inside their mops lay a selection of east European munitions).

Danger Man would occasionally feature cameo roles from famous actors, one episode featured John le Mesurier; I never wanted to be Sgt Wilson, but in increasing old age, can identify with Private Godfrey and his constant desire for the toilet; today I am more great-uncle rather the Man from!

"Is there a doctor in the dry cleaners?"

It was watching *Emergency - Ward 10* that I decided I was probably not best cut out to be a doctor. Even in black and white, blood looked pretty gruesome. However, I'm sure the ITV series which ran for a decade between 1957-1967 inspired many people to be asked "what's the bleeding time?"

In the 60s there was precious little TV choice - even when the third channel, BBC2, was added in 1964. Although, as a seven-year-old, this seemed to involve watching lots of men with beards sitting around talking about the meaning of life. Very late at night, in the 70s, if you couldn't sleep and turned the TV on you would be confronted by (probably the same) men wearing tank-tops and shirts with collars nearly touching their elbows pointing at complex charts or doing unspeakable things with pipettes.

However, in south London, with careers officers at school telling you to be a secretary if you were a girl and an armed robber or accountant depending on which type of boys' school you attended, TV could have possibly given that much-needed career-inspiration.

Perhaps 'All Gas and Gaiters' encouraged people to join the church or a Reg Varney-induced moment would have made being a bus driver appealing, although running a motel in the Midlands would not have been attractive as you would be forever sorting out the love life of the village idiot.

TV did inspire me and, despite having often seen the actor who played Mr Verity in Balham Sketchley's, I have enjoyed 40-plus years working in the Home Guard.

A-roving, a-roving

There was a time when you could travel from Balham (if you lived there) to (almost) the outer limits of the universe (as long as a London Transport bus went there) for only 10 bob.

A Red Rover was a frequent purchase for me and my mates in the late 60s to early 70s; a time when we were young teenagers and had irresponsible parents who would cast us onto the streets, armed only with 10 shillings, a Tupperware cup full of Coke and/or milk (depending on how nauseous you wanted to get), a Penguin and a selection of (one) sandwiches made with the pride of the Shippams factory. Travelling from Balham, most of our packed lunches had been consumed by Clapham North.

I had a paternal aunt and two cousins who lived in North Harrow (which, when looking at the bus map at Balham underground station, might have been outside the universe, let alone at its furthest boundary). I decided we should take a selection of ostensibly 20 buses and go and visit my dad's remote family. It seemingly took several weeks but, having successfully arrived, starving by this point as we had mistimed our food intake (which is why none of us joined the Commandoes), we discovered they were out.

No mobile phones those days to say: *"Hi, Auntie Betty, we're coming to visit"*, not even a couple of old yoghurt pots to communicate our impending arrival. So, skint, hungry and tired we ventured back to south London with my friends assuming this extended family didn't exist.

I go nowhere these days without the aforementioned yoghurt pots (in case of emergencies) and always have a 10-shilling note hidden inside the secret heel of my shoe – the one next to the beaver footprint.

When I see a coelacanth fly

As a kid I never took much of an interest in coelacanths (or any other higher form of maths for that matter); in the 60s travelling to the museums in South Kensington, I would give the exhibit of one (ostensibly extinct) caught by fishermen off the coast of Africa in the 30s a swerve.

Even though the Natural History Museum had several floors, I was interested only in seeing the blue whale, the diplodocus (I remember being vaccinated against that as a child) and the dodo. There was about 99% I never saw. Rare insects from Patagonia didn't grab me (probably no bad thing or I might have gone down with a mild strain of diplodocus).

The Science Museum was the same – all those fascinating things to see and touch, but all I wanted to do was press the button which opened a door automatically.

But there was always a gift shop?

I think you can tell how good a sightseeing attraction is by the numbers of bars of Kendall Mint Cake there are on offer in the gift shop. You could probably buy a badge your mum could sew on. I had one of those from Ventnor.

I vaguely remember lots of stationery on offer: pens, pencils, rubbers (the sort you get at museums, not at the barber's) and in the Science Museum a card which had ion filings on which, using a magnet, you could design facial and head hair designs. I assume Vidal Sassoon was a regular visitor there?

Once I inadvertently stumbled into the (surprisingly (not) defunct) Geological Museum. I didn't like the Kendal Mint Cake there – tasted of rock (and not the sort you buy in Brighton either, more what stuff you'd scavenge in Alum Bay).

But as Rupert Brooke would have said: "Is there coelacanth still for tea?"

Re: cycling

Unless I had suddenly acquired a shocking sense of direction, after being given a new bike, living on the fourth floor of a block of flats, may have been life threatening.

However, I never owned a bike (new, old or jet-propelled in case of emergencies). My parents clearly realised that turning right from our lounge would have led me to become more lemming than Lance.

Because of my devotion to Twix, Lycra is not my clothing of choice. Although, men of my age in their droves are switching to cycling from playing golf. However, I'm better off holding a putter rather than looking like I had one shoved down my Lycra shorts (especially in cold weather).

In the 60s, growing up in south London, few people had bikes, going everywhere by "Shank's Pony"; which I realised, later on in life, didn't mean they owned horses.

I did have a bright blue scooter and was allowed to propel myself (supervised) around Wandsworth and Tooting Bec Commons. This may be why I have one quadricep bigger than the other as I never mastered changing legs. I became very proficient at accelerating past The Priory on Tooting Bec Common as that was very menacing.

There were no cycle lanes back then. The only markings on the roads were hop-scotch grids – and the occasional chalk outline of a man on Balham High Road – I assume this was some prehistoric cave painting, like the Cerne Abbas Giant – he would have certainly looked good in Lycra.

I always wanted a Chopper – but perhaps that's a question for my gynaecologist?

"Steamin' and a rollin'"

I don't think I could have ever have been a train driver as the hat would have messed up my hair (being daubed in soot wasn't a major attraction either, even for a 10 year-old boy who loathed washing!). Until it was withdrawn in 1972, watching the Brighton Bellle through the railings on Wandsworth Common – the only thing which ever stopped our games of football there - was a fleeting glimpse of railway magic, where you contemplated becoming one.

Although, running towards the track invariably resulted in our opposition team scoring a goal while our entire defence were peering through the rail-side railings wondering if any of us would ever become Casey Jones (the late 50s Californian TV train driver, not the burger shop).

If you played against the bigger boys on Wandsworth Common there was the inherent danger that your jumper-cum-goalpost might be nicked. So, a few, fleeting moments of pre-Dr Beeching joy, frequently ended in pain (and a subsequent slight chill).

But Wandsworth Common has changed since the time the Brighton Belle would make its daily visit. As a kid, kicking a football or sending down a leg break, instead of fancy wine bars and Michelin Star restaurants, the poshest shop on Bellevue Road was Budgens. No doubt the current residents there pronounce every consonant too; whereas in my day, the only thing we had in common with the French was in inability to pronounce the letter H at the start of words.

I'm envious of people who witnessed the steam train days as the nearest I ever got to seeing Mallard was feeding one on Wandsworth Common ponds.

I always fancied being Big Chief I-Spy as I collected several of the pocket-sized books he began publishing from his office in Bouverie Street, throughout the 50s and 60s.

Because I rarely travelled outside the SW17 postcode as a child, books like I-Spy on The Farm, I-Spy at The Zoo, and I-Spy Country Crafts remained largely empty. Although I did once make my own entry of 100 points for spotting a Woolly Mammoth on an imaginary farm.

I nearly completed I-Spy in The Street – spotting a belisha beacon, a zebra crossing, and if you took your A6 book out at night and walked up Bedford Hill in Balham, you would get fifty points for spying 'a lady of the night'.

The most marks you could get in I-Spy on The Train was ticking off a severed head which had been poked too far out of a window you used to be able to pull down.

In 2011 new editions were launched to bring the series more up-to-date: I-Spy on A Car Journey In France being one. Within this the top points were: seeing the suspension go on a car carrying far too much cheap, Beaujolais; a French policeman nicking the car in front just because it had GB stickers on and General de Gaulle saying "Non!" (all a bit academic after Brexit).

The idea was actually first thought of in the seventeenth century with I-Spy at The Public Execution, where you were encouraged to look out for a basket (extra points if it contained a head); an axe and a woman with no teeth, knitting and swearing at the same time.
Keep 'em peeled, as Big Chief I-Spy would say*.

*With apologies to Shaw Taylor

Very fuzzy felt

Lionel Messi has probably never played Subbuteo before as, roughly translated from its original Argentinian, means, *I've been substituted*.

With World Cup fever still gripping (like the last Ice Age) memories of playing Subbuteo in the bedroom of my 4th floor Balham flat in the 60s and 70s still puzzles me. Why did the little men break so easily? If the pitches in England were as unironed as the Subbuteo playing field felt were you would never play a single game. And why was it so hard to get the Red Star Belgrade away kit in any toy shop on Balham High Street? Was the loathing of Marshal Tito so bad in SW17 in the late 60s?

I learned to iron attempting to flatten out my Subbuteo pitch, although a consequence of this is that I can now only iron shirts made out of green felt – and having given up modelling for canned and frozen vegetables, this is now a rarity.

Many Subbuteo games for me were ruined before they even started – I had a mouse who would eat more Subbuteo goal-nets than he did sunflower seeds. My knees, as a kid, clearly had a mind of their own and were obviously anti-football as they would, with unerring accuracy, invariably break several players before kick-off and there was always that inherent looming fear of getting carpet burns on my index finger (which was needed to play the violin badly).

Rather than having penalties in World Cup games, I would like to see an introduction of 30 minutes of Subbuteo with the winner being the person with the most intact figurines remaining at the end of that half an hour. Or, if it were held in my Balham flat, the fewest mouse turds on the pitch was the deciding factor.

A nod's as good as a wink to a Ford Cortina

There was a time when Kensington Olympia was the gateway to Devon. All you needed was a nervous driver, a Ford Cortina and a Motorail.

In the summer of 1972 I was taken, by my dad, from our home in Balham to Kensington Olympia – the Motorail terminus. I sat in the back of my uncle's Ford Cortina as we travelled the 100-yards to board the Motorail. When we parked and my uncle had applied the handbrake I remember thinking that Devon was not all it had been set up to be and the beach smelled of exhaust fumes; there wasn't a cream tea in sight, either. Having never been to Devon before, it looked suspiciously like West London.

I didn't have to spend the entire time in the Ford Cortina – my only companion, after my uncle had got out of the now stationary car, was the model dog in the back of the car. Not much conversation, although it did seem to agree with everything I said; it certainly nodded a lot.

I realised, after what had seemed an eternity, that Dawlish was the end destination. Luckily the house where I stayed backed onto the railway line, so it felt, for the entire fortnight, that I was still on the Motorail.

I rarely went on holiday with my dad; but he would visit for the odd day. He made a special effort this holiday to come to Devon as he'd heard Dawlish were playing a Chelsea XI in a pre-season friendly. I subsequently realised my dad was more interested in Marvin Hinton than me. More Marvellous Marvin than Marvellous Micky.

The Motorail no longer runs, probably because Ford Cortinas are no longer that popular. As are nodding dogs.

Steering committee

As a Christmas present in 1963 I was given a pretend steering wheel.

This was jointly given to me by my mother, who had passed her driving test the previous months in fog, snow and hot pants and my father who, after a span of 20 years consisting 11 unsuccessful and one complete freak of driving nature successful driving tests.

I inherited my father's poor driving ability and really should never have progressed to anything further than a pretend steering wheel made of light plastic, not having any electrical power and only able to affix itself to something with the use of a big rubber sucker.

My steering wheel had many levers. One was the indicator (this is something Volvo drivers won't understand) and a gear stick; this often came off in my hands, but had an extra use as I'd emulate my dad's road rage by shaking the detached gear stick at passing (invariably innocent) drivers. In the middle of the wheel sat a hooter, which sadly didn't play *Colonel Bogey's March* when pressed.

I enjoyed making the noises small children think cars make and would couple this by copying my vituperative father. It brought pretend driving to life for me; Dad put the F in Ford.

I failed my first driving test in Sutton. Having to sit next to a complete stranger and having no plastic steering wheel to manoeuvre were distinct disadvantages; saying "parp, parp, said Noddy" as we did the emergency stop didn't exactly help my case.

Spud-U-Dislike

I've never touched an actual gun, courtesy of having no second amendment in the 1904 Balham Constitutional Club founding declaration.

As a kid, however, to protect myself from strangers and head of my one-man vigilante group, I did possess a Sekiden gun. I also owned 50 silver balls (these were the Sekiden gun's ammunition not something I had miraculously acquired during one of my many hernia operations).

Before you could progress to owning a Sekiden gun, you'd have to prove your responsibility with a spud gun (it is an apocryphal thought that the 1845 Irish Famine was caused by the over-use of spud guns within the Emerald Isle).

Armed with my spud gun and a couple of potatoes past their sell-by date courtesy of the Du Cane Fruiters, I would stalk my south London flats seeking out the cleaners - their sole protection being a mop, set of rubber gloves and a tin of Duraglit. Luckily for them my aim was less Jack Ruby, and more Ruby Murray.

Balham was a gun-free zone as far as I knew growing up in the 60s and the biggest chance of dying was of embarrassment if you'd had your jeans bought for you from the local Tesco Home 'n' Wear.

The postman doesn't even ring once!

Around this time of year, when I was growing up in London in the 60s and 70s, I would anticipate copious amounts of postcards from friends and relatives arriving showing pictures of a place within the town they were staying where they would never visit, but locally it was iconic, and/or telling me they wished I was there (which begs the question: why wasn't I invited in the first place?).

Cards would come from far-reaching places such as Bognor, Bournemouth, Bideford – having been brought up in Balham it seemed that my friends and relatives were incapable of travelling anywhere which didn't begin with a 'B'. These days people will travel to Belize, Bolivia, Bogota – nice, but do they do a nice cream tea there?

No one sends postcards anymore; instead of *"wish you were here"* on the back of a card featuring a beach, historical monument or a cartoon of a large-breasted woman berating her diminutive husband with an innuendo like *"why can't your sand castle be that big?"* you get a text or an email which says: *"arrived safely"*, swiftly followed by over 100 Instagram photos of the baggage retrieval area of some distant airport and bemoaning the fact that why is it so few people speak English in the Belgian Congo?

One of the last postcards I sent was in 1973, around this time of year, wishing that my mum and dad were *here* and hoping I'd done well in my O-levels. I hadn't. The punishment being the next year with two weeks in Benidorm – also beginning with B – like *Bubonica Pestis* (a little-known Greek island).

Rings a bell

You no longer have to answer phones with your number. Somehow reciting the words "Balham 0557" still rings (no pun intended) favourably with me and was gutted when, sometime in the 60s, the *Balham* prefix BAL changed to the very impersonal 673 – where is the magic with that? At least make it 666 – infinitely more comedic; the telephone exchange number of the Beast.

I had an aunt who had a phone voice. If you rang her she started off as Princess Margaret and if she knew who you were would instantly (subsequently moving several rungs down the ascendancy to the throne scale) became Margaret Powell (who might have driven a Princess, but certainly wasn't one).

My family's first phone was red and was a step up from the yoghurt pots and string we'd owned before; although more expensive, you never got cross lines on a yoghurt pot and there were no party lines either – it was YOUR yoghurt pot – no waiting for the old woman downstairs to come off the phone to the chimney sweep.

Until Trimphones came along phones were quite cumbersome – only slightly smaller than the *Colossus* built at Bletchley Park. The receivers were good, however, if you wanted to practice rounders in your lounge.

Phone boxes aren't as popular as they were, either. No wonder there are loads of ads on TV for printing your own business card, the former major advertisers within phone boxes now (allegedly) use the Internet. And pressing "Button B to get your money back" was how fruit machine addiction began.

"Putting you through now, caller."

Ex-directories

There must be a massive market for old telephone seats.

With the advent of modern phones there are several pieces of unwanted furniture no longer needed. The old-fashioned telephone seat, much loved in the 50s, 60s and 70s, is sadly one – along with locks on the phone, wires and telephone directories.

In London there were the four monster books; when they'd arrive you'd always check your own entry and then see if there were any rude names to ring. I was always disappointed to find there was no Mr Knob living within the London postal district. They were great door-stops, but not very good if your telephone seat was bit wobbly at one end.

I was never encouraged to sit too long on the telephone seat as my mother told me this was how you got piles. *"Piles of what?"* I always thought to myself not having been professionally trained in rectology.

But there was something even more dangerous than falling off an unbalanced seat or haemorrhoids: that was the address book - not a simple one you'd add people whom you'd met on holiday and would swap Christmas cards with for a respectable period of time until you realised that Hayling Island was a long way from London and did you *really* like them?

The device with the letters down the side, which, when pressed, opened up at a speed like that of a hunting cheetah. If you had bad eyesight, like me, you'd need to be close to check the number you were about to ring – consequently there was always the danger of just prior to making a call, you'd re-enacted the most famous bit of the Battle of Hastings.
I often dreamed of being able to rip a London telephone directory in two. I clearly never followed the instruction manual which came with my Bullworker that accurately.

I miss "Take Your Pick" not being on every Friday evening. I would sit with my nan in her Balham flat urging everyone to fail at every opportunity.

The first hurdle for the contestants was the yes/no interlude, when questions would be asked where the obvious Pavlovian response would have been yes or no. *"Is the Pope Catholic?"* being one of Michael Miles' trickier questions. If, after the longest minute of their life to date, the contestant had successfully avoided saying neither yes nor no, they'd be given five bob (25p in new money).

Five bob was double my pocket money in the 60s when *Take Your Pick* was aired and I believed that five bob could probably have bought the universe – certainly could have bought Rediffusion, the programme's producers.

If the contestant failed, their ignominy was doubled by having former *Pathé News* newsreader, Bob Danvers-Walker, banging a gong next to them to make their ears bleed.
I especially enjoyed the climax of the show when the contestants could potentially win a booby prize. The use of the word *booby* on TV before 9.00 pm amused me. I was only 11, I hasten to add.

During the show the contestants would have accumulated money and were faced with the ultimate choice of betting against their current winnings (take your pick – *get it?*) – on offer by selecting "Box 13" – this could have been a holiday in Totnes, or something equally exotic or an aforementioned booby prize, like a mousetrap. It was when the word stress was first invented.

My nan and I would hope people would select "Box 13" but very few people did; no bad thing as some weeks inside was a three-headed dog who guarded the gates of Hell.

Marginally worse than going to Totnes.

Titch and clackers

One of the most dangerous things in a London school playground in the 60s and 70s wasn't the chance of getting cholera from the school fountain, it was clackers.

How did this get past any research group and actually make it into production? "You get two, heavy when moving at 100 mph, plastic balls and bang them together". The noise was one thing, the potential wrist breaking a mildly bigger problem.

But these toys' life didn't last long within playgrounds, although during its reign of terror made the Eton Wall Game look like a cream tea with an elderly aunt. They were soon banned; not by schools directly, the local hospitals were running out of supplies of plaster of Paris.

During these times, clackers were not the only life-threatening injury one could get in a playground: a hoop and a stick could, if out of control, crash into ankles and if not treated in time could easily turn to gangrene. I was a connoisseur of cards inside bubble gum packets and here a paper cut courtesy of Alan Tracy coming out of the Roundhouse was always lurking when flicking said card up against the playground wall; conkers was always potentially dangerous if your opponent had a violent allergy to acetic acid.

I've not been in a primary school playground since 1968 but I'm assuming hop scotch is now played on an app; one potato, two potato is deemed offensive in case any participant in the playground's relatives lived during the 1845 Irish famine and marbles are things you tend to lose now rather than play.

Three and in, anyone?

Perpetual balls

Last Monday I moved offices and pondered how the contents of my desk differed to that of my first desk, which was situated just off the Strand in 1974 (in an office building, obviously, not me sat, on the Strand, at a desk outside the Stanley Gibbons shop).

The fundamental change on my desk being there is a PC now and no sign of a Newton's Cradle (certainly no drinking bird with its nodding head slowly filling up with (in my case) Civil Service tea) – a must for any executive desk. Not that I was anything like an executive in 1974.

I did have a typewriter – for younger readers this was like a PC, only with slightly more dexterity needed to type, although it did come with a selection (red and black) of typewriter ribbons; sadly, it didn't have Tetris.

As well as the example of conserving momentum and energy (who said physics was useless at school?), aside from Newton's Cradles being on desks, during the 70s, there would always be some form of calendar involving wooden blocks; and if you really were an executive, an angle-poised lamp.

The most senior person in the room would possess the pencil sharpener – scarily not dissimilar to ones you'd have had at primary school, so talking to your boss always left with you the feeling that you'd hope you'd not be tested on your four times table.

But no executive desk was complete without having some form of balancing toy. The trick was to tap the toy and set off the perpetual motion without being too cack-handed and knock it off. It would be the nearest any of us got to doing gymnastics.

Tomorrow I'm off round the shops in Covent Garden to seek out a 70s executive toy. I wonder if the drinking bird likes Irn Bru?

Flowers in the train

One week back in Covent Garden, after nearly four decades away, I have discovered they've moved the London Transport Museum from Clapham.

As kids in the 60s we would walk the along the A24 (probably a Roman Road which linked Watling Street to Offa's Dyke via Gaul) from my flat in Balham to the huge hangar which housed more trams than you can shake a stick at just past Clapham Common Station. We walked, as this saved on the bus fare, plus we wanted to feel like Centurions.

No one was especially interested in 19th century Tube trains, but it made a change from going to South Ken to see a blue whale, a dodo and a couple of coelacanths.

Also, in Covent Garden, there seem to be nicer shops than when I was last here. Indeed, the office where I was is now a Gap store. When I had worked there previously the only *gap* was in the window next to where I sat giving me the impression of feeling like Bert Trautmann for my 18-month tenure in WC2.

One thing I have seen is a lot of men in black jackets carrying square-shaped brief cases – presumably they are carrying portable chess boards – there are a few who look like Bobby Fischer, although with handshakes that they're giving out, would struggle to move any chess pieces.

Because of the theatres round here I've already seen various celebrities – yesterday I saw Mark Thatcher – I assume he's in *The Lion King*? I guess it's just a matter of time before I see Eliza Doolittle.

Big Boys' (and Girls') Breakfast

Just as King Arthur sought the Holy Grail, as a young man starting work in London in the mid-70s, my goal was, during my lunchbreak, to find the best sausage, egg 'n' chips; and preferably all for under four and six (even though Imperial currency was no longer legal).

To help him on his most Holy of quests, King Arthur had people like Lancelot, Gawain and Sir Percivale (whose close friends called him Lance); I had a book of Luncheon Vouchers.

As my work took me twice a day for three months to Fleet Street, I was tempted by one establishment: Mick's Café (if I had a café that's what it'd be called – wouldn't be a proper caff if it wasn't called Mike's Café). However, as a very innocent 18-year-old I was rather scared to go in– I imagined the entire printing staff of the *Sun, Daily Mirror* and *Reveille* would be gathered there devouring all the eggs and leaving only streaky bacon and black pudding to mere mortals such as I.

As I became more senior, people would take me to breakfast and the attraction of pubs serving breakfast suddenly appealed; there were several in Fleet Street and a few in Smithfield, where the meat was fresh even if the people serving it weren't.

The only danger was that you'd come out smelling of what you'd just eaten and, as you got older and forced to have annual medicals, the word cholesterol would become part of your vocab. In the mid-70s cholesterol sounded more like a type of frothy coffee rather than something brought on by having too many BBBs.

More tea, love?

It's gone all over my suit

Sooty is 70.

My first-ever glove puppet was one of Sooty. One of the rare pictures of me ever taken was as a four-year-old in 1961 in my parents' Balham flat with me holding Sooty in the style of the Boston Strangler.

What a lot of people didn't know was that Sooty suffered from hydrophobia and his constant squirting wasn't him being naughty, but simply trying to allay his deepest, water-borne fears.

Sooty was also an accomplished magician and dated Debbie McGee before dumping her for Soo.

While working for the BBC the producers there were told that Sooty and new girlfriend Soo could never touch on screen; Sooty is reputed to have been the founder of tantric sex. Sooty's owner was also very accomplished; as well as (literally) having a hand in Sooty's success, he was very good portraying Harold Steptoe.

Sooty's inability to speak loudly was due mainly to vocal-chord damage attributed to his constant haranguing in 1948 across to the steps of 11 Downing Street of Sir Stafford Cripps about his austerity plans.

During the show, Sooty's owner, star of *Carry on Screaming*, invariably had his suit ruined; the show was sponsored by Burtons and the suits actually free.

It was above a Burton's where Sooty initially met Sweep, who, in 1948, was running an illicit snooker hall. Sweep spoke as he did as he'd previously had an unspeakable accident with a couple of billiard balls, a spider rest and several pieces of chalk.

Bye bye, everybody, bye bye

Strike a light

A new *A Star is Born* film is out; a new one was a due as it keeps the sequence of one every other decade going. Although -3 in 1954 when the second one came out, it is my favourite, as I enjoyed James Mason playing Rommel in it.

However, it was the 1976 version which I saw at the pictures: The Granada, Clapham Junction.

It was a time when they still had B-movies at the cinema. The B-film before the Barbra Streisand classic was a grainy, black & white film about Ernest Rutherford and him splitting the atom. There were no songs like *Evergreen* in this film; not even a clip of the future 1st Baron Rutherford for Nelson humming *Don't Rain on My Parade*.

Aside from me and my aspiring Barry Norman mates, there was a bloke sitting down the front (arguably better than sitting in the back)) of the cinema. Thirty-minutes into the atom-splitting film the nutter turned around to me and my mates and asked: *"Is this the Barbra Streisand film?"*

The lack of naked bath scenes and an aging star driving into the distance (not to mention the lack of songs) were the giveaways. We suggested it wasn't but stuck with it as we'd paid our 4/6 (or whatever cinema entrance was in 1976) and there is a bath scene.

The main attraction started. Towards the end, the Streisand character sings at a concert and several lights are lit from within the audience. This was the cue for the nutter to get his powerful, out-of-control French lighter out to join in the memorial of a lost friend.

Within seconds the Fire Brigade was called, he was frog-marched out by a fleet of usherettes and submerged in a giant water tank, lighter held aloft, singing *"Hello Dolly"*.

That's showbiz.

Trains and boats and planes (but mainly boats)

It's been many a year since I submerged U-Boats into my Mr Matey; bath times are different now I'm older.

In my south London flat, growing up in the 60s, no bath time was complete without a fleet of plastic destroyers and rather too much Mr Matey acting as dangerous mid-Atlantic cliffs and waves as I re-enacted the Battle of Jutland and scenes from *The Cruel Sea*. I was Noel Coward in my bath (without the smoking jacket, obviously).

However, as you get older, and as a boy discover there are other things to play with in the bath other than replica *Bismarck*s, a sophistication comes over you and Mr Matey is eventually replaced by *Radox* and then anything from *Kiehl's* as you get older still. Plastic boats and rubber ducks are replaced by candles as you try and re-enact scenes from Barbra Streisand's *A Star is Born*.

I can only assume Queen Elizabeth I only bathed once a year as no-one had invented Mr Matey or, in her case, Miss Matey. It might have saved Sir Walter Raleigh's head if he'd brought some *Bronnley Bath Cubes* back from the West Indies rather than tobacco.

I still enjoy a bath; although I just lie there these days, my myopia bearing testimony that I should really have stuck to manoeuvring my replica *HMS Victory* more during my adolescence.

Triumph of the windscreen wiper

The moment, after a journey of not 100-yards, when I'd crashed my mum's Triumph 2000 into a tree next to a garage behind my Balham flats, I knew I was destined never to become a driving examiner.

I failed my first car driving test in Sutton and aside from having far too few lessons, it was an incredibly bright day and I realised how Saul of Tarsus must have felt on his way to Damascus (he probably wouldn't have gone via Sutton).

On the notice board inside the test centre, there were posters encouraging people to become examiners; the ones I'd met weren't the happiest: dicing with death several times a day and getting no reward were key reasons. Ironically, the test centre was close to the local hospital where I'd once been given Pethidine (if Jimi Hendrix had been a driving examiner, he'd have worked there).

When I was 14 in 1971 my mum was keen for me to learn to drive. The garages behind our flats were quiet and an alternative as the open fields in SW17 were long gone.

It was an automatic car but took me no time to get the two pedals mixed up as we hurtled towards a tree. I didn't drive for a decade – deeply scarred, although not as scarred as the Triumph 2000.

I had more success with a motorbike and passed first time. Nowadays, the instructor follows behind giving instructions via a walkie-talkie; in 1978, when I passed, you were sent off and told to return in fifteen minutes; as long as you made a hand signal leaving the test centre and returned with a limited amount of blood on your bike, you passed.

I'm still not a good driver; it is inherent. My father took 12 tests to pass. It took me two and was glad to rid myself of L-plates, which for me meant liability, rather than learner. It still does.

An absolute shower

During my school days in the 60s I was in danger of making school nit nurse redundant.

While I never had a specific bath night, I do remember regular washing of my hair. It wasn't the actual washing I didn't like – I quite liked the smell of *Vosene* or the occasional *Fairy Liquid* when we were cutting back on shampoo – it was the methods my mother employed to get my hair clean.

We didn't have a shower attachment which you affix to the bath-taps, but we did have a massive sink in the kitchen. If my mother washed my hair while cooking, there was the danger of coming out of the kitchen smelling of a combination of *Vosene* and egg 'n' chips.

My hair was washed over the sink with a plastic device which hung over the edge of the sink to help ease the shock of cold enamel on nape of neck; people facing the *Guillotine* were more comfortable. I preferred my hair to be washed while I faced the ceiling, as the yellow nicotine patch was preferable than looking at the potato peelings.

A cup was used to rinse my hair – most times it didn't contain my mum's *Guinness*, although I'm sure the iron might have strengthened my follicles.

My hair would then be vigorously dried with a tea towel from the Isle of Wight. As my head was being rubbed as if I were an old English Sheepdog I would see visions of Ventor, Alum Bay sands and Parkhurst Prison passing, at sub-liminal speeds, before my eyes.

I never did get nits, but then I'm told they don't like clean hair. Or perhaps all head lice are allergic to potatoes?

Glued to the… gerbil!

I had the remains of an ME109 in my bedroom once; although this sounds like a quote from a cab driver, it is the result of my first (and only) attempt to construct an *Airfix* model.

As a child I'd go to tea with other kids and invariably see the Battle of Britain being fought out on their ceilings. I was very envious of this and decided I'd have a go. I'd start slowly and build up – I could, with one plane, re-enact Rudolf Hess's lone flight to Scotland – on *my* ceiling.

Off to the model shop in Tooting Bec I went and procured an *Airfix* model kit of an ME109. I told the shopkeeper I was a direct descendant of Willy Messerschmidt and asked for a discount. With the Cold War still raging, this wasn't bright, so set off home, together with my over-priced miniature plane.

Half an hour later I realised how tricky it was getting glue off carpet; and hands; and gerbils! The glue went everywhere except on the crucial hinge bits of the ME109. Half hour after that, with many pieces of balsa wood having been scattered to the four corners of my bedroom, it looked like Kenneth More and Robert Shaw had been in personally and destroyed it.

I never attempted to construct another model. I did keep the bits of balsa wood on the walls, carpet and various rodents with the vain hope of winning the Turner Prize; sadly, Tracey Emin had thought of this first!

Trig of the dump

My failure to pass Maths O-Level three times (1973, 74 & 75) was not helped by my total misunderstanding of what a slide rule was meant for. If you wanted a straight line, with a little bobble in, then a slide rule was just that – forget that it was designed for complex multiplication and duplication; although, when I first got mine I thought it was broken as the middle bit kept sliding out.

Log tables were also useless if you were destined to regularly fail maths exams; however, if you had a slightly uneven desk, then a log table book was the ideal thing. Many restaurants use them for wobbly tables when they've run out of beer-mats.

My question is: what was the set-square for in the student *Helix* geometry set? Compass, yes – if you'd forgotten your darts; protractor, yes – if you needed to draw half a moon or an ox-bow lake. But a set-square? It would remain, gathering dust like Miss Haversham's dining room, in your protective plastic wallet, with no ostensible use. Perhaps my school believed Tooting was going to be the source of budding architects?

It wasn't until I failed my third maths O-level that I realised that trigonometry wasn't a type of dinosaur, cosine was not a type of lettuce and Pythagoras' theorem was not an ancient ruin just outside Athens.

Pi's off, love.

Ducking: The question

Walking through a south London park the other day to show the expensive consequence of eating too many mint humbugs to my dentist only to notice a sign saying not to feed bread to ducks. Since when has this become a thing and why, after generations of duck-feeding with bread perilously close to after its sell-by date, have the entire duck population, in a dodo-like fashion, not become extinct?

The sign suggested fruit (must ducks now eat five portions of fruit a day? And are they now more susceptible to colds?), birdseed and nuts (I have found, to my peril, walking through St James's Park that Canada Geese are quite partial to nuts – I would always wear a reinforced surgical support whenever I went to watch Trooping the Colour).

People will now be taking their children and grandchildren (duck feeding being something you don't tend to do as a lone adult) to feed the ducks, armed with a basket suitable for a Harvest Festival offering and packets of Trill.

Duck's not off, love, it's gluten-free.

Blind dates

My fear of heights precluded me ever becoming the *Milk Tray* man. As Christmas approaches, thoughts turn to what we can possibly buy which will heighten our bad cholesterol count as we contemplate the annual purchase of a box of dates.

1968 saw the first *Milk Tray* man ad on TV and ran, with several actors, into the mid-2000s. I was 11 in 1968 and watched as the man leapt from building to building, through numerous avalanches, combating three-headed dogs along the way to delivering his milk chocolate selection box.

If I'd been better at PE at school, I would have quite fancied that – black is my favourite clothes colour; in my mind, I was halfway there. The SAS-type training being the other half, was an aspect which needed work! I couldn't vault over a horse during PE, so there was no way I'd be seen on UK TV screens across the land with my important package (my own personal important package being my main concern while attempting to leap over a wooden horse in my Tooting school gym).

"And all because the lady loves *Milk Tray*" – really? Even "Perfect Praline" which isn't perfect as so few people know what praline is? I'm surprised this hasn't been discontinued as it is the only one which remains in the box after the decorations are put away, the cards taken down and box of dates stored back in the loft.

Milk Tray has been around since 1916; coincidentally the sell-by date on my box of dates.

Rum 'n' raison baby Jesus

I would like to know when the baby Jesus got replaced by a KitKat?

It is now Advent and Advent calendars are in evidence; in some shops they've been available since August Bank Holiday.

Advent calendars these days contain sufficient chocolate to raise your cholesterol levels by 10%, but when did this start?

Growing up in the 60s, when you got an Advent calendar at the start of Advent and not at the beginning of the grouse shooting season in mid-August, behind the 24 tabs were pictures of likely presents and Christmas-related things: a spinning-top, some holly, a snowman (especially if your town was twinned with Reykjavik - I think Balham was, but only for 1963).

The flap with the number 24 on hid a picture of the aforementioned baby Jesus. Today, people are disappointed when it's not the daily output of the Bournville factory behind any of the flaps.

If I were the Archbishop of Canterbury, my Christmas Message this year would be directed at the British Dental Association. I blame them; although KitKat is marginally tastier than cardboard!

Lo, He comes with clouds descending – only this year with added caramel filling.

Vinter Vonderland

"Holidays are coming" says the Coca Cola-fuelled TV ad six times, as the British public awaits the now famous ads for Christmas.

Growing up in south London in the 60s there was never that anticipation of exciting TV ads – mainly because there was only one commercial TV station and the only thing anticipated was how much Cinzano Leonard Rossiter might spill over Joan Collins or the shock of the inarticulate Lorraine Chase talking about Luton Airport. Says he who bunked off elocution lessons when 10.

However, there was one which I remember vividly and was in that box of things (like dates) that you only devoured at Christmas; that was promoting Advocaat (particularly the brand made by Warninks – pronounced with a "V" as if you were playing a German in *Hogan's Heroes*). Suddenly a snowball wasn't something you remembered making in 1963, or a leading character in *Animal Farm*, here was something your parents gave you in an effort to put you off drinking alcohol at Christmas – and subsequent decades. It's like if custard was alcoholic.

My favourite Christmas ad from times gone by still remains the one marketing various forms of fragrances for Morny's talc – although rather than the line: *"Morny – the natural choice for Christmas"*, I'd have preferred: *"Because everyone suffers from chafing sometime"*.

Probably why I never made it in a creative department of any ad agencies in which I worked. To which I say *"Bols"*.

Blob on the landscape

The record which topped the charts during my first Christmas, in 1957, was Harry Belafonte singing *Mary's Boy Child* which is *When a Child is Born* played backwards. It wasn't until 1967 with The Scaffold's *Lily the Pink*, that the Christmas songs became novelty songs – you'll never hear the choir of King's College Cambridge singing *Ernie* during any of their Nine Lessons & Carols services.

1956 had Johnnie Ray singing *Just a Walkin' in the Rain* – if he'd had released that during Christmas 1962 he'd have had to have changed the words to *Just a Walkin' in the Snow* as Britain witnessed its worst winter since the Black Death.

Is it, that at Christmas, peoples' music tastes change so dramatically that they are bound to buy the worst record that week?

Why would you buy *Long-Haired Lover From Liverpool* (1972) sung by someone who'd rarely travelled outside of Utah? In my view the 1980 hit *There's no one quite like Grandma* is correct – my maternal grandmother had no teeth, stockings which were never fully pulled up properly and the most vituperative person ever. And *Mr Blobby* (1993) – if Mr Blobby had been one of the three wise men, then fair enough, he deserves a Christmas No. 1; but he wasn't unless there were actually *four* wise men carrying gold, frankincense, myrrh and a yellow, spotted bow-tie.

Bring back Johnny Ray singing *Just a Walkin' in the Disturbingly Mild for the Time of Year*.

Sponge, anyone?

Growing up in the 60s, Balham Woolworth's was the place we'd get our Christmas tree each year.

They weren't as easy to nick as the contents on the *Pick 'n' Mix* on the counter, so temptingly near the entrance, so we bought ours. This was also the place where we'd also purchase our decorations: which, because they were so fragile, by the time we'd get them back to our flat, and with an attrition rate of around 67%, we'd leave a trail of shattered glass/plastic in our wake along Balham High Road.

The biggest argument, however, was what to put on the top of the tree. As a small child we'd have a fairy/angel and then a star as I got older. Upon entering teenage years there was a perennial internal family fight as to what perched at the top of the tree.

We all had varying hobbies and interests: my mum wanted a packet of JPS, my dad, despite being a massive Chelsea fan, wanted a picture of Vanessa Redgrave and I wanted a model of Gerd Müller. We compromised, and for several years the pride of place atop our tree was a model of Tommy Baldwin wearing a Germany shirt made from old cigarette packets.

Candlewick green

It is that time of year when you have a momentous decision to make: is it time for the winter duvet?

Growing up in the 60s in London duvets were things people only used in northern Finnish ice huts. It wasn't until the 70s when Brits realised that duvet didn't rhyme with rivet.

Now everyone has a duvet; and most people now know that tog is a unit of thermal measurement, as well as being some bizarre creature in Pogle's Wood.

But was there, in the late 70s, a massive chucking-out of sheets, blankets and, most importantly, candlewicks? Were there suddenly heaps of discarded eiderdowns at the local tips?

I had a blue candlewick, which, over the course of many years constantly picking (which prevented other potential adolescent nocturnal activities – and still I have dreadful eyesight), ended up with more holes than actual bedding – I'd have been warmer with a giant Polo covering me!

Perhaps "continental duvets" featured heavily in The Champions or The Persuaders which encouraged us and our parents to hurry down to Brentford Nylons to purchase this Scandinavian wonder night-time protection?

I miss my candlewick, holey that it became, and would be comforted by it in the dead of night in my quiet Balham flat, if ever I woke, to see the beaming, and comforting, face of Captain Scarlet – half hour later I'd wake up thinking the Mysterons were in the room – they weren't – they were burglars

Three Amoebas

In September 1968, after a series of exams and interviews, and having gained a place at my Tooting Grammar Sschool, I was amazed that the first set of homework was to cover our text books.

I was anticipating in my first week to have gone home to split the atom, remembered the dates of the reigns of all the Anglo-Saxon monarchs or knowing that in binary 01000101 is 69 (which, when you're 11, is just another number).

Over the next few days we would all come back to our school rooms with our books adorned in whatever material our parents had left lying around our houses.

Most had used brown paper, one or two had gone down the wallpaper remnant route, with one boy coming in with his books covered with red flock wallpaper which looked suspiciously like the same wallpaper which decorated the Granada Tooting. I never went to tea at this boy's house, but I'd have bet his carpet would have had the word 'Granada' inscribed into the weaving.

Another lad came in with his books bedecked in Thunderbirds wallpaper. Sadly, for him, in the teachers' eyes, Thunderbirds were not "GO" and he consequently got a detention – even Virgil Tracy couldn't rescue him from that.

The homework did get harder; the toughest assignment being charged with looking after the class amoeba (this was a grammar school, so no run-of-the-mill hamster) for an entire weekend, making sure it didn't die or get impregnated by other organisms.

River deep, Streatham High (Road)

In the '60s, my mum took me twice to the Streatham Odeon. Once to see Mary Poppins and then to see The Supremes.

I saw them both in quick succession and wondered, halfway through Love Child, why Julie Andrews wasn't in the line-up, and why they ended the concert singing Baby Love and not A Spoonful of Sugar?

When I saw The Supremes, Diana Ross had left the group to commence a career starting World Cup finals and I thought I was well within my rights to expect the expert nanny, together with her magical umbrella, to be on the stage singing You Can't Hurry Love. This song was originally written for the 1937 Cockney musical, Me and My Girl and the version was to have been called, You Can't Hurry, Love.

I'm thrilled, however, that the Streatham Odeon is still functioning as a cinema; the Balham Odeon is now a Majestic Wine House – not so much Kia Ora more a fine Beaujolais, and the Mayfair Tooting is now a bank (via, in the '70s, an upmarket snooker hall – which of course in Tooting is oxymoronic) and will probably end up being a pub – as most old banks do.

I suppose there is a link, as the grocer where Mary Poppins bought her sugar was called Nathan Jones.

Finger lickin'

My walk to school in the late '60s would, every day, take me past a stamp shop. The shop, near Tooting Bec Station, was next to a baker where the smell emitting from the bakery was so foul I was drawn ever nearer to the stamp shop next door for comfort, and often considered collecting stamps.

My dilemma was not knowing the difference between a Penny Black stamp and a Green Shield one. Although I look back and think, if I'd owned a Penny Black, I wouldn't have needed to lick as many Green Shield stamps as I did to collect the required amount for a flannelette sheet.

Most Saturdays I would journey to the stamp shop with a peg on my nose to avoid the acrid smell emanating from the next-door bakery to buy some stamps.

I bought an album, a set of hinges and an implement which you dipped the hinges in so you didn't die of thirst with too much licking. I nearly bought one using Green Shield stamps but had dehydrated by the time I got to the shop in Clapham Common.

I quickly realised that my half a crown pocket money was never going to buy a Penny Black (or even a perforation off one) so my plan B was to buy stamps with modes of transport on.

Most people would collect stamps from specific countries (or Penny Blacks), but I was content with stamps with Concorde on or the occasional hovercraft. My album consequently had no value, but I believed it could float on water or travel at super-sonic speeds.

It was only when I was older that I discovered the official word for collecting stamps was fellatio; more of that next week when I talk about my rare Blue Mauritius.

Dogging is not just for Christmas

I never encountered Janet and John when I began to read at my south London school in the early '60s. My class was given Mac and Tosh (do you see what they did there? I assume the authors also ran a chain of raincoat shops?)

I missed out on Here We Go (Janet and John become football hooligans), Off to Play (Janet and John discover the joys of truancy) and I Know A Story (where Janet & John learn the art of pathological lying).

No, I had two Scottie dogs helping me improve my four-and-a-half-year-old reading skills.

The early books were Mac and Tosh Learn to Read and Mac and Tosh Learn to Write. I moved on from this series quite quickly and assumed the next editions covered: Mac and Tosh Learn Elementary Computer Programming and Mac and Tosh Secure World Peace.

Because I progressed away from books with lines such as: "Here is the dog," we like the dog," "John likes dogging". It wasn't until I was in my mid-20s that I learned that dogs can neither read nor write. I blame this on Dr Doolittle and watching too many episodes of Mr Ed.

Part A

I never got a party bag when I left any party I attended as a kid. In the '60s you'd get a piece of cake for your mum and an item of stationery: pencils for the girls, the boys would get rubbers (you can't be too careful – even at eight!).

Neither did I go to a party where they had a child's entertainer. You made your own entertainment: musical chairs (always won by people interested in Feng shui), pass the parcel (where you got your first paper cut and the chance to get another pencil) and postman's knock (which was a marginally more accurate introduction to sex education than learning about the reproduction system of amoebas at school).

Party bag ingredients these days is a serious and highly competitive business; personalised cup cakes are popular (just in case you've not eaten enough cake at the arty) and Slime.

If you're of a certain age (61) think Play Doh, only more malleable. In the '60s the only slime you saw was if you were watching The Quatermass Experiment or your nan hadn't probably cleaned out her larder during an unseasonably hot summer.

Growing up in the '60s there was no slime given out at the end of parties, just your parents explaining to the returning parents why Keith had had a nose bleed, how Stephen had fractured his ankle on a removable chair and that Josie was sick into the parcel being passed. We never played blind man's buff; it was too dangerous as we lived on the fourth floor of a block of flats with dodgy windows.

Hotel du Lack

Due to a pathological fear of cheese, I'd have never have made it as a chef

Having failed a vast majority of my O-Levels in 1973, my father took me to an industrial psychologist in Gloucester Place to establish which career I should pursue; Astronaut was out due to a morbid dread of flying, postman was never an option due to a teenage propensity to getting verrucae and the role of prime minister was already taken by Ted Heath – although I did hoard candles – handy during the three-day week power cuts.

At the psychologist's I was given a series of tests. One was a list of hundred potential occupations grouped in pairs; I had to choose one of the two. One couple was: bishop or miner? This was a no-brainer as I don't like getting dirty and as a choir boy looked quite charming in cassock and surplice.

Lastly, I had an interview with the psychologist who, having analysed the results, and me assuming I'd be a shoo-in for the next Archbishop of Canterbury, suggested a career in hotel and catering.

I had immediate visions of running a hotel but suddenly realised I'd have to start at the bottom and wouldn't have suited being dressed as a chambermaid. I haven't got the legs.

And so, I went into advertising – where you don't have to wear a pinny – unless the client is particularly demanding.

So, what was room service's loss became the world of conning people into buying something they really don't want's gain.

You can check out any time you like, but you can never leave. Unless you don't want your 10-bob deposit back.

Snooker loopy

I wanted to be Joe Davis when I was growing up. The five-foot folding snooker table, which took up 90% of my bedroom, was the investment I needed to help this dream materialise. I already had comedy glasses.

As I grew older, and was allowed out of my bedroom unaccompanied, I discovered, during the '60s and '70s, there were as many snooker halls then as there are Prets and Costas now.

Many were above Burton's, meaning you could buy a suit and get a century break (OK, eight) within the same building.

Many halls were temperance; the strongest drink you could get was black coffee – unless you included WD40 for the squeaky doors – although this doesn't mix too well with Bovril.

The greatest expense, aside from the table hire, were pieces of chalk. I'd always forget my chalk and collected over 100 small, used-only-once, blue cubes. I finally ground them down and gave them to my mother stating they were the new, exotic range of Bronnley bath salts.

Snooker was made popular in July 1969 with the introduction of Pot Black. The thrill of this game was somewhat negated as a majority of UK TVs in 1969 were still black and white, thus meaning the grey ball scored one as well as seven – given the vertical hold on the TV was always on the blink in my flat, I always thought snooker was played at sea during a force 10 gale.

My favourite player, once colour TV was more prevalent, was Perrie Mans. He, like me, had clearly made his waistcoats out of discarded curtains. Although, being professional, he'd have removed the hooks.

Bleak house

My father was always trying to improve me intellectually and would frequently organise visits to stately home and places of interest (just what you want when you're a teenage boy).

Around this time, in 1970, my parents had agreed to move out of Balham and look further afield.

One Sunday we took the train and a series of buses to Bloomsbury. Our journey ended at 48 Doughty Street, WC1 (this'll be a bugger in the morning to get to school in Tooting, I thought to myself).

We were let into the building; it was dark, foreboding (a word I used frequently as a teenager), it became ever darker as we climbed the several flights of stairs (not one step was the same height, but I realised I'd certainly get my money's worth out of my new Slinky).

"So, Michael," said my father, (this didn't bode well as I was normally called Mick unless I'd been naughty, set fire to a relative or not tidied my room) "do you think you'll be happy in your new home?"

I suddenly realised what the Princes in the Tower had felt like – the only thing this house lacked was a scaffold and a bloody great axe.

But before I could run away (which would have been interesting as I had no money and bus drivers tended not to accept half-eaten sherbet dabs as payment), my dad informed me we weren't moving here but this was in fact where Charles Dickens had lived.

My joy of not moving was as evident as was the relief of not having to rewrite Hard Times – only with fewer gags.

We did move two years later – to Carshalton – famous for its ponds rather than greedy orphans.

No plaice like home

In the late '60s, years before "take your child to work day" was introduced, my Dad would occasionally take me to his advertising agency office in Gloucester Place. It was like Mad Men, only set just off Baker Street rather than Madison Avenue.

I never spent a single minute in my Dad's actual office but was relegated to the bowels of his building and put in front of a drawing pad which was bigger than me and more writing implements than the annual output of the Cumberland Pencil Company. I was in stationery heaven.

The other men in this subterranean office would have paperclip battles with one another and several people would come in and swear badly. If you're only 10, this is hysterically funny. If they'd had a swear box in this office, they'd have been spending half the year on a cruise.

Both my parents were vituperative; these people made them look (and sound) like Mother Teresa.

Paperclips wars, more pencils you could shake a pencil-shaped stick, at and gratuitous swearing – a career in advertising clearly beckoned.

At lunch Dad would take me to The Golden Egg restaurant in Baker Street. I was a fussy eater and would only ever eat plaice and chips there. My diet never really extended and still, for me, the mark of a good restaurant is one where the food is served with a wedge of lemon.

I miss the giant pad. I could have been the next van Gogh, only with more ears.

Passport to Puerto Banus

Summer holidays in the '60s did not start at Palma, Penzance nor at Puerto Banus. They began at Petty France.

A trip to London as an 11 year-old in 1968 to get a passport was exciting as we passed New Scotland Yard, where I hoped to steal a glimpse of Shaw Taylor, Stratford Johns or Officer Dibble.

The need for passports was to enable my parents and I to travel to Majorca. I couldn't find Majorca in the London A-Z so assumed it must be abroad. As we waited in the interminable queue, and my parents practiced their pigeon Majorcan, I wondered if there was a Significant France, which had more counters and fewer queues?

What passports don't take into account is fashion – nor differing hair lengths through the ages. You keep your passport for a decade and, sometime into the '80s, there was a part of people's passports which was forever Les McKeown.

They do say if you look like your passport photo you're too ill to travel. But neither can you smile; if you wear glasses you must be photographed without them. Because of retina recognition at Passport Control, if you wear glasses (as I do) you must remove them. I now grope my way officially back into the UK like Mr Magoo.

These days passports can be renewed online. There is the inherent danger, however, of also visiting Amazon, Ocado or eBay. A consequence of which is you may receive a used passport the next day for £1, a substitute passport as they'd run out of the original or you've sold yourself to a man who's coming around later to collect you.

Weather or not

If my surname was Fish then I think I'd probably be somewhat the wiser. Although, given its current misbehaviour, as far as weather prediction is concerned, I might as well be Captain Haddock.

Growing up in London in the '60s and '70s, it was cold in 1962/63 and hot in 1976, you also knew the next day would be the same; not these days. Is it because we all used too much Harmony hairspray or Brut anti-perspirant during this period?

Clothing, to cope with the changes in temperature, is different too. In the '60s we had duffel coats, a plastic rain hat and a mac with a belt you could tighten so much it was like wearing a Victorian corset. I never had a rain hat as a kid as I wasn't allowed plastic near my mouth.

Today you can have multi-layer coats, usually made by unpronounceable named Teutonic companies – the harder the maker's name is to articulate the warmer it'll keep you.

To cope with the unseasonable heat, we are now seeing more public water dispensers. I don't quite know when bottled water was invented, but certainly wasn't evident in Balham in the '60s. Unless you include the two water fountains in my school playground. Who can't forget the "refreshing" feeling, after a successful and energetic game of three-and-in, of the dribble of lukewarm water emanating from the playground fountain?

If it's windy, eat less cabbage.

Dressing-down day

I'm unsure when dress-down days were introduced. If you're a bloke, it was a hard thing to convert to. Simply talking off a tie (which you'd worn for several working decades prior) isn't really dress down.

Despite working in the City, I never wore a bowler hat (the intricate folding of the accompanying umbrella failed me miserably) but I did wear a suit and tie for years.

My first suit was purple (it was 1974!) – a strange choice given my only eye ailment is myopia rather than colour-blindness. Deep Purple were a fashionable group at the time, but the eponymous name didn't translate well into work clothes. Many fellow travellers thought I must be a bishop in mufti.

During the early days of dress-down you got an insight as to what people looked like at weekends. Posh people would wear cords, the colour of which made my purple look surprisingly normal. Posh people also wear shoes (loafers which have seen better days, but that's how the rich get rich) with no socks – a sure-fire way of contracting pneumonia.

Before ties were deemed unnecessary in the workplace there was competition within workers as to who had the best tie. This contest became null and void when workers from the suburbs would visit with their ties adorned with Homer Simpson, Taz of Tasmania or any Thunderbird pilot.

Virgil Tracy always beats anything from Hermès.

The term "smart casual" has entered our vocabulary. However, initially this was misinterpreted as I remember one day arriving at work and a fellow worker had dressed in army combats. He looked like he was more likely about to invade Angola rather than help out with some filing.

I was often confused as a kid as both parents and grandparents would tell me things which, with the small knowledge I've gathered over sixty-plus years, were either horribly inaccurate or a total lie.

If ever I made a face (which tended to happen if my nan was cooking boiled fish in parsley sauce – a concoction which should be considered as an alternative to anthrax in biological warfare) she would say "if the wind changes, you'll stay like that". The UK is situated in the path of a polar front jet stream – winds are frequent, facial disfigurements for me fortuitously were not.

My mum would use the word "bleedin'" so much, growing up I realised that an urgent learning of the rudiments of first aid was going to be a must. Luckily, however, it seemed there was nothing inside our flat which was haemophiliac.

Bob's your uncle was recited many times. I never met Bob – even with much genealogical research. My mum would "entertain" many people – several had the epithet "uncle" – in our flat, but none featured on my home-made family tree chart, even fewer called Bob.

And as for fairies being at the bottom of my garden, living in a fourth-floor flat (unless you can get apparitions among your begonias in your window boxes) there was never going to be a Fatima-like vision which I was perpetually promised.

And the word wireless these days doesn't necessarily have to involve Lord Haw-Haw.

Tubs, tubs, tubs

In 1970, me and three others were in the Granada Tooting, a cinema built in 1931 to accommodate 4,000 people. I was watching Tora, Tora, Tora, a film about the attack on Pearl Harbour. The cinema was therefore 0.1% full.

With me there was my dad, a friend of my dad's and the usherette. There was a fifth, but he didn't count, as he was the projectionist. He had to be there, the usherette didn't. Tubs were quite expensive and it wasn't until my mid-20s that I realised I didn't have an allergic reaction to raspberry ripple as my dad had suggested when I was younger.

The Granada Tooting closed as a cinema in 1973. With dwindling cinema goers and over-priced wafers, they had committed their own economic and cinematic Kamikaze.

Also, there was no atmosphere, unlike when I went to see Jaws at the Ruby, Clapham Junction (another cinema also sadly playing in the great picture house foyer in the sky).

It had been raining heavily during this 1975 winter's evening as I trudged across Wandsworth Common to get to the cinema; I was glad of the protection once inside the Ruby. Sadly, the Ruby had seen better times and, due to the excessive rain, had sprung a leak in its roof. A consequence of this was, as I watched the film, that it felt as if I was on the boat with Messrs Scheider, Dreyfuss and Shaw, as I became increasingly wet.

It was like being there except they weren't holding a Kia Ora on the boat and nor did they develop trench-foot a week later.

Plus the passive-aggressive usherettes in the Ruby were scarier than any Great White Shark.

Go to Jail

Easter holidays have kicked in and with it the need to entertain kids/grandkids/aged aunts.

Do the kids of today play board games like Monopoly (slightly out-dated as you can't get a packet of crisps for £400 in Mayfair, let alone build a hotel there)? Or Totopoly (before Ray Winston demanded you gamble responsibly and where Old Kent Road was replaced by Arkle) Or Go – the international travel game (a typical game now takes several years due to the USSR now being 15 different countries, Yugoslavia is spilt –no pun intended) – and Czechoslovakia has never been the same after Jim Prideaux was brought back)?

Today there is X-Box (like Pandora's box only containing more of the world's ills), Minecraft (a 1957 hit for Frank Sinatra), and anything by Nintendo (easily my favourite '70s wrestler).

Kids of today probably believe rolling a dice might dislocate their wrists; the thought of taking on the persona of an old boot for a couple of hours would seem abhorrent if they've never had anything second-hand and playing with pretend paper money is something they'd expect to see on Antiques Roadshow as surely everything is contactless.

They are unlikely to know what a billiard room is, let alone knowing what a candlestick might be used for – and (literally), Heaven forbid the local vicar's a murderer.

We might have to wait a long time before we see Grand Theft Top Hat

Freudian slippers

It beats holiday snaps, pictures of other people's children and any unnatural bruising – people telling you about their dreams.

Do people assume you're perpetually carrying around a copy of Sigmund Freud's The Interpretation of Dreams with you? Ready to pronounce what giant snakes represent, being drowned by someone you don't like at work or why Pamela Anderson featuring heavily actually means?

While Freud led us to believe what these dreams possibly mean, they are not real life and didn't happen – it's like believing Coronation Street is real and wondering why, after Martha Longhurst got killed when the viaduct collapsed, it wasn't splashed all over the front page of the next day's Sun.

Anyone saying "I had this weird dream last night" should immediately be told: "Never mind that, here are many pictures of my goldfish, may I saw my arm off with a spoon or I'm about to go and watch some paint dry, perhaps tell me there?

Some people will often say they don't dream; you do dream, you just don't remember (thank the Lord) all of them.

However, if you do want to properly dream a dream everyone will want to hear about around the water fountain, a cocktail of Camembert, brown ale and Skittles, all consumed before midnight, should do the trick.

Although, funnily enough, last night, I did dream about Pamela Anderson. Again.

Chocolate is not just for Easter

Living on the fourth floor of a block of flats meant Easter egg hunts were precarious to say the least. My mother was good at hiding them, but I never felt confident with her scaffolding-erecting skills outside the lounge window.

In the '60s I'd get Easter eggs from benevolent relatives. They'd be from Cadbury's and would contain (inside) a small packet of chocolate buttons – as if you'd not had enough chocolate with the actual egg.

Nowadays you can spend hundreds of pounds in Hotel Chocolat (who can't even spell chocolate) or from Lindt (which, when I was growing up, was something you'd put on a wound).

Creme (what is it with the inability to spell correctly in the confectionary industry?) Eggs were introduced in the UK in 1963, the same year there was a rise in anti-emetic drugs.

I believe there is something in Easter eggs which make them even more addictive than normal chocolate. It clearly isn't just the sugar. Perhaps there is crack cocaine inside? I'd be very unhappy if I were to get an Easter egg where a Curly Wurly had been replaced by some Class A drugs.

Although it might explain the ads with Terry Scott in in the '70s.

Sing something painful

Sunday afternoons (when wireless meant something you switched on enabling you to listen to Lord Haw-Haw, rather than something you seek out in coffee shops) were epitomised in the 1958 episode of Hancock's Half Hour radio show. It therefore begs the question, as if Sunday afternoons weren't turgid enough: Why on earth did they invent "sing something simple"?

This was broadcast every Sunday for 42 years (more than the Krays got).

I was subjected to many of these episodes via the built-in radio in my Balham flat, which was constantly stuck on the Light programme.

It would begin at 6:30 every Sunday evening, a time when you already have a dread of, a) it's nearly time to go to bed, b) I'm about to be force-fed Bournvita to enable aforementioned sleep, c) have I done my Latin prep? D) I don't do Latin, but have I drawn a cat which was the weekend homework? And e) are these songs being played at Guantanamo Bay?

Earlier in the day, leading up to the very worst of British broadcasting, we'd listened to people stationed in RAF Oberammergau (or somewhere like that) requesting anything by Pearl Carr and Teddy Johnson, swiftly followed by former pygmy, Jimmy Clitheroe annoying "Our Susan" (who sounded, inexplicably, nothing like Jimmy). Top of the Pops was good if, like me, you liked to list things, but you were simply being lured into a false sense of security before you heard the refrain of "sing something simple, as cares go by" – well, they clearly didn't care and why were the songs simple? I'd have liked to have heard "Sing something complex", "Sing something by Stockhausen" or "Sing something so quiet only bats can hear".

These days you have the Internet for Sunday afternoon entertainment and the ability to watch The Cliff Adams singers on YouTube.

Spam (sadly), isn't off, love

I rarely ate school dinners as I lived next door to my Balham primary school. Plus I had an intolerance to caterpillars – which the school salads had in abundance (the dinner ladies thought it a substitute for ham – although you rarely get that with an Ocado delivery, "We've no ham, but we've substituted it with a punnet of caterpillars").

As an only child – and subsequently a fussy eater – my weekday lunch at home was a decade of egg and chips – I look back and wonder why I have such high cholesterol.

However, growing up in the '60s there was a regularity about what I had for my tea:

Monday	Cold meat and bubble – "you can never have enough sprouts, Michael"
Tuesday	Mince, made from the meat originally used on Sunday, but chewed and digested as if it had been cooked in the 17th Century
Wednesday	Spam
Thursday	Possibly more Spam as my mum refused to buy any recipe book other than "Cooking with Spam"
Friday	Cod fillets – to be enjoyed alongside watching The Champions
Saturday	Sausages – made from 95% old bus tickets, so low was the nutritional value

Sunday Never happened as mum would invariably have one of her "heads"

Diets have changed over the years (mine hasn't, although I rarely have spam twice in a week these days) and more foodstuffs have been introduced.

However, for me, avocado is still the colour of your bathroom, not something you eat on toast.

Two half a sixpences

Occasionally, as a kid, I'd be given an extra sixpence pocket money to buy sweets; I believe the local dentist was in league with my nan and her sugar-loving sisters, who would supply the bonus money.

In the mid '60s there were more sweet shops along Balham High Road than there were traffic lights – this resulted in the whole of SW17 having high cholesterol, few teeth and an abnormally high ratio of road traffic accidents.

My sweet shop of choice was Nugent's, run but a woman, seemingly 200-years-old (you think that as a kid and she was probably only 150).

Sixpence was almost too much to possess as this produced the dilemma of choice.

There were many items – Fruit Salads, Black Jacks, Shrimps (made from 200% sugar) – where you could get four for a penny. With my order only 16.7% complete, there was the executive decision to make as to whether you continued to build a glucose mountain in your hand – 24 pretend bananas would have had me climbing the walls – or did you plump for a 3d Jubbly?

I would spend an eternity in the shop doing mental arithmetic and wishing I'd bought a copy of Calculus for Idiots with me, an abacus or a slide-rule.

I think, looking back, I probably went the 24-shrimp route as I consequently needed several fillings before I was a teenager. Sadly, you don't get four of anything for a 1d these days – which is why you never see a rich dentist.

Monsieur "Chopper" Guillotin

My Nan introduced me to French knitting while growing up in her Balham flat in the '60s. She did this for two reasons: one, to stop me playing outside the confines of my block of flats and two, in case they ever reintroduced capital punishment via La Guillotine on Balham High Road, she would have a ringside seat. Because, if you see paintings of any execution during Le Terreur in late 18th Century France, you'll see depictions, aside from the poor, cake-offering toffs about to have the severest of all haircuts, old crones with no teeth, smoking clay pipes and knitting.

If public executions were to return to the UK, my Nan wanted to be in the thick of it and I would be her vehicle – who is going to stop a 10 year old kid brandishing an old cotton reel, four nails and two-foot of something which wouldn't even work as a draft-excluded, even for The Borrowers, moving, with his Nan, to the front?

Being introduced to handicrafts such as French knitting (I wasn't allowed a crochet needle as I'd have taken my eye out, apparently) in retrospect was possibly a mistake as, strangely enough, we didn't have use for things like this at an all-boys school – the ability to create some very long piece of intertwined wool didn't stand me in good stead on the rugby field.

I was expected to conjugate Latin verbs as an 11 year-old, not provide the entire class with matching hat and scarf. Plus, I needed to know the exact dates of Gladstone's periods as PM – crocheted coasters were never ever needed for that.

Milking it

Diphtheria is not only tricky to spell, but you never wanted to catch it as a kid. I never did, but did contract most of the other children's diseases during the '60s.

My mum used to have a book which had a table listing all potential ailments, their symptoms, how long they lasted, and the incubation period. The latter column being the one most used – you'd be innocently sent to a children's party where your parents knew some child there had chicken pox – you came away from the party with a balloon in the shape of a penis, a piece of cake and a highly contagious disease.

In my Balham flat I remember my dad having to get up in the night to put calamine lotion on me in front of our two-bar fire. I assume it must have been winter, unless he was deliberately getting me to lose weight as I had a ride on the 3:30 at Newmarket the next day.

I had measles as a baby, chicken pox at six, mumps when I was seven, German measles (it was the only German thing allowed in the flat) at eight. At nine, I contracted a mild form of Scarlet Fever. The treatment for this was to dab the inflamed parts with milk. I had an aunt who did this while smoking one of her 40-a-day Embassys. I was concurrently cured of Scarlet Fever while enduring passive smoking.

But prevention being better than cure, I was force-fed sprouts as a kid, as my mother told me this would stop me getting consumption, Black Death and Marsh Ague (winds from the River Wandle could have brought them, apparently).

Going Virol

There are many smells from my youth growing up in the '60s and '70s, which have stuck with me and ones I fear may never smell again.

Last week I talked of applying calamine lotion on anything burning during a childhood ailment and, if you'd suffered, one smell you'd never remove from your olfactory sense.

Virol too, is a smell I'll never encounter again, as people now know obesity is not the name of an Afrobeat band from the '70s. Virol was a malt extract (made of 200% sugar) which you were given as a kid if you were skinny; I was like a character in a LS Lowry painting and got given it by the vat load.

Excessive use of chlorine is another long-forgotten smell. Due to an altercation with a swimming instructor aged eight (I was eight, the swimming instructor wasn't, as that would have been dangerous, unless they were half-haddock) I didn't swim much, but, am aware chlorine in swimming baths has subsequently been watered down – although the faintest of smells bring on my hydrophobia. I don't foam at the mouth as much these days.

Burnt milk is another (courtesy of Costa, Starbucks etc) waft you don't get. Before any Seattle-based coffee shop entered the UK, my nan would boil up milk for a "frothy coffee" is her saucepan. Invariably she'd forget, having gone off in pursuit of a Player's Weight, while the milk, originally destined to become a frothy coffee, was fast becoming more like the top of a crème brûlée.

I can only think the need for lepidopterology is rapidly declining as, whenever you used to visit an aging relative, you were hit by the overriding smell of mothballs. Perhaps moths are now on coat-free diets?

Water, water, not quite everywhere

These days no one is more than six-feet away from a bottle of water; the summer signs at Tube stations actively encourage you to carry one. So how come none of us living in London in the '60s and '70s died of dehydration?

Growing up I'd play outside for hours, either trying to become the next Alan Knott or Gerd Müller, but I'd never have any form of liquid near me. I'd return to my Balham flat and be given orange squash diluted by tepid (at best) water from the tap, not some chilled bottle of Perrier or Evian.

I always judged people as being posh if I was ever invited anywhere for tea and offered lemon squash. We never had fruit juice either (how I never contracted scurvy I'll never know!) and the Du Cane Fruiters opposite my Balham flat never sold anything from outside the UK (they were advocating leaving the EU before we even joined in 1973), so the only fruit intake I had was at half-time during school football matches. Accessible water, unless you were having it flown in from the Perrier factory in the Gard departement in France, was restricted round my way to the school water fountain or the horse trough on Mitcham High Street.

These days water bottles proliferate and the substances inside manifold. But, if you'd have asked me in the mid-60s, after running around Wandsworth Common like a banshee, if I'd have liked an Elderberry Press, I'd have assumed it was the name of a local newspaper.

Sushi and the Bandit biscuits

Contents of a Tupperware box have changed over the years.

During summer holidays in the '60s and '70s I'd purchase my Red Rover ticket at Balham underground station and travel as far as possible, believing Ongar was not only (then) the end of the Central Line, but also that beyond that, you'd drop off the end of the Earth.

With me would be my Tupperware box full of '60s/'70s foodstuffs: Spangles; Blue Riband biscuit; a meat-paste sandwich consisting more paste than meat and another Tupperware receptacle holding water with just a hint of squash (as the combination of e-numbers, the depths of the Northern Line and 80% of all Spangles eaten by Clapham North may have had a detrimental effect on mummy's little Mickey Mouse's tummy).

These days the Blue Riband would be replaced by something which is now 90% cashew (even though it is called "chocolate something" on the wrapper); water will be the only drink – preferably flown in from a mountain stream feeding Lake Geneva; Spangles replaced by the most exotic fruit from an island which hadn't even been discovered in the '60s and all forms of bread would have been replaced by sushi.

In the '60s sushi was likely to be the name of someone who worked alongside Steve Zodiac, Troy Tempest or Captain Scarlet.

Tide up

I was never a dirty kid growing up, but the moment I discovered you got free plastic soldiers in packets of Tide, I became a mudlark overnight.

I would seek out dirt and puddles round the back of my Balham block of flats to increase the necessity of clothes washing: therefore, more soldiers.

My desire was to create my own Terracotta army (only in plastic – and slightly shorter).

Looking back, my mum could have taken in a year's washing for the entire SW17 postal district and I'd have still come up short of the 8,000 soldiers which the aforementioned army comprises. That's a lot of Tide. As Balham's not in a monsoon area, we would never have had enough puddles.

Growing up in the '60s there were often things inside grocery packets – PG Tips and their cards being an obvious example – cereal packets would have toys inside too (small, blue, twisted packets of salt weren't toys by the way), but this seems to be a thing of the past.

My journeys accompanying my mum to the supermarkets on Balham High Road would always be governed by my desire to buy products with free items inside – never mind the quality, feel the gift.

Washing powder has now mainly been replaced by washing liquid – the last thing you want to be doing is fishing out a soldier covered in a viscous cleansing agent; it'd make a mess of your fort for a start.

And if I'd been challenged on my doorstep – I'd have always taken two packets of Tide.

Holding a candle for the dustman

If I'd been an entrepreneurial 13 year-old in December 1970, I should have been buying and selling candles from the bedroom of my Balham flat. If there'd been a queue, the punters could have occupied themselves in the next-door bathroom with my model of Stingray and fleet of plastic U-Boats.

During the "winter of discontent", fuel supplies were low, and Ted Heath warned of power cuts. I knew it was Ted Heath speaking to the nation on the TV and not Hughie Green (who was normally on the telly) as he never said the word "sincerely".

Each day I'd be sent to fetch a copy of the Evening Standard as they published when SW17 was going to be plunged into darkness.

Because my block of flats was quite labyrinthine, once the lights went out, the corridors became a black abyss. If you were an early teenager this was tremendously exciting, but then, when you realised you were completely lost, there was the overriding sense that you really should have eaten more carrots when younger.

These were the days before scented candles. There wasn't the chance, during these blackouts, to have your flat suddenly smelling of Fresh Linen, Jasmin or Schnitzel with Noodles. There was one sort – the types you get in churches, only smaller; a strong relationship with the local ironmonger was key (or knowledge of someone who had moved on from stealing church roof lead).

If you'd asked anyone in December 1970 what Yankee Candle was, most people would have thought it was a film with James Cagney in.

Much bindweed in the marsh

It's that time of year when private gardens are opened up to the more green-fingered public.

Having lived during the '60s and '70s in various south London flats until the age of 25, I never had a garden of my own. And living on the fourth floor, unless I'd been Red Adair, a window box would have been spectacularly dangerous. So, the decision of having some finely-cultivated begonias combined with plummeting to an early death versus life was quite a simple one to make.

But this lack of horticultural knowledge means the gardens I have owned are highly unlikely to be opened to the public – unless the RHS introduces "Best in class bindweed" at the Chelsea Flower Show.

As a teenager I did buy the I-Spy book of clematis, but, due to lack of spelling ability, was sadly disappointed. I watched Bill and Ben avidly for gardening tips.

At primary school we were given bulbs to plant; the success I had I might as well have planted one from Philips – such was the greater chance of growth.

I'd love to write into Gardeners' Question Time and ask: "I think I have Japanese Knotweed; can the panel recommend a good ointment?"

As far as I'm concerned nettles is the bloke who played Bergerac.

Un petit pas

I blame Neil Armstrong for me not being fluent in French.

On 16 July 1969, towards the end of my first year at my Tooting Grammar School, a TV was hurriedly bundled into the classroom during a French lesson, for us to watch the moon landing.

I welcomed any excuse to miss French and would have been happier watching an old episode of The Clangers (which inspired space travel) in preference to conjugating verbs like avoir, être or faire la grève (a popular verb in late 1960s France).

I look back 50 years and wonder if Neil Armstrong (whose cameo in Hello, Dolly I particularly enjoyed) regrets not taking a golf club like one of his successors? I'm not a trained astronaut, but given the choice of essential items between a six-iron and more oxygen, I'd opt for more breathable air.

Despite being a frequent flyer, I probably wouldn't make it as an astronaut. During any hint of turbulence, I'm grabbing the stranger next to me's arm as if I were a human tourniquet. So, going at 6,164 mph, as the Saturn 5 rocket did, wouldn't appeal – unless Buzz Aldrin wanted his blood supply cut off.

I've never walked on the Moon (unlike Neil Armstrong and Sting), and I still don't know the past participle of the verb atterrir.

Yours sincerely,

Clair de Lune

Sofa so good

Hiding from the TV detector van was easy if you lived on the fourth floor of a block of flats. I had surmised that the van would not only have never get through the revolving doors at the entrance to my Balham flats, but also, it'd never get inside the lift as the antennae would probably snap off.

There was no warning of the van's impending arrival – no theme tune from Jaws/Psycho/or the little known Confessions of a TV Detector Van Cleaner.

I'm sure people (whose dwellings were at street level) would hide behind their sofas, a plethora of Habitat scatter cushions or a life-sized cardboard cut-out of a TV detector van – to ward it off like an evil spirit.

This, of course, would be the antithesis of being out by leaving the radio on, thus giving the impression (especially to potential burglars) that someone was actually in. This stems from the urban myth that burglars have a pathological fear of The Archers, the long-range shipping forecast or stumbling into a house at a time when Sing Something Simple was on.

But sometimes there are programmes on when you want to hide behind the sofa – if there are too many such programmes broadcast on the BBC, could you apply for a rebate?

The eagle hasn't landed

Living in Balham in the '60s the chances of being taken by a wild animal was unlikely.

Even when the circus came to Clapham Common, the animal security was quite tight, so you'd have had to have been very unlucky to have been trampled to death by marauding elephants running down Balham Hill.

However, in February 1965, shortly before my seventh birthday, Goldie the eagle (no avian relation to Eddie) escaped from London Zoo. My dad worked near there, in Gloucester Place, and would go and see the errant bird during his lunchtimes.

My immediate fear of him doing this was: could an eagle carry a five-foot nine man in his beak, thus rendering me 50% of the way to becoming an orphan? And if this happened, what sort of work could I do as overnight I'd become head of the household?

As a six year-old my options were few: chimney sweep was out of the question as we lived in flats; my fear of horses (or any animal larger than a gerbil) preventing the course to becoming a jockey and although Willy Wonka and the Chocolate Factory had been written the year before, casting for the film had yet to begin.

I pondered in my mind that, because Dad smoked about 40 Senior Service most days, would the eagle pass on capturing my dad as the eagles could be more partial to filtered fags or even Consulate?

My fears were abated 12 days' later as the eagle was recaptured – dead mice being preferable to 20 Kensitas.

Security was enhanced at London Zoo shortly after that as Pipaluk never escaped.

I'll be dummy

I started commuting in 1974.

Activities within train carriages have changed somewhat over the decades.

These days everyone is in their own space, their own world, together with their headphones, which are now in all shapes, sizes and colours: they no longer just come in orange foam.

Some like to share their travelling experiences: although I realise I'm never going to be a big fan of rap (also, I'm more Alfie Bass than drum 'n' bass).

In 1974 I remember people bought newspapers; I got mine from a man outside Balham Station who called everyone "John" – which was why he was selling papers and not writing for them as his attention to detail was poor.

I'd like to say I'd completed the Times crossword by Stockwell, but this is the boy who struggled on most return journeys with the picture puzzle inside the Evening News.

You can't smoke in trains anymore, plus the luggage racks aren't made of rope, thus making Tarzan impressions harder as you can't swing from one side of the carriage to another.

No longer do I sit on trains where there are bridge schools going on, French tuition being held outside the Buffet carriage or Pilates in First Class.

But the good news is that if you want to play Solitaire, you don't need the entire table anymore.

People still stare at my Walkman (this isn't a euphemism).

The ice pole cometh

As the hot weather persists, so the reward of a lolly after a sweltering commute becomes attractive.

Yesterday I bought a Fab.

I was, however, disappointed on two fronts: first, they don't cost 6d anymore and nor, on the wrapper, does it feature Lady Penelope (the woman who invented the word and spelled it out every episode except the one where Alan takes Tin-Tin up the Round House – a scene subsequently deleted by censors).

For me, a lolly isn't a lolly unless it features a Gerry & Sylvia Anderson puppet on the front.

As a kid growing up in south London in the '60s my lolly of choice was a Jubbly (I'd like to say Mivvi, but that was only available if you were posh and rich).

A Jubbly was 3 old pence, but each time you bought one you'd forgotten that the juice only lasted for about 5% of the devouring. 95% of the remaining time you were sucking on a pyramid of ice. You might as well have visited a newsagent in Trondheim rather than one in Tooting.

Ice poles were better value and, if you were trained in sword swallowing, you'd appreciate 100% of the available juice.

These days there is far greater choice – especially since salted caramel was invented. The danger of these excessive options is, you open the freezer chest and, by the time you've scanned the contents, inspected the likely e-numbers and wondered if you really would like a Cola-flavoured Calipo, the freezer is on its way to defrosting. If this happens you're going to have to find another newsagent to buy your lottery ticket in.

I understand Linda Lovelace was a fan of ice poles (whoever she was).

Thermos, the Greek god of travel

In an effort to save the planet from becoming one big plastic bag, everyone nowadays seems to be carrying around a reusable cup.

This is not a new thing and is basically a modern-day thermos flask – only they're no longer in tartan.

However, these relatively new containers are designed to carry one liquid, unlike the old thermoses, which would hold multiple liquids. They will contain only coffee, water or, if you're currently reading any Jean-Paul Sartre, absinthe.

Thermos flasks had a different function, but with a built-in obsolescence. Thermos flasks were invariably solely used for picnics but, after several uses, regardless of the historic liquid inside, the contents would eventually taste like oxtail soup – regardless of whether it had ever contained oxtail soup or not.

In the '60s, as a young teenager, I'd often set off on an Orange Luxury coach trip from Balham High Road to a destination I would hate with picnic basket, containing a thermos and two parents. The problem arose with the lack of cups. As the youngest in the family, while orange squash was ok, drinking chicken soup from my hands was tricky. They might have been able to do that sort of thing on Kung Fu, but I struggled at places like Hever Castle. However, the vending machine within A&E at Pembury Hospital did do a nice Bovril. Or was it Earl Grey tea?

Look, three hands!

Everyone has at least one thing in their hands these days: mobile phone, takeaway coffee cup; miniature juggling kits.

Gone are the days when the only thing you'd have in your hand was the handle of a basket on wheels as you headed to the shops.

I wonder, if in many years' time, nature will start growing a third hand on humans? If there is a re-introduction of the use of semaphore flags, having a third arm is going to be essential as there would be an inherent danger of spilling hot coffee on yourself if you were suddenly called on to send a message.

You never see a Hindu deity struggling, but this might be because Durga, the Hindu warrior goddess, didn't live near a Starbucks.

Penny for your thoughts?

With Brexit looming does this mean we'll revert to using Imperial currency? If so, how many euros will you get for an old 10-bob note?

I shall look forward to shop windows displaying their clothes' prices in guineas and going to a greengrocer where there are hand-written cards showing bananas are 1/6 for a pound

In 1971 I remember buying a set of the "new" decimal coins from a Post Office on Balham High Road. I'm assuming they were the real thing as the bloke running the Post Office was Polish and he could have been selling me a set of out-of-circulation zlotys for all I knew. They were in a Perspex box and remember thinking how any of those coins were going to fit in a gas meter which only took half-crowns. I bought several candles too, just in case.

If this money does return then I'm getting my half-full jar of threepenny bits (insert you own gag here) down from the loft, where it has lain dormant since the bank amnesty ended for pre-decimal coinage. I shall also be curious to see how much a farthing gets me.

I think I may invest in some sheep too in case bartering comes back and will bird-feeding still only cost tuppence a bag?

PE or not PE?

In September 1968 I beheld my first wooden vaulting horse.

It lived in the gym in the labyrinth under my Tooting secondary school – where no humans dared venture and probably housed a three-headed dog – there were suspicious teeth marks on the wall-bars.

This horse, at first sight, seemed the size of a Shetland pony. However, when we were told what we had to do on it and over it, suddenly it was the size of the one I'd imagined had been plonked outside Troy.

I'd watched, admiringly, the success of the Czechoslovakian gymnast, Vera Caslavska at that year's Olympics, as she glided over the wooden horse as if she were being operated by strings. Much as I looked like Joe 90, I had no strings attached and certainly nothing which was going to help me over the horse. I was, having watched the eponymous 1950 film, also surprised there weren't sprinklings of discarded soil around the wooden horse.

My turn came to vault over the horse: I ran and promptly stopped like a runner in the Grand National who doesn't fancy Becher's Brook. I couldn't do it and subsequently found out during that academic year that I could neither climb a rope nor do anything vaguely precarious on wall-bars.

This inherent danger was greater than what I'd experienced at my Balham primary school when all you had to do during PE was run around in your pants pretending to be a tree.

At secondary school we were told that all the trees had got Dutch Elm Disease and so would we if we didn't vault over a horse.

I guess I was more Ronnie than Olga Korbut

You're probably not allowed to wear just pants these days.

Bish, bash, Bosch

The moment an Athena shop opened near me, my bedroom in my Balham flat overnight became festooned with death and destruction, mainly provided by Hieronymus Bosch and Pieter Bruegel.

As if Sir Kenneth Clark had lived in my flat, I had become an art expert overnight – as long as the paintings gave the impression that you'd have loved to have had a pint of whatever the artists had been drinking.

I'd spend a fortune in the Athena shops buying famous pictures replicated on postcards, posters and small blocks of wood; I'm sure my neighbours always enjoyed my random nail-hammering after a shop visit.

I was never tempted with any Picasso cartoon, though, as I was more an Andy Capp man.

Dali was hugely popular within the stores and if he'd bought his watches which he depicted in his paintings, you could see that Gerald Ratner had had a point.

Before its advent in 1964, very few people had art in their houses unless it was The Laughing Cavalier, a bowl of fruit, or a Chinese woman whose face was so green it looked like she'd eaten too much fruit.

However, one of the more popular images was something I never bought: Leonardo da Vinci's Tennis girl scratching arse. Although the eyes do follow you round the room, a sign of a good painting.

A toffee apple a day...

Toffee apples, despite purporting to being part of your five-a-day, would not be a food (unless he or she'd been struck off by the BDA and you'd not been informed) your dentist would recommend consuming.

But because toffee apples tend to only be eaten on one specific day (like dates on Boxing Day), and unless you've an appointment on the 31 October, this warning will never be relayed to you.

It is odd that toffee apples tend to feature only on Halloween. Whilst studying Macbeth for English Lit O-level in 1973 I cannot recall, whenever the three witches appeared, that they were doing unspeakable things with apples – they tended to stick to frogs and newts.

Apple-bobbing would feature at many of the children's parties I attended in the south London area as a kid, although, once parents realised this was much like water-boarding, it was quickly replaced with pin-the-tail-on-the-donkey; much safer – small child, sharp object, blinded – what could possibly go wrong?

For me, the novelty of toffee apples stopped the moment the last piece of toffee was eaten. I had no interest in the actual fruit. I look back and wonder, if I'd have known how much crowns cost, should I have opted for candy floss? No, because that's bad for your teeth. Hang on a minute...

Bombes away

Everywhere these days, a previously bare wall, has been covered in graffiti; usually with uninterpretable hieroglyphics people have tattooed on their upper arm for a bet assuming it's Japanese.

I blame Banksy (the man with the spray can and mouse stencil, not the Stoke and England World Cup hero).

As a kid in the '60s I can only remember one piece of graffiti in my formative years. As you entered Wandsworth Common from the Balham end, displayed on the first wall, you saw Ban the Bomb.

When I was five, I could read, but not having lived through the Second World War, assumed, having been subjected to lots of music as a child, that The Bomb were a group and this message had been daubed by fans of The Beatles; The Stones or The Swinging Blue Jeans.

As I grew older and realised that CND wasn't a shortened form of the Irish group Clannad, it dawned on me which bomb they were talking about.

Shame it didn't read Ban the Bombe as I've never been a fan of circular ice cream desserts.

Scent from above

In the early '70s I discovered that Aramis wasn't just a third of a band of musketeers, but was a brand of after shave available in Balham Boot's and something to daubed on in the unlikely event a girl might talk to me. I could have owned Estee Lauder and girls were unlikely to talk to me.

I was a massive fan of Aramis and Paco Rabane (having not studied 17th Century Spanish literature in any great depth meant I never thought he might have been Don Quixote's little helper). These were my scents of choice as a teenager. I tried Kouros (not one of the remaining 66.6% of musketeers) but always came out in a rash – not a good look unless the girl you fancied took an inordinate interest in dermatological problems.

As my taste in after shaves became increasingly more sophisticated, I was appalled one Christmas when my paternal grandmother gave me a bottle of Avon's Windjammer. If I'd have wanted anything to jam my wind, I'd have bought a packet of Carter's Little Liver Pills.

Whilst my perennial search for the perfect scent continued, I often admired the girls' perfume selection. I was fascinated by the elegance of the packaging of YSL's Rive Gauche – arguably one of the best right back Paris St Germain have ever had.

Whilst the shop assistants in Balham Boots were quite persuasive, they had nothing on Valerie Leon.

A Meccano bridge too far

I was never destined to become a civil engineer with the toys I was given as a kid.

In my Balham flat, growing up in the '60s, there wasn't a sniff of Meccano; although my mum was constantly hoovering up discarded pieces of an Airfix ME110 I'd scattered in a fit of pique to the four corners of my bedroom. Mum was careful hoovering as she thought she might find a miniature Rudolf Hess, although may, in the '60s, have been more constructive looking for Martin Bormann.

I only had one rectangular piece of Lego – with which I could pretend was a table, a sentry box or bench depending on which side I laid it.

So, my creative construction juices were never encouraged as a kid. I did have a Willy Wombat glove puppet but, as anyone who's ever watched the National Geographic TV channel will know, marsupials aren't renowned for their construction skills (although very good at transmitting urgent messages).

So the much-needed bridge over the River Wandle was never going to materialise with me as the project manager.

I did, however, play with my Spirograph a lot, which might have been the cause of my myopia.

You say Sudoku…

I've been commuting for 45 years, and the activities on my journey home have changed considerably.

In 1974, when I first started journeying back to south-west London, having got on at Embankment, I'd have finished the Evening News picture crossword by the Elephant and would have (unsuccessfully) spotted the ball by Clapham Common.

The only time you'd have heard the word wireless on the Underground would have been people telling you what they were going to listen to on it later that evening.

Now papers are packed with things like Sudokus and other things which sound vaguely like types of motorbikes, martial arts or members of the Imperial Japanese Navy. Ironically, the No. 1 when I first started commuting was Carl Douglas's Kung Fu Fighting, which is a martial art.

No more do people get the Evening Standard to look for the stop press to see the teatime cricket scores, they can listen on their phones to former public-school types telling you exactly that, while throwing in cake recipes.

These days you'll know in pretty much in advance what the next day's newspaper headline will be and no longer will reading "Queen Anne, dead" be a surprise.

Futoshiki? Thank you, but I'm allergic to most fish.

Is Chris Tavaré out yet?

In the 1970s, when foreign travel started to take off, access to information at home was limited to your daily newspaper, News at Ten or a set of reliable homing pigeons; the lack of news, once abroad, was frustrating and people would scour kiosks in Spain and France hopeful of a two-day-old Daily Telegraph sent from Blighty.

Your holiday would be ruined, not just for NOT drinking the water or failing to take your Enterovioform three years before your trip, but if you weren't up to speed with the Test or County Championship cricket scores. You wanted to be that person, like the major in Fawlty Towers, who goes back to the (almost built) hotel and announces that "Hampshire won!"

But was there that same demand in this country?

I remember the man who sold newspapers and magazines outside Balham Tube station, who called everyone "John"; was he visited by people who'd wandered off the beaten track (as Balham rarely gets a mention in any Michelin guide) looking for a copy of Paris Match (seeing how the latest strikes were going), Süddeutsche Zeitung (sending off for the deck-chair-sized towel offer) or El Pais (how many Brits had drunk the water?) and if he was, did he call them Jean, Johann or Juan?

Chalky White, whom you'd could identify and win £5 if you were carrying a Daily Mirror on holiday (invariably in Shanklin), is alive and well and waiting to be spotted in Bali. Hope he's taken his tablets.

You can ring my bell (unless you're selling something)

I could never have made a career in campanology.

As a teenager I sang in a church choir which would perform two concerts a year. As I lived in the flats next door to the church on Balham High Road, my task was to call on the 600+ flats to sell tickets.

I didn't know, in the mid-70s, that so many different doorbell chimes existed.

The task of selling tickets to hear Handel's Messiah or Mendelssohn's Elijah was hard. The residents were more likely to listen to "Chirpy, chirpy, cheep, cheep" than Chopin, "Ernie" than Elgar or "Shang a lang" than Shostakovich.

We thought we'd have more luck with people whose door chimes played a sophisticated tune, sadly they had the sound because they liked the tune in a cigar advert.

The most worrying noise was the bark of a clearly dangerous dog. Either the dog behind the door had trained at Wandsworth Prison or had three heads, and therefore guarding the gates of Hell (I was in my mid-20s before I realised that Hell wasn't on the fifth floor of my block of flats).

Many doors had spy-holes and the chances of the door being opened to a long-haired git in a cassock and surplice was never going to happen unless the Archbishop of Canterbury had moved county.

However, the most disturbing thing for a shockingly naive teenager, was the sound of "My ding-a-ling" playing as Mrs Robinson, the siren of the third floor, opened her door. I could have died and gone to Heaven. A bit like Elijah.

Toffee-nosed

As a kid, growing up in south London in the '60s, around this time of year I often balanced the preference of being hanged, drawn and quartered with that of root canal treatment.

Our firework displays, in early November, would be held near the garages at the back of our Balham flats; the oo-ing and ah-ing would be interspersed with offerings of home-made toffee from a "responsible" adult who clearly moonlighted as the local dental nurse.

Guy Fawkes obviously never witnessed a firework display and I wonder whether he'd have been proud of his eponymous day being celebrated by people succeeding where he spectacularly failed on that fateful November evening in 1605

Toffee was introduced into Western diets around the turn of the 19th century, just before the time the cost of dental crowns surged.

1868 was the year of the last public execution in this country and coincided with the advent of Starbucks and Pret, thus occupying people during their lunch breaks in the absence of a hanging.

So, when you're next in line for your convenience lunch, spare a thought for the man who inspired sparklers, bangers and Roman Candles and think: "It could be worse, the avocados might have run out, but at least I've not been chopped into four pieces and my penis is still intact!"

Next time you're ordering rocket, make sure there's no blue touch paper attached.

Dungeness monste

Once a year, during the summer, in the '60s and '70s, I would leave the safety of my parents' flat on Balham High Road and temporarily set up camp with my paternal grandparents in a rented house on the coast somewhere.

For several years, we rented a house at Greatstone, on the Kent coast; we were so close to the Dungeness nuclear power station, I'm surprised I never grew a third arm.

Money was tight and our humble abode reflected this (even the squatters had given it a bad review on Trip Advisor) and for our evening meals we were given a budget of 8/6 (42.5 new pence for my younger readers).

As we sat, waiting to order our evening dinner at a cafe in New Romney, mathematical juggling was the name of the game. (8/6 in 1970 is worth £6.24 in today's money). Being good at darts as a 12 year-old stood me in good stead.

However, my dilemma was that I wanted sausage, egg AND chips AND cassata siciliana – the combined cost of which was ten bob – one and six over my allotted allowance.

Did I go the high cholesterol route or a lump of multi-coloured ice cream with random bits which'd stick in your teeth most of the holiday?

New Romney is famous mainly for smuggling during the 18th century. I bet Dr Syn, the fictional anti-hero who operated around these parts, had more than eight and six to spend for his tea? I couldn't even afford sherry trifle, let alone anything with brandy in it.

Pippa Dee Pippa Dum

I remember vividly the first Pippa Dee party I ever attended.

My mother would throw such parties for her friends in our Balham flat.

The invitation was never officially extended to me as I'd have been sent to bed earlier after a mug of warm milk, a chocolate digestive and above the legal limit dose of Gripe Water (I can never drink Ouzo now without conjuring up scary bedtime stories).

I can recollect entering a lounge through a fug of Embassy cigarettes, the bouquet of Blue Nun and witnessing rather a lot of Innoxa make-up to see several women holding up Baby Doll negligées.

The nights were drawing in and my practical, eight year-old brain, calculated that the length of this garment wasn't practical and probably wouldn't have been for the guests' daughters' Barbies.

My stay (before I could be offered a fag or a sip of Black Tower from a glass procured courtesy of the local Esso garage) was short-lived and my return to my bedroom was threatened with less Gripe Water the subsequent evening.

I'm assuming that Pippa Dee parties were replaced with Ann Summers parties – with even shorter negligées, although probably more fire retardant?

Whatever happened, a Baby Doll night dress nor a vibrating rabbit could never replace a container which kept food fresh. But then, there's nothing sexy about a Tupperware box and certainly wouldn't make you smile quietly to yourself.

Buckle up

The nights are drawing in and with that the advent of cold weather.

I look back to my childhood in 1960s south-west London and wonder why I never had hypothermia more frequently.

My winter attire was a mac (I've seen thicker veils) with a belt which, when my mother put it on me, acted as a tourniquet; a yellow and black school scarf which itched so much it was like having Scarlet Fever permanently; and gloves, which were attached to a long loop of elastic, taken, I think, from my Nan's knickers as she coincidentally never left her flat during winter. I refused to wear a balaclava as I found the thought of messing up my hair abhorrent and one of the major reasons I never joined any terrorist organisations.

Everything was marked "Michael Richards Class 7" and all this while wearing shorts. Captain Oates had more protection.

Nowadays there are so many German-sounding layers of clothing to keep you dry, warm and to cheat the wind. I was not allowed to wear such things as my Nan thought there was a danger I'd look like Himmler. Given his uniform was made by Hugo Boss, I fear she may have missed a trick; still, I enjoyed the sanatoria which were located by the seaside.

Do you want to build a cardboard snowman?

When did Advent calendars become the monsters they have?

Gone are the days when you'd have a flimsy piece of cardboard, as near as you could get to being homemade, adorning your mantelpiece.

In my Balham flat, in the '60s, the moment December arrived I'd erect mine (Advent calendar) and wait, with childlike anticipation, until the 24th (the night before Christmas when I'd also be hurriedly, and badly wrapping, my mum's Bronnley bath salts).

However, my brain must have been like a goldfish as, when the 24th came, the only number with a double door, behind which was always the same: the baby Jesus lying in a manger.

You'd be lulled into a false sense of security all month as you'd open one each day to reveal a picture of a snow-covered post-box, a robin, an old fish (if you'd got your calendar free from that month's Trout and Salmon magazine) – items vaguely relevant to Christmas and then, bang! The baby Jesus again.

Don't get me wrong, I'm all in favour of the baby Jesus being there – certainly in preference to a dead trout. However, these days the windows are no longer pictures of sugar cane sweets, holly or an immolating Christmas pudding, but actual gifts.

They are now as big as houses and many theme-based.

The Wise Men weren't in Frozen, but if you were to look at any Advent calendar today you might be fooled into thinking that Elsa, Anna and Olaf were the bearers of gifts.

In 4 BC you'd have not been able to take Myrrh or Frankincense back to the Bethlehem branch of John Lewis.

Cards on the table

It is that time of year when Christmas card arrivals gather pace.

In my Balham flat, growing up in the '60s, my mother would hang cards over hastily-erected pieces of string which, the more cards we received, the greater the chance of being garrotted.

In those days you'd buy a box of mixed cards, marginally heavier than greaseproof paper adorned with various winter and/or biblical scenes; the hierarchy of your friends and family would be determined by whether they got the (un-Christmassy) robin, a snowman in the shape of a wise man or the baby Jesus surrounded by donkeys, incense and virgins.

However, something which has crept into Santa's postbag is the round robin letter from people you've not heard from since exactly a year ago.

Sadly, and this might be an only child thing, I couldn't give a toss about the successful summer's holiday, how (insert your own pretentious child's name here) has integrated into the local Kindergarten or how the entire family is learning Italian – such was the triumph of the aforementioned trip to Tuscany and everyone now knows how to correctly pronounce the word Latte.

Also enclosed in the envelope is a picture of the entire family (many of whom you'd not have babysit your own kids) all dressed in the same onesie taken at Christmas last year; which begs the question: why do people dress normally for 364-days of the year only to have a total sartorial brain aberration at Christmas?

Five portions

As an eight-year-old, at Christmas I believed there were two ways I could get drunk – like my relatives.

The first was Pimm's. My auntie, who also lived in our Balham flats, while being sponsored by Embassy before they ventured into supporting snooker and darts, would have bottles of virtually everything alcoholic in her flat except potcheen (and she didn't have that because of her allergic reaction to potatoes).

It was tradition on Christmas evening to go to my auntie's and, while everyone else got Pimm's, I had a glass full of half the contents of the greengrocers opposite the flats, lots of lemonade, a tiny umbrella, as used by The Borrowers, but not a sniff of Pimm's.

The second route, I believed, was with the help of the mandatory Christmas box of chocolate liqueurs.

However, after eating a third, I'd already began to feel nauseous. Given that you need to eat 700 grams (that's 14 Picnics!) to get one shot of liqueur, I'd have had to have eaten one anti-emetic tablet every time I'd tuck into a Tia Maria Bounty (never did quite learn the names)

A consequence of this lack of alcoholic intake meant I remained stone-cold sober, although often felt sick and burped a lot courtesy of more than enough chocolate and a surfeit of lemonade!

A third route could have been with Advocaat, but I didn't like the taste of "Snowballs", having massive doubts about the colour and felt the texture was like that of blancmange which was past its sell-by date.

So, needing to go to meetings saying, "my name is Michael and I think I have a problem" was never necessary as an eight-year-old!

That's a cracker!

In 1847 Christmas crackers were invented.

As a child in my south London flat, a disturbingly cheap cracker would sit next to my turkey dinner. As I grew older, so I realised what a massive disappointment its contents awaited me with its unveiling.

Coupled with the shock of the noise from the actual cracker (the cheaper the cracker the more likely you'd get second degree burns from the errant sparks) was a useless plastic toy.

For someone who takes pride in their hair, the thought of covering it with a flammable paper hat was abhorrent. When this occurred you hoped there'd be a temporary wig inside rather than a compass which was clueless about where magnetic north was!

Less than an hour after the last cracker had been pulled (despite the awaiting disappointment you still wanted to be pulling with an aged relative and thus claiming two-thirds) the remnants would be gathered up and thrown away, sometimes in a bin, sometimes, if your host was particularly myopic, into the cold meat and bubble for the next day!

The only evidence there'd been any crackers was the most elderly relative still wearing theirs who, when suddenly waking up, would ask which one was Morecambe and which one Wise? The answer being neither of them as neither appeared in The Great Escape.

I always knew that Christmas crackers were fundamentally wrong as you never saw the Queen delivering her message wearing one or reading, from a small piece of paper, that a mince spy is the person who hides in a bakery at Christmas.

Making a diary note

Which diary will I get this year? Desk or pocket? Page-a-day or five-year one, complete with padlock and key? Or a Samuel Pepys one, which is already filled in for you?

As a kid my dad would always buy me the MCC diary, which I'd pour over in my Balham flat in the 60s discovering which far-flung places the England cricket teams would be travelling to over the next five or six years.

Growing up, Lett's was invariably the diary brand of choice.

In 1967 an ancient relative mistakenly gave me the Lett's Brownie diary; while the dates worked ok, I spent the entire year desperately trying to lend a hand.

As I grew older and didn't feel the need to train for any more badges (having learned how to tie knots, clean my shoes and make a receptacle capable of containing an emergency sixpence) but received diaries containing all manner of information: maps, geo-political statistics and the posher ones, a linen bookmark.

But much of this information – like the GDP of southern Tanganyika – I'd learned through my old school exercise books; on the back covers of which were housed data which could have enabled me to have been the first six-year-old to appear on Mastermind.

As well as showing you simple multiplication tables, you also learned that four noggins made a pint, four farthings made a penny and twenty-one shillings made a guinea. Although my later diaries would show an actual map of Guinea!

I even know how many mickles make a muckle.

For this year's birthdays I'll be sending everyone 36lbs of hay, which is a truss, which, in my day, used to be a type of surgical support.

Winter Hondaland

During the evening of December 24th, 1978, it snowed in Balham.

It wasn't until after I'd sung the last verse of 'Hark! The herald angels sing', and stepped into a scene from a Bing Crosby film, that I realised the change in the weather.

For a nanosecond it looked idyllic, until I realised that my transport home at one o'clock in the morning to Carshalton, was my 400cc motorbike.

The trains had long stopped running, plus my mother had warned me that travelling on the night bus was how you caught VD, so motorbike, that evening sponsored by Captain Oates, it was.

I immediately regretted not asking Santa for a John Curry annual rather than the Barry Sheene one I'd requested at the Balham Co-op earlier that month.

This was the winter of discontent; an appropriate noun as I anticipated the slowest motorbike ride ever. However, going along the relatively flat Balham High Road was fine until I reached Church Lane, which, at that moment, looked like the top of the ski jump at Garmisch-Partenkirchen!

I clung to my bike like Marcel Marceau fighting against an invisible wind, to the bottom, to Amen Corner (famous for its joke shop, which seemed decidedly inappropriate that evening).

From there on it's flat and I got back on my bike, thinking it must already be Easter!

I arrived back safely, only to face the return journey the next day.

I have yet to get the feeling back in many of my five extremities!

Horror of horrors

I changed secondary schools in 1972.

As well as studying different syllabuses, I was introduced to different hobbies.

At my new school, my new friends had two hobbies: discussing what girls were really like. And plane-spotting (if the latter hobby continued into your thirties, you'd never find the answer to the former!).

Plane-spotting involved journeying to Heathrow Airport (pre-Piccadilly line extension and Heathrow Express). We took a train from Balham to Clapham Junction, another train to Feltham, a bus to the airport (where was Sherpa Tenzing when you wanted him?) and finally on to the observation tower within the main terminal, where we stayed for what seemed like the length of time it'd take for a return journey to Brisbane.

My interest in planes had been soured in the summer of 1968 by having to drag my nervous (and very drunk – too much Campari) mother across the tarmac at Luton Airport to board a plane to Majorca (she wasn't content having gastroenteritis at home!).

My previous experiences of transport-spotting were ticking off 88, 155 and 181 buses (and the occasional Green Line to make my hobby seem exotic to my new school buddies) as they trundled down Balham High Road.

I ticked these buses off on the back of a Basildon Bond envelope stolen from my nan's secret stationery store; plane-spotting meant having a pad the size of an *Encyclopedia Britannica*.

I lasted two trips. The journey tired me out – I assumed this was jet lag?

However, to ingratiate myself with my new schoolmates, I invited them to the top of my block of flats, so they could spot their planes there.

And from that time on I've always been able to tell my Qantas from my El Al.

Plane sailing

A supply teacher at my Balham school in 1968 proved I was never going to make it as an aeronautical engineer.

Instead of doing maths, history (always the bloody Tudors) or geography (the field trips were always to the field adjoining our school – so not much of a trip), we were taught origami. The supply teacher was from India, so closer to China than Balham, so he had credibility with us ten-year-olds.

While my efforts to fly paper airplanes were similar to watching grainy and speedy footage of man's earliest "flight", I did become very adept at other things which involved the intricate folding of paper.

Although I should have been learning important dates in history, capital cities of the world and times tables past twelve, because of the supply teacher, paper folding became my new obsession.

The making of water bombs resulted in the entire class going up before the headmaster as we'd doused the dinner ladies during morning playtime.

The thing I was best at was creating 'chatterboxes'. However, this talent was not one I should have taken with me to an all-boys secondary school. My schoolmates, amazed at the proficiency of my origami, became slightly confused (the more sexually advanced kids in the first-year, slightly angry) when, after much swift action between both thumbs and forefingers – and vigorous counting at pace – they read, "kiss a boy" or "I love you". These had worked as a precursor to mixed junior school kiss chases, but rather made me a target during inter-house rugby matches.

There were many who wanted to tell me my fortune – many without the aid of a carefully folded sheet of A4 paper.

Chainsaw messenger

Ernie Binks, the caretaker at my school, could multitask: not only did he have a very useful left foot, but he was also very adept at scattering sawdust.

There was no such thing as after-school club in the '60s in Balham, but at my primary school, if you stayed in the playground after the 3.30 bell, the caretaker would give impromptu football lessons. He played in goal for Balham United; as far as we were concerned, it was like having Sir Alf Ramsey coaching us.

Mr Binks did have a very cultured left boot (probably the only thing cultured in Balham in the '60s) and this was demonstrated in the playground on many an early evening as he tried to encourage us ten-year-olds to 'let them know you're there'. Even though I played for the school football team, my interpretation of this was to involve your opponent in some philosophical debate (while also being concerned whether I'd ever get dubbin off my hands).

Unless you played football, Mr Binks was largely absent, unless, as they say on announcements on London Transport, there was a Code 3 incident. In which case he would enter our classroom with his bucket of sawdust, scatter it liberally, but accurately, after which we would return to advanced calculus or hitting a glockenspiel very hard, depending on whether it was a Tuesday afternoon or not.

Mr Binks lived on-site, probably with a forest of pine trees (native only to Balham) in his back garden, all ready for sawdust preparation. Thankfully, he never mistakenly came into our classroom with a chainsaw rather than a bucket.

They won't forget Ernie.

Cream crackered

I never read as a kid (the *Beano* and *Shoot!* don't really count), but one book which I would absorb, lying on the shagpile carpet in the lounge of my Balham flat, would be the *Guinness Book of Records*.

I wondered if I'd ever be in it.

I was quite tall as a kid and pondered whether I'd ever reach 8' 11" – diet being key in height development. However, I can attest that egg 'n' chips consumed daily only gets you to six-foot, slightly smaller than marginally under nine-foot.

I deliberated if I could balance fifty spoons on my body? The fact that we didn't have five, let alone fifty spoons in our flat, meant I'd have to attempt this world record in the ABC cafe on Balham High Road. Assuming you'd have to be partially naked, this would have only been practical in the warm weather. Either way, it'd have got me banned, and I did so like the iced buns and cups of tea with more head than tea you got at the cafe.

What we did have in our flat were cream crackers. Could I eat three of these in under 49.15 seconds? Did you know it only takes ten seconds to become totally dehydrated? I found this out aged ten.

At sixty-two, some records are now beyond reach. Sitting in baked beans for over 100 hours would never work – at my age I'd be needing a wee after half an hour.

Making an impression

In my Tooting secondary school, during the early '70s, I discovered that, as well as bringing in sweets, being able to mimic helped you to not be bundled – the medieval secondary school event which involved thirty boys piling on top of one another, preventing the entrance of the divinity teacher (and this was a bloody grammar school – no wonder Mrs Thatcher made no effort to keeps ours going).

Mimicking of teachers was the greatest and most revered talent to have, second only to being able to imitate a Trimphone (very popular in the '70s) – a great asset to have to confuse people in the silence within Balham Library.

I couldn't imitate a single teacher, or phone apparatus, but could mimic an assortment of other people, including most of the Goons, Bernie Winters and Dudley Moore. However, my pièce de rèsistance was my impression of Fyfe Robertson. Fyfe Robertson was a roving TV reporter in the '60s and '70s and would be sent to report from obscure places, invariably surrounded by sheep. He'd start every report with, "Hello there, I'm Fyfe Robertson" and would confirm the obscure place where he was standing. I could sound like him and announce to my classmates, "Hello there, I'm Fyfe Robertson and I'm standing on a traffic island in the middle of Balham High Road."

I could also imitate the actions of Reg the greengrocer opposite my flats. As this greengrocer wasn't terribly well known, my likelihood of auditioning on *Opportunity Knocks* was never on the cards.

I often toy with entering *Britain's Got Talent*, but sounding like Bluebottle, Minnie Bannister and Eccles is never going to be as powerful as a song by Susan Boyle.

Alphabet soup

I was eleven when I properly mastered the alphabet.

At secondary school we'd be seated in alphabetical order for every lesson. Thereby, that's how I learned my A-W (we didn't have anyone in our class named Xylophone, Yacht or Zither – it stopped at Williams).

At primary school we could sit wherever we liked. I avoided the girl who wanted to be a golden retriever when she grew up (she'd be 434 now).

The other difference was being called by your surname. No teacher called me Mick at secondary school. Nor did they call me Michael, a name which meant I'd not cleaned my room, I was late for my tea or both, so Richards was preferable.

Rather than learning more complex times tables, obscure African cities or historical events before Christ, we would, in a very regimented way, learn the procession of the alphabet because, for every lesson we'd be sitting, in order: Atkinson, Bates, Bird, Bower until Williams.

Although we all sat in the same order for academic year after academic year, from this group of ordered individuals came an alpha male. He was Mark Finch, or Finno, as he deemed Mark to be far too effeminate for the classroom role he portrayed.

Finno was self-elected leader of the form for three reasons: he wore Cherry Red Dr Marten's; he was the tallest and he was the first to develop pubic hair. By default, he became a demigod.

We were at a grammar school, but in our class, you didn't need to go past the letter F.

And as we all know, there is no F in haddock.

Foiled again

In the '60s, growing up, one obsession I had was collecting silver foil to send off to *Blue Peter* to help provide guide dogs.

I was an avid viewer of the programme and keen to do my bit.

I had two sources of silver foil (aside from nicking my mum's Bacofoil so we didn't eat a roast for several months): the tops of milk bottles and the insides of some cigarette packets.

Within our Balham flats there was a grocer on-site. I was insistent my family visited every day to 'drink a pint a milk'. I'm sure there will have been dairy farms serving the SW17 area on high alert to produce more milk because of my calcium-intake keenness.

(As the only child and only grandchild, I was always treated to the 'top of the milk' to put on my tinned fruit cocktail).

My dad smoked Senior Service. Once unwrapped and the top of the packet opened, covering the fags was a strip of silver foil. During the *Blue Peter* campaign, I'd got my dad smoking sixty a day.

While I never understood, how *Blue Peter* turned my offerings of silver foil into Labradors and Golden Retrievers, I innocently assumed John Noakes must have been an alchemist?

Get down, Shep.

Under the Moon

The closest I ever got to witnessing any form of diabolistic activities growing up in Balham in the '60s was during a full moon.

My nan and my great aunt would take me (I always feared I was about to be offered as a sacrifice to some pagan god who lived in the River Wandle) into the gardens of our block of flats, with their purses, and 'turn their money over' (or in my great aunt's case, rearrange her collection of Embassy cigarette coupons).

Animals weren't allowed in our flats, so there was little chance of having your path crossed by a black cat and, because the flats reached the height of eight storeys, you rarely saw any ladders to inadvertently walk under. So, my chances of becoming superstitious (like my aged relatives) were limited; we were too poor to have mirrors.

There were receptacles for putting in eyes of newts, toes of frogs and wools of bats, but these were meant to be for rubbish – people tended to use them for discarding old copies of the *TV Times* and *Reveille* rather than dismembered reptiles. Again, little evidence of witches.

Every November there would be a big fire in the garages where we lived. After the release of the 1973 film, *The Wicker Man*, and after all the coin-churning, I'd half expected Edward Woodward to suddenly appear round the back of a Ford Cortina.

I'm not allowed matches, so it wasn't me.

Lavez-vous maintenant les mains

The NHS has suggested singing 'Happy birthday' twice as the recommended duration for hand-washing. Alternatives are the national anthem or 'La Marseillaise'.

While every good Cub would have learned the national anthem (if you were a good sixer you'd learn the verse about 'knavish tricks'), few, being brought up in south London, would have had 'La Marseillaise' high on their musical repertoire, unless your dad had been Charles de Gaulle, Charles Aznavour or Asterix.

Or, of course, if you had a French teacher at your school who decided to introduce a 'Continental Evening' (as if the recent introduction of Scandinavian quilts wasn't abhorrent enough).

At my Tooting school in 1970 we had just that.

Our class was to sing 'La Marseillaise'.

It has fifteen verses.

Fifteen!!! (If you washed your hands singing that you'd end up with fingers like ET).

In 1970 we'd not even joined the European Community, let alone left it; many of us were still smarting after the 1967 *NON!* rebuke by the aforementioned Charles de Gaulle (who, after retiring from being President of France, became an airport).

We simply learned the French words. This was to protect us knowing the last line translated into English is: 'To cut the throats of your sons, your women!' In Tooting, in the early '70s, the only person who was likely to cut your throat was your barber if you'd tried to hide a copy of that week's *Parade* up your jumper.

We duly learned the song and performed it in front of our parents. However, this foreign lark didn't catch on in my house and, after a week of being served *escargots*, mum reverted back to egg 'n' chips.

Vive la Révolution? Bugger that, thought my mum.

Generation (Dure)x

The day you felt you'd become a man (certainly in the rituals in place in south London in the '60s) would be the time you no longer needed the bench to sit on at the barber's. In effect, you'd only started to enter adolescence and the well-thumbed copies of *Parade*, *Reveille* and *Health & Efficiency*, almost overnight, became more interesting than the *Beano* or *Charles Buchan's Football Monthly*.

The time you did, at least in the barber's eyes, become a man, was when your mum no longer took you. Although in the late '60s and early '70s, with so many people opting for longer hair (I blame *Chicory Tip*), I'm surprised anyone went to the barbers, unless they needed something for the weekend and knew too many people working in their local Boots.

I can remember sitting for ages in my Balham barber's knowing, when accompanied by my mum, that the magazines could have been housed in Fort Knox, such was the chance of me touching one, let alone opening one.

You would wait patiently looking around the shop at photos of hairstyles you could have (although many of the photos were quite old, so if you wanted to look like Clement Attlee, this was the place to go). There were also many displays of Brylcreem, some magic stick which stopped you bleeding after shaving, and combs. Things for the weekend were not in sight. When you hadn't yet entered puberty (some days I think I'm still waiting) things for the weekend were footballs, Jimmy Clitheroe and roast beef; this might explain why I have fourteen children.

Cheap, cheap

When people are asked to name their favourite album, no one ever mentions *Top of the Pops – Volume 18*.

I would play it endlessly in my south London flat, listening to the songs which were in the charts at the time. I'd listen to them under my eiderdown on Radio Luxembourg. But, on these records, none were by the original artists.

I was fourteen in July 1971 and had the lowly weekly income of 50p; these LPs quenched my musical desire cheaply (which was ironic, given one of the songs on the record was 'Chirpy chirpy cheep cheep').

During this time there was a proliferation of impersonators on the TV. It was my naive belief that if they could mimic Harold Wilson, they could also do Harold Melvin. I did not appreciate at the time that these covers were done by professional session musicians who were as good at doing Ted Nugent as Mike Yarwood was Ted Heath.

During these times there were rivals to the *Top of the Pops* LP series, with Hot Hits being one. However, you tended to be loyal to one, a bit like preferring *Monty Python* to *The Goodies*, Max Factor to Rimmel or Harry Potter to anything by Dostoyevsky.

But, dear reader, I bought these LPs purely for musical pleasure and not because of the album covers showing women in provocative poses. I was fourteen and still thinking about which new *I-Spy* book to get. Honest, guv.

WFH; WTF; VPL

I'm one week into working from home, or 'WFH', to give it its abbreviated title. It would seem these are the words used by WFH novices; veterans of WFH call it 'working remotely'.

However, with the closure of anywhere where you can sit for hours on end tending an increasingly cold cardboard cup of something which originally housed a large latte, these 'remote' people will be restricted to WFH and, therefore, be on the same level as us WFH newbies.

This could go on for three months – or, if you're a gynaecologist, a trimester. I am not a gynaecologist, and the nearest I will get to being one is that I own several pairs of gloves, most of which have remnants of begonias on them. None, as I'm sixty-two, have a giant loop of elastic attached.

What are the essentials to a three-month imprisonment? There could be a lot of downtime, so read everything by PG Wodehouse; this is essential to keep your spirits up and, also, books by John Buchan to read about the derring-dos you'll be re-enacting once you're released from your confinement.

It is also important to have one DVD – the BBC version of *Tinker Tailor Soldier Spy* being my DVD of choice, and have my own competition with myself before I say 'dead, mate!' to the TV screen.

You must still take on liquid – you don't want to be the person who doesn't return to work because they've dehydrated. Drink Benecol drinks if you have high cholesterol, Irn Bru if you don't. Don't start eating more cake as your gym has been closed; time to get that Bullworker down from the loft if you're tempted by a Victoria sponge.

Learn another language. Esperanto will probably be the favourite, as we're all in the same boat and we all need one thing which will bind us together. If you can't get hold of a copy of *Teach Yourself Esperanto,* then buy John Buchan's *John Macnab* and learn how to capture salmon off posh Scottish people.

Knitting, crochet and cross-stitch will become less important as most people tend to only create toilet roll covers, and soon we'll be out of that. If you have a garden, build a pine forest – suddenly you'll start to get on with your neighbour (wouldn't that be nice, to quote the Small Faces).

But it's worth occupying your heavily-washed hands (opticians will soon be closed, so you don't want to be doing too much self-isolating) so, building the *Bismarck* out of discarded matches might help pass the time – unless you're a convicted pyromaniac, in which case carry on sniffing glue while constructing an Airfix ME1019.

And if you're looking for live sport, badminton is still on, but I bet you've not watched it longer than five minutes before you're saying: 'Stone me, they hit that hard, don't they?'

Stay safe and remember, it's just a matter of time before they are reshowing *Mind your language.*

Vole steam ahead

Bit like being in the Scrubs, you are now allowed to leave your house once a day for exercise.

Because of the closure of gyms nationally, and therefore the need to find a replacement to my cancelled Zumba classes, I am taking advantage of this allowance from the correctly advised government-induced curfew.

A few days in and I'm witnessing things near my house I'd driven past previously (probably quite badly, as Lewis Hamilton I'm not) but can now stop and think and wonder which aspect of flora and fauna I'm looking at.

However, the disadvantage of having been brought up in urban south London means my limited knowledge of nature is confined to the ability of being able to identify different dog turds. We did have trees, but they would either be goalpost one, goalpost two or a very thick cricket wicket. No one ever returned home saying, 'Mother, dearest, my friends and I managed to scale the entire height of a Canadian Redwood earlier.' (Also, because this was Tooting Bec Common and not a park in Vancouver)

Having escaped, like the TV programme, to suburbia, the nature-identification needs are far greater. Aside from identifying a dead mouse (it could have been a vole or a shrew, I'm assuming here), I'm struggling with my lack of knowledge.

Because of this ignorance, I'm thinking of taking a series of educational books with me on my daily hike: *The Observer's Book of Birds*; *The Observer's Book of Trees*; *The Observer's Book of Dead Rodents*.

Carrying the contents of a small mobile library could also act as a replacement for the free weights I use at the gym. I could strengthen my biceps courtesy of a book with several pages devoted to pictures of deceased gerbils.

I'm going out early in the morning for my walk. I'm at that age when I wake up early and have invariably done the ironing by half four. Walking around, you notice many things about peoples' houses: the porch lights which come on when you walk past (handy if you're an aspiring burglar – which I could be, as I suit black); as the houses get bigger, so the car number plates become more personalised (my car's number plate is MDZ, which would work if my surname was Zither); and whose nets need cleaning.

Today, during my hour-long traipse, I passed four people, two running, two walking like me (the two walking probably having a copy of *I-Spy in Suburbia* tucked inside their newly bought cagoules). The normal British response would be to ignore any passer-by, but these are different times and I'm wondering what the correct protocol might be? Should I have said anything or even doffed my cap (or in today's case, my Bayern Munich bobble hat)?

As this process continues, I'm sure we'll all be talking – albeit shouting across various roads to each other (while keeping a safe distance, obviously), 'Did you see that dead mouse on Banstead Road?' 'That was no mouse, that was an aardvark!'

This in turn will prompt me to return home and order *The Observer's Book of Anteaters*.

Time to wash my nets.

Haircut 100 (days of solitude)

When will I get my hair cut (properly) again? As the amount of conference calls grows, so is my consciousness to look professional but, if my hair isn't likely to get cut for another three months, there is the danger it will be the length it was in 1970, the only difference being, I'm no longer thirteen and Mungo Jerry's not number one.

I wonder if that's what will happen with contact only via a phone or computer screen? If this is the route we're going, I might as well get my flares down from the loft now and buy as many different coloured pieces of wool to create the mother of all tank tops.

I will probably have a fear of girls, as I did when thirteen. My insistence on wearing tank tops, which would have made the biblical Joseph look colour blind, didn't exactly help my cause.

When this is all over and I get invited to my first party I will be taking a Party 7, a bottle of Blue Nun together with the Simon & Garfunkel album, *Bridge over Troubled Water*. And all that while smelling of too much Aramis. If the latter is correct, that will ensure my own social distancing will continue.

(Although there is a certain irony that the eighth best-selling single in 1970 was the England World Cup squad singing *Back Home*. I'm surprised this isn't played during any messages given by Boris Johnson).

I'm at that age when I can remember great details about 1970 but cannot remember much about yesterday (oh yes, I stayed in).

1970 was the first year of Glastonbury, a town previously only famous for King Arthur having rented a flat there. Half a crowns were no longer legal tender and, given that these were the coin fed to the gas meter, I feared my teenage years would be in perpetual darkness (and owning such a selection of tank tops I'm surprised there weren't).

Will my return to work show a 1970s-length hair or will everyone have thought themselves an amateur Vidal Sassoon? Or return looking like Yul Brynner, Duncan Goodhew or Uncle Fester?

I shall miss going to my barber. To whom will I be able to tell where I've been on my holidays, that I don't work locally and that I am the person who last cut my hair?

I think I might watch an episode of *Desmond's* for some ideas.

It's Wagner

I like to think my Man Cave is slightly more sophisticated than Fred Flintstone's.

While I haven't got a pet dinosaur (walking it day and night in mid-winter doesn't appeal), I do have everything I need in my self-appointed self-isolation room.

Because I'm working from home, and with no one to talk to (or as I'm an only child), I need to have elements of distraction and comfort. I have a desk, an ergonomic chair, a sofa for lounging on in the style of Noel Coward, when I'm not having to look at Excel spreadsheets, Word documents or participating in Zoom video calls.

But, above all, I have BBC Radio 3.

I realise classical music isn't everyone's cup of tea but, I sang in a church choir (arguably when I looked my most angelic) and also played in the school orchestra. I was third violin (mainly because they didn't have a fourth, fifth or six – I wasn't brilliant, but it did get me out of maths), although if Richard Wagner had ever heard me playing his overture to Die Meistersinger von Nürnberg, he'd have turned in his Bayreuthian grave.

This exposure, throughout my life, has endeared me to the genre of music they play on Radio 3 (although I do struggle with Jazz Record Requests), especially Essential Classics, which is on during weekdays mornings; it offers great, accessible music with some light-hearted banter too. It keeps me sane, plus sometimes I can sing along or pretend I still own a violin.

However, because it is on in the background, I tend to forget it is on, and on it remains during my newly-increased habit of video conference calls. While no one in my offices or any of my clients believe I'm training to be one a concert pianist, I was asked the other day, 'What is that noise?' (the overture to Fidelio) I now know not everyone likes Beethoven, and many people with whom I have these calls think it is a film about a giant dog. I have yet to fully master 'mute' during some of these calls, although there is a part of me which believes I'm educating and entertaining my fellow video call participants.

A video conference call in itself is a curious thing: several people on my computer screen, in their own contained box, make it like watching an episode of Celebrity Squares. As, at sixty-two, I'm invariably the oldest one on the call, and think of myself as Arthur Mullard or Pat Coombs.

I must encourage more of my video callers to listen to Radio 3. Who knows, some might come away knowing that Wagner isn't just some random bloke who appeared on X-Factor.

I'd do anything

As a football fan, I've been lucky to have watched the beautiful game at the Bernabéu, the San Siro and both German Olympic stadia in Berlin and Munich, but the zenith of my footballing viewing has got to be Sandy Lane, former home of Tooting & Mitcham FC.

Here I watched a charity game between Tooting & Mitcham and a team of celebrities – think Robbie Williams' games, only in 1968 – and in Mitcham.

I went because my comedy hero, Marty Feldman, was playing. Great writer and actor, but no Charlie Cooke.

The game, like most charity games, had an unexpected celebrity kick it off. In this case it was Mark Lester, who played the title role in the film *Oliver*. Like Diana Ross at the 1994 World Cup, only with more begging.

I am one year older than Mark Lester, but even at that tender age, although you dreamed of playing with grown-ups, when reality kicked in (literally) you wanted to hurriedly produce a note from your mum excusing you from the first half.

Mark Lester kicked off and immediately trotted back to the safety of the dugout, changing rooms or Nancy.

But imagine if he'd stayed on and discovered that Tooting & Mitcham had Oliver Reed in their starting XI? He'd have terrorised the poor urchin for ninety minutes.

Picture the scene: young Mark gets the ball from the comedy equivalent of Jimmy Greaves, dribbles inside several Tooting & Mitcham defenders, is about to shoot, balances, raises his leg and then suddenly hears the death cry behind him of 'Bullseye!'

This was 1968; you couldn't do that now: FIFA have introduced a rule which says you can't have a pit bull terrier playing at centre-half.

Speaking Mandarin segments

Panic buying is now a way of life, like watching *Corrie* or turning the gas off before you leave the house. And, as it becomes so, will our diets change? Or perhaps we might revert to things we'd forgotten about since childhood, but now remain the only things on the shelves?

Over the decades, with the introduction of increasingly exotic foods, there must have been a point when you told yourself: these are the last tinned peaches I'm eating.

I think many of us of a certain age can remember refusing to eat corned beef because of its connotations with typhoid – not a good marketing gimmick. (This was before the Falklands War, but blaming the Argentinians came naturally even in the early '60s).

Opening up a tin of fruit in syrup used to be perceived as a treat, especially if it involved a glacé cherry, although an inevitable family fight would ensue over whose cherry this was, as there was usually only one half in each tin. The scuffling would be good practice for shopping these days.

There does, though, seem to be a surfeit of hundreds and thousands – always a treat to top off a tinned pear, but less so corned beef.

Along from the pear halves, mandarin segments and peach slices are tins of prunes; given the paucity of toilet roll, this is far too much of a risk. And as such, my loft collection of *Charles Buchan's Football Monthly* magazines are now beginning to look highly endangered.

If it's Tuesday, it must be Rapunzel

What bloody day is it?

I've not felt this day confusion since my last six-week school holiday and, given my last playtime was forty-seven years ago, I've lost count of which day it is.

Given the lockdown could last for months, I've decided I might get a set of seven underpants and, together with my name tag, sew in a label stating which day of the week it is.

The only problem, given the current shortages and delays in deliveries of certain items, is that you can't guarantee what you want and might end up with a substitution, like when the Ocado delivery person gives you spam when you'd ordered sun-dried tomatoes.

Having ordered my daily pants, I notice from the confirmation that they will all be Disney-themed. Therefore, no need for any sewing-in of any day tags, I shall simply create a mnemonic to remember which day it is: Mickey; Tigger; Woody (insert your own gag here); Tinkerbell; Anyone from *Frozen*; Simba and Snow White.

The inherent danger here is if it's Thursday and I have an accident with Tinkerbell pants on.

My favourite Disney character is Pinocchio – sadly there is no day of the week beginning with P, so I won't be wearing those; no bad thing if I ever started to lie wearing them. Mind you, in this cold weather, that's largely academic.

Do you want to build a snowman?

Cheese is off, love

These days, everyone can pretend to be David Bailey. Most people have phones, in which are built-in cameras which would put Lord Snowdon to shame.

I am conscious, while growing up in south London in the '60s, that these photo opportunities for me were rare. The one I use on social media was taken when I was four, in 1961.

I remember the preparation and actual taking of the photographs took an age, plus there was the added resentment that my bedroom had become the makeshift studio. I did not want my photo taken (an attitude I still have, fifty-nine years later) and I think it shows as poor Sooty, with whom I am posing, gets strangled, making me look like I've been brought up in Boston rather than Balham.

The desire to play with Sooty and my thirty-odd other hand puppets, rather than looking angelic, never faded. With the exception of the mandatory primary school photograph (without Sooty), there remain few photos of me. Neither parent owning a camera didn't aid matters. Although my mum did borrow an ageing relative's Box Brownie during one summer holiday, she held no ambition to become the next Annie Leibovitz (although she did like her posh biscuits).

Other families usually had one relative adept at taking still and/or moving pictures of their offspring, and you'd dread the invite to someone's house to witness their holiday that year with a blurry, shaky, grainy silent memory of that summer in Bognor courtesy of their cine-camera.

I wonder if I'd had a puppet of Sweep things might have been better. And smile ☐.

SOS

Given the current lockdown, 1967 was a very important year for me.

As a ten-year-old living in south London, this was the year I attained my Cubs Signallers' Badge.

As I still work, my communications these days involve Zoom (not the lolly, nor the 1982 Fat Larry's Band hit); Webex (like Zoom, only with more spiders) or Teams (not ideal if you're an only child). House Party isn't perceived as professional, plus I'm at an age when most things are too loud anyway, so this method won't ever feature with my client calls.

The novelty of video calls has worn off, so I've ordered a set of giant semaphore signalling flags, as my future communication will be waving these frantically from the roof of my house.

My training, back in 1967, involved several wintry weeknights of going to a house in Tooting to be taught semaphore by a man so old he could have been Samuel Morse. There was no bell on the front door, just a selection of tom-tom drums in the porch with which to send messages saying you were outside the house (oh, and please either open the door or pop an umbrella through the letterbox).

With my work cap on, as opposed to my Cub cap (and matching woggle), I will be starting business meetings with no introductory pleasantries, but with messages I learned during my 1967 communications course: 'My boat is sinking', 'Can anyone erect a tent?' and 'I think I've burned my sausages'.

In case the latter is construed as a euphemism, I've also ordered a set of Aldis lamps.

Mrs Mills solves a problem like Maria

Despite doing am-dram around south London in the late '70s, I rarely went to the theatre before the lockdown. Now thespians around the world are bringing their offerings, using live streaming, into your front room.

To make this experience even more intimate, I believe you should take part in the actual screening: if it's *Les Misérables* then sling all your cushions onto the carpet and build a barricade; if it's Lloyd-Webber's *Joseph and The Amazing Technicolor Dreamcoat*, get that crochet kit down from the loft and help the Family Jacob out. It doesn't have to be any special material – any wool will do (see what I did there?). And, if you're watching *Macbeth* and you have lodgers, try not to murder them in their sleep, and watch what's being put into that evening's stew.

It's your chance to be the next Vanessa Redgrave or Neil Pearson (good Tooting boy) and say the lines as your favourite character. Take the TV remote, hover your finger over the mute button and, when it's your turn, say 'To be or not to be', sing 'I dreamed a dream' or re-enact the fight scene from *Women in love* – although mind that fire.

Give it everything – no one will see you (if you've got nets), no one will hear you (unless you've not got double glazing) and no one will say anything unless the nets are in the wash, the windows are wide open, and you've left the living room light on.

And if all that fails, get that nun's costume out and pretend to be Julie Andrews singing about a goatherd with no mates and potential altitude sickness.

Plus, who needs an excuse to put on an excessive amount of make-up? Oh dear, time for the lockdown to end.

Ready for you now, Mrs Mills.

Fete worse than death

It's that time of year when normally we'd be attending our local village/school/church/ diabolist commune fairs.

Sadly, none of us, this year, will be winning anything you wouldn't dream of buying on a tombola stall.

Discarded bottles, costing no more than 67p, from day trips to Calais in the late '80s, will still be remaining in the loft for another year.

I'm reminded of the only success at my Balham school fetes. Having previously won goldfish with shorter lifespans than the average housefly, one year I won a goldfish who lived for eighteen years.

If it hadn't had such a dreadful memory, it would have been old enough to drive – remembering stopping distances would have proved a problem, as it was constantly smashing into the side of the bowl.

During these eighteen years I tried to make its life as pleasant as possible: added a plastic diver for company, green foliage modelled on Tooting Bec Common (I assume it had been caught in one of the ponds, so this was a glimpse of 'home') and a signed copy of *Moby Dick*.

When it died, I wanted to give it a decent burial. They weren't too keen at the South London Crematorium (my suggestion of playing 'For those in peril on the sea' as the curtain closed was the nail in the coffin), so I packed him into a tin of daphnia and threw him in the Wandle.

The next time you're watching Tooting & Mitcham and you hear splashing from the nearby river, please remember Flipper.

Highly strung

Women have always frightened me. It stems from a concert I was part of when I was ten in 1967.

In a ruse to get off maths at my Balham primary school, violin lessons were offered. The consequences of this were me failing maths O level three times, the irony being I'm not first violin at the Royal Opera House.

I have a musical ear. I can sing, and, as a ten-year-old, adapted to playing the violin so proficiently I was invited to attend rehearsals for a concert to be given at an all-girls' secondary school in Tooting: Garratt Green.

In my formative period of ten years, I'd been mainly shielded from girls – apart from looking curiously at the covers of magazines (we never had in our house) at the barber's and my mum, twenty-four years my senior (girls in my class didn't count; I'd known them since I was four, and they were all soppy anyway).

What I'd not encountered were 'big' girls – those taller and older than me and, especially the other violinists, which was more threatening.

As an only child, most of the girls in the string section were like older sisters to me and I was put at ease. I think sharing my rosin helped.

I look back and amaze myself none of them put me inside my violin case. I like to think, being a bit nerdy, they felt sorry for me. Whenever our cross-country runs from Bec took us near the school, I look back fondly at those girls, to whom I'm grateful, for preparing me for adolescence, something I'm probably still going through.

Complete and utter…

On January 22nd, 1966, 'These boots were made for walking' entered the charts. To celebrate this fact, I erected a life-size poster of Nancy Sinatra, sporting (there is no other word) a pair of pink boots, across my bedroom wall.

This was, in my nine-year-old opinion, arguably the most artistic thing hanging in SW17 that year. The next year, Nancy was usurped by a picture of Julie Andrews confronting the Gestapo.

A nine-year-old interested in thigh-length boots, I hear you say? Not what you're thinking. At nine I was still recovering from seeing Action Man naked (my parents had taken the cheaper option and *not* ordered any uniform) and was quite content playing with my Hot Wheels (this is not a euphemism) to worry about leather-clad women. No, the real reason is that I wanted to work in a shoe shop.

Clark's in Tooting High Street had a pneumatic money carrier which, as a nine-year-old, I assumed launched you into space. The woman who worked there also looked a bit like John Glenn, so my assumption seemed valid. Although, given the sandals my mum forced me to wear, defying gravity was going to be tricky – there were more holes than shoe. There was also this secret desire to be able to say (without being smacked) 'Uranus', should anyone ask where I was heading.

As I got older, nude action men and Hot Wheels took a back seat and thigh-length boots came to the fore. As did increasingly more frequent trips to the opticians.

I never worked in the shoe shop but, ironically, throughout my career in advertising, I have talked a load of old cobblers.

Three-day weak

Because I'm not having to commute to work, I've replaced the time I would normally be on a train playing I spy with unsuspecting passengers, by walking.

Aside from taking photos of various flora and fauna and keeping them in a folder ready to show anyone out dogging (regardless of whether it's a Doberman, Chihuahua or Ford Cortina), I'm listening to documentaries on my radio.

These past few weeks I've been listening to the BBC's 25 years of rock. This week, I listened to 1973. It is, as the show title suggests, mainly songs, but interspersed with clips of news items. Really good if you were a fan of Ted Heath or Richard Nixon!

One of the songs, 'You're so vain', I thought particularly apt, as I like to keep my hair in place in my local park, even when going through particularly dense undergrowth – David Bellamy I'm not.

1973 saw us enter Europe, work three-day weeks, wish we'd bought shares in Wandsworth's Price's Candles and sit in cars for hours, queuing for petrol, when the question 'Are we nearly there yet?' had the consequence of having your Green Shield stamp allocation being taken away by an equally-bored parent.

It was also the year of the release of 'Tubular Bells' – bought mainly for the B side, which, played backwards, got you a small part in *The Exorcist*.

For me it was the year I managed to obtain one-seventh of the O levels I took, my excuse being I was trying to learn the words to 'Tubular Bells'. Sadly, I only got as far as 'two slightly distorted guitars'.

Although, I did learn that a mandolin wasn't a small French cake.

Kerb your enthusiasm

After leaving the Communist Party in 1961, I joined the Tufty Club – I felt Stalin was no longer in a position to help me cross Balham High Road safely.

I was four and my membership provided me with a badge and a Tufty Club handkerchief – this also acted as a tourniquet in case you didn't properly observe your Kerb Drill.

Imagine my horror when, in 1975, a TV advert saw Tufty replaced by a six-foot-seven bodybuilder called the Green Cross Man. How could this be real and taken seriously? Surely no one was that tall – not even Tufty's road-crossing weasel buddy. The giant's premise was *'stop, look, listen, think'* – you can now add *'hope ('it's not a Prius')'* onto the end of that.

Because I lived next to my primary school, I never needed the use of a lollipop man or woman. I did see them at a distance, though, and assumed that, a) you had to be over 100, b) they hated kids and c). they would probably have been very proficient with a Kendo fighting stick in a previous occupation. They would stop speeding traffic on the A24 with one step into the road with their 'lollipop' as if on the set of *Enter the Dragon* – this was in itself quite dangerous, and we often nearly witnessed *Enter the Cortina* – lollipop first.

Tufty Fluffytail was first created in 1953, he would be sixty-seven and is probably now a grumpy old lollipop squirrel somewhere or living in your loft. Wherever he is, he'll be moaning the music's too loud.

Mind the roads.

School holiday of rock

Blue whale, magic door or lump of rock? This isn't a playground game, but were the alternatives, during my summer holidays in the late '60s, offered by the Natural History, Science and Geological Museums respectively in South Kensington – a 49 bus ride from the stop outside Tooting Bec Station.

However many visits we made as kids there, I don't think I was ever destined to become a scientist.

I liked the idea of a door which opened the moment you walked near it and the ball you could never touch, but this indicated to me that I was unlikely to be called on to walk on the Moon, split an atom or discover fire.

Similarly, I marvelled at the blue whale and the dodo in the Natural History Museum, but with the extinction of one, and not enough maggots in my mum's fridge to capture the other, I was never going to make it as the next David Attenborough or Jacques Cousteau.

This left the Geological Museum, which we went in to escape the rain. You can only look at a few pieces of sedimentary rock before the risk of pneumonia becomes very attractive. Now closed (I rest my case), but part of the Natural History Museum, if you don't fancy it, its memory lives on through *The Flintstones*. Or take an umbrella.

The rock museum gets the last laugh, as there is no Museum for Paper and Scissors.

Milking it

Now there is avocado milk to go with the trillions of other dairy products you can get.

Growing up in the '60s, we had three types: red, silver and, if you'd come into a few bob, gold-top; avocado was the colour of your bathroom.

Can you imagine the chaos in the '60s at school milk time with thirty different alternatives? Hancock advocated, during the 'Blood Donor' episode, to: 'Drinka Pinta Milka day'. Poor spelling, but a strong message. Mrs Thatcher was clearly not a Hancock fan.

My first departure from straight milk was when my mum once bought a tin of Nesquik. It did involve a lot of stirring; if you drank a lot of it, one arm would be much larger than the other.

Such was the desire to have a more varied dairy diet, I once asked for the popular '60s dessert, raspberry ripple. At the time it was quite expensive, and we didn't have much money, so my mum created it serving a block of vanilla ice cream you'd normally have in a wafer, covered with Ribena.

And I wondered why she never made it as a Michelin-star chef?

Humphrey is currently in HMP Wandsworth serving time for armed robbery.

Go on my son et lumière

In the bedroom of my Balham flat, growing up in the '60s, I'd always have a night light on. I'd have one on now, but at sixty-three I'm 99 per cent certain the bogeyman doesn't exist. I would, with the light's reflection, enact shadow dramas onto my bedroom wall.

My dramas would involve a rabbit's ears, Dennis the Menace and a pre-historic bird with a beak which could open and close.

In my teenage years I travelled one night with my mum to Hampton Court to watch a son et lumière (with Balham's cafe society being like Paris in the '70s, it was the natural thing to do).

The drama employed actors whose silhouettes were the only thing you'd see; they depicted some violent scene from the life of Henry VIII.

After this, I decided my career lay in film direction, using only silhouette. I felt I could create anything – except *The Invisible Man*.

Returning, excited, to my bedroom that night, I hurried to bed early, turned on my Flopsy Bunny night light and felt like Balham's answer to Sergio Leone.

In my bedroom, in total darkness save for a 40-watt bulb, I thought Shakespeare would be the best place to start. I'd start to study him at school and felt my wall would do him justice. It was at this point I realised there are no rabbits, birds or Dennis the Menaces in any Shakespeare play – except the opening scene of *Macbeth,* when all three are ingredients in the witches' cauldron.

But, as we say in Balham, *je regrette rien* (looks like rain).

Barbie and Däniken

In 1968, immediately after the publication of *Chariot of the Gods* by Erich von Däniken, I would gaze expectantly out of the bedroom window of my Balham flat, anticipating the imminent arrival of aliens – and by this I don't mean people from south-east London ☐.

I would trawl over Tooting Bec Common, desperate for signs of a spaceship runway from 50,000 BC – perhaps on the Tooting Bec running track, or pondering whether the Lido was in fact a giant (or tiny) fountain built by Martians?

Von Däniken suggested many biblical events were carried out by alien races. I once saw a ladder with Jacob written on the side and believed this was a prophesy of von Däniken, only to discover that this Jacob was in fact a painter and decorator from Clapham.

The destruction of Sodom was probably not done by people from outer space, but executed by a group of pyromaniacs from neighbouring Gomorrah.

Such was the success of the first book, it spawned many others – invariably with *Gods* in the title. It all got a bit hard to believe when *Confessions of an Ancient God* and *Carry on Corn Circling* were released.

I'm writing this from a condominium in Roswell; the neighbours are lovely but do keep churning up the local park making it look like the East-West runway at Heathrow Airport, saying they've relatives visiting.

The Hoss has bolted

During lockdown many people have been lucky, once they've had enough of Lorraine on *This Morning*, to have a subscription to Netflix, Amazon Prime or have a reel of an 8mm cinefilm they found in the loft, to watch to while away the times they've been stuck indoors.

Imagine if this had happened in the '60s, assuming we'd had the technology? Would we have binge-watched all 431 episodes of *Bonanza*? Had Zoom calls talking about 'have you got to the episode when Hoss goes to the dentist yet?'

Today we have a plethora of Scandinavian murders to watch. In the '60s, in my Balham flat where I'd be hoping perhaps this week I might see Alexandra Bastedo naked, I'd not even heard of Scandinavia, (these were the times when Iceland was still *Bejam*) let alone know what *noir* meant (I thought he played for Paris St-Germain).

The problem with many of these series is that eventually they have to insert a dream sequence. You never got that with *Tales of the Riverbank* – suddenly Hammy wakes up and Southfork has been sold!

On far too late for a youngster like me, the daily eight minutes of *The Epilogue* would have made a good box set. Although would it have been worth waiting for the big fight scene at the end between the Devil and St Michael?

But there were always circuses to fall back on. On the BBC sixty years ago, to this day, there was *Chipperfield's Circus* starring Mr Pastry. Remembering how annoying he was, I'm hoping it was the episode when he gets eaten by a lion. Too soon?

Wolf in sheep's clothing

A sheepskin coat is not just for Christmas – unless your paternal grandmother has given you one.

Each year I would receive a big present, bought off my nan's Grattan catalogue.

Fashion ideas, however, differ when there's a sixty-year age gap.

I'd travelled on Boxing Day 1970 from our flat in Balham to my nan's flat in Marylebone, filled with great expectation as to what the 'big' gift might be? The year before I'd been given an identity bracelet with 'Michael' engraved on it (my full name, which meant *you're late for your tea*, *your room needs tidying* and/or *you're never going to get any O levels reading the Beano*). The bracelet was so heavy, my arm would hang like an orangutan.

Would this year be different?

Once settled, I was presented with a package half the size of my torso (not another bracelet, then?). Upon removing the *Clangers* wrapping paper I discovered a sheepskin coat which, if you were fifty, a football manager, selling an old *Cortina* or all three, was the ideal present. If you were fourteen, you almost wished for another bracelet (at least *both* shoulders would droop).

But there was always a second, smaller present. After more unwrapping – this paper adorned with *Atom Ant* – it became evident my nan had succumbed to the sales skills of the local Avon lady. As I unravelled, I found a bottle of *Windjammer*; a fragrance which sounded like it should be a cure for flatulence, and certainly smelled like it.

In years to come I had visions of sitting in a football dugout, 1600E logbook at the ready, knowing no insect would come within 100 yards of me!

Lava and lime

In the '60s, you didn't have to go to the edge of Mount Vesuvius to see lava; if you'd saved up enough Green Shield stamps, you could get some in a lamp. If the lamp had faulty wiring, there was that ever-present danger the eruption of AD79 would be re-enacted in your flat.

But if globules resembling something out of the *Quatermass Experiment* wasn't for you, then a fibre optic lamp was the thing to adorn your bedroom in the (in my case) highly unlikely event that a girl might visit.

In the 70s, in my Balham flat, I would turn my light on in the hope that it would act as a homing device to any unsuspecting girl in our flats (preferably one who liked cricket, *Thunderbirds* and Sven Hassel novels).

However, the only danger (there was no danger of anyone visiting) was that the fibre optic lamp, though wonderfully pretty when lit up, would moult more than the hairiest German Shepherd dog.

This was not advertised on the packaging and you only found out – given the room was in virtual darkness – when you trod on one. Think pieces of Lego, only with a skin-piercing syringe attached.

I was clearly never going to make it as a hippy. My mother had installed fire alarms in my room, so joss sticks were out of the question and the only flares I'd see would be my mother firing one out of our flat window signalling my dad had gone to work.

How to find a clematis

Living on the fourth floor of a block of flats made gardening precarious. While my Balham flats had a communal garden, it was not the same as having your own begonias or clematis to tend to; if you were to become Percy Thrower, you were restricted to indoor plants.

Consequently, we had a flat with more plants than Kew Gardens.

With my mother suffering from arachnophobia, we didn't own spider plants, nor did we have anything made out of macramé, as mother didn't like pasta. We did, however, have cheese plants (even though most family members were lactose intolerant).

Aspidistras were few and far between, as this was thought to be a child's illness which gives you a sore throat and fever. Rubber plants were acceptable, as Mum believed these acted as a form of contraception (constantly reading books past midnight on indoor plants ensured I remained an only child).

Indoor plants are designed to be fairly indestructible. However, if you're a teenage boy, the leaves make a very good camouflage hat in case the Nazis invaded again, and a father who'd once seen a documentary on Fidel Castro thought he could make a fortune selling cigars made from mother-in-law's tongue.

But the most exotic plant in our flat was the Venus flytrap – not wonderfully pretty, but we saved a fortune on tins of Raid.

Off topic

In my final year at my Balham primary school, apart from the playtime bell ringing, my favourite time there was when the teacher announced: 'It's time to work on your topic.'

A 'topic' was a project which lasted several terms and had nothing to do with hazelnut-covered chocolate.

In 1967 there were thirty of us in the class (I was one of the few not called 'Susan') and our topic was to write about a county. There had been thirty-six English counties, so the chances of getting Rutland (and consequently no work) was high.

I got Middlesex. I wanted Kent as I was, even as a ten-year-old, a massive fan of the county's cricket club and obsessive about cricket generally – which became horribly obvious as my topic progressed.

Two years earlier, Middlesex had officially stopped being a county. Surely better than getting Rutland? No: new county boundaries meant for nothing in SW17 (not part of Westmoreland).

I could have written about Harrow School, Chiswick House or the 15th century font in West Drayton; I chose solely to write about Middlesex cricket.

My topic could have included facts about Hampton Court and its inhabitants and history; I chose to write about the inhabitants of Lord's (not even in Middlesex).

Leading up to my eleven-plus, rather than plumping for Thomas Cromwell, I wrote (at length) about Fred Titmus. I even referred to the English Test cricketer probably being a better off-spinner than Katherine of Aragon.

So, not so much divorced; beheaded; died; divorced; beheaded; survived, more stumped; run out; caught; stumped; run out; hit the ball twice.

Bunkered

As an only child, I would often have to amuse myself with whatever toy raw materials I had around me. I was obsessed, as a ten-year-old, with golf and would spend hours at night in the bedroom of my Balham flat putting a golf ball into a lone, empty yogurt pot (pointless having two yogurt pots, as I had no one to call).

One year I was given the *Arnold Palmer Pro Shot Golf* game and, as golf courses tend to close during the hours of darkness, at night I'd set this up. Using the six available clubs, two bunkers and four out-of-bounds fences, I'd try to complete eighteen holes.

My golfing ability, due to playing too much *Pro Shot Golf*, never improved, so I'd never win the Morden Pitch 'n' Putt Open, let alone the US one.

I never completed eighteen holes as, invariably, I'd get my finger stuck in the levering device which enabled mini-Arnold Palmer to swing. I would then walk the walk of shame into my parents' lounge, implement still attached to my finger, and ask for some butter to remove it. As I walked back to my bedroom, I'd hear them talk:

'All he does at night is play with himself.'

'He'll probably go blind.'

As I walked back, I thought: *I've got my finger stuck; it's not taken my bloody eye out!*

Vested interest

There was a spectacular difference between physical exercise in primary schools to that in secondary ones.

And what a surprise I got during my first PE lesson at my Tooting grammar school. It wasn't so much pretending to be a tree (something I'd done successfully the previous seven years). This was trying to jump over objects which looked the size of a fully-grown oak!

Previously, I'd dressed only in vest, pants and ill-fitting plimsolls, prancing gaily around my Balham primary school hall, listening to a BBC employee who sounded like she'd a whole orchard of plums in her mouth.

At secondary school it was not called 'Music and Movement', although there was certainly movement (mainly avoiding the PE master's eyes), but no music, although any funeral march or anything towards the end of Wagner's *Götterdämmerung* wouldn't have seemed out of place.

Music and Movement was very innocent; I still have days when I wish I could suddenly become a horse chestnut (usually during endless Zoom calls).

When we didn't have the radio, we'd have a kind, elderly teacher who'd play the piano (she probably tinkled on her church organ at weekends, like Violet Carson, only without a hairnet). This contrasted with secondary school when our master who, should you have tracked his genealogy back to the late 15th century, would have taken you directly to Tomás de Torquemada.

The only good thing at secondary school was you didn't have, chasing you throughout the lesson, a girl who wanted to become a Golden Retriever when she grew up. Especially if you being a tree was slightly too realistic.

78 trombones

I'm at that age when I'm starting to mishear and mispronounce things. I blame events in 1978 and ageing relatives.

During that year, every Tuesday I'd go to Karachi. At least that's what my great aunt told anyone even remotely interested in my whereabouts in the grocer's housed in our Balham flats. I wasn't an employee of the Pakistan International Airways; every week, I'd go to St George's Hospital in Tooting to learn karate (a kind of medical paradox). Only 5,000 miles out (perhaps the Proclaimers did this trip and inspired their hit song?)

That year also saw the release of The Motors' song 'Airport'. I was still living with my dad (my mother having successfully constructed a tunnel four years earlier) and we'd always have the radio on. 'Have they just sung "eff off"?' asked my dad. 'No,' I replied, 'airport.' He went off muttering something about Frank Sinatra being more articulate.

Later that year, while getting ready for work, doing up our respective Van Heusen shirts and arguing about the Old Spice being stolen again, we heard on the news that one of the members of the band Chicago had died. The newsreader went on to inform the listeners that, 'one of their biggest hits was *If you leave me now*.' 'Effing appropriate,' said my dad (well, that was the gist of what he said). And he wondered why he failed the audition to appear on *Fifteen to One*!

Wheelie bin TV

There was no better feeling of euphoria inside my Balham classroom during the '60s than when the school TV was wheeled in.

As a schoolkid, you couldn't have given a monkey's that you were about to witness the funeral of a great statesman, the launch of an ocean-going liner or the exploration of other parts of the universe.

Neither Churchill, Queen Elizabeth II (the boat, not the monarch) nor Neil Armstrong could take away that feeling of *soon, we'll not be working*. Only double playtime, or an inset day, had that ability of relief from the monotony of learning about the Stone Age, the four-times table or the tricks of the baby Jesus in later life.

It would be the school caretaker who would wheel the machine into the classroom (there were no IT assistants in the '60s – the only IT we knew about in those days was the creature from *The Addams Family*). The TV was housed in a wooden box (the size of which wouldn't have looked out of place outside Troy) and placed in the centre of the room, in front of the blackboard, thus hiding any trick way of remembering that four times four is sixteen.

And so, plugged in, warmed up (this took the best part of a week), we then sat watching corteges, yachts and automobiles (OK, moon buggies).

At the end of it there was a sense of anti-climax, as many of us had never heard of Churchill, were unlikely to go on a cruise or fly to the Moon. We'd resume our daily tasks.

I don't think we missed much schooling, as I know my four-times table (up to twelve), how to slay a mammoth and that the adult baby Jesus wouldn't have needed flint to have started a fire.

Stage fright

In the late '70s, I joined an am-dram group (still have shirts with stage make-up on). We'd mostly perform in a Balham school hall, where there was more a smell of rotting plimsolls than greasepaint.

Having started with one line, I worked my way up to be given larger parts. This impressed some of the younger girls in the group. Well, one in particular.

We'd just performed a revue at the old Tooting Bec (Mental) Hospital. Tough gig, as many of the audience couldn't clap, as they still had their straitjackets on.

During the revue I'd sung, danced (albeit in a ballerina costume) and acted.

It was at this time when I'd started my career in adverting and, earlier that day, had bought the book, *Teach yourself advertising*. I still haven't finished it, nearly fifty years on.

The show finished, and Tooting's answer to Nurse Ratched had returned her cares to their rooms, and we left the hospital to return to our respective homes.

As we approached Hurley's on Balham High Road, there were just two of us left: me and a girl in our troupe. As we got to her house I was invited in for coffee, except it wasn't for coffee – it was for '*coffee*'.

With a fear of girls even now, being alone with one filled me with dread, especially after the door had been locked, the pet Alsatian, Himmler, had been tied up, and there was no obvious sign of a percolator. At the announcement of 'Mum's out for the evening,' I went into blind panic.

I stood up, announced that I had bought a new book and needed to read it before the morning, and left, coffee-less.

Oddly, I have three children, but back then, you could get all sorts of things off the Freemans catalogue.

Seven deadly syns

Whenever I go on holiday, I like to read about the place I'm visiting: *Jamaica Inn* in Cornwall; *The Mayor of Casterbridge* in Dorset; the *Clangers* annual if ever I make it to the Moon.

As a teenager, I'd spend many summer holidays on the Kent coast; my reading there was the *Dr Syn* novels. Dr Syn was a clergyman by day and head of a Romney Marsh smuggling gang at night.

The seven novels were written between 1915 and 1944 and two films came out of the writing. I only saw part of the 1963 adaption. I was so traumatised by Dr Syn, terrifyingly dressed as a scarecrow, my mum had to take me out of the Balham Odeon, probably before the usherette called the local health visitor or hit me with a Kia-Ora to shut me up.

Dr Syn was ultimately hanged in the final book, but in current times he'd have escaped that fate, as he'd not have been able to carry anything out if he was working from home. You cannot offload stolen barrels of French rum from a boat via a Zoom call.

I'd have made a dreadful smuggler: fear of water (worse than that of hanging), don't like rum (even in a bar of *Old Jamaica*) and don't look good in a scarecrow outfit.

Also, at my age, I'm quite susceptible to marsh ague. Rum Baba anyone?

Not-so-little fishy

During the early '60s, I associated the *Dick van Dyke Show* with smoked haddock.

Every Saturday evening, as the activities of everybody's favourite cockney would be played out on our TV screens, my mum would serve up smoked haddock. Having flirted with the fishmongers in Balham Market to get their finest fish, I still, to this day, cannot stomach the taste, and whenever you go to a restaurant (remember those?), the fish of the day is invariably haddock. There clearly is no God – which is more than can be said of the omnipresent haddock.

The opposite effect on me is with roast beef: my brain conjures up images of Ted Moult. He'd be on the radio (wireless for older listeners) every Sunday (he'd alternate with Jimmy Clitheroe on the *Brain's Trust*) and there is still this association. Whenever I'd see an Everest Double Glazing ad on the telly, I'd start salivating. I do that now, but that may be an age thing.

However, I do blame Lucille Ball for my allergy to prawns. My mum's divi must have come in one week, as she decided to buy prawns instead of the haddock. Fine by me. Shortly after another slapstick episode of the US situation comedy, I decided that I didn't love Lucy that much and her show should have been sponsored by Kaolin & Morphine.

But the worst taste and smell for me: boiled fish in parsley sauce. My nan would make it and it was the worst smell ever. I am reminded of it whenever I read Dante's *Inferno*; the recipe had come from the tenth circle of hell – so awful, it wasn't even in the book.

Lightweight and bitter

I've not drunk alcohol since 1976; I blame David Vine.

Before then, albeit for one legal year, I'd have the odd half in pubs near where I grew up in '60s and '70s Balham. I wasn't cut out for drinking, but I'd tag along. On Friday nights, when the Salvation Army sellers of *War Cry* would come into The Hope on Wandsworth Common, I'd be one of the few in our group capable of finishing the picture crossword in their weekly newspaper.

On 5th April 1976 (my 19th birthday), I went with my mates to the Surrey Tavern. We'd play pool there and put millions of pounds into the jukebox to listen to 'Save your kisses for me', 'Fernando' and 'Music' by John Miles. These were the top three singles on my birthday. You really got your money's worth with 'Music', as it went on for about a week.

As I was singing along, 'Music was my first love' etc. etc., my mates thought it'd be hysterically funny to empty that month's Smirnoff factory output into my half a pint of lager and lime.

Later that evening, when the world was spinning faster than anything they'd ever had at Battersea Funfair, I decided alcohol wasn't for me.

The next month I went on holiday to Austria with my dad. He tempted me with what he called 'innocuous' light ale. What I didn't realise, despite him being very well-read, was that this was one big word he didn't fully know the meaning of. The words from the Tony Newley hit 'Stop the world I want to get off' rang round my head again.

Travelling on a coach around Innsbruck the next day, I've never felt so ill. I still can't listen to the theme tune to *Ski Sunday* without feeling nauseous!

Not-so-floppy Flopsy

Before discovering Radio Luxembourg, I was more than capable, as an only child, of entertaining myself at bedtime in my Balham flat.

As soon as it was lights out in HMP Mick, the wall of my bedroom would become a giant control panel, which would transport me to wherever I wanted to go – I rarely thought past Morden, though.

I'd pretend where there was actually Flopsy Bunny wallpaper (neither parent was regular decorators), there were buttons to push, enabling me, in my ten-year-old brain, to travel, out of SW17, into a parallel universe (Morden).

During the day this same wall had been a goal into which I would head one of my dad's nicked squash balls. By night I was Neil Armstrong; by day I'd be Gerd Müller.

To re-enact some of Müller's many goals, I'd throw myself across my bed, oblivious to the fact there was invariably either a violin bow or pair of glasses lying there.

I gave the violin up as soon as I could but, as I got older and found the spaceship wall less and less appealing, so my need for stronger and stronger glasses became increasingly necessary and visits to the opticians seemed almost weekly. I couldn't work out the correlation. Seems my nan had been right all along ⬜.

To infinity and beyond (well, the southern end of the Northern Line).

The postman only rings after playtime

In December, during the '60s, in my Balham primary school, there would be a temporary postbox put in the playground.

Its use was for pupils to put our Christmas cards into. It was purely for our fellow pupils – although some didn't realise this, and those with relatives in far-away countries were quite disappointed that Auntie Gladys in Brisbane would moan she'd not received a single card for years.

The cards would be delivered; unless you had siblings at the school, you tended to get twenty-nine cards – from your fellow classmates.

I realised, after I'd finished full-time education, that you only tended to know your actual classmates, apart from the boys' names announced at the Monday morning assembly for their sporting prowess or those who were (yet again) on detention.

Receiving so many cards was great; the problem was that twenty-nine also had to be written. I got very bored signing every one, 'Happy Christmas, Mick', and so mixed my signature up with people I'd seen on TV or were sporting heroes. I'd sign many as 'John Drake' or 'Amos Burke'; many girls in my class would wonder who Gerd Müller was, and several boys would get excited thinking they'd got a card from Nancy Sinatra or Mandy Rice-Davies.

This Christmas I shall be confusing friends and family with my Christmas signature of 'Be lucky, Pol Pot'. Confusing as, a) he's dead and, b) wasn't terribly Christian. You certainly wouldn't have wanted to sit on his knee, let alone enter his grotto. Be lucky, Mick.

Postcards from the Devonian Age

The last time I got a postcard, the price of the stamp was 3d.

No one sends them any more – not even the ones featuring very small men with wives with enormous, Pamela Anderson-like chests, looking at marrows or any odd-shaped vegetable mentioning its size, etc.

As a kid, during the summer, I had two great aunts who, upon their arrival in Ilfracombe (might have been Pluto for all I knew, it sounded so far away from Balham), would write to me using every conceivable space on the card. There would always be a picture of the beach – not a sniff of a giant marrow ☐.

It was lovely to receive, but the *quid pro quo* was that you had to send them one back and would be forced by elder relatives – seemingly for the entire duration of the holiday – to write them.

'Wish you were here' was the obvious inclusion but, however large you wrote it, it wasn't covering the entire message area. I would lie and write about the remains of a pterodactyl I'd found on Dungeness beach and wouldn't be able to write a second card due to having been abducted by Ellen Terry (we were forced to visit her house in Kent one year). So, when I returned, having been released by the leading 19th theatre actress, some ageing relatives were quite surprised.

And the weather; you'd be in the same country and the weather probably similar, but you were, because you were British, obliged to mention it. You said it was hot, but then you'd never travelled to the Sahara Desert, the Grand Canyon or Mars.

I'd send more postcards, except they cost more than 3d to post and my marrows aren't at their best in this cold weather.

Halfpenny for your thoughts

Boxing Day in the '60s for me meant an early introduction to gambling and the chance to win my bodyweight in halfpennies.

We would travel from Balham to Wimbledon Chase (which sounded more like a horse race than an actual place) to visit a family who'd previously lived in my block of flats but had emigrated to SW20 – could have been Borneo, it seemed that far away.

At the end of the four-mile journey south down the A24 would be the largest ever collection of bottled beer, two packs of cards and a pile of halfpennies, which to me looked like Everest (the mountain, not the double glazing).

The game we played was Newmarket; it was simple and easy for a ten-year-old (me) to play. The games would seemingly go on long into the night (probably about 9.30!), and amid the continual clinking of light ale bottles, you stood to have a pile in front of you, if you were lucky, adding up to nearly a shilling. I'd never felt so rich – plus I had already been given a £1 Premium Bond at birth – surely only members of the royal family were better off?

The lady who lived there looked very much like Dusty Springfield (this was preferable to looking like Myra Hindley, as my Auntie Vera did), so it was no coincidence her songs were played throughout the evening.

When the beer had run out, and the halfpennies usually in one person's sole possession, we began the trip home – back to wonder how easy it was to mend a broken Action Man.

Who's got the ten of spades?

End of the tier show

As we approach the end of a rather bizarre year, there are words in 2020 which have slightly different meanings to when I was growing up in my Balham flat in the '60s.

Corona: this was the brand of cream soda and cherryade I'd buy from my school tuck shop.

Quarantine: if you travelled back from a foreign land, this is what Rover or Tiddles had to do for the best part of a decade.

Mask: unless your occupation was a surgeon, highwayman or the Lone Ranger, the only time you wore a mask was playing Blind Man's Buff or Pin the Tail on the Donkey.

Lockdown: when you've lost your door keys. Or someone's escaped.

Social distancing: what you did if you wanted to avoid certain people at your local whist drive.

Trump: a word used during a whist drive either pertaining to a suit of cards or flatulence. Or both.

Tier 1: what you give guests at a wedding.

Tier 2: what you give guests at a Christening.

Tier 3: what people who really don't need to eat more cake tuck into during a wedding.

Tier 4: opening words of Ken Dodd's signature tune.

Bubble: a thing you blew, and in the process, got washing-up liquid all over your hands; now you need to douse your hands in Fairy while singing 'Happy Birthday'.

R: used to be a letter, now it's a number.

Zoom: was a lolly until 1982 when Fat Larry bought Lyon's Maid.

COVID: what Glamorgan is now called.

A little bit of elephant's

Bank Holiday TV viewing, when I was a kid growing up in south London in the '60s, invariably involved a circus.

As a ten-year-old keen to get some career ideas, the circus was no help at all.

One year, I visited the travelling circus on Clapham Common. This was like an appointment with a school career officer.

If you had a head for heights, owned a whip and a small stool, liked sharing a Mini with heavily made-up men (and tonnes of fire hydrant foam) or, to paraphrase Robert Duvall, loved the smell of elephant dung in the morning, then there were potential jobs for you.

These ticked none of employment-prospect boxes for me.

This was confirmed when I'd watch the circus on TV (and you'd only watch that because there were only two channels and no one could be arsed to get up and physically change the channel as they'd overeaten the cold turkey and bubble, OD'd on dates or had alcoholic poisoning through consuming too many chocolate liqueurs).

I remember watching Billy Smart's Circus. I thought to myself that he couldn't have been *that* smart, as one of his main tasks was collecting elephant poo – why else would he need a top hat?

Also, the smell of sawdust reminded me of when someone had been sick in class and the long-suffering school caretaker would come in and scatter sawdust onto the problem in question as if it were some form of fairy dust with magical powers to ensure the smell disappeared.

This New Year Bank Holiday, I won't be watching the circus, and I'll be keeping any fruit buns to myself .

Yes, we have some bananas

This year, 2021, will be the year for injections – my question is, will the syringe be as big as it seemed when I was a six-year-old in my Tooting doctor's surgery awaiting my booster jab? And will I get a *Mr Bump* sticker saying: 'I've been a good boy at the doctor's'?

I remember my doctor's in the early '60s and the abiding smell of ether – I was always surprised none of the staff were comatose by mid-afternoon.

And there was, if you were only six, nothing to read – unless you wanted to learn forms of needlework, in which case you were lucky as there were always decades-old copies of *Woman's Weekly* (famed for its knitting) strewn across a table which would have been deemed too old for *Going for a Song*. The magazines were so old, in one there was a pattern on how to crochet a gas mask.

I'd often be taken to the doctor's, as my mum was a hypochondriac and clearly fancied the doctor; this attraction was mutual. My mum would have a paper cut and the doctor would gladly do a house call.

The best thing I remember about visits to the doctor's was banana-flavoured penicillin. I had a connection with Alexander Fleming, having been born in St Mary's, Paddington, where he'd discovered how to make antibiotic from an old Hovis – I'd have my own plaque erected there if it wasn't for him.

Such was my love for this medicine, I'd make up illnesses just to get some – Mum wasn't to know typhoid wasn't *that* rampant in SW17 in the '60s.

So, is there a doctor in the house? No, because he's round my mum's flat.

And cough.

Don't forget your gym kit

New year, new calendar. Will it have kittens on? A favourite football team? Twelve pictures of Claudia Cardinale (I'm buying a calendar for a friend)? One thing is certain: mine won't have the new moon turning up on the fifteenth of every month.

We never had a calendar, as my mum rarely attended school and so it never mattered what date it was as she couldn't count further than thirty-one. My Nan, however, in her Balham flat, had a very simple one showing the phases of the Moon. She'd have been an astronaut had she not had a fear of heights – and Martians.

More men would have had Pirelli calendars, only there was a general fear of foreign food in the '60s.

These days most shopping centres have pop-up stalls (seemingly all year round, thus catering for anyone who has just come out of a coma) serving every hobby and interest (unless you're a budding astronomer). But you only really need one with several columns, making sure no one forgets their gym kit, so it's academic what the pictures are. I created a calendar one year for my household with a different Nazi each month; we'd got to October (Hermann Göring in a swimsuit) before anyone noticed.

Because I'm still working from home, I've erected a bird table outside my study window, a consequence of which is that my calendar for 2021 features garden birds. I'm looking forward to August – the index has promised 'Great Tits'.

Sixty-three and only now going through adolescence :)

Having a wobble

Blancmange – the literal translation being 'only eat if you've absolutely nothing in your cupboard' – was a curious dessert I rarely had (I may have been given it as a punishment, but am clearly too scarred to remember).

Growing up in the '60s, desserts (or puddings, as we tended to call them in SW17) offered little choice and would normally consist of tinned fruit (my mum told me she wasn't travelling to Jamaica just to get me a banana) and the top of the milk. If either parent came into some money, there was the occasional investment into a block of raspberry ripple. But blancmange rarely featured; I was clearly protected by St Ivel, the patron Saint of milk-based desserts.

It was 1967 when Angel Delight was introduced to the UK – thus striking the death knell for blancmange. Even though you had to whisk the living daylights out of it (and still had remnants of the powder on the bottom of your bowl at the end), it was a sensation at my ten-year birthday that year. It helped everyone forget the party entertainer, who could only make penises out of balloons, rather than swans the other ten-year-olds at the party had requested.

The only good thing about blancmange was the receptacles they were constructed in. We had one shaped like a rabbit – you could see where Elmer Fudd got his bunny hatred from.

Slotting in just nicely

These days you have to tap in for everything. In the '60s and '70s, the only tapping-in being done was by the *Stasi*.

Back then, coin-operated machines were the '60s equivalent of our near cashless society (well, cashless except for the odd half a crown). Imagine your horror during a '60s Christmas dinner, together with the 365-day anticipation of getting a sixpence in your slice of pudding, only to have both cheeks pierced by an Access card. (Not very flexible now, is it?)

There was a cigarette machine on the pavement near Tooting Bec Station which, with the correct change inserted, twenty Senior Service would magically appear. For an old penny you could watch the trains in the model shop along from that same station – you could wave every modern-day card you carried from Visa to Kidney Donor via The Tufty Club – if you didn't have *real* money, you'd see no train moving.

The launderette would pose similar problems if you'd travelled back in time with your current wallet (or phone). You could try all you like – if you didn't have a couple of shillings to buy a small packet of Tide, you'd very quickly become like Queen Elizabeth I and only wash once a year. Imagine how angry the launderette manager would become if you thought waving the handset of an old Bakelite at the spin dryer would make it rotate.

There still are vending machines for those who have kept a collection of florins; these are for people who haven't cleaned their teeth, have headaches or haven't had a vasectomy. If you've still not found solutions for the first two, you needn't bother with the third.

Do keep the change, waiter.

A knotty problem

I still have my school tie.

I'm unlikely to wear it again (unless I receive a very belated detention) – even if tied properly, it would be far too short and the bottom bit would only sit pointing to the part of my chest which meets the excessive, biscuit-eating part of my body. I blame the school tuck shop.

At my Tooting grammar school this was a major part of the uniform.

In our first year we also had to wear the school cap which, if your journey home took you past the next-door comprehensive school (which housed a million pupils), provided an ever-present danger of having it knocked off, nicked or turned into a burning sacrifice – before your very eyes and satchel.

Luckily, my journey home took me in the opposite direction, thus allowing me to retain my cap until the end of the year.

We were allowed to leave school ahead of next door to avoid any cap conflagration. I still think 4.10 is time to go home. This happened several times when I first started work and would often walk out of late afternoon business meetings saying I had physics homework to do.

Long trousers (once you'd ignored the chaffing) were a bonus during the winter months, but the tie was the most important adornment to your uniform. It seemed the larger the knot, the greater your standing within the class. These days people wear lapel badges denoting their company, nationality, membership of the Bazooka Club. In 1968 Tooting, the tie was the lapel badge and a big knot said: 'I have pubic hair'.

I've worked from home for nearly a year now and haven't had to wear a tie. I may put my old school one on, get an iced bun and pretend I'm in the school tuck shop. And wonder if pubic hair turns grey and falls out?

Fondue fondle

I always knew, in the '60s, when they were popular, when my parents were having a fondue party. I'd smell molten cheese wafting down the hall of our Balham flat and hear Edith Piaf songs, played on a continuous loop, echoing around my bedroom, from which I'd been banned from leaving until daylight.

Fondue was not, as my mum thought, French – it's Swiss. However, my mum owned an old atlas, so playing French music was close enough for her. She didn't have the proper kit and made do with an old saucepan and a Primus stove. To her, Zürich was something you cleaned the toilet with.

It was hard to sleep during these fondue evenings as, the drunker the guests became, the louder the singing of 'je ne regrette rien' would be. My mum would come in with 'ear plugs' – which turned out to be Dairylea segments.

Not that I'd have known it at the time, but I think the fondue evenings were a front for wife-swapping. We lived on the fourth floor of our flats, so branches of pampas grass outside the flat wasn't practical.

I can remember helping clear up the morning after one such party and finding a Ford Cortina key fob at the bottom of the saucepan-cum-fondue bowl. I assumed the owner must have walked home, although there was often a strange man in our flat watching TV and holding a tin of Dulux whenever my dad was at work. He didn't like it when I said, 'It's not going to paint itself, is it?'

None of the fun of the fair

It was 1961 when I first discovered my fear of polar bears.

I wasn't travelling in the footpaths of Oates, Scott or Amundsen – attempting to reach the North Pole before tea-time – I was four years old and I was in Battersea. At this early age I'd still not fully received all my cross-tundra training and was shocked to have been accosted by a polar bear in SW11 – well within the Arctic Circle.

At five, and you've not yet played the back end of a pantomime horse attempting to kick-start your thespian career, you can't comprehend that's there's an actual human inside the bearskin.

As well as this new-found fear, it also put me off having taxidermy as a hobby.

The 'polar bear' was one of many attractions at the Battersea Fun Fair. Despite the journey taking only ten minutes from Balham Station, we only went a few times – mainly because of my recently acquired fear of Arctic fauna. Also, the water chute gave me aquaphobia, the helter skelter vertigo and the ghost train enabled me to be a regular, if unwilling visitor, at the Balham branch of Sketchley.

The only place I enjoyed was the small booth (claustrophobia never a problem) in which you could produce a record onto a floppy piece of plastic. My dad and I whistled the theme tune to *Supercar*.

I'd have been Mike Mercury, only I had a fear of flying. Quite coincidental given, to this day, I still look like Joe 90.

You're Not Nicked

I've never stolen anything in my life.

As a kid, the likely reprisals from either parent would have been more daunting than facing a multi-tattooed, hooded torturer in the Tower.

Temptation was certainly there. The pick 'n' mix counter in Balham Woolworths was so near the front of the shop, it might as well have been on the High Road pavement!

But, when I walked past, the kola cubes, pineapple chunks and jelly snakes remained intact. I like to think they stayed this way and almost gathered dust – but this was Balham in the '60s.

My not stealing anything was quite the opposite to my dad; he stole ashtrays – from pubs, restaurants, stately homes. He was a heavy smoker and there was the need (he would say in his defence) for an ashtray in every room. It was like the flat was sponsored: Watney's Lounge, Playboy Club Kitchen and Chartwell Small Toilet.

But the bug never caught on with me. I'd watched *Papillon*, and the thought of spending my days on an island off the coast of French Guiana, kept me from straying.

I also believe, had I started a career of petty crime, I'd have panicked and gone into the wrong shop. Instead of swiping a load of fruit salads from Balham Woolworths, I'd be down the road in Boots, filling my pockets with lipstick, and none of them my colour.

Slopping out time!

Encyclopedia Britannica rules the waves

Back in the day, when google was something you wrote when you'd spelled goggle incorrectly, if you'd needed access to any information, you relied on an encyclopedia.

As a young teenager, I travelled from Balham to Purely (might as well have been Pluto, it seemed so far away) to collect a set of ten 1928 Chambers encyclopedias from my dad's boss. I still have them – there is so much dust on them, it looks like Miss Havisham could be my cleaner.

There are, however, many wonderful colour plates inside and, being nearly 100 years old, some interesting entries: Benito Mussolini, up-and-coming Italian politician; Dodo, flightless bird, in danger if humans ever visit Madagascar. It is also a great place to discover what countries used to be called, showing why you can never find a holiday brochure for German South-West Africa at your travel agent's.

But there are probably many encyclopedias in peoples' houses, perhaps acting as doorstops or being used to create a set of steps if you've mislaid the ladder which gets you into the loft?

And what happened to door-to-door sellers of the *Encyclopedia Britannica*? Are they now trying to path over peoples' drives with old books? I used to feel sorry for the salesman and bought the first once, thus making me capable of only knowing about things if they began with an A or a B. Perhaps they gravitated towards double glazing salesmen? All thirty-two editions of the *Britannica* would certainly cut out a draught.

Next time any of my children/grandchildren ask me anything, I'm getting all ten volumes down, placing them on the floor and telling them the internet's down.

Two pints of Milk of Magnesia, please

Hidden away in a cupboard inside my parents' Balham flat was a large tome entitled *The Home Doctor*. Mum was a hypochondriac, so here were 400 pages of opportunities for imaginary illnesses.

However, growing up – and hiding in the cupboard – in the '60s, I would look at only one of the 400 pages. Towards the end of the book there was a page with a chart detailing all the 'child' illnesses, their incubation period, signs and days of contagion. If it wasn't for the dread of seeing blood, I'd have been a leading paediatrician by the time I was ten!

These were the days before Calpol, Sudafed or Imodium (which sounds like a Roman god).

The '60s alternatives had been invented in the Middle Ages. Two teaspoonfuls of Kaolin & Morphine (forerunners to Bonnie & Clyde) would be enough to make you stay away from any toilet for several months. The precursor to Calpol was gripe water (which tasted like Ouzo – of which we had a lot of in our flat as both parents were fans of the film *Zorba the Greek*) – and contained alcohol, to allow little Johnny to sleep.

If you had a cold, there was no Lemsip – you needed a bowl, a towel, access to boiling water and a few drops of Friar's Balsam; it wouldn't stop your cold, but it'd make sure you stopped moaning about it.

Another horror was Milk of Magnesia – like drinking chalk – and *that's* meant to settle your stomach?

Of course, back then, the most used anaesthetic was cocaine. My dentist was in Clapham and I fear that, should I want some now, rather than going to the grand old house where I went, you probably have to wait outside Clapham Common Station and wait for Stephen Ward to turn up.

In a Binary Bind

Going from primary to secondary school in 1968, while being traumatic enough (small fish, big pond to amoeba, Pacific Ocean, etc. etc.), was made worse by my introduction to 'new maths' – so awful, it would have driven Alan Turing to have given up computing and take up darts.

At my Balham primary school, we'd be given the statement: Janet has six apples, John has five apples – the resulting question would have been: how many apples have they got? At secondary school the questions were: why has the greengrocer's security camera failed? Is Janet a sociopath? Have you translated *Janet & John go shoplifting* into Latin yet?

In my Tooting school in 1968, I was introduced to binary, courtesy of the then three-year-old School Mathematics Project. It sounded (and certainly felt) like it was a dangerous estate just outside Marseille.

There was not a single mention of apples in the book – or any item of fruit for that matter. At my new school there was no bringing in an apple for the teacher – you brought in a book of logarithm tables.

The first thing we learned was the binary system. We learned that two was ten – up until then, for seven years previously, I'd been taught that ten was ten (and had successfully committed this to memory without the visual aid of Bo Derek), and I wonder why I failed maths O level three times on the trot. I'd have got more marks by drawing Carmen Miranda's hat!

Colonel Mustard and cress

The only nature I experienced growing up in the '60s, living between Wandsworth and Tooting Bec Commons, was as I wandered across them identifying (largely unsuccessfully) various flora and fauna. (Until I started learning Latin, I thought Fauna was Flora's brother or a type of small deer).

These days, as an adult, what you did with plants and flowers back then, has changed.

No longer, due to social distancing, can you ascertain whether someone likes butter or not – unless you've a two-metre-long stick with a buttercup stuck on the end.

The moment you own a garden, the thought of blowing off dandelion spores (regardless of whether you want to know the time or not) would be abhorrent – as if you haven't got enough weeds! Also, I'm at that age, and up in the night so frequently, that picking them and thereby running the risk of wetting the bed is largely academic!

When you're older you tend not to throw sycamore leaves into the air and watch them descend, pretending it's a Messerschmitt 109 you've just shot down.

And bending down to pop open a snapdragon's 'mouth' is far too onerous – although, Antirrhinum does sound like something you'd use to stop chafing.

I'd have made more daisy chains, but this was 1960s Wandsworth – not Woodstock.

This afternoon, I'll be making mustard and cress as, over the years, I've collected a lot of old flannels.

Balham's Mrs Malaprop

If you were to ask a young person today to put the wireless on, they'd go into complete panic, thinking the internet had been turned off.

I'm conscious there are many words and phrases we and our parents would say that are no longer in use.

No one rings in work saying they've a bilious attack any more, it's never five and twenty to when telling the time and no one in shops says 'Gawd bless yer' unless they have Hue and Cry on in the background.

I had an elderly great aunt who would impress Balham shopkeepers with the fact that I would go to Karachi every Tuesday evening. I went to karate (in Tooting!). Besides, if I'd missed the connection with the 155 bus, I'd never had made it there and back in an evening to one of Pakistan's major cities!

To guess peoples' ages, you had to know the twenty-times table thoroughly (tomorrow, 5th April 2021, I shall be sixty-four, not three score and four).

And what and when was 'supper'? This is a posh thing, and I would often be asked round to peoples' houses for supper. I'd think, if I wanted a hot, malted drink and a couple of biscuits, I'd prefer to stay in my own house.

And, without wishing to cause offence, the adjective bleedin' (if you've been brought up in SW17, there is not consonant at the end) is now rarely used. It was my mum's favourite word, and I remember coming home from school after the cough 'n' drop test with a card saying I had an 'ascended right testicle'. Mum understood one third of the card and asked why they'd not diagnosed 'bleedin' malnutrition' – double Virol for me that evening.

Anyone got change for a guinea?

Fish with everything

For sixty of my sixty-four years I have eaten fish 'n' chips; high cholesterol precludes me from eating them every Friday these days. The one thing that strikes me is that, certainly over my lifetime, the only thing which has changed is the cost (nothing much for under a shilling). The menu has stayed almost the same.

In Balham and Tooting, we went to three chip shops: The Lighthouse near Tooting Bec station (to eat our chips watching the model railway in the shop next door), the one diagonally opposite the 211 Club (to learn how to say plaice, skate and haddock in Greek), and the one in Chestnut Grove (where I'm sure they'd give discounts to West Ham fans and let them jump the queue). In the latter there was so much memorabilia emanating for '60s Hammers glory – I remember an old matchday programme they had on the wall (next to the gherkins) which had the words and numbers *TSV 1860 München*. I assumed this was the code for the toilet.

For research (and yes, I take writing these weekly ramblings seriously), I looked up the Superfish menu. It could have been from the '60s. The only notable absence was rock salmon (like smoked salmon only whiter, cheaper and covered in more batter). This was a stalwart for us if ever we had a rise in pocket money and a portion of chips wasn't going to suffice.

It's ages since I've been to a chip shop, so I may venture down to one, wearing Greek national costume, with a Billy Bonds shirt on top and ask for six penn'orth of chips and have they got any scraps.

And then wait for the police to arrive. 'Is that large or small cell, son?'

Hello, Matey

Because, these days, you can buy soap which exfoliates, you see fewer pumice stones lying around bathrooms.

The bathroom in my nan's Balham flat had one; she was the relative charged with washing off all the grime I'd accumulated during various playtimes. She'd say my neck looked like the Black Hole of Calcutta. From this I assumed she'd been a missionary in India – in actual fact she had been a waitress in a central London Lyon's Corner House. She did watch a lot of documentaries, though.

No longer do we have to cobble together old bits of soap or have receptacles stopping soap turning from being a solid. Perhaps this was how liquid soap was discovered? Someone who'd lain in the bath for so long, the soap had turned to mush. Archimedes, perhaps? Eureka does sound like the name of a soap – I'd have bought that in the '60s over Lux, Camay or Imperial Leather with its built-in stand. Wright's Coal Tar Soap was only necessary if you had miners as lodgers.

The only time our bathroom accessories changed was just after Christmas, after we'd accumulated enough Bronnley's bath salts to build miniature Pyramids.

Rather than Mr. Matey, Mum would put Fairy Liquid in my bath. It did the job, and my hands were as soft as my face ▢.

Although most bath times I didn't care what was in it; all I wanted to do was sink the *Bismarck*. This is not a euphemism, and nor is it the make of a German soap.

'And don't forget to wash behind your ears, either!' – could never have imagined Karl Dönitz saying that.

Noddy's offside

One thing I miss, whenever I'm eating boiled eggs, is the Noddy eggcup I had, together with its accompanying blue hat with a bell on, to keep the eggs warm.

A kitchen table is probably much changed from mine in my '60s Balham flat.

Gone is the Formica (which looked suspiciously like an old piece of lino) used as a tablecloth, and I bet kitchen tables these days don't tend to have mangles built in underneath (because you're always thinking about wringing out a damp vest when you're tucking into your muesli).

Do people still have novelty cruet sets? My nan's was so old, she had representations of William and Mary on her salt and pepper pots. Those were the days when the sell-by date simply said: 'the end of Pitt the Elder's government'.

The thing which confused me as a kid was when mustard was prepared. It was put into so small a dish and served with so small a spoon I thought the Borrowers were doing the catering.

If you're a football enthusiast, it was important to have a fully stocked kitchen table. Especially if you were to re-enact a spectacular goal you'd seen (or indeed scored for your Cub pack on Tooting Bec Common), you needed as much condiment action on your kitchen table as was possible. You cannot explain the offside rule without the use of a jar of marmalade, a pile of salt and a couple of kippers.

Pass the toast, please, Jeeves.

Slings and the occasional arrow

I was around five, and sitting in my Balham flat, when I had to take a career decision: would I become a sailor or an outlaw?

Weekend afternoon TV in the early '60s had two excellent TV shows: *Sir Francis Drake* and *The Adventures of Robin Hood*.

I would sit, transfixed and inspired, in front of the telly wondering whether a life on the seas would be preferable to a life constantly trying to thwart the Sheriff of Nottingham?

My complete inability to swim and possession of a toy bow and arrow made the decision easier.

I would prowl around the block of flats where I grew up knowing that King John could possibly own one of the maisonettes – I can now assume he never left Runnymede.

I'd have struggled on the Golden Hind. They never had Kwells in the late 16ᵗʰ century, I'm not a massive fan of scurvy and, although I also speak German, I'd struggle in a port-side gift shop as we circumnavigated the globe if they didn't speak either of those two languages.

So, robbing from the rich and giving to the poor would be my *metier*. However, this was Balham in the early '60s – a town not renowned for its billionaires – a place where Elon Musk was thought of as a type of perfume.

So, the new Magna Carta would have to wait to be written, decreeing that no robber baron could live in SW17, and Iceland would remain undiscovered. In the late 16ᵗʰ century, it was still called *Bejam* anyway.

Land ahoy!

Hello, my darlings

I was lucky as a kid, as my dad would frequently take me 'up West' to the pictures and the theatre.

Soon after it was released in 1966, Dad took me to see *The Professionals*.

There were mixed emotions for me during the film: the highlight being when Claudia Cardinale appears – washing topless. This was then followed by mortification, as I realised my dad was sitting next to me! I didn't know, as my nan used to say, whether to laugh, cry, poo (not her actual word) or have breakfast.

On the Tube back, Dad asked which part of the film I liked best? This was probably a trick question; I suddenly became the Northern Line's answer to Barry Norman and suggested that they could have given Lee Marvin more song numbers?

But this world of nudity had peaked far too quickly for me, as Dad and I then travelled to see Charlie Drake in panto – not exactly *Oh! Calcutta!* We then saw *Ice Station Zebra* – no women allowed on board the submarine, let alone any having a wash. Finally, we walked up Balham Hill to the Odeon to watch *Patton* – I was more likely to see Rommel naked in that film then any Hollywood star.

Growing up, I watched TV with my nan. As TV programmes got riskier, there was the ever-increasing chance of seeing some nudity; any desire was soon quashed as Nan would shout at the TV, in a style of a more common version of Mary Whitehouse: 'Get some bleedin' clothes on, love.'

TV or not TV

In the early summer of 1968, I was on the telly.

I wasn't the person on the test card, neither did I feature on *Police 5* and nor did I have my own chat show (producers tend not to give them out to 11-year-olds).

The BBC cameras had caught me at Lord's, watching the visiting Australian cricket team practising in the nets there. I'd travelled there, from Balham, courtesy of a Red Rover ticket, and featured on an item covering the Aussies' arrival on *Sportsnight with Coleman*. I did wait by the phone for many weeks after, as I saw myself as the next Simon Dee.

Sadly, a career in TV was never going to be a possible due to genetics.

After the 1966 World Cup there was an ad in the *Radio Times* inviting people to apply to be the new commentator. My dad applied. Sadly, for him, Motty got the job – and didn't we all know it – especially during *Match of the Day* – as Dad berated the TV screen saying, in the style of Yosser Hughes, that he'd taken his job.

It was also this natural inclination to swearing which brought my dad's audition on *Fifteen to One* to a very abrupt and vituperative ending.

My TV career was ended as soon as it had begun; I'm sure TV executives do an MI5-type search of potential show hosts. Although I guess I should be grateful, as my dad's lack of anger management and extensive swearing vocabulary stopped me from being attacked by an emu.

'Quite remarkable!'

Das Experiment

Nearly 200 years ago, Victor Frankenstein was in his German laboratory creating life; fifty years ago, I was in the kitchen of my Nan's Balham flat hoping to create something more powerful than anthrax.

I never owned a My First Chemistry Set, so my science knowledge was purely self-taught.

I would be allowed to use anything spare in Nan's kitchen, as I created my 'experiment'. Having been given an old milk bottle, and after I'd half-filled it with water, I'd add some Bird's Custard and some pre-Boer War curry powder, and then venture next door to the secret supply of 19th century medicines, hidden behind Nan's cistern.

After several spoons of sulphur, there was Andrew's Liver Salts to be included; they gave my concoction some added fizz as Nan tended to not have much Moët lying around. I also added Timothy White's Lavatory Cleanser – safety first was always a priority – and a sprinkling of Instant Robin Starch to give it a bit of body, not unlike Victor Frankenstein.

However, the *pièce de rèsistance* was Senakot – as if the other combined ingredients weren't going to make you regular enough!

Once my experiment was complete, I needed a willing patient. My great aunt lived next door and, because she smoked forty Embassy before she'd had breakfast, had precious little sense of smell. She was a good sport and pretended to drink some of it; my punishment was to count her Embassy tokens later that week.

With 99.9 per cent of my efforts still intact, we would sell it, in Balham Market, as a deterrent for foxes; something to ward off vampires or a carpet cleaner if you didn't like your existing carpet.

Exterminate

On 21st December 1963, the Daleks first appeared on UK TV.

Such was their popularity (anyone who owned a sink plunger wanted to be one when they grew up), the *Radio Times* ran a competition asking kids to draw and name their own Dalek. I can't remember the prize – probably a promised trip in the TARDIS – the thing which influenced *Honey, I shrunk the kids!*

Dalek drawn, my dad (who worked in advertising so, by default, creative) suggested, 'Ironside' (I spent years thinking Raymond Burr was inside the chief, black Dalek).

I didn't win first prize, but did receive a cardboard kit, so you could create your own model Dalek. As I wasn't allowed scissors until my early twenties, the Dalek remained unconstructed.

I did continue interacting with various TV programmes and collected a copious amount of silver foil for *Blue Peter* – much to my relatives' chagrin. I'd nick the foil protecting their cigarettes inside the packets, whip the tops off milk bottles and steal sixpences and florins to melt down with my Amateur Alchemist kit. My dad smoked so much, he could have created a life-sized guide dog from the insides of one week's fag packets!

My last creative submission was for my school magazine in 1968. I drew a spider so terrifying it has subsequently been removed from all back copies due to protests from the Tooting Tarantula Protection League – the people who believe arachnophobia is a fear of medieval torture.

Pots, pans and sprinkling of rosemary

Growing up in my Balham flat, I didn't exactly share rooms with Fanny and/or Johnnie Craddock. While my mum had many kitchen utensils, she rarely used about 98 per cent of them.

She had a percolator, but this percolated so infrequently that, rather than have a sprinkling of chocolate, you were more likely to receive a smattering of dust on your freshly brewed coffee.

My mother never baked, so the Kenwood Chef might as well have been in Kenwood rather than Balham, although it did make a rather good doorstop – unless you were allergic to meringue, which would sometimes form on the doorknob.

The things which did get the most use, if only by me using them to explain the offside rule to a very disinterested mother, but rather than adding some literal spice to our food, was the collection of brown (everything was brown in kitchens in the '60s) pottery herb and spice containers.

Such was the lack of use, we were more likely to get attacked by Parsley the Lion, weed on by Dill the Dog or assaulted by Bayleaf the Gardener than see any of them in the ingredients at mealtimes.

Mum's *pièce de rèsistance* was her egg 'n' chips; luckily, she never added bergamot!

If you'd have asked her what she liked best about coriander, she'd have said Ena Sharples. Henry VIII was her favourite turmeric and she thought holy Basil was a local priest.

Chive anyone?

Window of opportunity

Car window activity has waxed and waned over the years. There are fewer things happening on car windows; even tax discs have gone.

During the '60s, I would travel in a relatively naked Ford Popular with my parents in and out of Balham with nothing more than 'AUG 64' displayed in the bottom corner of the windscreen.

As things developed, people would add where their car had taken them (we had a sticker proclaiming 'VENTNOR' – I'd have preferred something more exotic like Vienna, Vietnam, the Viking Coastal Station).

People then began adding their names (it was always a couple – having BILLY NO MATES plastered, in a green laminate, across the top of your windscreen, wasn't ideal). You'd walk down the streets and see RENÉE RENATO, BURKE HARE, ADOLF EVA and suchlike adorning the cars.

Behind the names, dangling, would be a pair of furry dice the size of which made them look like they'd come from a Brobdingnagian Monopoly set.

I could never understand the use of a nodding dog (usually an Alsatian) – hardly a deterrent to car thieves.

Furry dice has since been superseded by worry beads (with the state of my driving, I should have a Vatican's worth of rosary beads hanging from my rear-view mirror) or tiny fir trees, like the ones the Borrowers would use at Christmas.

Nowadays you know how many kids people have 'on board', their other car is a Dinky and, if you're Scottish, a sticker saying 'ÉCOSSE', as the French dislike the Scots marginally less than they do the English.

Taxi!

One of the first books I remember reading was Ladybird's *Tootles the Taxi* (an early Dostoyevsky work, I think).

The book included other vehicular stories, aside from Tootles, who, stated in rhyme, why he wasn't going south of the river after 8 p.m. I was a fan of Mickey the Mail Van (he doesn't exist any more as he's been replaced by delivery drivers who send you a text saying you're seventh in the queue, although the sixth is in Truro, so don't hold your breath), as we shared the same name, and Willie the Water Cart, as his name (when you're four) was comedic (although that never quite worked with Willie Whitelaw).

My love of this book was a consequence of going in a taxi, aged two, having had my fingers caught in a Tooting toy shop door jamb. I cried (obviously) but shut up the moment I was in the cab. Luckily, my fingers were saved by a janitor with a couple of old plasters and a needlework kit working at the now defunct Balham hospital, St James' – you wouldn't have trusted any of the doctors there.

In later life I once asked a cab driver if their taxi was called Tootles. I never asked a second time, although I was told, for the best part of an hour, how Mrs Thatcher would have handled COVID.

My next book was Emile Zola's *Thérèse Raquin*, which was a shame, as it put me off boating for life.

The game of the name

You can usually tell a person's age by their name. In the '90s I worked in a hospital shop; my co-worker was called Dorothy – she was about 100.

Because of the success of the *Thomas the Tank Engine* books, published in 1945, many boys were subsequently called Thomas, Gordon or Percy (being called Percy made you tougher at school), although Duck and Fat didn't take off as much.

I would sit in Balham Library in the late '60s devouring these books, wondering why I was called 'Michael'? Had my mum had a visit from an archangel? Did she aspire to buy her underwear at Marks? I so wanted there to be an engine called Michael.

The *Famous Five*, published shortly before *Thomas*, would have had an influence on girls being called Ann or Georgina (the consumption of ginger beer surged during this period too).

With the advent of TV, I wonder how many twins were called Willy and Jenny or Bill and Ben or Ron and Reg (little known characters from *Tales of the Riverbank*)?

When I was born, in 1957, the top girls' names were Susan (90 per cent of our class were called Susan, including a couple of boys), Linda, Christine and Margaret (everyone wants to be called after a princess). Michael was the fourth most popular boys' name, with David, John and Stephen being the top three – all four named after kings – England, Israel and Heaven.

I got off lightly, as modern culture is hugely powerful with children's names. Michael is preferable to Kylie, Peppa or Laa-Laa and, given *The Lone Ranger* was at the height of its fame when I was born, I could easily have been called Tonto.

Welcome map

In 1972, during our fourth year of secondary school, our year were let loose on/in Guildford.

Part of our geography O level course involved studying Ordnance Survey maps and knowing the difference between a Roman *Tumulus* and a motorway (you can't drive a chariot on a motorway).

We were bussed from our school in Tooting and dropped, ostensibly, in the middle of nowhere (if you'd rarely ventured outside SW17, then the outskirts of Guildford *were* the middle of nowhere), armed only with a 1937 O/S map of the South Downs, a compass and a year's supply of chicken paste sandwiches (no one had said it was just an afternoon, so I'd come prepared).

The more astute, but geographically challenged, had brought a French phrasebook – they assumed, like our day trips to France, that Guildford was *the* place to procure flick-knives and lighters with flames so high they scorched most of your fringe. The coach journey was so long, and so far south, many of my fellow pupils thought we'd travelled to Senegal (where the phrasebook certainly would have come in handy).

We were left, with our map, to find our way back to the city centre, remembering everything we'd been taught about contours and railways (disused). Having not paid too much attention during the class we did ask, in very broken (and slow) French, the way to the *Centre Ville* – ironic, given this was nearer Dorking than Dakar. We'd have been better off talking in cockney rhyming slang.

We arrived safely, but disappointed the tourist shops had nothing with which you could start a fire. We did get lots of very small bottles of marmalade and enough Kendal Mint Cake to make us feel nauseous before we'd got to Leatherhead.

Threepenny Bitcoin

I've never owned Bitcoin. I've played bit parts in local am-drams, was an avid subscriber to *Titbits* (I bought it for its gardening tips) and, as a kid, collected threepenny bits, but have not succumbed to the latest fad of cryptocurrencies (itself sounding like something Superman would be allergic to).

I've only just mastered decimal currency, so the last thing I'm going to do is invest in something in the ether (a thing which used to pervade every doctor's surgery).

However, growing up (when Elon Musk was a fragrance and not an entrepreneur) I would devise ways, from the confines of my Balham flat in the '60s, to pay for things without using actual money; ten bob notes were like gold dust back then (although, if they'd been made of gold dust, they'd have been worth a lot more than ten bob).

I would collect all manner of things, hoping I'd invented a new currency: what might the Esso 1970 World Cup star coin of Peter Bonetti be worth down the local newsagent? Could I buy the latest copy of the *Beano* with a kidney donor card? If I pressed enough silver tops off milk bottles together, could I create a sixpence?

Might there have been an opportunity for barter? The complete set of *Thunderbirds* bubble gum cards in exchange for a flock of sheep? This was never going to happen, as I was never given the Freedom of Balham, thus allowing me to walk my sheep over Wandsworth Common.

If I was given some Bitcoin, I'd try to buy the card of Thunderbird 3 going through the Roundhouse (I lied about the set being complete).

Colin the Caterpillar pet

Living in a fourth-floor flat was impractical for keeping most pets.

Goldfish were always an option. I would regularly win one at our Balham school fete. However, the quality was so poor, the fish would invariably have visited that great fish tank in the sky before I'd even got out of the lift on the fourth floor. A fete worth than death ☐.

Because there were large communal gardens in our flats, I would seek out potential pets with the hope of developing a deep bond.

I would often find caterpillars (the bonding lasted between seven and fourteen days due to the evolution the caterpillar goes through).

The (un)natural habitat of the caterpillar is, of course, a matchbox (always many around the house due to my dad being sponsored by Senior Service). Obviously, it needed feeding, so a variety of cabbage leaves were stuffed into the box (saved me having to eat my greens). Friend for life (well, a fortnight, tops).

However, caterpillars grow into moths – which I discovered after opening its matchbox once and seeing it make a beeline for my mum's coats!

I would have to mark the matchbox with a label, 'Mr. Caterpillar', or my mum would take hours trying to light the stove with it.

Lady Lucky peg

I've had a few people tell me my fortune, including one was while I was legging it out of Balham Woolworths when I was a kid.

However, I have sought more professional routes: when I was seventeen, an industrial psychologist told me I should seek a career in hotel and catering. As I assumed all hotels were on the coast, I feared it would bring back an attack of the ague (and other diseases prevalent in the 17th century), plus I can't cook; my guests would soon become disillusioned with nothing to eat but toast (my *pièce de rèsistance*) and an array of broken biscuits on one of my home-made doilies.

As a kid I often bought fortune fishes to tell me my destiny. While they didn't show me which career path to take, they did tell me whether I'd be jealous, indifferent, in love, fickle, false, tired or passionate. As a nine-year-old, I'd had to look up half the words, so tired it was, regardless of the position of the fish.

Most fortune fishes are made in Taiwan – it took me three sets to realise this and become even more tired translating the instructions from its original Cantonese.

I tried it with real fish once (I'd lost my Mandarin/English phrase book) – after a while it remained motionless (it was dead rather than tired, as the explanatory chart said) – it curled up more than the fortune fishes.

These days, if I want my fortune told, I go to the Derby and buy as much lucky heather as I can until I hear what I want to hear: 'In the future you'll be less tired.'

Say goodnight to the folks, Micky

People don't have catchphrases like they used to.

Growing up you'd hear, 'Can I do you now, sir?' – after ITMA stopped, you'd only hear it if you drove, very slowly, up Balham's Bedford Hill. Former resident of my block of flats, Tommy Trinder, would say, 'You lucky people' – that wouldn't be allowed these days, as it's unfair on people who are generally unlucky. You could never say to a cleaner, 'Look at the muck on 'ere,' as they'd probably sue you.

I would also question some of the catchphrases of yesteryear. Did Hughie Green really mean things 'most sincerely'? As long as he got his salary from Rediffusion and didn't get into a fight with the Muscle Man, he probably couldn't give a monkey's.

Columbo episodes may have been shorter had he not had 'just one more thing'. *Hawaii Five-O* showed Steve McGarrett's ability to delegate all the unnecessary admin to Danno. Dick Emery showed, as Gloria, that he/she had a split personality. Harold Steptoe introduced us to the importance of hygiene (albeit in a kitchen sink), Bruce Forsyth to palindromes and Jack Regan to the correct dress sense if being arrested.

Perhaps I just don't watch enough TV these days, but there just don't seem to be as many – or as memorable. Am I bovvered?

Good night, John-Boy.

The goose who cooked in the Golden Egg

With diets having changed over the past decades (back when you thought tofu was a make of Hungarian car), some London eateries no longer exist.

My dad worked in Baker Street. When he grudgingly took part in 'take your son to work' day, we would go the Golden Egg. I'd always have the plaice and chips and, having been brought up in Balham and rarely subjected to any form of nature, I always thought lemons were an eighth of their actual size.

My first job involved me going to Fleet Street twice a day for three months. I would frequent Mick's Cafe most days, as I felt empathy with its name. It's probably now a Starbucks.

In the late '70s I worked in Paddington, where every other restaurant seemed to be a Micky's Fish Bar. Again, unswerving loyalty ensured most days involved some form of fried fish – accompanied by a portion of chips and increasingly higher cholesterol.

Healthier eating means these shops now sell nutrition bars, which taste of wood; this is because 85 per cent of it is made from balsa wood and is invariably made from a recycled Airfix ME109.

Balham, my hometown, had shops which suffered similar fates. The ABC turned into a branch of Abbey National – no good if you wanted an iced bun and a cup of tea, but handy if you needed a mortgage.

And all the bricks from the Lyon's Corner Houses are being used to build the Northern Line extension.

Plaice is off, love.

Overcoming the first hurdle

I've been inspired with the recent Olympics. However, I've never threatened to get a place on the GB Olympic team.

At our Tooting secondary school, we had a term of athletics which would eventually lead to finals day. There was no podium, as the woodwork teacher was rubbish.

I tried the shot put and discus, but struggled to pick the things up, let alone throw them halfway to Tooting Broadway Station. I had even less luck with the javelin, as I nearly created the climax of the Battle of Hastings with my poor aim.

The hurdles were tricky if you wore glasses, as you'd approach the actual hurdle and, with NHS ill-fitting glasses wobbling all over the shop, you'd see several hurdles and invariably hit the wrong one. David Hemery I was not.

I tried to introduce a note from my mum, but such was the ferocity of the PE master, it'd have been less painful impaling myself with one of my more errant javelins.

I could run about 100 yards (these were the days before metres were invented) – but anything more was torture; the cross-country run we'd be sent on was like me taking an urgent message to Marathon.

We had no swimming pool and boxing only occurred when the comprehensive school opposite invaded the rugby pitch separating our two schools. Our school caps offered little protection.

I would've liked to have done tae kwon do but have never been any good at foreign languages.

On your marks …

Pier group pressure

I've been lucky and, for many years, I've holidayed abroad. The past few years, however, have been spent in this country.

It was 1968, as an eleven-year-old, when I travelled abroad for the first time, taking that famous 18th century European travellers' journey from Balham to the Balearics.

But since the last time I was in the UK for a holiday, I noticed many of the things were no longer there.

Try as I might, I could not find a single knobbly knee, glamourous grandad or best pub singer competition to enter (I was never going try out in a beauty contest – I haven't got the legs).

Many of the piers in existence in the early '60s had either caught fire, been hit by the storm in 1987 or had sunk.

There were restrictions should I have wanted to see an 'end of the pier' show – many of the venues required you to bring either your own snorkel, windcheater or extinguisher. And if you have a full deep-sea diver's kit on, then it really would be a slow stroll down the promenade.

This year, the only show on offer was *The Little Mermaid*, but you had to produce a swimming certificate to gain entrance. It was worth it, as Jacques Cousteau was playing Ariel. Red Adair was the prompt.

I was quite skint but fruitlessly scoured the beaches with my *Daily Mirror* looking for Chalky White to claim my £5.

The weather was good, especially if you were either a duck or trying to improve your Gene Kelly impression.

The candy floss man can

Carrying on with my holiday theme, and before we all go back to our chimney sweeping jobs in September, I've been reminded of the singularly unhealthy foods we'd have all eaten on holiday.

I think, looking back, that the stallholders must have been in league with (in my experience) all south London dentists.

I'm talking initially about 'rock'.

Only a struggling dentist could have thought this confection up. A mint-flavoured sweet and 99 per cent guaranteed to break a tooth or at least loosen a filling. The type I would buy, if you cut it in two, would have 'root canal treatment' running through the middle.

Also, candy floss – more addictive than crack cocaine, but slightly more sticky and certainly enough ingredients to make you even more susceptible to gingivitis. The best bit for me was watching it being made – a bit like seeing how a spider spins its web using a time-lapse camera. Actually, I lied; the best bit was eating it and still having most of it round your face several hours later.

But the one thing we eat in the open, only during our holidays, is fish and chips. But if you'd have known the seagulls were going to have such an absence of fear, you'd have bought two portions!

So, tooth decay, diabetes and high cholesterol – highlights from summer holidays gone by – and that's before you've bought the mandatory postcards.

Are we nearly at the pub which sells Double Diamond yet?

Key Balham

I was brought up in a block of flats in south-west London with various relatives.

I lived one floor away from my Nan, but was trusted to go back and forth, on my own, from my flat to hers.

I was also entrusted with a key: three times. Such was the ease with which I lost each passkey, I was finally never assigned another – three keys and you're out.

So, my Nan taught me how to break into the flats.

This was the same woman who'd told me she'd been a waitress at a Lyon's Corner House, when, clearly, she must have been breaking and entering throughout the '50s.

All I needed, she instructed, were very thin wrists (easily done as I didn't 'eat enough to keep a fly alive'), a belt (which I owned, despite my daily intake of Virol) and knowledge of the outer workings of a doorknob.

I was taught to put my wrists and belt through the letterbox, above which was the knob, attach the belt, get some traction and – *Open Sesame* – I was in.

As Balham's answer to *Raffles* of *Arsène Lupin*, I was able to get into Nan's flat.

With this success, literally under my belt, I thought I'd try it out next door – where my aunt lived.

I assumed she'd be counting her trillion Embassy coupons but, unbeknown to me, she was getting dressed. Successfully in her flat, I revealed myself, only to find my aunt peroxiding her hair – dressed only in her industrial bra and panties.

When you're only ten, there are some things you simply cannot unsee.

It is the sole reason I've never became a hairdresser.

Paderborn Calling

In the '60s and '70s I lived in a block of flats in Balham which had radios built into the wall.

My Nan, whenever she went out, would leave the radio (or wireless as she called it) on, to give the impression (mainly to potential burglars) that someone was at home. One Yale, two Chubbs and an assortment of chains you'd not find at Fort Knox was clearly not enough for peace of mind.

In my view, some background noise works as a far greater deterrent than others.

If you want to discourage burglars, then have 'Mother of mine', 'There's no one quite like grandma' or anything by Reginald Dixon on a continual loop blaring out. These will work like the thing you put in your garden to ward off foxes.

Playing anything by Mahler will make the burglar believe you're about to top yourself and won't want to engage in conversation.

At weekends, any burglar hearing *Two-Way Family Favourites* will assume you have a relative based in West Germany and therefore will seek reprisals when home on leave. Or you have Judith Chalmers held captive.

Back in the '60s the option was the Light, Home Service or Third Programme – so your burglar prevention could include *Music While You Work*, something involving Dame Isobel Barnett or sixteen hours of *The Ring Cycle*. It depended on how valuable your cigarette card collection was.

Nowadays you can simply say, 'Alexa, play something which'll frighten burglars.'

Poles apart

FDR once said, 'We have nothing to fear but fear itself.' Growing up and being pushed in a buggy across Wandsworth Common in the early '60s, I developed a pathological and irrational fear for one particular telegraph pole.

I've since acquired other fears: birds. It's why Rod Taylor got the lead in the Hitchcock classic. And thunder: if God had furniture, because He is God, He'd have someone move it around for Him. Quietly.

There was a cafe on Wandsworth Common, in front of which stood this odd-looking (in my mind) telegraph pole. I could not go past it without shouting, screaming and, literally, throwing my toys out of the pram (Sooty never got so dirty than on these trips). My perambulating relatives never reached the cafe as I believed I would be sucked into some electrical void, ending up inside an Earl Grey tea bag in the cafe's industrial tea urn.

On my way to the cafe, we'd pass hundreds of other telegraph poles, but this one, in front of the cafe, had at its top these two eye-like things – the shape of which could have been modelled by Charles Laughton for his screen test for *The Hunchback of Notre Dame,* or something Picasso would have created on a bad day.

This fear may have been the reason I never applied to be a BT engineer (also I haven't got a head for heights) and, because the Wandsworth Common tennis courts were behind the cafe, was another reason why I never became Balham's answer to Emma Raducanu.

Never a crossword

'Hot beverage' (three letters)?

You didn't have to be Alan Turing to be able to complete the *Evening News* crossword.

In the '60s, the evening paper would be delivered to our south London flats. I'd be given the page containing all the puzzles – including the children's picture crossword. (This was easier, as I didn't drink tea or any hot beverages!)

It was here that I learned how to identify a cat (the no-pet policy in the flats made that trickier than you'd think) and how to spell it.

I'd have tackled the grown ups' cryptic crossword, except my knowledge of Greek mythology lets me down. I think Hermes sell expensive scarves, Apollo took people to the Moon and Athena is where you went to get a picture of a woman scratching her arse.

After solving all the picture clues, I'd move on to 'spot the ball'. I never won, and assume the players chosen to feature in the competition had dreadful eyesight and simply had a guess where the ball might be before they tried to head, kick or punch it if they were Gordon Banks, Gordon West or Gordon the Big Engine – such was the difficulty of this prediction.

I miss the evening paper, as I rarely commute – so I struggle to see where can I get the result of today's 3.30 at Newmarket or find out the latest County Championship scores?

Hot beverage is off, love.

Five ages of slippers …

The slipper is an item of clothing, like that of a medieval chastity belt, which can bring pleasure or pain.

One of my favourite shoes, bought at *Clark's* in Tooting in the early '60s, was a pair of slippers, not only with Noddy's head on each foot, but also sporting a bell.

As an adolescent, you'd not admit you wore slippers in case a prospective girlfriend asked who was on them – answering 'Willy Wombat' didn't necessarily lead to a successful courtship.

One particular slipper at my secondary school took on a very sadistic form; the geography teacher would employ it should you get signs on an O/S map wrong, failed to draw an acceptably accurate ox-bow lake or forgot a South American capital city.

I played five-a-side once with a Geordie friend of mine. After the invitation to play, he asked, 'Shall I bring my slippers?' My instant reaction to this Tyneside approach to football, not knowing he meant his trainers, was if I wore my slippers, they'd likely slip off. Also, the bells would be in danger the moment I made contact with the ball. Top half Gerd Müller, bottom half, Noddy – not a good look or feel.

I've never owned a dog, as they savage slippers like they do tins of Winalot and, most likely, would take half my foot off – fine if you want to be the next Fred Titmus.

I'm now at that age where slippers are essential footwear. And, as I sit, wearing them by the fireside, rereading my *Noddy* books, I'd have a pipe on, only I'd look like one of the women who hung around the foot of the guillotine, although many would have had more teeth.

Anthromorphic Powder

Growing up in south-west London in the '60s didn't offer much guidance on nature and wildlife.

I was, therefore, confused, having watched Billy Smart's circus one wet bank holiday, as to how Terry Hall got Lenny the Lion to be so docile. No stool, no whip and, ostensibly, only one arm. Probably no bad thing I never went on safari as a child – who knows what damage I'd incur with an innocent, wandering hand!

Also on TV, accompanying Wally Whyton (how 'The wheels on the bus' was never used as a Eurovision entry still amazes me), was Ollie Beak. Before watching this, I'd assumed owls, a) lived in trees and not in guitar cases; b) didn't speak – 'twit' and 'twoo' aren't real words and. I also wondered if all owls become Brownie leaders the moment they reached adulthood?

I'd worked out that cartoons were not based on real life (except *The Flintstones*, obviously, because I studied cavemen at primary school – plus I've been to Cheddar Gorge). Mister Ed? I rest my case.

But, as a child, these creatures were real to me; it wasn't until I was in my second year at agricultural college that I realised that Pinky and Perky weren't actual pigs. I'm not afraid of the big, bad wolf either.

No time to … go to the toilet

I've just been to the pictures for the first time since 1970. If I'd have known the film was going to last two and a half hours, I'd have taken a couple of empty Lucozade bottles (if it's good enough for Sir Alex Ferguson …).

The cinema was much smaller than I remember (although I was much smaller in 1970) – it was like being in my lounge only with more flock wallpaper and fewer abandoned copies of *Woman's Weekly* (I get it for the cricket coverage).

The seat wasn't as sticky as it had been in 1970 in the Tooting Granada watching *Tora! Tora! Tora!* with two other people and an ice-cream girl, who looked a bit like Admiral Tojo – this was more like being in a DFS commercial!

There was no intermission – I could have murdered a tub halfway through. The upside was that I was, during the entire film, neither pelted by a full carton of Kia-Ora nor a Jubbly.

I was disappointed not to have seen Ursula Andress or, before the main film started, a travelogue, a documentary about splitting the atom or an episode of *Emil and the Detectives* (I'd willingly pay the best part of £10 to see groups of people chasing one another through 1930s Berlin).

In the cinema there were no usherettes – people have torches on their phones these days, I assume?

But I did get out before the national anthem and Reginald Dixon started up again.

A Trill a Minute

I've developed a fear of birds.

As a child I'd be taken to Trafalgar Square, bought threepenny's worth of bird seed and put in the middle of Sir Edwin Landseer's lions to be savaged by more birds than Burt Lancaster.

No fear – just a higher-than-normal dry-cleaning bill.

Years later, I'd cross over roads like the people who'd walked past before the Good Samaritan to avoid any pigeons, such was my avian terror.

In the '60s and '70s I'd play football on Wandsworth Common and call for a mate *en route*. He owned a budgie (he'd actually owned several, except his myopic dad would invariably tread on them, although he would secretly replace them with ones with totally different colouring).

If my mate wasn't ready, I'd have to wait and sit in the kitchen, where the family did 99 per cent of their activities – and where the budgie was caged. Because the family's favourite film was *Born Free*, the budgie was encouraged to fly around.

Budgies sense pathological fear (and hate).

In my mind's eye, this budgie was as threatening as a pterodactyl and would make a beeline (or budgieline in this case) for me as if I were a giant cuttlefish or had Trill in my hair.

Such is my fear these days that, if I ever visit anyone, I have to ask: 'Are there any small mirrors with tiny bells in this house?' I've also stopped watching any TV series involving Adam Faith.

Windmills of my mind

Half-term activities are different now to the '60s and '70s when I was at school.

Growing up, I'd often be seen running up and down Balham High Road with my hoop and a stick.

But the activity which has stood the test of time is crazy golf. During school holidays, mere mortals and their children and grandchildren mentally turn into Tiger Woods – without the lack of driving skills, or sex addiction, one would hope.

As a young teenager I honed my golf skills at Morden Pitch 'n' Putt and have played regularly since.

However long you've been playing, these skills become academic on a crazy golf circuit.

Even if the putter they give you (and skanky old ball) had a grip and was the right size, your putting ability (and any innate golfing talent you may possess) goes out the window. However, if people know you play, there is added pressure. But why should this be? At my course, south of south London, the opening hole is 551 yards – you need more than an antique putter to get you close if you're to get the required par five. Plus, the ball would probably disintegrate before you've even got close to the green.

The other fundamental difference between crazy golf and my local golf course? There's no massive clown's mouth ready to gobble up your Pro V1 golf ball, there is no giant windmill in the middle of the fairway and, although you can hear the A217, there is the complete absence of dinosaurs roaring.

Horsing around

I knew I was destined never to become a professional actor when, after my first audition for the local am-dram society, I was offered the part of the front end of a pantomime horse. On reflection, I realise that this wasn't (actually) starting at the very bottom.

The disadvantages of this are that you have no lines (just the odd whinny and comedic shake of your mane), there's no chance of being spotted by talent scouts and it's tricky signing autographs, as hooves aren't renowned for gripping writing implements.

I was determined to make the most of it, and introduced method acting into my theatrical learning.

I'd spend a lot of time watching episodes of *Mr Ed*, eating hay and trotting, like Arkle, up and down Balham High Road. I'd have popped into the local Sainsbury's, but they had a no-horse-allowed policy. Ironic, really, given that Princess Anne had actually opened the store – and if any member of the royal family is half-horse, half-princess, it's her.

Due to work commitments, allergy to stage make-up and metaphorically being sent to the acting glue factory, my 'career' was short-lived.

If I hadn't given this up, we would never have witnessed the greatest acting talent to come out of Tooting – Neil Pearson – treading the boards. There was only room for one thespian in SW17 in the mid-70s.

Knock Me Down with a Feather

It's 100 years since the first public telephone kiosk was introduced in the UK.

If any of the original booths had one of those sheets on the wall stating when they were last cleaned, they'd probably say '1922'.

In my Balham block of flats, we had the use of two public phone booths; I have nothing but bad memories of them.

The phones were just outside the dairy which operated within our flats. I remember once summoning up the courage to ring a girl, walking up and down for nearly an hour besides the two phones, going, via the dairy and unnecessarily buying a pint of milk, carton of yogurt and three rashers of bacon, only to be told she thought my friend Trevor was funnier.

There were also phone booths in Balham High Road.

I would often go in them hoping to find some odd coins previous callers had forgotten to collect. I'd also look up my number in the L-R directory (and to find Trevor's number to get some better gags) and, as a teenager, wondered why so many women had left their business cards – most of them promoting French lessons – futile for me, as I was learning Latin. Plus, they all seemed to be called Delores, which was quite exotic for 1970s SW17.

Once, when looking for coins, the phone actually rang. I answered and was asked if I worked for MI5, I replied that I didn't and wasn't a fan of pre-pack furniture.

And, as Trevor's girlfriend said, don't ring us …

Two pints of lager and …

Although introduced into the UK in 1957, flavoured crisps only became popular a decade later.

I remember when, to paraphrase Henry Ford, 'You can have any flavour you like as long as it's ready salted'.

Unscrewing the tiny blue bag of salt was often painful if you'd a paper cut you weren't aware of and suddenly had what felt like a cat o' nine tails over your hand.

Golden Wonder introduced smoky bacon, which was quickly rivalled by Smith's gammon flavoured crisps. When I first saw this, I assumed that, rather than a small bag of salt inside, there'd be a slice of pineapple or a fried egg instead.

Very soon the world's food ingredients would be found inside one solitary crisp packet:

I could be inside my Balham flat and allow Chipitos to culinarily transport me to Mexico; Monster Munch to Transylvania and anything containing prawn cocktail to a sophisticated restaurant in the West End. Well, this was the '70s ☐.

But having prawn cocktail and steak and onion crisps was almost like having a proper meal; I'm surprised they've never introduced Black Forest gateau flavour to literally cater for all three courses.

But, for me, the worst thing was Tudor Crisps' pickled onion flavour. They'd blow your head off – ironically, something not uncommon in Tudor times.

Mere bagatelle

If you asked anyone of my generation what *Minecraft* was, they'd probably say it's something decorative made out of coal you'd put on a mantelpiece. For those without grandchildren, it is a computer game.

In the '60s growing up, a computer was as big as a house, and you only saw one if you lived next door to Alan Turing.

One of the things which entertained me indoors was a bagatelle board. If you were to describe it – a wooden slab, full of nails, splinters and with ball bearings hit viciously with a wooden stick – it sounds more like medieval torture than a schoolboy pastime.

A good Balham primary school mate had one and, because neither of us had school dinners (both had allergies to caterpillars – which were prevalent within the salads), we'd play most lunchtimes. I think we both secretly hoped we'd have an international bagatelle scout come and watch us. This was unlikely, as my mate always kept his bedroom door shut – plus, we'd been warned at a very early age to look out for bagatelle scouts.

We also had a shove halfpenny board but, after decimalisation in February 1971, frantically stowed it away in case the Inland Revenue came to our flat looking for illegal currency.

Penny up the wall anyone?

Roy Wood, would you?

You could have been on Mars for several years and returned, not knowing what day it was, until you walked into a shop only to hear Mariah Carey's 'All I want for Christmas is you' and know it was approaching Christmas – or, in some shops, early October.

It seems that Christmas music being played in shops is introduced ever earlier – it does beg the Band Aid question, do they know it's Christmas?

I'm not sure, while looking for the mandatory bath salts for my mum, that I want Noddy Holder screaming at me. Nor do I need to be reminded of the unnecessarily long car journey Chris Rea's embarking on – move house, Chris! Or, get an Uber.

Would I, as Roy Wood might suggest, wish it could be Christmas every day? No, as, a) I'd be skint and, b) there isn't a factory providing an infinite amount of bath salts that's yet been built.

I'd happily rock around the clock with Brenda Lee, except I've developed *plantar fasciitis* – which is not the Latin for cactus.

It's handy, if you're looking for a row at Christmas, to know all the lyrics to the Pogues' Christmas offering; if this is the case then 'Step into Christmas' would be renamed 'Step outside'.

And Dean Martin's 'Let it snow, let it snow, let it snow' would have been banned by the BBC in 1962.

No levels

I failed most of my O levels because I listened to far too much music, although I did think it would help with my revision.

Listening to The O'Jays' 'Love Train' – as they mentioned England, Russia, China, Africa, Egypt and Israel (too) – would have been helpful had I not been meant to be revising the physical landscape of Canada.

Learning the very descriptive lyrics to Boney M's 'Rasputin' would have been constructive had I not had a series of questions about Gladstone and Disraeli during my history exam.

I knew little about trigonometry and knew even less after constantly listening to Barry Manilow's 'Bermuda Triangle'.

A favourite song to listen to was Jane Birkin's 'Je t'aime' – again a waste of time, as the question with the highest marks was: 'Write to your pen friend in Antibes about your summer job'. Had I worked as a high-class prostitute, I'd have got full marks. It did help a bit with biology, though.

I feel I could have done even better with science should My Chemical Romance have been around.

The set work for music was 'Ceremony of Carols'. This, I discovered when the results were out, was by Benjamin Britten and not, as I'd written, Neil Sedaka.

However, I do know what a slide rule is for: it is for neatly underlining your name, date and subject of your exam. Also, as this was the summer of '73 (almost another good song), you could use it to swat away flies – although this was Clapham, not Rwanda.

You can turn your papers over now.

Annuals of history

Every Christmas during the '60s I would be given – alongside two tangerines, a handful of walnuts and two packets of last year's dates – the mandatory annual.

Which subject would my parents choose? Had they been listening to me throughout the year to get a feel for what I was interested in?

As, for several years on the trot, I received the *Rupert* annual, they clearly hadn't. Unless they thought I was a secret *Daily Express* reader, I was always slightly disappointed. I didn't possess a matching distasteful yellow scarf and trousers – if I had been posher, I might have, but this was Balham in the '60s, so that was never happening.

I'd have liked to have got the first edition, published in 1936, featuring stories where Rupert trains with Jesse Owens and Hitler invades Nutwood, with the pretence that there were German speakers living there.

After a while of the annuals still being in pristine condition the following December, my parents changed tack.

The *Coronation Street* annual was never the same after 1964, as it no longer featured pictures of Martha Longhurst.

I was thrilled, in 1967, to get *The Man from U.N.C.L.E.* annual – I'd always wanted to be Illya Kuryakin and had, as a teenager, an interest in east European female gymnasts.

My parental procurement of my annual annual stopped in 1972. Aged fifteen, you really don't want your mates coming round to your place and seeing *The Clangers* annual taking pride of place on your bookcase.

There were some great soup recipes inside, though.

Burn Baby Burn; Honda Inferno

Comment [BE]: 'and' shouldn't follow a semicolon.

It was, in the mid-seventies, standing, in the pouring rain, next to my burned-out motorbike on Clapham High Street, as the local fire brigade extinguished the sparks emitting from my bike's electrics, when I realised that I'm a salesman's dream.

I had bought this "second-hand" bike from a dealership in Tooting some months before Clapham's answer to *Towering Inferno*; the sign saying "one previous owner – vicar's wife" – had got my attention. I can only assume the vicar's wife's husband has since been defrocked, as the 11th Commandment stipulates: "Thou shalt not lie about the mileage."

But these salesmen see me coming. I think it may be the fluorescent light – invisible only to me – above my head, which says "MUG" the moment I walk into any vehicle sales room.

The eternal fear of not wanting to get my hands dirty (I'd never take a throw-in at football) would ensure my blissful and complete lack of awareness of any form of car/bike maintenance. If you'd asked me, aged sixteen, when first allowed a motorised vehicle, "What is a spark plug?", I'd have suggested he was a puppet who had a magic piano.

In trying to buy my first moped, the salesman was so crafty, before I knew it, he'd sold me a Cortina – and I'd never even been to the Dolomites!

Cold Cuts

I wonder when people stopped having larders?

My nan's Balham flat had one, as she didn't have a fridge.

Electric refrigerators were invented in 1913, but she didn't like anything newfangled, and if larders were good enough for the cast of *Upstairs, Downstairs*, who was my nan not to have one?

What she did have was a room, which remained permanently cold, inside which was a small cupboard, with netting on the front (probably to ward off foxes – animals renowned for scaling three storeys). Inside the cupboard was milk, butter and a life-size cardboard cut-out of Captain Oates.

The other ingredients of the cold cupboard were cold meats, many of which were leftovers from whichever Sunday roast we'd had.

However, one meat product I could never understand which dwelt in the larder was tongue. I don't remember having roast tongue hot on a Sunday. Was tongue cold lamb? Which animal did it come from: cow, sheep, aardvark?

My nan would serve it with mash. Well, I say mash. While I'm no culinary expert, I rather assume that mash only becomes mash after more than three pumps with an implement which wouldn't have looked out of place at a medieval jousting tournament?

Although sometimes I'd wake from a nightmare when some aged relative had asked "have you lost your tongue?" – I had a vision it was in my nan's larder, resting next to a beetroot.

Flush with Mornay

Within her Balham flat, my nan had an inside toilet.

An outside toilet would have been, three floors up, singularly impractical. Also, her sense of balance was poor, and she constantly refused abseiling lessons.

My nan's toilet did suggest many a mystery: did every old person's toilet always contain a tin of pre-war talc, smelling salts (you didn't sniff those by accident twice) and an empty bottle of 4711 eau de cologne? I often wondered whether eau de cologne was some form of Franco–German mouthwash?

Which leads directly on to, and begs the question: who on earth came up with "toilet water"? Not even *eau de toilette* lightens the thought of popping something behind your ear which smells like Harpic. I assume the "before" toilet water is more expensive than the "after" version?
☐

Did this idea come from people escaping from revolutionary France armed only with a secret selection of toilet ducks containing toilet water? And what marketing whizz suggested calling it that?

However, it was in this "smallest room" that it was determined why I'd never become a plumber: within the cistern, my nan explained, was the ballcock, which helped the actual toilet function.

When you're eight and prone to giggling at comedic words, I felt my credibility would be blown as a professional plumber should I ever have to utter the words: "I think it's your ballcock, love."

Comment [BE]: A popularised term now, so no italics.

Comment [BE]: QUERY: Please check. There seems to be missing text.

A Not Very Alive Fishy, on a Little Dishy

When you left a school fete, which I did during many a summer from my Balham and Tooting schools, the very least you'd want to leave with was a goldfish. Or a coconut – although, in most of the fetes I attended, the coconuts tended to live longer.

You'd take your prize-winning goldfish home, in its plastic bag, only to establish that your flat was a flat, not an aquarium, and thus not set up for any form of aquatic creature.

You would leg it to the local pet shop where, when you mentioned your plight, you discovered the overnight increase in the cost of fish tanks had far outpaced the rate of inflation for the past two decades!

In addition to the tank (you had the water, which, if you didn't, the pet shop owner would have willingly sold you some with a price similar to that of petrol in the early '70s), you'd be flogged daphnia and hydra (which were neither great-aunts you'd long forgotten nor a US detective team). But, the pet shop salesman wouldn't have done his job if he'd not sold you a pretend deep-sea diver.

Fish have a memory span of four seconds, but why a deep-sea diver? Make them feel at home? No, because they are freshwater fish, and few make it to the depths of the Mariana Trench.

If I was to get a goldfish now, I'd have a replica of the *Mary Rose*, a book to improve memory loss and a statue of Johnny Weissmüller to stop the fish from slacking.

You Batter Beware

Comment [BE]: QUERY: Do you mean 'chipped'?

Before Red Bull was invented, I had a great-aunt who would send me on my way to work fuelled by toast – with the entire contents of the local Tate & Lyle factory sprinkled on top. I think she was in league with the local dentist.

I look back to my family's answers to Fanny Cradock with horror and think of the things they got me to eat.

My nan would cock for me each morning, as my mum often had one of her "heads". She wasn't content with frying eggs, bacon and sausage; her next thoughts would be: why not soak up the fat with a slice of bread? Because making toast involved a giant fork, a one-bar fire and a week's wait, I could understand her reticence.

On Sundays, my nan would cook giant Yorkshire puddings. My dad could have some cold, with jam on, the next day – was Angel Delight a banned substance in early-60s SW17?

So, before my family were sponsored by Statins (surprise, surprise), the thing I remember being adored, like some demigod, was dripping. The thing sounds like a medieval torture. The evidence would sit in some old cup (the more chopped, the better) – these days it would have a hazard sign on it; there certainly wasn't a sell-by date to be seen!

I'm still surprised I wasn't, as a youngster, offered it – with sugar liberally dusted over it, obviously!

Another crisp sandwich, vicar?

Bang Bang

There are clearly more small motorbikes on the road than there were fifty years ago. Without buying a back copy of *Motorcycle News* from 1972 to prove it, I just know.

Many of these motorbike owners gather outside various food establishments, like something out of *The Birds*, waiting for their order to take something in a polystyrene box to someone very hungry. Or very lazy. Or both. You half expect Tippi Hedren to tentatively come out of the local KFC, only to be cajoled by waiting bike riders randomly shouting out items of fast food.

These riders are mounting the 2022 equivalent of the Honda 50 (a bike many of us probably had, to enable us to pass the bike test or appear in a very poor sequel to *Quadrophenia*).

Fifty years ago these riders weren't leaving McDonald's or Burger King, together with their produce – they were learning 'The Knowledge'. As a kid, when I got my first moped, I'd pretend I was doing it too – memorising every Balham street in case my plans of going into advertising failed. I imagined being able to talk loudly to people behind me about "if Mrs Thatcher were alive, we'd have never got into this mess".

Nowadays, if you randomly stopped a bike rider, they'd not be able to tell you the quickest route to Charing Cross Station, but they would be able to hand over a bucket of bang bang chicken and chips.

I am the Queen of Sheba

"Well, I'll go to the foot of our stairs," my nan would exclaim in abject horror of something I'd done. Given she lived in a one-storey Balham flat, I wondered if this was physically possible? Was there a secret tunnel which led to the other side of the high street? Did she own some collapsible stairs? Was there an emergency carpenter as a lodger?

Either way, it leads me to things people said years ago but rarely heard these days.

She clearly had tremendous powers as, if I pulled a face, she would tell me if the wind changed, I'd stay like that; I was never going to run the risk of having my tongue permanently on show the moment the levels of the Beaufort scale rose.

She was obviously unaware of the abolition of slavery, as she'd often ask what my last slave had died of?

My nan clearly never did history at school, as the retort to any of my many lies – "Yes, and I'm the Queen of Sheba" – was clearly inaccurate. My nan was old and had no teeth, but she was neither 3,000, Arabic (she was from Clapham) nor royalty!

Cat's got your tongue? Well, of course not, as we don't possess any pets.

Given that time travel doesn't exist, it would be hard, unless you're Superman or Dr Who, to knock someone into the middle of next week.

Unless you've a 120-year-old greengrocer, you're unlikely to hear "much obliged", "thanking you" or "that'll be tuppence, three farthings, love".

Gertcha!

The Pools Boy

Every week I'd do the pools. Well, I didn't, but my nan did. I was her expert adviser.

We'd sit in her Balham flat, and she'd have a pen, a Player's *Weight* having out of the side of her mouth and a selection of farthings. I'd have a copy of *Charles Buchan's Football Monthly.*

As Jimmy Hill used to live in our block of flats, we felt the gods were with us — assuming the gods had a pointy beard (which, in hindsight, is more like the Devil).

I'd played football for the school team, had a subscription to *Shoot* and several decent players in my youth were called "Mick", so, for some reason, my nan thought I had some magical insight. She never scooped the potential million on offer; I was more orifice than oracle.

My nan would ask if I thought St Mirren might be good for a score draw? I didn't have the heart to tell her that a) I didn't even know who, what or where St Mirren was, and b) wasn't she the patron saint of reflective glass, anyway, so unlikely to be a footballer?

We would watch *Grandstand* on a Saturday afternoon — having turned over from watching Kendo Nagasaki being goaded by Jackie Pallo — and listen to the intonation of the score announcer's results and his slight delay if it was a score draw.

Every week we'd be praying that the same inflection would only be used on the eight games of the boxes we'd ticked.

If that happened, we'd be millionaires, nan. □

A tea towel is not just for washing up

Whenever I'm doing the washing-up, I'm immediately transported back to Shanklin.

My family were obsessed, regardless of the quality of the holiday, with buying a tea towel denoting the resort they had visited.

Not for them bringing me back a bottle of wine, a straw donkey or a stick of rock – I got a tea towel.

For me, who didn't do a lot of washing-up as a kid in our Balham flat, it was only useful if I wanted to look like a member of the PLO. Although, I'm quite sure Yasser Arafat didn't wear a headdress with tourist attractions of Ventnor plastered all over it.

People would come round for dinner with my parents and would help with the washing-up. They'd spot my mum's tea towel she'd brought back from a holiday in the Balearic Islands in 1968.

"How was Majorca?"

"Didn't see much of it. I had gastroenteritis the entire fortnight."

Still, good to feel nauseous every time you picked up a tea towel with a map of Alcúdia on it.

Visiting National Trust places was the same: it would have been great to have received a bar of Kendal Mint Cake or some fudge, with the stately home emblazoned on the wrapper. No, I'd get a tea towel of Polesden Lacey.

I didn't really want a tea towel from Cliveden, either – I'd have preferred Mandy Rice-Davies to come round and help me with my biology homework.

Well, I would do, wouldn't I?

Cutting the Mustard

I think my maternal nan had lodgers. I think they were the Borrowers.

Every Sunday I'd walk, with my parents, down one flight of stairs in our Balham flats, to lunch at my nan's.

Everything was laid out on the table. The roast was brought in, then the condiments: salt, pepper, and this is where my suspicions were alerted, a very small bowl, full of mustard, plus an even smaller, exceptionally tiny, tiny spoon!

All through lunch I'd be looking around at cracks in the skirting board for any evidence of stunted human life.

I assumed the Borrowers didn't have Sunday lunch. Was this part of the rental agreement with my nan – you can live here, but we want your spoons every Sunday? Did the size of the spoon affect the taste of the mustard? Did the Borrowers insist, as part of this bartering system, on it being *Colman's* own brand and not some muck from Dijon?

My nan had an old Crimplene house coat she'd wear permanently. It had two pockets: one would store the sprouts I'd not eaten, having deflected my parents' attention before whipping them off my plate; the other might have the Borrowers' bedroom?

My paternal nan also had tiny spoons. Whenever I'd make the journey to Marylebone to see her, dessert was always served with a tiny spoon with "LCC" on it. Perhaps another side of the Borrowers family lived there – a family of kleptomaniacs who stole from local council offices?

Keeping abreast of things

Like me, my dad was in advertising.

His speciality was industrial advertising; most of his clients' ads appeared in magazines like *What's New in Hydrocarbon Processing* – he would read it for its gardening tips.

He would often bring these magazines home – they often had riveting articles about heating, ventilating *and* riveting promoted on the front covers.

So, when I found a copy of *Playboy* in a dark cupboard in our Balham flat, I was very confused.

Had Dad won a bra advertising account? Was this research? Was one of the "contributors" going to feature in one of my dad's ads?

I'd never before seen an ad which featured a naked woman holding up a tunnel support.

My next question was why this magazine was in the cupboard and not lying on our coffee table alongside the *Radio Times* or *Woman's Own*? Or my *Beano*?

Because as a ten-year-old I wanted to follow my dad into advertising, I thought I'd do my own research.

I was *researching* away when my mum found me in the darkened cupboard.

"You really shouldn't be looking at magazines featuring ladies' bare breasts, Michael."

"Bare breasts, Mother?" I replied. "I'd not noticed; I was reading the very well-written, in-depth articles."

She took the magazine away, probably to be used as a rolling pin later that evening on my dad, muttering, "No bleedin' wonder you're always having to go to the opticians!"

Sling and Arrow

In 1972, in the fourth year of my Tooting grammar school, we had a term of learning first aid.

A few lessons of Latin and suddenly everyone thought they could be a doctor.

Sadly, we were so badly behaved in those eight weeks, the only thing we learned was how to make a sling.

Broken leg, typhus, West Nile fever? We'd have been quite hopeless – unless any of those conditions could have been cured using an old Cub scarf.

These days, most homes will have sophisticated first aid kits. With the contents, you could carry out minor operations – although you'd have to keep your work surfaces clean and clear.

Growing up in the '60s, if your ailment wasn't treatable with Germolene, Friar's Balsam or three miles of lint, you'd be put on the cart the moment it entered your street.

If you broke a limb playing sport at school, the deranged PE master would say you had another one. The school first aid kit consisted of a sponge, a bucket filled with water from the River Wandle and a junior hacksaw from the metalwork classroom, should anyone have gangrene before the master put them on the 155 bus home.

To paraphrase Robert Duvall, "I love the smell of calamine lotion in the morning."

Having a Butcher's

Nicknames can be a cruel thing.

I wasn't wonderfully grateful to Gerry or Sylvia Anderson introducing the British public to *Joe 90* the moment I entered my second year at secondary school! If only I'd had his magic glasses – I could have suddenly sworn in Russian to the boys in the playground who likened me to the string puppet!

But it was the school holidays which were the most ignominious.

My mum would insist on dragging me the length and breadth of Balham High Street, introducing me to numerous shopkeepers as her "little Mickey Mouse". When you're ten or eleven, and you're first contemplating asserting your masculinity, you really don't want your mum referring to you as a cartoon rodent!

As if being mistaken for her younger brother wasn't embarrassing enough, mum was stunning. She couldn't add up or spell but had certain assets which were seemingly very attractive to the male shopkeepers of SW12.

We'd visit various butchers, where the staff were excellent examples of the fare they were selling, as their arms looked like giant hams.

Because we rarely had much money, juggling her housekeeping would involve me adding up various items of meat. This was rewarded with the question: "What shall we have this Sunday, chicken or beef? What do you think, my little Mickey Mouse?" My career as a butcher was instantaneously and metaphorically chopped off in its prime.

What was advertising's gain was a piece of scrag end's loss.

Pass the Bloody Parcel

I've had a fear of cheese for exactly fifty-eight years now (I'm writing this on the 5th of April 2022, the day I turned sixty-five).

My parents had thrown a party in our Balham flat when I was seven. There were twenty kids all in one small lounge, together with two heavy smokers and an assortment of matches and lighters scattered like cushions in a Habitat furniture display. What could possibly go wrong?

One lad from my school at the party was very susceptible to nose bleeds – they were so regular, if we'd been allowed watches, you could have set your time by him. Of course, during a very competitive postman's knock, my mate's nose began to bleed. The flat turned into the set of *Emergency Ward 10* as my mother's Bracklesham Bay tea towel quickly became a tourniquet. Several of the guests (can you call seven-year-olds guests?) thought this was real-life "doctors and nurses" and had replaced the much-promised pass the parcel round.

Not content with the salmon and chicken paste sandwiches, I asked my mother for a cheese sandwich. When it arrived, I decided I didn't want it; my mother made me eat it and my relationship with Camembert, Edam or even a Dairylea triangle ended on that fateful April 1964 afternoon.

Still, everyone got cake and an item of stationery (as one did in those days), although my mum got the rubber order wrong, thus avoiding many young pregnancies.

A Jumper's not just for Christmas

A joke within my family, at Christmas, would be, who was the previous owner of your present?

My dad and I would travel from Balham to Baker Street to see his side of the family. They never bought us new clothes. My aunt, his half-sister (different fathers, not that she only had 50 per cent of her torso), would give Dad jumpers from her local charity shop or from her (recently dead) husband.

Dad would have preferred the charity option, as his brother-in-law had been a foot taller, so the arms of the jumper would hang down, making Dad look like a bespectacled orangutan. Didn't make his tree-hanging ability any greater, though.

One year Dad was given a jumper, and for once, the label had not been cut out (my aunt should never have been allowed near scissors). My dad didn't like it much, so decided to return to the shop from whence it had come.

These were the days when you didn't need a receipt. Dad handed over the jumper, hoping he'd get a refund or coloured jumper other than the yellow he was handing back (handy if there was a fancy dress party and you had to go as a condiment).

After a while, the assistant returned to my dad saying this line had been discontinued – for seven years. My dad had been waiting a while, but not seven years.

Next Christmas, my dad got his own back on his sister and gave her a ration book. This was 1973.

Stone Me

I wouldn't have made a good caveman.

I remember in one of my first history lessons, at my Balham primary school, seeing pictures of cavemen. I lived in a centrally heated flat, so that gaping hole at the entrance to the cave would have simply prompted cold after cold for me. Remember, they didn't have Lemsip in Stone Age times.

Before Tesco started in the Neander Valley, food was mostly obtained by slaying woolly mammoths (imagine the Green Shield Stamps you'd have got with one of those).

Once slayed, you'd soon get tired of variations on the same meal day after day: roast mammoth; cold mammoth; cold mammoth sandwiches; mammoth curry. The job to have would have been spear maker or owner of the local flint factory, such was the ever-present need to ward off hunger.

I can only assume no one ever got told off for drawing on the walls. Everyone was very capable, it seems, of drawing bison, but precious little else. The day after fire was invented, the health and safety officer was appointed.

If you were the local outfitter, you'd have asked if the mammoth suit was to be three-piece or not? And did you want the design to be houndstooth or sabretooth?

Of course, you didn't need a coat in the summer months. It was warm 2.6 million years ago; this was when outdoor badminton was invented and *Health & Efficiency* first published.

Roast coelacanth, anyone?

Auf Wiedersehen . Petting

It was 1972 when I first learned that heavy petting had nothing to do with animals.

Attending my school swimming gala at Clapham Manor Baths, on display, as a warning I now know, was a sign: "No Heavy Petting".

My pets, prior to 1972, had been a mouse and a West Highland Terrier – animals not renowned for their excessive weight.

As I looked at the sign, I thought about animals I knew to be both heavy and aquatic. I began worrying that an alligator or great white shark might suddenly appear during the 100-yard butterfly relay race.

Before this visit, to me the word "petting" meant a tiny zoo with goats, guinea pigs and gerbils (most small animals beginning with "g", basically).

Might very fat guinea pigs feature as floats for the participants who could not swim, perhaps?

My next worry was the potential disease one might get if a load of rodents were in the pool? Getting a verruca would have been the least of my worries.

After the swimming gala, whenever I was asked if I was interested in any heavy petting, my response was that I had a fear of water, and an even greater fear of crocodiles.

A consequence of which was I attended my first date wearing water wings.

Ballet High

It was November 1973 when I decided never to wear women's clothing again.

At the tender age of sixteen, I was asked to appear in a sketch my Balham amateur dramatics society was producing. I'd been overlooked for many large parts, so this was my chance for glory.

The sketch was entitled 'We're the only girls left in the ballet'. It was a three-handed sketch. The other two were six inches taller than me, a generation older and had beards. I didn't start shaving until I was around thirty-five, so could not compete in the facial growth stakes.

Aside from performing in the church hall, we would travel with our revues; these were invariably held in local mental homes (that's showbiz!). The downside to this was that the audience rarely laughed at what we thought were the right places. We could have performed *King Lear* and they'd have probably complained that was too funny.

Meanwhile, with my first venture (that I'm admitting here) looming, I had to be helped into a tutu. If Margot Fonteyn had ever visited SW17, she'd have had kittens.

The dress cut into my crotch (almost acting as a vasectomy). I've still never taken to blocks of wood in the ends of my shoes, and a mixture of muslin, gauze and nylon brings me out in a rash.

So, if ever you go to the ballet to watch *Romeo and Juliet*, if my stage career had taken off, I could have played the latter – although I'm not good with heights, so they'd have to cut the balcony scene.

You Say Potato

Mr Potato Head has just turned seventy.

I would have hours of endless vegetable-related fun in my Balham flat as a kid, although potatoes became quite dangerous if the plastic hat and moustache were still impaled while being roasted.

But, seventy years ago, were Mr and Mrs Potato (Senior) sitting down with their son asking whether he was going to be a chip, crisp or dauphinoise, only to be disappointed to hear he wanted to be a model?

Also, in 1585, when Sir Walter Raleigh first brought potatoes to the UK, did he think their prime aim would be for children's entertainment? Perhaps, when looking for El Dorado (the mythical South American city, not the BBC show), he saw someone with a head shaped like a potato with stumpy legs, sporting a small hat and moustache one would normally associate with risqué films in the '60s?

Growing up, when you had the introduction of 'celebrity' chefs, you'd never see Fanny Cradock sticking some comedy ears on a potato she was about to show us how to cook. Perhaps Johnnie did this behind her back? If so, you'd have thought it would have had a monocle like his?

Thick As a...

I was five when I decided I'd leave my Balham flat and head for the high seas.

In the early '60s, on Sunday afternoons, I'd watch the ITV series *Sir Francis Drake*. I was hooked (no pun intended with the seafaring *Peter Pan* character).

I'd only just started school, and a chance to explore exotic lands and get into fights with Spanish people seemed an idyllic life. I was desperate to be transported back to the late 16th century.

However, at the SW17 naval recruiting school, I was informed of the possible disadvantages outweighing the fact I could earn my own body weight in doubloons.

Did I like rum? Well, as a five-year-old, I'd have preferred Ribena. What's my view on scurvy? Having had both scarlet fever and chickenpox, more itching didn't really appeal. Walking the plank if punished? Well, my singular inability to swim would prove hazardous. How was my Spanish, should we have to negotiate? I could say, "Do you know the way to the library?"

At the end of the interview, which was tricky as I was still quite small and kept slipping off the cushion I'd been given as a booster seat, thereby not showing my ability to balance (key on board ship), I had no credibility left at all!

I was encouraged to go back in twelve years' time, but only after I'd got a certificate from the local duckling club.

In the early '70s, a 99 ice cream cost 15p. Last weekend it cost £3.25 – and only had one flake in so, technically, it should have been called a 49 and a half.

On the side of the ice cream van this weekend was a poster offering almost 99 varieties. In the '60s and '70s, the only choice was "Do you want sprinkles with that?" Now you can have a wafer, a cone, an oyster (try tapping one of those on the machine at the entrance to the Tube), tub, or just put straight into your hands, because that's where most of it is going to end up if it's sunny, so you're missing out the middleman, in effect.

From my Balham flat in the '60s, I'd hear the metallic tune coming from the ice cream van. Because I was on the fourth floor of my block of flats, by the time I'd got to the ground floor, it would have taken me so long, the ice cream seller would have run out of Flakes or, worse, retired – the lifts weren't terribly reliable.

Last Saturday, after I'd remortgaged my house to buy my 99, I gave the man my money, to which he replied, "Be lucky." I thought I'd been transported back to the '50s.

Mr Whippy always sounded quite innocuous, until Ambleside Avenue became famous.

Flake's off, love. Be lucky.

Lovely Jubilee

This week, in the UK, we are celebrating a jubilee.

This is the time when you buy a celebratory tea towel – probably overdue, as your existing one still has Edward VII on it.

I've never attended a street party; being brought up on the fourth floor of a Balham flat made it dangerous hanging bunting between windows. One false move and you'd be threatening the livelihood of Albert Pierrepoint.

I've never erected trestle tables either, as they look like they could dismember a finger as if it were a bacon slicer.

I haven't got any flags except my giant FC Bayern flag – most people would find this tasteless, although we are celebrating a family who used to be called Saxe-Coburg and Gotha.

I'm assuming every street will have an old piano pushed out onto the street?

Once you've established someone in your road is named Chas and/or Dave, you've got the makings of a party.

To get in the mood for 1952, all you need are jam sandwiches or anything which has come out of a container with the name "Shippams" emblazoned in its front. My allergy to beef paste will prevent my attendance.

No, I shall be waiting for the dessert, which must be a Jubilee Jubbly. A dessert alliteratively fit for a queen – and hopefully still costing 3d.

I just hope that Brian May's not on top of my bloody roof again.

Dad, What's a Tumulus?

Are we nearly there yet? The plaintive cry I'm sure we've all heard (and probably said).

With modern-day satnavs, the answer to this can be given to the nanosecond. When you had a series of Esso road maps, a compass which was originally in the heel of your shoe and an old London A-Z, those ETA predictions became harder to determine.

We struggled whenever we drove anywhere outside of Balham High Street – our A-Z was so old it only had Watling Street and Offa's Dyke marked on the pages; if friends or relatives lived in Roman villas we'd get there, otherwise it was very hit and miss.

Travelling abroad was trickier – the countries were physically bigger and so, it seemed, were the road maps.

It's tricky enough going round the Paris *Périphérique*, let alone trying to navigate it with a map larger than the windscreen in front of you and flanked by irate Parisians. It's no fun playing pub cricket driving through the Loire Valley, either.

I thought, having begun to study map-reading preparing for geography O level, that I could be more useful. However, driving from Balham to Dawlish (not quite Paris to Dakar), my dad needed to know how to get to the A303. Me pointing out, using my school Ordnance Survey map, slag heaps, narrow-gauge railways and coppices added several days to our journey.

Are we nearly there yet? No, but I think we're near an area with non-coniferous trees. Handy for logs, but not if you want a cream tea.

Scampi in a Basketcase

People rarely serve food in baskets these days. Is there a world shortage of baskets? Is eating from a basket one of the ways to catch consumption? Were there outcries from the World Scampi & Chicken Protection Society?

Every Friday night, during the '70s, after choir practice (this isn't a joke), we would go to a pub on Wandsworth Common, where I would pad out half a pint of lager and lime for several hours and eat chicken or scampi and chips out of a basket.

During the evening, the Salvation Army would enter and flog the customers *War Cry*. The more drunk were enrolled and would find themselves playing a tambourine the following Sunday.

Friday night was complete: meal in a basket, lukewarm beer and a crossword puzzle to do where most of the answers were Biblical characters. Having sung about most of them earlier in the evening, I had a distinct advantage.

But the basket gave it its own magical flavour – like hot chocolate after you've gone swimming or been rescued after several weeks down a pothole.

I would often wonder, during Sunday dinner, why the most chipped plates in the world were brought out and the food not served in a basket? I guess gravy could have proved messy had the weaving not been as tight as it should be.

One day, they stopped serving food in baskets. I went up to the bar and said, "Basket?" I was banned for a month.

Making a Right Old Red Rackety

If you buy a comic these days for a grandchild, child or yourself (if you're still thinking you'll get a decent idea of dress sense from a copy of *Bunty*), there are always free gifts attached.

If you were brought up in the '60s, as I was, then a free gift with a comic was a rarity. You were more likely to see a Penny Black, unicorn or hen's tooth attached to your *Dandy* than a set of stickers, pencils, or transfers.

And so, when one of my *Beanos* arrived in the mid-sixties and had a "Red Rackety" attached, I didn't know whether to laugh, cry, poo (I've cleaned that up, as this is a family blog) or have breakfast, as my old nan would have said, such was my excitement.

However, it was my poor old nan who got the wrong end of this DC Thomson act of goodwill.

The "Red Rackety" was something you whirled, like some dervish, above your head, and it created a strange noise. The secondary (unscripted) noise was the smashing of my nan's ceiling lampshade. This was not in the instructions.

Another week there was a "whoopee cushion" – a trick to play on old relatives. As you become an old relative yourself, you realise there is no need for any form of artificial stimulus like a whoopee cushion ☐.

Iron Filing a Complaint

The only job I could have done in the police, should I have chosen that career path rather than advertising, would have been creating photofit pictures.

I'd watched *Z-Cars*, *Police 5* and *Softly, Softly* as a kid, but owning a kit with a man's face, a magnetic pen and a pile of iron filings gave me the feeling this was the vocation for me.

Living equidistant between Tooting Bec Police Station and Wandsworth Prison, I feel it was fate I should own such a toy, and possibly become the next Albert Pierrepoint (he began life creating photofits, until he won some rope in a raffle).

But, watching Stratford Johns in *Softly, Softly*, I was always surprised, when a victim was asked about their assailant, that the iron filings toy wasn't produced!

If the assailant looked like The Hood from *Thunderbirds*, they'd be easy to catch, or a pirate with an eyepatch or with a moustache so outrageous it wouldn't have looked out of place on a WW1 German general. Although I don't remember anyone in the Great Train Robbery looking quite like any of those?

Sadly, I never really mastered the art of iron filing face painting. I think the magnetic pen was faulty, as my faces wouldn't have looked out of a place in a Picasso painting.

If I had got that job, the police would constantly looking for a woman with an eye where her ear should be.

Keep 'em peeled (wherever they are on your body).

When You Wishbone Upon a Star

The best bit about Sunday lunch, when I was growing up as a kid in south-west London, was the thought that your future was about to be changed by the successful pulling of a wishbone.

However unprepared you were, if you won, you still had to make a wish.

My enduring wish was, as my nan subscribed to *Titbits* and *Reveille*, that she'd leave the room long enough for me to look through her magazines, or search for the ladies' underwear section of her Freemans catalogue.

I should have known that no wish was ever to be granted, as the ominous signs of chicken gravy suddenly splattering over my Sunday-best shirt wasn't that encouraging.

The pulling of the wishbone was an excellent diversion from my parents, who would stare like Victorian schoolteachers at my uneaten sprouts. My parents would watch the wishbone-pulling competition as my nan, with her non-pulling hand, whisked the unwanted sprouts into her many-pocketed housecoat. Although, always unnerved as to the origins of her next day's bubble .

Comment [BE]: QUERY: The meaning of this is unclear.

It was the ancient Romans who invented this tradition and believed it gave them luck. Sometimes, with my nan's roast chicken, I think that's the period in which she'd bought her joint.

We tried pulling a T-bone steak bone one Sunday – I nearly dislocated my little finger.

Trollied

The one thing about working from home is that the trolley doesn't come round. If I want a bun, cup of tea or a Wagon Wheel, I'm going to have to get up and get it myself.

I worked in an office once where the keeper of the trolley would announce, around 11.00 each morning, *"Trolley!"* in a voice like someone demanding a light be put out during the Blitz.

In the days before the confusion of which type of continental coffee you wanted and the shops supplying them not existing, trolleys would be rolled round offices. They were like the school tuck shop, only on wheels and pushed by a woman seemingly over 100 with a fag hanging out of her mouth, adding an unnecessary layer to her doughnuts.

It was also a welcome break in the day; fag breaks were a thing of the future during the '60s and '70s. Plus, if I'd got on the smoking carriage of the Tube from Balham Station, I really didn't need a fag break.

The tea lady was scary and/or predatory. Did I want to sample her iced buns when I finished work? Probably not, and I always had a note from my mum excusing me from such *liaisons dangereuses*.

So work, for me, at around 11.00 in the morning, became like school PE lessons: full of dread and the fear my pants would fall down while doing a handstand, thus risking getting third-degree burns off a giant tea urn.

Saying Cheese is Off Love

There was a photo booth by the ticket office of Balham Underground Station. I used it once.

I would walk past, during my commuting days, and wondered if I'd ever venture in there to produce four photos of increasingly inane grins, as if practising for a gurning competition?

I never did.

Would I go in there with a girl and take loving photos? No, I rarely talked to girls during my teenage years, let alone persuade any of them to spend time in a darkened, underground cubicle with a protective veil.

The one time I entered this magical photographic world was to provide photos for my first passport.

I wore a maroon suit and matching maroon double-Windsor-knot tie. If I'd have worn any more maroon, people would have mistaken me for a bishop – or a giant plum.

After the photos which appeared, it surprised me I was allowed into Luton Airport, not to mention the Balearic Island of Mallorca! (They do say, if you actually look like your passport photo, you're probably too ill to fly!)

I was very much aware that many of these booths were used by couples. I, however, stood outside, for what seemed like a millennium, alone, waiting for my four photos to drop into the receptacle. It simply shouted: "Billy No Mates".

It was like waiting for Godot or, more to the point, waiting for Godot's passport photos.

And smile.

No Smoke Without Playing Cards

As an only child, grandchild and nephew (not that you can tell!), it was my parents, grandparents and great-aunts and uncles' job to entertain me. One uncle decided he would introduce danger into playtime within my Balham flat.

There was always a pack of cards lying around when I was a kid (my mum always wanted to be a croupier, but never got further than the church whist drive); my uncle would build towers with them. My uncle was a heavy pipe smoker, so his pipe was invariably on – nothing like going to school smelling of your uncle's finest shag (insert your own gag here).

He'd inhale and blow the smoke through the bottom of the cards. The smoke would drift up and eventually exit through the hole he'd made in the top. The first time I ever saw the election of the new pope on TV, I thought, once the decision had been made, my uncle had been in the cellars of the Vatican blowing smoke up the papal chimney.

We would lie down on the carpet of my flat (which wasn't shagpile, so no running gag this week) to get the best effect of the smoke rising. It is only now, with my mental health and safety handbook going crazy, that I realise how dangerous this would have been!

Highly flammable carpet, burning tobacco embers, child who wasn't allowed matches until he was twenty-six – what could possibly go wrong?

Either we've elected a new vicar of Balham, or the fire brigade needs calling.

What's On the Other Side

Comment [BE]: QUERY: Is this correct? I might be misunderstanding, but Martha Longhurst died of a heart attack in The Rovers?

Shall we view the test card, comment on the Open University lecturer's sartorial elegance or watch *The Likely Lads*?

This would echo round my Balham flat in the '60s because, invariably, each night, this was the choice of viewing. Having seen Martha Longhurst's death by viaduct, I was always too traumatised to watch anything on ITV.

Nowadays we are spoiled for choice, but you still hear the perennial utterance of, "There's nothing on TV tonight."

In the '60s, there were no remotes, so getting up and down to change the channel was part of an evening aerobics class. The other challenge was making sure the aerial was correctly positioned.

As part of my parents' child labour activities, I'd often have to stand behind the TV with the aerial held high in the air so they could watch *Compact* clearly. For years I thought it was a radio series.

Because the screen was so grainy, you couldn't see the strings attached to many of the puppets. I was always amazed that Andy Pandy could jump into his box like a Harrier jump jet. The sound wasn't brilliant either. I'm sure, if there were modern-day flowerpot men, Bill and Ben would sound quite articulate.

I'm still not used to a remote and often try to change channels with my glasses case.

Squirreling Away

When you saw your careers officer at school, you were never encouraged to become a squirrel.

I wanted to be a squirrel as, on TV, growing up in the '60s, they had the best jobs, were massively popular and hugely responsible.

I'd have liked to have been Tufty. He had many friends. One was called Willy Weasel (which wouldn't be allowed on TV these days, and actually sounds like some kind of STD). Tufty's full name was Tufty Fluffytail. I think, if ever I consider a role as a drag queen, this would be my stage name.

Slightly more adventurous, and without the nagging mum, was Secret Squirrel. He had a coat which housed many weapons to fight crime. Although, because I have bad eyesight, I probably would have been better as his sidekick, Morocco Mole.

I can only assume, as I was told a career in advertising is what I should seriously consider, that the lack of O levels I achieved in 1973 meant that being a squirrel was never on the cards.

It was, however, while revising for my O levels in my Balham flat (Squirrel was an O level option you could take back then), that I discovered squirrels only lived for about five years. Advertising it is, then! Atom Ant would have to find another crime-fighting partner.

The smells are different between primary and secondary school. You go from rotting plimsolls (and the feet therein) to various acids waiting to be turned into stink bombs, freeze the head boy or tools for encouraging pyromania.

You weren't allowed matches at primary school, let alone Bunsen burners you'd try to emulate a North Sea oil rig fire with. The only way I'd have started a fire in my Balham primary school would have been by hitting my glockenspiel too quickly.

I remember the first moment I entered my Tooting secondary school chemistry lab, with its associated smells. Was I going to fall off the stool? Would I get to wear the long white coat (I assumed the physics teacher had just come from umpiring a school cricket match)? Was I going to end up being part of *The Quatermass Experiment*?

During one physics lesson we learned about propulsion from fireworks to manned spacecraft. I remember thinking to myself: "Well, it's not rocket science, is it?" Which, of course, it was, and one of the many reasons I failed all my science exams. Or wasn't the first man on the moon.

He Always Calls Me Donkey

I started work in September 1974 and became a regular newspaper buyer off the man at Balham Station who called everyone "John".

The thing you miss most about going to work are the lengthy school holidays.

Suddenly, you go from having had the only person of authority as your PE teacher, to having everyone as your boss.

If you're the lowest in terms of seniority, you cannot tell anyone what you did on your school holidays – something you would have written about on your first day back at school after you'd covered your new text books with unwanted, normally distasteful, wallpaper.

You have no one to tell the only words of Spanish you learned on holiday were "I think my brake pads need replacing" (when actually you were trying to ask where the nearest chemist was); no one to tell about the third-degree burns you suffered because your mum had misread the "how to make your own sun cream" recipe; no one to tell of the singular lack of food served in a basket.

One my first day of work in September 1974, I stood on Balham Station, the only one peeling and holding a straw, almost life-sized donkey tucked under my arm. I wasn't to know I wouldn't have a desk, let alone one to put a straw donkey on.

"**Bitte, Hat Kent Gewonnen?**"

You no longer have to dust off a 100-year-old encyclopedia to find out anything: the answer will be on your phone.

As a bloke, sports results are key. These are readily available now but, even before Ceefax, how did we establish what was going on in the world of sport? Or, if you were intellectual, the world?

Even harder, what if you were abroad? Because *Le Monde*, *Süddeutsche Zeitung* and the *Buenos Aires Herald* were certainly not reporting on how Kent's cricket team were getting on during the summer.

I remember, before wireless meant something other than the thing you listened to *The Goons* on, being abroad, listening to a short-wave radio and getting ever deeper into the Normandy countryside, I'd try desperately to listen to the Test match before the reception went, the local radio station took over and you suddenly went from John Arlott to Edith Piaf before you could say baguette.

But it was the quest for a three-day old *Daily Telegraph* which was the high point of many holidays for me. Apart from the dress code of Brits abroad – long shorts, socks, sandals, hat made out of a hankie – we'd spot one another, in quiet anticipation, milling about inside a French newsagent for the out-of-date papers to arrive. And I'd pay a bloody fortune just to see how many runs Colin Cowdrey had made.

But these French newsagents could be devious, and I remember buying a paper which was so old it had turned yellow; the headline proclaimed: "Queen Anne dead". Never mind that, I thought, have Kent won? And my secret hope – was it still raining in Balham?

Not Gone Fishing

Even with Jack Hargreaves' weekly invitation to do something *Out of Town,* I was never going to become the world's greatest fisherman. The fear of maggots (I'm sure there's a long word ending in "phobia" for that) being the reason.

I had several ponds nearby on Wandsworth, Clapham and Tooting Bec Commons where I could have pursued an angling hobby.

I had a mate who invited me to go fishing. This sounded good and so, armed with a bucket and net I'd bought a decade earlier with "Bognor" emblazoned all over them, I called round.

We entered his kitchen, he went to the fridge, opened the door and pulled out a tub. Would we be taking some raspberry ripple with us, or some haddock paste sandwiches to eat as we sat on the banks of Wandsworth Common ponds looking for stingrays? No, these contained maggots.

I thought of the culinary errors which could occur from having a tub of maggots in among foodstuffs: the tub containing mince could remain in the fridge as the errant tub was used to create a shepherd's pie; mistaking it for Neapolitan meant the addition of hundreds and thousands would create utter chaos in the bowl. Plus, going round to a mate's house, their mums never asked, "Have you a maggot allergy?"

I assume, if you do this far out to sea, where the fish are much larger, the conversation is going to be: "I think we're going to need a bigger maggot!"

Crazy Horses

Through abject fear, I've never touched a horse.

Playing Totopoly was the nearest I ever got to going anywhere near the likes of Arkle, Mr Ed or the Woodentops' Dobbin.

Living on the fourth floor of a block of flats made it impractical keeping a goldfish (they don't like the altitude), let alone having my own little pony.

You rarely saw horses running wild across Wandsworth Common as if they were on the Argentinian Pampas.

I had one stand next to me as a kid, as I queued to get into Stamford Bridge; it was hard to determine, as a nine-year-old, which was the scariest – a seemingly giant horse or the travelling Leeds fans in the late '60s?

When I was in the Cubs, I once visited Tooting police station – as a visitor, not on remand – they didn't have a badge for that (I assume a hand-woven depiction of a pair of handcuffs would have been the motif). Luckily for me, our Cub pack visited the day the horses were out: probably performing at Badminton (the place, not the game – horses have very poor hand–eye coordination).

I've never even ridden on a seaside donkey (probably, wearing the obligatory "kiss me quick" hat put me off, as it'd mess up my hair).

Unless they start filming the Lloyds Bank ads on Tooting Bec Common, I fear I will never, ever touch one. At six-foot, I'm unlikely to make it as a jockey – we won't go there regarding making the weight, although, during this summer, there were days when I thought I could easily be involved in the 3.30 at Newmarket.

Not So Glorious Mud

As a kid, growing up in my Balham flat, I had central heating, *Hot Wheels* and thirty-five glove puppets. It begs the question: why on earth did I play in puddles the moment it rained?

We had no running rivers with bridges over them (I'd have built one, but wasn't terribly adept with Meccano), so there were no opportunities for playing poohsticks.

But, when it rained, we had puddles and would re-enact Pearl Harbour.

Because I wasn't well-versed in laundry matters, I would get very dirty – and wet. Having built dams using stones, half bricks, mates' satchels, we imagined we were fighting Admiral Tojo until I had to go in for my tea.

Thrilled with the fact I'd subverted the Japanese navy, and knowing I wasn't about to have sushi for tea (this was Balham in the '60s), I would re-enter my flat.

The moment my mother saw my clothes, she went berserk. I immediately apologised, to which I heard the all-too-frequent refrain: "You're always bleedin' sorry, Michael." Being called "Michael" meant trouble; I was no longer "my little Mickey Mouse."

It was a quiet teatime that evening; we watched *I love Lucy* in total silence while eating our smoked haddock.

As I explained to Sooty and Sweep – two of my glove puppets, who were on each hand – how was I to know mud was difficult to get out of a new school shirt? Was I sponsored by *Dreft*?

Sooty never did answer.

Not Very Hungry Caterpillar

Even though I only lived feet away from my Balham primary school, my mother thought it best I attended school dinners. I lasted one day.

I remember sitting down on a mashed potato-ingrained table and chair.

What I'd not anticipated – never having had it at home – was a caterpillar in the salad. Lettuce, yes; tomato, yes; the odd spring onion.

Never a caterpillar.

We did live on the fourth floor of our flats, so I assumed, as I sat staring at said caterpillar moving slowly over a slice of beetroot, they weren't capable of climbing up 100 feet of brickwork?

I'd never seen mashed (this was a masterpiece of overstatement) potato like it. The original King Edward they used was more mashed. And why was it grey? Had they used grey butter? Lurpak had grey packaging; perhaps they'd used that?

But it was the sponge pudding which was the *pièce de résistance*, as we like to say in Balham. If you wanted the quickest way to dehydrate, the sponge pudding offered this. Adding the chocolate sauce would have had Lady Isobel Barnett not knowing which clue to give the listeners!

When asked, after I'd arrived home, what I'd had for my school dinner, I said roast swan, as I dreaded my mum ordering hundreds of caterpillars to make me feel at home.

I'm still waiting to fully digest the sponge pudding.

Cane and Unable

I was a goody-goody at school; this made receiving my first detention a big shock.

At my Tooting secondary school we had exams for everything, including PE.

PE was not a strength. Give me a ball to hit, kick or head and I'd be fine, but get me to vault over anything larger than a matchbox and I wasn't.

We were about to start a geography exam – I had an image of what an ox-bow lake looked like in my head – when the PE teacher entered to read out the results of the PE exam we'd recently taken: "Richards, 0 per cent" – you couldn't even get a mark for writing your name. The consequence of this was a detention.

So, because of my inability to do a forward roll, leap over a buck or climb a rope, I had to spend an hour after school writing, "Please give me a rope to climb, because it's not at all futile" 100 times.

I also had to do a cross-country run – running round Wandsworth Common – seemingly 100 times.

And that was the only punishment I had – I don't count mental punishment after every parents' evening – "Michael could do better" – and wasn't Michael told about that later those evenings!

I never got the cane, which was still in use.

However, the only violence I witnessed was after I was caught singing Wizzard's 'Angel Fingers' during O level music revision. A blackboard rubber was hurled at the speed of light, with the accuracy you'd have wanted on *The Golden Shot*.

"Bernie – the blackboard rubber."

Sycamore or Less

With the proliferation of computer games these days, I assume no one plays with flowers any more?

Are daisy chains still made? I assume, if you live next door to a family of ageing hippies, they probably are?

I'm at that age when I don't need plucking a dandelion to remind me to get up several times during the night!

Do I like butter? Nowadays you're asked about food allergies rather than food preferences.

As you get older, you're more likely to worry about dandelion spores creating more weeds, not whether someone loves you (or not).

As a kid, growing up in the '60s and wandering across Wandsworth Common, I'd collect conkers. Don't know why: the fear of breaking the wrist which bowled a decent leg-break when I was eleven was never going to be risked in a school playground with a weapon baked in vinegar.

Walking along the street these days you never see people with green tufts of goose grass sticking to their clothes? It was how Eric Bristow started. Goose grass was also called "sticky willy" – you can insert your own joke here, or, if this affects you directly, order some ointment.

Every time I walked past a sycamore tree on Tooting Bec Common, I'd dream of becoming a helicopter pilot.

Luckily, rationing has stopped, so I don't have to drink coffee made from acorns any more.

Nettle tea's off, love.

Don't Tie that Kangaroo Down Sport, He'll Dob you In

One of the disadvantages of being brought up in south-west London in the '60s and '70s was that none of the parks or ponds encouraged the local animals to help out the police.

If there'd been an Outback within Tooting Bec Common, a Cockney Skippy could have helped identify villains. Local police could have been trained to speak kangaroo. "What's that, Skippy? Someone's selling eggs past their sell-by date in Tooting Market?"

If Clapham Common ponds had been at the same temperature as the waters off the coast of Florida, Flipper could have made a second home there and been a massive assistance to the constabulary operating out of the Cavendish Road Police Station.

However, my question is this: why did the law enforcers, who, in Dr Dolittle vain, spoke to the animals, always assume there was a problem? Was there not the outside possibility that both Skippy and Flipper, having befriended the local Bobbies, were simply trying to exchange pleasantries?

I can imagine Skippy and Flipper chirruping and squeaking away wondering, *why do these people think a lifeboat's adrift, or a body's been found on Ayers Rock? All I want to know is if they think it looks like rain?*

I've always wanted to talk to dolphins and went to evening class to do so. In the first lesson, I learned to count to ten in dolphin, ordered two beers and mastered saying, "You have the right to remain silent."

Dingo took your baby? Sorry, Skippy, that's another series.

What's it Harry Worth

The BBC is celebrating 100 years of broadcasting. Growing up in the '60s and '70s, it had a major effect on my life.

As a kid, I would frequently walk down Balham High Road wondering why I couldn't lift both feet off the ground in shop doorways.

My mother always wanted me to have elocution lessons; this would have been pointless in south-west London – I'd have been better off copying Bill and Ben.

It was a great vehicle to see what possible lines of career you might take. I couldn't have been a rag 'n' bone man due to my fear of horses. Life on the open seas looked attractive, except no episode of *Captain Pugwash* ever mentioned getting scurvy, being attacked by Spaniards or being only ten years old on board, having been press-ganged into joining the navy. Nor could I have been Bluebottle, as I don't like big bangs.

The Good Life encouraged us to become self-sufficient. Having a goat in a fourth-floor flat wasn't terribly practical, but we did always have nice mohair coats.

The BBC connected people with one another. Every Sunday you always wondered where Paderborn was, thinking it must be so awful that the people there were constantly looking forward to coming home for Christmas! Even in January.

But there was little choice. If you'd been living on Mars and returned and turned the TV on and it was showing *The Big Country*, Billy Smart's circus or Val Doonican with a particularly thick jumper on, you'd know it was Christmas. There was no escape – especially not from Stalag Luft III, which usually preceded Val's Christmas jumper fest.

Goodnight children, everywhere.

Goose Feathers are Off Love

I'm not so old that I remember writing with a goose feather, but writing implements have changed over the years.

I remember my first day at my Balham primary school. I sat at my new desk, wondering when my afternoon rest was going to start, when I had a lump of slate and chalk thrust into my hand. Was I expected to start a fire with them? Was this a type of drum? Was I to write the odds of the 3.30 at Newmarket?

Before this I'd only had crayons. My nan had a biro to do the *Evening News* crossword every night. I wasn't allowed that as, the only time I'd been given one, I bit the end off and got blue ink all over my mouth. My mother assumed I was part of a royal family; biology was not one of her stronger suits.

When I was ten, we were introduced to italic pens. After ten years of mastering writing with crayons and the occasional pencil, suddenly everything had to be slanted – like I was doing my classwork from the other side of the desk.

At secondary school the desks were so old, there were still inkwells in every desk. With the advent of cartridges, the only use of the redundant inkwell was to place your mid-morning tuck shop iced bun in. Although, if you found you suddenly had royal blue icing, the inkwells were clearly still being used.

But if your cartridge had run out, there were always the geese running amok on the rugby field.

When I'm 65

When you're a kid, there are various (usually medical) things you observe that only old people use.

Last week, after sixty-five years, I had to buy corn plasters. As a child, I was aware of ageing relatives using them. My question is, will I be using medical aids I'd witnessed in my Balham flat in the '60s?

Perhaps I'll start dabbing myself with 4711 eau de cologne. I may start protecting my clothes with mothballs or begin sucking cloves for toothache (one of the few things not mentioned by the witches in *Macbeth*)?

I wonder if the bottles of Kaolin & Morphine, Milk of Magnesia and Friar's Balsam I currently have in my loft are past their sell-by dates?

Obviously, medicine has progressed over the past sixty years. The doctor no longer visits with a black bag, but can give you a password for a Zoom call.

One thing is for certain: I won't be creating my own laxatives. I had a great-aunt who lived in our flats. Once she invited me into her bedroom as she was getting ready to go to work. Aside from the overriding smell of peroxide, on her bedside table was a cup, full of brown water, in which floated several actual rotting senna pods. The mere sight of these sent me rushing to her toilet. I guess they worked.

Pass the smelling salts, please.

Lavender Fields Forever

I don't quite remember when the site of Morden Station was lavender fields. Nor do I remember when the Hanging Gardens of Babylon were part of the Battersea Park Festival Gardens in the years before Christ. What I do I realise is the buildings I knew as kid are no longer there.

When I first started work, in 1974, my job was to collect regional newspapers from their London offices in Fleet Street. Most of these buildings are now law firms. So, if you need to get a copy of the *Hull Daily Mail*, *Helston Packet* or the *Isle of Wight County Press*, it'll cost you £1,000 just for someone to fetch it.

Many old banks are now wine bars, old pubs are now wine bars and you can't find a decent milliner for love nor money. I now have my own anvil.

The Balham Odeon, where my mum and I watched 50 per cent of *Dumbo* (we left early as it was too upsetting) and 30 per cent of *The Scarecrow* (too much set in Dymchurch), turned into Majestic Wine. I'd moved away, came back, sat in the shop waiting to watch *Emil and the Detectives,* only to be sold a case of Rioja. Not even close to a Kia-Ora or a tub!

The Mayfair cinema, Tooting, turned into a snooker hall and then a bank. I assume it's a wine bar now? It certainly won't be a haberdashery shop.

But the most disturbing thing, given that everyone is being told to drink more water, is where have all the horse troughs gone? They're probably very small leisure centres now!

"75 per cent of heat loss is through the head" – Dr T. Savalas (retired)

I never felt the cold as a kid.

I had the mandatory duffel coat, which made me look like a very small protester on the Aldermaston March, but rarely felt I needed it, even in the winter of 1962/3. *Ice Cold in Balham* would have made a good film.

But now, with the duffel coat no longer fitting (I blame chocolate Hobnobs), I need several layers. When I go out, it looks like I could be assisting Sherpa Tenzing, only without the ice pick.

I had an uncle who had a string vest. He would eat his tea wearing it. I often wondered what the point was – there were more holes than things stoppings drafts. "Don't forget your vest" was a much-used adage. Why, if 90 per cent was holes?

Nowadays everything is "thermal". When I was a kid, the only thing which was thermal was a flask, or a wind from the Gulf of Mexico.

Years ago, if you had layers on, you'd look like the Michelin Man. These days, everything is more streamlined and energy efficient. If you still look like the Michelin Man, it means you're not cold, but simply eating too many cakes.

If we were still living in the '60s, as we approach Christmas, we'd be getting ready to welcome Perry Como into our houses.

What did he do the rest of the year? What happened to all those jumpers? Did he sell them to Val Doonican? When we watched Val Doonican's Christmas specials, was he wearing Perry Como's hand-me-downs?

Were round-robin letters describing the events of the year a thing in the '60s? Did we read them by the light of our fibre optic lamps? (I think I have one of the fibres still stuck in my foot.)

My great-aunt, who also lived in our Balham flats, owned a *Pears' Cyclopedia*. I didn't need a letter telling me about "Melissa and the girls finding a lovely inn in rural Tuscany" to enlighten me as to what had happened in the previous year.

More and more Christmas cards are sent electronically. It's not quite the same having a PC dangling overhead on a piece of string.

I wonder if I'll still be scared of the Alastair Sim version of *A Christmas Carol*? In recent years, I've found Miss Piggy scarier.

And so, as Tiny Tim (the Dickens character, not the singer) would say, *"God bless us, every one"* – even those sending round-robin letters.

Hot under the collar

We rarely wear things our parents wore.

I've never had recourse to wear armbands to keep my shirt sleeves up; I never wore a flat hat to go to football; my mother had a different chest size to me, so I never wore any of her bras – well, not since the psychiatrist visit, anyway.

Fashions change. You don't see people wearing togas these days or coats made out of mammoths.

As a kid, I'd be dragged, by my mum, into various clothes shops along Balham High Road. I remember a milliners. I wasn't allowed to touch a single hat and realised, at a very early age, I was never going to sport a fascinator, bonnet or boudoir cap.

I'm also neither posh enough nor old enough to wear braces; I don't use string to hold my trousers up and luckily never had a demob suit.

However, I did secretly wear my dad's old football shirt – although I did think Roy Bentley was a type of car rather than the centre forward for Chelsea. Probably best not mention my mum's thigh-length boots – if only to say how tricky I found walking in such high heels.

Our children are unlikely to go out wearing loons, anything made of velvet and possibly think Biba is a far-away planet.

Time to starch my collar and attach my cuffs.

Blowpipe dreams

I'm surprised I never ended up in the Madame Tussauds Chamber of Horrors given the toys I had as a kid.

By the age of six, I'd become very adept at using a tomahawk. Luckily, it was made of rubber and therefore the chances of me chopping people's scalps off was remote.

As if encouraging the art of decapitating wasn't enough, my father once brought home a blowpipe. A German client of his had sent it to him. I scoured all my Christopher Isherwood, Goethe and Sven Hassel novels, but never found any mention of blowpipes.

When I was given the gift, I had the sudden fear we'd be leaving the safety of our Balham flat and moving to New Guinea, with my new-found blowpipe prowess ensuring we'd become self-sufficient the moment we got off the boat or plane from Croydon Airport.

The blowpipe darts were, of course, rubber-tipped. The worst I could do was take one of my parent's eyes out as they entered my bedroom brandishing my evening hot chocolate.

As you get older, there's a medical test where you have to demonstrate your ability to blow. Little do these doctors know I'd been trained by Pygmies from an early age with my blowpipe and, during the test, I imagine I'm trying to kill a mammoth.

It was a few years ago now.

Thriller minute

I was eight when I wrote my first novel. It was called *The Windy Night*. It was a thriller and had nothing to do with cabbage.

I only wrote four pages, and most of that was drawings (the sign of a good book is one which contains pictures).

One evening my dad brought home a few sheets of slightly used Letraset letter transfers. My book suddenly had a very professional front cover, courtesy of these discarded sheets.

The book was never published. My theory was that it was down to the lack of semicolons in the prose (or perhaps, too many?). Sadly, there were no vowels left on the sheet, so the title became *Th Wndy Nght* – possibly many publishers rejected it as they thought it was written in Welsh or Shakespearean English?

There was a shop in Balham High Street which sold stationery. They not only sold these transfer sheets with letters (including ones with all vowels still intact), but you could also buy a piece of card depicting landscapes where you could create your own scene. I had sheets which had a beach showing the D-Day landings (with soldiers and tanks to manoeuvre) and a field, where you could place flora and fauna.

I mixed the two and had a giant caterpillar landing on Omaha beach and several Wehrmacht officers blowing dandelions.

99 scary balloons

My paternal grandmother owned several Royal Doulton figurines.

When I was quite young, the journey from Balham to Maida Vale would terrify me, as I found the ornaments scary.

One was an old crone (probably about my age now) who had several balloons. I envisaged that, aside from selling balloons, she would wait besides the guillotine, cackling, smoking a small clay pipe and swearing in French.

There were also plates on the walls. This confused me – did my north London relatives stand up to eat – and eat sideways?

Comment [BE]: You only need one of either "also" or "too", not both.

The plates mostly depicted hunting scenes – I assume my nan went out, after I'd left, to look for stags running wild up and down Baker Street?

None of my south London relatives had ornaments or plates defying gravity. We had no hunting on Wandsworth Common so, if we'd possessed plates, they'd have shown a Black Maria, Princess Anne opening the new Balham Sainsbury's or local lad, Mike Sarne, inviting *EastEnders* stars outside.

If I didn't have a pathological fear of birds, I'd have loved three ducks hovering over my fireplace – readying themselves to dump something on balloon lady below. Now, that *would* have made her swear!

Antlers & Decking

It's that time of year when you open your Christmas cards with apprehension.

Will they contain exploding glitter? Will it open to 'Away in a Manger' being played on a stylophone (too soon)? Or will it contain a round-robin letter? Personally, I'd prefer to have shards of glitter imbedded into my face than receive a letter from a frightful family I'd met on holiday in 1968.

Cards are more imaginative these days. The actual card is certainly less flimsy.

In the early '60s, deposited through my Balham flat letterbox, would be an envelope. Inside was a card featuring a robin, covered in snow, chewing a sprig of holly. The card also felt like it could disintegrate at any moment.

I've friends in Germany and have received cards which, when opened, played oompah music to the tune of 'Jingle Bells'.

I felt like I was in a Bavarian beer house, especially as there was scratch 'n' sniff Glühwein on the envelope.

I'm lucky that I wear glasses, as some cards open out with such force, it could have my eye out – and no one wants to be in A & E at Christmas asking for a pretend antler to be removed from both pupils.

And now I have to write to all my "friends" to tell them about how Melissa and Persephone are doing Grade 4 castanets and the pet labradoodle is nearly fluent in Esperanto.

Mini Banister

Until my Auntie Vera took me on a trolley bus from Wimbledon to Belmont (which seemed so far away from Balham, I could have been on Neptune), my second favourite mode of transport was banisters. (My first was the train, as I enjoyed climbing into the rope luggage rack. I think I was a monkey in a previous life).

In my Balham flats, the cleaning ladies had done such a fine job with their tins of Pledge on the banisters that going down them was like the bobsleigh at the Winter Olympics.

Perhaps it's a boy thing, but going down the flight of stairs from my fourth-floor flat, I'd slide down the set of banisters rather than testing my multiplication skills by taking eight or nine steps at a time or taking the lift.

Oddly, I never did this on the stairs at Balham Tube station. I think the metal studs fixed regularly on my potential downward "course" were off-putting. "Vasectomy" was one of the first Latin words I learned.

A consequence of this constant sliding meant one side of my trousers became quite worn. When questioned by my mother about this one-sided wear and tear, I said that one of my thighs was larger than the other and therefore rubbed. Explaining why I'd drawn Olympic rings on her best tea tray was less convincing. You win some, you *luge* some.

Counting the pennies

This week I tried to pay for something using my kidney donor card. Another restaurant I won't be allowed back in.

Years ago "tap in" would have been something your plumber mentioned and "contactless" was when you were removed from someone's Christmas card list.

This system of payment is a far cry from having a plastic-covered National Savings paying-in book. I miss waiting in the queue of my Balham sub-Post Office and furtively looking at the magazines I'd never have the courage to buy. I always thought both health and efficiency were very laudable attributes to have.

And the wait was invariably to pay in ten bob, a present from a generous aunt or the results of a money laundering scam during bob-a-job week.

My first experience of "money" was the pretend coins my dad would get from the Co-op. Because he bought Senior Service by the vat-load, he'd get plenty of these to save up for his divi.

I'd play with these coins, sharing them among my thirty-eight hand puppets, telling them about communism and the redistribution of wealth. Sooty always knew what I was talking about, Willie Wombat less so.

I found my old paying-in book in the loft the other day. I have £3 17s 6d. Not even enough for another hand puppet.

Wonder how much credit I have on my library card?

Taping over the cracks

I've slung out my old Betamax machine. I realise *Antiques Roadshow* is never coming to a town near me. Arthur Negus is clearly allergic to suburbia.

I don't need it now as I have "catch up TV", "download series link" and various programmes one hour later.

As a kid, VHS was something your mum said you'd catch off other people's toilet seats. Betamax was the ointment you'd use to get rid of it.

With the *Radio Times* you planned in advance what your viewing would be. As an adolescent I knew Alexandra Bastedo was on Friday evenings, *Andy Pandy* was Tuesday – I can't remember which day *Sunday Night at the London Palladium* was on.

You had to watch things live. If I missed any episode of *The Persuaders*, I'd have to wait until playtime at my Balham school before catching up. The quality of the retelling made it obvious none of my mates would ever become screenplay writers. However, you could miss a decade of *Crossroads* and still get up to speed with plot before the first ad break.

And then came video tapes – almost the size of your lounge – and with a slit for inserting the tape which could be as vicious as a piranha.

But the ever-present danger was taping over something precious.

I once recorded the 1989 FA Cup Final over *The Sound of Music*. Instead of the Nazis turning up, suddenly you had Ian Rush marauding into the Everton penalty area. "I am sixteen" was suddenly replaced with "You'll never walk alone". The remote buttons were never allowed in my hand again.

Peanuts!

My father, as part of his unofficial education for me, once took me to see Stan Kenton.

We travelled from our Balham flat to see the great jazz artist. As a ten-year-old, jazz was not something I could easily get my head round. I was still coming to terms with the complexity of the songs Wally Whyton would sing on *Ollie and Fred's Five O'Clock Club*.

Because I didn't complain, and kept humming the tune to *Peanut Vendor* during my bath time, dad organised for us to travel to Croydon to watch Gil Evans, the Canadian (also jazz) pianist. I have never been so bored.

I was lucky as a child and subjected to many types of popular music. I'd have listened to more Sibelius, but my mum thought this was a type of waterborne disease and wouldn't have it in the flat.

I was old before my time musically; by the time I was eight I knew the lyrics to most Frank Sinatra songs. I really did do it my way.

Not all my relatives had this musical passion. My nan only owned one 78, 'Underneath the spreading chestnut tree'. That 1938 classic you will all now be doing the actions to! Hearing it over and over again as a kid, I'm surprised I never developed a nut allergy.

Peanuts!

Little sun-ray lamp of sunshine

Aside from attempting to increase my cholesterol by serving me egg 'n' chips every lunchtime throughout my school years, my mum was actually quite keen for me to remain healthy.

Being force-fed Virol and given a Haliborange tablet every day, they became staple additions to my diet.

I never realised just how powerful Haliborange tablets were until, realising I'd missed a day, once took two in one day. That was the day to have bought shares in Andrex.

However, living on the fourth floor (of eight) of our Balham block of flats, my vitamin D intake was minimal. So, my mum invested in a sunray lamp.

She had toyed with the idea of dangling me out of the window at certain times of the day when the sun came round, but could never get any rope strong enough. Also, she'd bunked off the lesson about knot-tying when she was a Brownie.

Instead, I had to endure several minutes, on a regular basis, in front of this powerful lamp (my mum got it cheap, as it had previously operated the North Foreland Lighthouse) wearing tiny black goggles whose string dug into my head.

So, what with the sunray lamp and Mum drinking Rioja while preparing my egg 'n' chips, it was like being in Majorca in the mid-sixties.

'Viva Franco' – and other great summertime songs.

A little bit elephant's

As a kid, in my Balham flat, we had radios installed into the wall. I would avidly listen to see if my request for 'Nelly the elephant' was ever played on Stewpot's *Junior Choice*. It never was. Nor was the ending of *Götterdämmerung*.

Through my mother's guidance, I discovered I preferred Motown to 'Right, said Fred' (the song, not the group), 'Puff the magic dragon' or 'A windmill in old Amsterdam' (a song which encouraged rodent infestations – and that's how plagues start – we all remember 1665, don't we?).

Your request would invariably be linked to someone's birthday, going to big school or thanks to a nan for doing something.

I've been listening, as a baby boomer, to *Boom Radio*.

Having got over the shock of listening to various DJs I thought were long dead, the requests are very typical for our generation (forgive me if you were born after 1964, and therefore not a baby boomer).

This week I heard someone hoping the replacement hip operation had gone well. When we listened to radio as kids, we couldn't even spell hip, let alone know it could be replaced. Also, you thought lumbago was a Caribbean island and sciatica was a Greek philosopher.

Still, one song rarely requested on *Junior Choice* was 'Mustn't grumble', probably because, when you're eight or nine, you don't understand the concept. However, when you're sixty-five ...

Comment [BE]: The usual style for italics is to use them for larger bodies of works, so books, for example, films, operas, albums, but not individual songs, which get single quotes. A series would normally get italics, but an individual programme within it single quotes.

Are you sitting uncomfortably?

Watching children's TV in my Balham flat was a great way of establishing which career I might (or might not) follow.

Monday's *Picture Book* asked children, "Do you think you can do this?" Well, no, because it is lunchtime, I'm only four and I'm on my break; I can erect a box girder bridge after my afternoon nap.

Tuesday's example showed *Andy Pandy* – a man in a clown suit, whose only friend was his teddy. As an only child, I could identify with this; for many years, my best friend was a glove puppet. Living in a box didn't appeal, though.

Living in a flowerpot with an inarticulate neighbour had even less of an attraction. Coupled with forever being on the run from the gardener, it would have meant totally frayed nerves by the time I was ten.

I always felt *Rag, Tag and Bobtail* on Thursdays was a recipe for social disaster. Hedgehog, mouse and rabbit respectively – you've only got to be living near a cat and it's *Goodnight, Vienna* (where *Mary, Mungo and Midge* was set).

Which left Friday – you're running out of days for any career guidance inspiration.

Did I want to work on a farm? Did I want to be subservient, as clearly Mr and Mrs Scrubbitt were? Watching *The Woodentops* ruled out potentially being a vet, cleaner, farmhand, twin-child psychologist or spotted dog.

It would take several years before I found my métier. I eventually became a dragon, making soup on a remote planet.

Comment [BE]: QUERY: Please check these changes convey your intended meaning.

Piano splinter group

I had piano lessons for two weeks. Sadly, this didn't qualify me for being the next Liberace, although I am fond of a giant candelabra.

My great aunt was my teacher, as she possessed a baby grand in her Balham flat. Her violent teaching skills were reminiscent of the role Harry Andrews played in *The Hill*. I've still got splinters embedded in my hands from the smashed rulers over my knuckles.

Her husband, my great uncle, was an amateur band leader. His piano was his pride and joy and he would cover the keyboard with old copies of *Melody Maker*.

I'd always look at this protective paper (when not being assaulted) and wonder why, in 1970, I'd never heard of anyone in the charts and wondered why, each week, Marie Lloyd's 'Oh! Mr Porter' was still number one.

Not knowing the paper was never changed, but anxious to keep up to date with popular music, I once asked for this song in my local record shop. I was disappointed to hear it was no longer available, but did I want 'Chirpy chirpy cheep cheep' instead? I decided not to, as this sounded more like a disease or type of birdseed than a song.

So, I was destined never to be the next Liberace. Also, I'm not allowed near matches. Plus, to me, Quavers remain a type of crisp rather than a form of musical notation.

Having someone else's cake and eating it

Today is Mothering Sunday.

When I was a kid, this meant cake. Not made by my mum – her two favourite things were Guinness and John Player Specials; you could scour every cook book by the Galloping Gourmet and you'd struggle to find any recipe combining both.

At my Balham church the vicar's wife was on a par with Fanny Craddock (only without the scary make-up). She would make simnel cake for people to take after the morning service. I would always try that end-of-party trick of asking if I could take a piece for my mum too? I'm surprised I've never had to enrol in WeightWatchers.

The idea was that you were actually meant to take the cake home to your mum. Mine would have been too engrossed with her latest Jean Plaidy novel, or still been in bed with "one of her heads". Throughout my formative years, I always thought my mum was some sort of hydra.

At my church I sang in the choir. Although, I started late and was never a choirboy, therefore, I missed out on all those sixpences I could have earned singing at weddings, shillings at funerals and ten bob for an exorcism. I did make up for this lack of earning by eating cake. It would have been rude not to.

So, to all the mothers, grandmothers, great-grandmothers out there, thank you, and just a small slice, please.

Overstepping the mark

I have a Fitbit and am obsessed with how many steps I do each day.

I look back to when I was a kid, a time when "school run" was something you'd do if you bunked off. I walked everywhere (when I wasn't running).

They suggest, like eating five pieces of fruit (pineapple chunks and Jaffa Cakes don't count), that you attempt to walk 10,000 steps a day.

I think I'd have achieved this walking to and from my Tooting school from my Balham flat.

Sometimes I'd skip. Sometimes I practised my bowling action while humming the main theme to *Patton: Lust for glory*. I was a mixture of George C Scott and Richie Benaud.

Couple this walk with running around like a maniac during playtime, and the 10,000 steps were invariably achieved before double chemistry. Road Runner meets Pipette Man.

However, all that walking and playing football in the playground during playtime, with school shoes on, gave you an appreciation of how Margot Fonteyn must have felt. At least I never had to wear a tutu.

My Fitbit also monitors my sleep; what it doesn't tell me is why I no longer dream about Claudia Cardinale every night. So, modern technology, not all it's cracked up to be.

It's Sunday morning – only another 9,995 steps to go.

None of the fun of the fair

I never went to a fair while growing up in the '60s and '70s.

If I wanted to see bearded ladies, there were plenty of nonagenarians living in my Balham block of flats whose LadyShaves had clearly run out of battery before rationing was introduced.

I wouldn't have trusted myself on any shooting range. I was more Mother Kelly than Ned.

Already having thirty-six glove puppets in my bedroom precluded the need of the addition of a four-foot-high teddy.

I would feel nauseous just looking at various rides, so going on any – even an innocuous-looking giant teacup – was never going to happen.

If I wanted to look odd in a mirror, I'd simply eat more cake.

On Clapham Common, there was often a fair with its accompanying circus.

The smell of sawdust brought back memories of what the school caretaker would bring into a class when a school dinner hadn't agreed with a fellow class member. So, the likelihood of me entering the big top was remote.

I remember being at the top of the Monument aged eleven and realising I'd never be an acrobat.

I think local dentists were in league with the fair organisers, as I don't recall candy floss and toffee apples ever being recommended foodstuffs by the British Dental Association.

I could never have been a lion tamer, either; I've watched *Mr Benn* and it's not as easy as he made it look!

Send in the clowns. Actually, please don't.

Comment [BE]: It's common to see ages in numerals, even if they're being written out in other instances, but I'll keep this consistent with what you've mostly done until now in the manuscript.

I am abseiling

Easter egg hunts were always precarious when you lived in a fourth-floor flat.

I knew the 1967 Easter in my Balham flat was going to have a hint of danger when, instead of getting an egg full of Chocolate Buttons, I was given a book entitled *Successful Abseiling*, a set of grappling irons and Sherpa Tenzing's autograph.

My parents could have put the Easter eggs in the communal gardens, except my mother believed there were killer coelacanths in the ponds. There were garages round the back of the flats, but there was the ever-present danger of being run over by a Ford Consul as you bent down to gather up a hidden egg.

For me, my mother had put fifty-odd eggs, dangling on bits of string, outside my bedroom window. It looked like the Hanging Gardens of Babylon, only Nebuchadnezzar never lived in south London.

The demand for the sugar rush chocolate gives you made me eager to climb down the face of the flats. Having attached the guide rope to my very sturdy Dansette record player, I was ready to descend.

The window open, my Dusty Springfield LPs safely removed from the record player and with me about to leap to claim my eggs, I heard a knock on my bedroom door – my nan had arrived with an egg filled with Smarties.

So, can someone tell Sir Edmund Hillary I'm not coming out to play, please.

Happy Easter.

Those were the daze, my friend

The moment my Bullworker arrived in at Balham flat in the late '60s was the moment I believed I could win *Opportunity Knocks*.

Every Friday I'd watch the programme and get inspired by the weekly winners.

Given I was only eleven in 1968, I could hardly go on and sing a song about nostalgia, as Mary Hopkins did. (She was very good in the ITV show where she played a ghost detective.)

I'd have sung 'Mother of mine', except there were so many things my mum did which were either a secret or couldn't be mentioned before the nine o'clock watershed. Plus, I haven't got the legs to wear a kilt.

Science was not a strength of mine at school; even learning very elementary physics, I could not understand how the clapometer worked. I assumed there was a team of hamsters working it from behind? The louder the claps, the more the hamsters ran on their wheels?

I look back and think about the Muscle Man, Tony Holland, and the fact he might have had more credibility if he'd had another winner's name – Bobby Crush.

Still, we did learn that someone saying "and I mean that most sincerely, folks" probably didn't.

Vote, vote, vote.

I've got some lovely plums

There was no scanning of items in the Du Cane Fruitier, the greengrocers opposite where I was brought up on Balham High Road in the '60s.

There was, however, a giant, dirt-covered cash register where, if your bill came to anything involving a halfpenny, you'd need several hands to press the keys down to display the amount.

There was no "bag for life". You had a string bag, a bag you'd bought years ago during a holiday in Ventnor or a basket on wheels.

Rather than you packing the fruit and veg, they'd be poured into your bag. If you were lucky, they'd be wrapped in a paper bag so flimsy it would have disintegrated by the time you'd transferred your purchase into your vegetable rack. The greengrocer was determined to get you as earth-covered as he was; I think they were on commission from Lux, Camay or the local pumice stone makers.

I loved the signs in the greengrocers, especially as I was very short-sighted as a kid. I couldn't miss the six-inch-high white sign displaying 1/6 in some gothic script.

My mum would invariably do the shopping in hot pants. Looking back, the greengrocers must have thought I was a bit of a hindrance, especially as my mum would insist I was her little brother.

To be fair, she never went to look at the special cauliflowers they kept out the back.

Bugger Bournemouth

In 1963, when I was six, I visited Bournemouth. I vowed never to visit again. The trip from my Balham flat to the Dorset coast was a succession of disillusionment.

There's nothing wrong with Bournemouth per se, but my multiple bad experiences there left me very biased against it – however Alan Whicker may have praised it in future programmes.

This was the first holiday I can remember. I stayed with my paternal grandmother in a rented flat by the beach. My grandmother had a food allergy – insomuch as she was a dreadful cook.

On my first visit to the seaside I was stung by a bee. This was very painful; the only way my parents would calm me down was by promising me a part in the next series of *Emergency – Ward 10*.

In the sea there was a boy of similar age. I asked him if he knew Keith Ranger (a boy in my class)? I was amazed and hugely disappointed that he didn't. Even his parents explaining that this random child went to school in Leeds still made the fact incomprehensible. It was only, several years later, when I purchased my first Red Rover, I realised that the morning commute from Leeds to Balham may have been tricky. Especially if you missed the connection at Nottingham Bus Garage.

During my "holiday", my maternal great-grandmother died. I was told she had gone to join the angels. I was about twenty when I realised, not having seen her for a while, that "The Angels" were not a pop group who were on the road a lot.

Wall-to-wall entertainment

Music was very important to me growing up. The bedroom wall in my Balham flat was bedecked with singers cut out from *Fab 208*. The life-size picture of Clodagh Rogers did dominate the wall; this didn't leave much room for Melanie, Aretha Franklin or Nancy Sinatra (nothing wrong with having eclectic musical tastes).

I'd inherited some records from my grandparents: the 1939 classic 'Underneath the spreading chestnut tree'; 'Caruso's greatest hits' and a full set of Gilbert and Sullivan operettas. Therefore, the desire to have my own music was paramount.

I bought a cassette player. I also bought several C60 tapes to record on. I declined to buy a reel-to-reel tape, as I believed this would make my bedroom look like the IBM building.

I'd plant my microphone in front of the TV during *Top of the Pops* – sadly I'd not only record the song, but I'd also record my mother asking "what's this bleedin' row?" DJs on the radio would interrupt the songs by talking over the start and finish. At night, I'd try to record the Radio Luxembourg top 20 underneath my candlewick. My mother would enter my room (without knocking) and say, "I hope you're not doing what I think you might be doing?" I was ten and my eyesight was bad enough.

Eventually, as I got older, and with more pocket money, I could buy actual records. I'd buy the *Top of the Pops* and *Hot Hits* albums. My mother knew why.

Pomp and Circumstance in Balham

Listening to 'Zadok the Priest' last week during the coronation reminded me of one of the many times I'd sung it.

To celebrate various royal happenings during the '70s, our Balham church twice put on pageants. Because I could sing and act, I was involved in both.

Having won the RE prize when I was ten, I believed I was a shoo-in for any major acting part (in fairness, this should have been given to Neil Pearson, a Tooting resident when we were all growing up – and marginally better actor).

We regularly inflamed the vicar's anger by messing about during rehearsals. This wasn't helped by one line in a sketch where the vicar's daughter had to deliver a line: "Peter, pass me your crutch." When you're a teenager and you hear the word "crutch", it's similar to hearing the word "sausages" when you're six. Sadly, for the vicar, we were all still mentally about six.

We sang many choral pieces in the two pageants – all of them related to royalty. But, for me, the best thing to come out of it was through a fellow chorister from Jamaica. During the rehearsals and singing "may the King live forever", "amen, amen, amen" and "alleluia" more times than you can shake a stick at, my West Indian mate taught us the entire lyrics to 'The Israelites'.

If the vicar had known, he'd have torn up our shirt and taken away our trousers, as the great Desmond Dekker suggested.

Eva Brown

In the kitchen of our Balham flat in the '60s, my mother had eight brown jars containing all manner of exotic foodstuffs: ginger; cloves; nutmeg; cinnamon; marjoram; mint; parsley and thyme.

Because of my utter loathing of boiled fish in parsley sauce, I'd hide the jar marked "parsley". I couldn't watch any episode of *The Herbs* without the fear of coming out in a rash.

What puzzled me, as a kid growing up, was why the contents of these jars were never used?

My diet was very formulaic; I had the same thing most days, most weeks. But I cannot remember my Saturday evening smoked haddock being supplemented with a sprinkling of nutmeg, Sunday's roasts rarely featured ginger instead of Yorkshires, and whose cloves were actually in that jar? The Borrowers? (At this point I'd not learned how to spell "clothes" properly).

Brown was a popular colour in our flat: brown three-piece suite; brown carpet – with both parents being heavy smokers, it tended to hide the burn marks (and an unruly Flake packet); brown coffee pot; brown cups and saucers; dark brown sideboard and stereo. The only brown not there was Eva Braun.

My dad had a brown suit. He could hide his head in his jacket and my mum wouldn't spot him sitting on the sofa for hours.

So, when someone says to you "brown is the new black", send them off for a colour blindness check.

Tiger, tiger – hiding in my grass?

It is No Mow May.

This is blindingly obvious if you step outside your house and are confronted with what appears to be Epping Forest. No one has mown the communal streets seemingly since the last Ice Age.

I never had No Mow Any Time Period growing up in my fourth-floor Balham flat. Mowing wasn't easy, four floors up. We were so far up, off the ground, it was more fly-past then Flymo.

I'm wondering, when they eventually get round to cutting the Serengeti-type grass outside my house, what they'll find? Butterflies, bees, beetles? Most certainly. However, it has grown so high I wouldn't be surprised to see hordes of wildebeest, the lost city of Atlantis or The Borrowers living there.

In the '60s, I'd wander over Wandsworth Common with my *Observer Book of Birds*. During this time, it seemed south-west London only attracted pigeons and sparrows. I was twenty-eight before I saw my first robin – unless you count Burt Ward.

My father, having been brought up in Marylebone (famed for its birds of paradise), got very bored trying to birdwatch with me, so we used the book as a goalpost.

From trying to be Peter Scott, I hastily had to become Peter Bonetti. Equally handy trying to spot cats. And talking of cats, outside my house, I could have a family of Siberian tigers living in the undergrowth. This would explain why Siegfried and Roy have moved in next door.

Saving the bacon

At sixty-six, I tend not to get invited to as many sleepovers as I did many years ago.

Within my Balham block of flats, there lived another family with kids my age. If our respective parents went out, I would sleep in their flat. I loved it, for one reason: crispy bacon.

My friend's dad was a salesman for a toy manufacturer, so there were always the best new toys in their flat. However, you could keep Flounders, Happy Families and anything involving attaching something to a magnet and a bit of string, because it was the morning fry-up I looked forward to. I probably already had high cholesterol at six!

I didn't need waking up the next morning, as the smell of frying bacon would waft into our bedroom. Auntie Sylvia (she wasn't my real auntie) could have won countless worldwide competitions for cooking bacon.

However, before the morning food fest began, we'd still have fun the previous evening – staying awake (to the babysitter's probable annoyance) until 9.30 – which we thought must be tomorrow already! We'd plan night-time expeditions to the kitchen – although, I did think to myself, we'd better not eat all the bacon or anything which would have made me still full the following morning.

At sixty-six, I'm still getting up at midnight, only not to raid the fridge – or to find Penelope Plod, the policeman's daughter.

Enjoy – or the rabbit gets it

Comment [BE]: This one's already on page 2.

n the Balham ABC, during the '60s and '70s, the ladies serving the tea – which they poured from a great height above their heads – would slide the mugs across the metal counter; no words would be exchanged. You certainly didn't say, "This tea has more of a head on it than my mum's Guinness." If you did, you'd find yourself, and your accompanying iced bun, in A & E.

What the tea ladies never said was "Enjoy!" Nor did they say it – which seems commonplace in coffee shops nowadays – with incredible menace.

There is clearly no alternative to not enjoying it. If you don't, the barista will find you and creep up beside you as you're devouring your blueberry muffin.

They will ask, if you had to state your level of enjoyment on a scale of one to ten, it must be eleven. Or else!

Iced buns were the only pastry option in the ABC on Balham High Road. There were no croissants as many of the people serving there still had very raw memories of the Hundred Years' War; the thought of having to speak French was abhorrent. These were the days before sell-by dates. If you couldn't eat it, you could use it as a weapon and re-enact the Battle of Agincourt on Balham High Street.

Clocking in

Growing up, I would listen to aged relatives (it was that, or have your pocket money come to an abrupt halt) and wonder if any of them were related to Stanley Unwin?

I had a paternal grandfather who, if you asked him a question, would always answer with: "I'll tell you for why." He was from north London, so perhaps, having been brought up south of the river, having far too many prepositions in a sentence was considered the norm? Or perhaps he was a precursor to Google Translate? To paraphrase the *Catchphrase* catchline – "it's good, but it's not right".

Where cab drivers dare not go after 8.00, my maternal grandmother, when asked the time, would answer "five and twenty past" or "five and twenty to". Is this a generational thing and people in SW17 were taught to speak as if they were still living in Georgian London?

I bet, these days, no one is told "wait 'til your father gets home" as, with the advent of working from home, most fathers are already home, albeit working in a room which originally housed coal.

With raging inflation, I wonder how much people should be paid for their thoughts? Certainly not a penny.

And you didn't have to do seven years at medical school to give someone a taste of their own medicine.

Curiosity has been reported to the RSPCA.

Outnumbered

"It's five to five; it's *Crackerjack*."

Any of us who have gone to work, and learned very quickly not to get on the empty smoking carriage of the Tube train as it pulled into Balham Station, would have been reliant on specific times and timings. We'd have been aware that nine o'clock was very important, but not half as important as five o'clock.

For me, at my secondary school, ten past four was the best time – the time the final bell rang, announcing the end of the school day.

You had five minutes before the school the other side of our rugby pitch and their electrified fence, had their own bell rang. That gave you five minutes to leg it to the sanctuary of the bus stop before your cap was either nicked, knocked off or made into a gag or, from some of the more creative boys, a doily.

Nearly fifty-years on since I left school for the last time, 4.10 pm still has a magic ring about it. A sense of relief. A time when I decided, shall I play football, perfect my leg-break or conjugate a few Latin verbs?

TV, aside from just *Crackerjack*, taught you the time and numbers. *Six-Five Special* taught you how to count backwards, as did *3,2,1*; *Beverly Hills 90210* introduced very big numbers; *Blake's 7* catered to the less numerate; Patrick McGoohan was determined not to help at all.

Although I can't remember when *News At Ten* was on.

Comment [BE]: QUERY: I'm not sure what this means. Possibly something like: You had five minutes before the bell rang at the school the other side of our rugby pitch, with an electrified fence.

357

Upper case twit

I had to buy a new phone this week.

What they don't warn you in the shops is that you'll have to remember every password for every app you have.

Having unsuccessfully tried Gerd Müller's birthday, Alan Knott's wedding anniversary and the square root of two, the words I no longer wish to see are "forgotten password?"

Before phones etc. the last time I needed a password was in the early '70s, doing am-dram in a Balham church hall, saying the words "open sesame" (This would have been good if we were performing *Aladdin*; sadly, we were doing *King Lear*).

I never did CCF at school (I visited old ladies in Clapham, which was far more dangerous than being on a school field with fellow sixteen-year-olds with pretend guns), so I never had the chance to say, "Who goes there?" The key to getting into the houses of the old ladies was to simply answer "yes" to the question "Is that you, Mick?"

The most complex thing you had to remember growing up was the combination on your bike's padlock.

Back when we were kids, you didn't have to invent a special word using upper and lower cases, a selection of numbers and liberal use of asterisks, exclamation marks and semicolons. Once I've mastered a way to remember such things, I shall be applying to work at Bletchley Park and you can all start calling me Alan Turing!

Wild, wild wildebeest

Do people still have room dividers?

I didn't in my Balham flat, but I would often go to friends' houses where the kitchen had a series of beads and/or coloured strips hanging down from the doorframe, separating it from the rest of the house.

What were they there for? Was it to give an air of mystery to the kitchen holy of holies? Hide embarrassing old relatives? Stop herds of wildebeest rampaging into the lounge?

Anyone going to the cinema in south-west London in the '60s would remember the ad for a local restaurant which advertised: "It's so good, even the cook eats here." The reveal would be the chef, behind the dangling beads, literally eating his own lunch.

I think budding cooks believed that the magic ingredient to a good meal wouldn't be to add a selection of exotic spices, but to erect a series of dangly things. Who needs Mrs Beeton or Fanny and Johnnie if you've got the threads of Joseph's coat hanging from your kitchen doorway?

How were these things created? My belief is that many a room divider was made out of beads stolen from school abacuses. This would explain why many people at my school could only count to five by the time they were eleven.

If there was to be privacy, you couldn't knock, as your hand would go straight through – thus knocking over the embarrassing relative. At least that would have saved her from the stampeding wildebeest.

Not one Cornetto

I never had as much as a chocolate sprinkle from the ice cream van growing up.

I lived on the fourth floor of my Balham flats; the moment I heard the strains of 'Greensleeves' or 'O Sole mio' (which means raspberry ripple in Italian), I'd put on my Tufty Club slippers and leg it down four flights of stairs. I'd reach the bottom and hear 'Greensleeves' dying in the distance as the van made its way down the High Street towards Clapham, a town where most people would do anything for an Oyster.

To get any form of lolly, tub or 99, you had to be as fast as Roger Bannister; I was more Minnie Bannister. I would arrive to see hundreds and thousands of hundreds and thousands lying on the street – evidence I'd missed out yet again.

Having attained a semaphore badge with the Cubs, I could have sent a message to Mr Whippy.

When learning semaphore, we tended to learn phrases like: "I think the boat is sinking" not "one cornet, please". By the time I'd have gone down the many flights of stairs, it would have melted.

Flake's off, love.

Great Scot!

When I first started work, I couldn't wait to get into the office. Not because I liked work, but because I always had a packet of Royal Scot biscuits hidden in my desk.

My Tube journey from Balham to Warren Street would have me drooling at the thought – I had to be very careful I didn't dribble over anyone's *Daily Mail* on the journey.

Other items in my drawer literally had my name on – I'd written "Mike" in Tipp-Ex on anything which could be nicked inside my desk. I had a calculator, as well as a stapler, a tin of boiled sweets (you never knew when you were going on a long car journey), paper clips, emergency packet of Royal Scots and a selection of foreign currency (MI6 could ring at any time).

These days, with paper being used less and less, the contents of desk drawers are vastly different: phone charger; spare lanyard; small French dog. For those who have been working from home, they will simply have a spare pair of slippers, surgical cushion and a manual showing you how to unmute yourself on a Zoom call.

Sadly, Royal Scot biscuits are no more. They are extinct, like the pterodactyl – a Royal Scot biscuit had a smaller wingspan.

For Royal Scot biscuits, it's "goodnight, Vienna". I hope this doesn't make Viennese whirls an endangered biscuit.

Shouting down

This week I was travelling to London, changing trains at Clapham Junction.

This is the Mecca for trainspotters; Clapham Junction is the busiest station in the UK. It's not actually in Clapham, which means, if you are a trainspotter, you will need to be good at orienteering too.

In the early '70s this station was one end of my daily commute.

I would walk to the station from my school every evening with several friends. One particular friend lived in Wimbledon. His platform was 100 yards away from mine. Mine headed towards the *Gateway to the South*. When you're fifteen, you couldn't give a monkey's about other people around you, and my friend and I would continue our conversation across several platforms – like human loudhailers.

Back then, there were no electronic indicator boards – for any form of transport. These days, you know exactly when the next bus or train will arrive. In the '70s, you could be at a bus stop and sometimes feel you were on the set of *Waiting for Godot*.

Back on the platform, I'd look hopefully at the station staff as they dipped into their four-foot-high box which housed the train destination boards. Until the one mentioning "Carshalton" was withdrawn and inserted into its rightful place, I continued shouting across many platforms, asking: "How do you draw an ox-bow lake?" and "Just how many bloody Pitts were there?"

Gute Reise, as my friend's Austrian mum would have said.

Deskbound

There were many changes for me going from primary to secondary school. Aside from getting used to my long trousers chafing, we had actual desks.

At primary school we had tables. Our new school, deep in darkest Tooting, had wooden desks.

There was much carving on my desk. It was so old, I almost expected to see drawings of buffalo or mammoths carved into the top.

The desk had a lid on it. I gingerly lifted it up, checking that no one had written "Pandora was here" on it.

Assuming that all the world's ills were not in the desk, ready to fly out, I continued to open the lid; the contents were disappointing. There were no Post-it notes on the inside with any instructions for finding secret tunnels, invitations for illicit liaisons (no bad thing, given I was only eleven and it was an all-boys' school) or the answers to that week's French vocabulary test.

There was, however, a fossilised iced bun. At first I thought this had been left by some Neanderthal who'd lived in Tooting when it was all lavender fields and/or marshy swamps? It wasn't until the first break, when iced buns were sold, that I realised I hadn't uncovered a neolithic food storage site.

I did discover, mainly during supremely dull French lessons, that the desk was very comfortable and easy to sleep on. That was one of the many reasons I failed French O level or became a palaeontologist.

Tempus fudge it

You rarely see young people wearing watches these days. If they do, it probably does tell the time, but also it tells them how much water they've drunk, how fast their heart is beating and the results from Newmarket that afternoon.

Comment [BE]: QUERY: I don't understand this line, so it probably needs clarification.

I was encouraged to tell the time from an early age and had my first Timex bought for me from a Balham jewellers in the mid-60s. The man in the jewellers was disappointed, as neither parent was buying any expensive rings or bracelets, but solely a watch where you got change from a ten-bob note.

My mum owned a perfectly good watch. However, this didn't stop her asking policemen (or anyone in a uniform for that matter) the time!

I had the Ladybird book on telling the time. I learned that "At 12 o'clock Mummy cooks dinner" – until my mum rewrote it to say: "At 12 o'clock Mummy opens her first Guinness."

The final page was: "At half past seven we are asleep." I could never understand this during the summer when there was still about three hours of daylight left! But, as you get older, so that's horribly near the truth again. What the book didn't tell you was, "It is 2.30 in the morning and you realise you really shouldn't have had that Bournvita."

Whenever I'm asked what the time is, I look at my watch and tell people where the big hand is. They soon seek their information elsewhere.

Mum's gone to the Ottoman Empire

Many people use social media. My activity on Myspace (something I thought was for people suffering from claustrophobia) and Friends Reunited (they really weren't your friends or you'd not need to reunite with them) isn't as active as it once was.

Another social media platform I no longer use is Twitter. It is now called X. Growing up in the '60s and '70s in rural Balham (I lied about the rural bit), X meant one thing: the film you weren't allowed in to see.

Looking as young as I did, I was more likely to see Charlie George starring in an acting role at the cinema than Susan George!

Changing Bejam to Iceland was just as confusing, especially with the tag line "Mum's gone to Iceland". This made many small children believe that one day their mothers would suddenly disappear to some Nordic wasteland. I was always asking my milkman if he was aware of where Reykjavik was?

No doubt Philippides is turning (he can't run any more) in his grave now his sporting-event chocolate is called Snickers (which is what Americans call plimsolls).

MFI is now called the Secret Intelligence Service. However, their bookshelves are better quality.

Anyway, what do I care? I'm about to go on holiday to Czechoslovakia via Abyssinia to get some Opal Fruits in duty-free!

"Shut up, Eccles

As a kid, I managed to get most of the childhood illnesses: measles, mumps, scarlet fever, chickenpox (I can still smell the calamine lotion) and German measles (which, oddly, the Germans don't call English measles).

I'd had all these by the age of ten, and wished there'd been an *I-Spy* book for me to have ticked them all off. I never got West Nile fever (twenty-five points), even though we did live near the River Wandle.

When I was ill, it was my dad who looked after me; my mum invariably had "one of her heads" – Balham's answer to Cerberus – so caring for the sick fell to my dad.

Whether it was dabbing calamine lotion on me, pumping me full of penicillin or just sitting on the bath while I occupied another piece of bathroom furniture, he'd chat away. Usually about sport or comedy.

Dad would ask whether the Tommy Baldwin/George Graham swap was good for Chelsea, how lucky Kent had been with wicketkeepers through the years, as he extolled the virtues of the (then) very young Alan Knott, and would suggest getting comedy records out of the library, as he wanted to introduce me to *The Goons*.

All this led me to feel better – however unwell I was.

If ever I'm unwell now, I talk to myself in the style of Eccles, Bluebottle and Minnie Bannister. More effective than kaolin and morphine.

Eyes wrong

I went to the opticians last week.

I've been going since I was five, a consequence of failing to pick my dad's googlies playing cricket against the garages by our Balham flats.

"Can you read that car registration number?" asked my father.

"What car?" Off to the opticians in Tooting High Street we went.

They now have many more tests than they did in the early '60s, but the one constant is the 1930s sci-fi apparatus they put on your head. This certainly hasn't been designed by Prada, Ray-Ban or Hugo Boss – some of the options for later, should you need new glasses.

By the time I was eleven, I couldn't see the large letter at the top of the table in my left eye. Back then they couldn't make the lenses thinner, so my left eye looked like the lens had been made by Unigate rather than Carl Zeiss.

The use of glass from this famous East German glass manufacturer worried me as a kid – clearly I watched too much *Emil and the Detectives* at Saturday Morning Pictures. I often assumed that, because the glasses came from there, all opticians were spies. Although at our local optician, Burgess & Maclean, they all seemed terribly nice people.

Deep, fat Friar

As if going to big school, and having to wear long trousers in September 1968, wasn't alien enough, what I didn't anticipate were the new words I'd have to learn.

We were told about prefects. At my first playtime I expected to see a fleet of Ford Prefects lined up on the rugby pitch. How surprised I was to see several bigger boys, adorned with their badges of authority, checking no one ventured onto the rugby field. The rugby field confused me too. Why had they built two longer poles above the football goalposts? Clearly they'd had a job lot delivered? And where was the penalty spot?

During the lunch break we learned about a thing called "the tuck shop". I was a massive fan of the ITV series *Robin Hood*, which ran in the early '60s; I thought we'd meet one of Robin's merry men. I was, however, praying it wasn't a travelling barber's.

We were also informed, should we ever need to temporarily leave our Tooting school, we'd require an *exeat*. At primary school we'd not studied Latin. We'd learned how to throw a beanbag, pretend to be a tree during Music and Movement and drawn lots of dinosaurs; we'd never had to conjugate Latin verbs.

But the most confusing word for me was: homework. My inability to get my head round this word was duly reflected in my 1973 O level results.

Gloria sic transit (Gloria was ill on the journey).

Comment [BE]: QUERY: Should this be 'Prefects', as in the former Ford range of cars?

A chocolate is not just for Christmas

I was given a box of chocolates the other day. The chocolates were made by Lindt, something I thought you found in a first aid box.

Inside was the list of contents. Some of the descriptions were so long, Tolstoy could have written them. By the time you'd read what was in the box, you'd have lost your chocolate craving and not worried about ordering a higher potency of statins.

At Christmas, inside my Balham flat, there would always be the obligatory tin of Quality Street.

Inside the lid, there'd be a chart showing which chocolates were inside: "Fudge"; "Coconut Éclair"; "Toffee Finger". What it didn't say was: "Flown, first class, from the cacao fields of Mexico; fermented, dried, roasted and grinded for your delectation and mixed with hazelnuts (because hazelnuts seem to feature in every chocolate these days) and lovingly shipped from Turkey."

All I need to know is, IS it a *COFFEE CRÈME*?

But what if you're colour blind? You really don't want to be mistaking a Strawberry Cream for a Toffee Penny. It'd be like eating a giant handful of Revels – your palette wouldn't know what day of the week it was; would it be hard or soft and would you be needing an emergency dental appointment later that week?

But one thing which has remained the same is: at what stage do you start tucking into the second layer? Probably when there are only Praline Surprises left on the top.

"...because tonight, Michael..."

There's always someone on the telly you feel is on every programme you watch.

Growing up, watching my TV and listening to the radio (or wireless, as my nan called it – she was ahead of her time), for me, it was Eamonn Andrews.

I was too young to listen to his famed radio boxing commentaries, but do remember *What's My Line?*

I often wondered – possessing the worst, most illegible signature in the world – what the panel would have made of me? Doctor would be the most courteous answer, psychopath the more obvious.

I noticed they never invited Lady Isobel Barnett to sign in – latterly, of course, her "line" was shoplifting. If they'd let her have a go, she'd have probably nicked the pen and drawing board.

Holding his red book for *This Is Your Life* was a must-see programme. Again, I often wonder who they'd have dragged out if I'd featured on it? When he last presented it, in 1964, I'd have been seven, and therefore not had much of a "life".

My guests would have been two nursery school teachers and the cleaners in my Balham block of flats – most of whom hated me and called me "Michael" – something I'd have found deeply distressing on live television.

Crackerjack for my generation was another programme he was on. I'd have never gone on that due to my allergic reaction to cabbages.

Setting a small bar

The few times I was allowed to go with my parents to socialise at other SW17 houses, I was always amazed where the drinks were kept.

In our flat, if you were a visitor, you'd assume my family were sponsored by Bell's or Gordon's.

The drink wasn't stored in some fancy cabinet; in our flat, it was in the mandatory brown sideboard, next to dad's old Chelsea programmes.

In other people's places the Black & Decker had been working overtime, as one wall had been transformed into a small bar – albeit without the dartboard and cardboard sleeve of packets of pork scratchings.

One family had a globe. The globe would open up and a selection of alcoholic beverages were instantly displayed – I assumed Marco Polo had a similar container? I tried spinning it once and nearly broke my wrist. Although, only until recently, I thought gin came from Abyssinia (it was an old globe) and SodaStream was a lake in Africa.

Some families had clearly won decanters at various fetes. Many had collected glasses from Esso. In 1970, they may have swapped them for a card featuring Martin Peters.

Once, trying to help out, I thought I'd move the pineapple off the Borrowers-sized bar. Having picked it up by the top, ice cubes suddenly scattered to all parts of the shagpile.

For the remainder of the evening I was condemned to sit, and not move, by the Dansette record player. It's not unusual.

Playtime conkers all

As you get older, so you complain more about the vagaries of the weather.

During my south-west London school time, during the late '60s and early '70s, I can never, ever remember there being "wet play".

We had two 15-minute breaks. (I still think of a quarter of an hour as one playtime).

As boys, we would invariably play football. However, there were two dangers in our playground.

The only boy who didn't play football ran round the playground pretending to be a Ford Zodiac. There was the danger that he'd take out our team right-back when mistiming his turn round the school water fountain. And a Ford Zodiac, for those who can remember, was a very big car.

The other ever-present danger was the girl who thought she was a golden retriever. Not only could her lead get caught up with your legs as you sped down the wing towards the opponent's goal, but there was the constant danger of catching rabies if she bit you (she had a note from her mum saying she didn't need a muzzle).

If it had ever rained, we'd have been in our class struggling against pretend carbon monoxide fumes and the smell of wet dog. Still, it was preferable to Music and Movement.

Let them eat doughnuts

Every morning, on my walk to my Tooting secondary school, I'd pass a baker's. The smell coming from the shop was so awful it deterred me from becoming a baker. I assume it must have been the yeast? Probably why I never enjoyed our family holidays on the hop farm.

In the early '60s, a shop, which you could have found on the Champs-Elysées, was brought to Balham High Road in the shape of La Patisserie. The pastries and bread were lovely and you'd almost expect Jean-Paul Sartre to be sitting outside, although this could have been dangerous should a 155 bus suddenly veer off the road.

I spent a lot of time in there as my mum was friends with the owners. Lots of French fancies, very few Gallic philosophers.

Being a baker is one of those occupations where you have to get up early. I couldn't have coped with that as a youngster. However, these days, in increasing age, I wake up stupidly early. So early, I'm thinking about getting *Debbie does doughnuts* out of the library and starting my own bakery.

I'd certainly continue with the French theme: I'd call the shop *Les beignets, c'est nous,* wear a beret, a Thierry Henry shirt and mock people when they try to speak French.

Chalky Purple

Is chalk used in schools any more?

When I went to my south London schools, it was always very evident.

I used it on my first day – as a drawing implement when I depicted my mum looking like a giant potato with no arms – and on one of my last days, when I had a piece imbedded in my skull, thanks to a particularly irate music teacher.

Having had a misspent youth, my O level results were reflected by the amount of chalk inside my waistcoat and behind my ears.

During my O level year, there was so much chalk on my hands, anyone would have thought I'd taken up weightlifting.

Chalk was much in use in my school playground. You knew who was best at maths, as the hopscotch grids went in the correct numerical order.

One of our class's dads was a toy salesman and, with a stolen set of Crayola multi-coloured chalk, we had yellow penalty areas, turquoise lines outlining the Double Dutch rope-swinging area and purple stumps.

We were the '60s equivalent of Kerry Packer!

Printed in Great Britain
by Amazon